THE BLOCKO TOWER

by

John Guy Collick

CHAPTER ONE

Moortown, Leeds, 1967

Sally had a best friend at infant school called Eva Benjamin. One day, Sally wet herself in the playground. She begged the others not to tell the teacher, promising each of them in turn that she'd be their best friend forever. It didn't work. They pointed and went AAAAAHHH, all round-eyed and round-mouthed, and told on her. An exasperated Mrs Ryan changed her into a spare set of knickers and shorts from the back of the class cupboard, asking her why on Earth she didn't say she needed the toilet. Because she was scared she'd be yelled at, like Mummy yelled at her, that was why. And now she was scared and sad and lonely, so at lunchtime she stood in the far corner of the playground, attempting to hide from the others in the shade of the conker tree, and cried.

"I'll be your best friend."

She looked up to see another little girl watching her. Pretty black ringlets and big brown eyes. The newcomer didn't smile or laugh at her, despite Sally's ragged gym bloomers and the fact she wasn't wearing any socks.

"I'm Eva. What shall we play?"

Sally shrugged, struggling not to cry again at this sudden kindness. Eva held her hands up like paws.

"I'll be your kitten, you can be my mummy cat."

They ran around under the trees until the bell rang. That afternoon the other children giggled and whispered about Sally.

It didn't feel so bad now because she knew Eva sat somewhere in the classroom behind her. At home time she waited, but her new best friend must have already left, so she walked out to meet Mummy with her wet things in a plastic bag and got told off again for being the last one out.

"Sally pissed her knickers at school. The teacher said we need to train her better or stick her back in nappies. The good news is that she's found a new best friend," Mummy told her father when he came home from work. She winked at him and mouthed a word Sally didn't understand.

"That's nice," he gave a brief smile from high up in his world. "What's her name?"

"Eva Benjamin."

Daddy rolled his eyes.

"That's what happens when we move to Moortown. I told you Sally's the token goy at all their birthday parties. When they deign to invite her," Mummy said.

"Can I have a conjurer for my birthday party?"

"Bloody hell," Daddy said.

"See what I mean? Conjurers, film shows, goodie bags stuffed full of diamonds. We're not rolling in it, unlike some round here," Mummy told her. "You'll have to make do with a cake."

"Can Eva come to my party?"

"Three friends, that's your lot. And all out by five." Mummy went back into the kitchen and started to bang things around. That meant no more 'nattering'. Sally climbed upstairs, sat on her bed, and tried to work out who else she'd invite.

A week later Mrs Ryan decided she'd had enough and reshuffled the class so she could separate Joe, Richard, Owen and Peter. Her 'Horrible Little Chemicals' she called them - fine on their own, explosive when mixed together. Sally ended up sitting next to Eva at the back of the room, near the long picture of the dinosaurs on the wall. Eva knew all the names and told Sally she had the same poster at home.

"Where do you live?" Sally asked.

"In the Blocko Tower."

Eva had to repeat it a couple of times before the penny dropped. Sally knew about the tall buildings on the other side of the ring road. She could see them from the playground. People lived in flats inside, including a few of the other children who, she heard, came from families with not much money. Yet those blocks were tiny in comparison to the towers rising up into the sky near the centre of Leeds. She'd seen them from the window of the Number 12 bus, on the rare occasions Grandad took her to the toy shop on Briggate. They rose from the broken ruins of the bomb sites, flanked by cranes that resembled skinny versions of the dinosaurs on that poster. She imagined them picking up concrete walls in their pterodactyl beaks and slotting them together, like the building kit the boys fought over at playtime.

"Are you poor?" Sally asked.

Eva shrugged. Sally looked at her friend's clothes. She wore a plain blue dress and scuffed Start-Rites like her own. Grandad called poor ladies 'shawl women' because, he said, they walked barefoot with scarves over their heads, though Sally had never seen anyone like that, certainly not Eva.

"I've got nice toys."

Sally's interest pricked up and she paused in her colouring-in of a Maori sitting on a beach.

"What ones?"

"I have a Driving Game, a Thingmaker, a ViewMaster and all the Krazy Kreatures from Outer Space cards."

Jealousy crashed over Sally in a wave. She was going to be six in a few weeks and just one of those would make the perfect birthday present. She daren't ask Mummy, of course. Asking was 'nattering'. Instead, she had to whisper all her wants into Daddy's ear when he brought up her Ovaltine at bedtime, and hope he remembered. You could make plastic bugs with a Thingmaker. The ViewMaster let you escape to other worlds full of strange wonders.

"You can come and play with them, if you like. In my Blocko Tower."

Sally returned to her picture and tried to focus on staying

7

inside the lines. She'd be too frightened to go anywhere near a Blocko Tower, surrounded by ruins and flanked by metal dinosaurs. It was far too scary, even if it was full of the most wonderful toys and her best friend lived there. It made her sad and angry, so she lost concentration and Mrs Ryan told her off before the whole class because her colouring-in looked like a 'dog's dinner'.

Her birthday present came early. A bicycle was waiting for her in the front room when she got home from school, a fortnight before the big day. It was bright red with white tyres, and had stabilisers to keep her upright while she learned how to ride it.

A couple of times, Daddy accompanied her down to the bottom of the road where a rough track ran alongside the woods. He took the stabilisers off and held her saddle while she wobbled along. After that he was always too busy, so she'd head on down there by herself, determined to learn to ride despite the scrapes, mud and complaints when she tracked it through the kitchen. After a week she could balance by herself. She trundled up and down the path, summoning up the courage to venture back to the pavement and up the long slope to their house.

"Hello Sally."

She looked up and saw Eva at the edge of the trees. A gate opened onto another trail that led through the woods. She knew it went all the way to a big road, beyond which lay the reservoir where they sometimes took their Sunday walk. Mummy had told her not to go down the track by herself, in case she got carried off by funny men. She was very surprised to see her best friend standing there all alone.

"Do you want to come and play with my toys?" Eva asked.

"In the woods?" Sally looked beyond her friend at the quiet shadows between the tree trunks.

"No, at my home. It's near here."

"The Blocko Tower?"

Eva nodded. It seemed a bit odd. As far as Sally knew, the tall towers were miles in the other direction, on the other side of Grandma and Grandad's house in Chapeltown, close to the shops in the middle of Leeds. She'd never seen one in Moortown.

"Come on. You can play with my traffic game and the Thingmaker."

"Mummy says I can't go in there by myself."

"You'll be with me, silly."

"Just for half an hour." Sally had only a hazy idea about how long that meant. It seemed to be the standard unit Mummy used to portion out the day - tea time in half an hour, half an hour till bed. She wasn't old enough to have her own watch yet. That was another grownup present she was desperate to own.

Eva led her into the woods. Sally kept her eyes down so the bike wouldn't topple as she half-rode, half-walked alongside. That wasn't the only reason. She didn't want to look at her surroundings because the forest was full of shadows and silence and it made her tummy feel funny. After hardly any time at all, the dirt track under her wheels turned back into tarmac, then concrete. They were out of the trees and Sally realised they'd arrived at Eva's tower.

She could sense it, a huge dark weight filling the sky, looming over her like the giant in *Jack and the Beanstalk*. She kept her gaze fixed down. Sally didn't want Eva to think she was scared. As a toddler, she'd screamed and screamed every time Grandad tried to push her buggy past Chapeltown Church. Its immense soot-black shard, silhouetted against the racing grey clouds, made her sick and dizzy. In the end he'd had to cross to the other side of the road. She'd been a silly little baby at that age and was supposed to be far too grown up now to be frightened. Even so, Eva's Blocko tower seemed much bigger and much scarier than the church.

They passed through a pair of glass doors and concrete turned into linoleum dappled with light. She looked up and saw a big room with a row of metal lifts, and stairs heading up to the right. Sally watched in awe as Eva pressed a button and the elevator doors opened. All fear vanished. This looked great fun and very adult. Despite the towers being for poor people and shawl women, she began to wish her family lived in this bright world instead of their pebble-dash house.

Sally had no idea how high up they were when they got out of the lift and walked down a white corridor to an orange door. It had a slanted sticker showing the number 239. Eva opened it. Just before she entered, she reached up on tiptoe, touched something on the frame, and pressed her finger to her lips.

"What's that?"

"A mezuzah. It's a piece of paper with the word of God to protect our home against dybbuks," Eva said.

Sally had no idea what a dybbuk was, and soon forgot Eva's explanation because the hallway opened out onto a kitchen with a table covered in everything to do with the Thingmaker. She'd assumed that her best friend had just one of the sets, perhaps the Zoofie Goofies or Mini-Dragons. This looked like the entire catalogue. The other girl hitched herself up on a chair and began to sort out the metal moulds and bottles.

"I'm going to make a Creeple Peeple," she announced, unscrewing a couple of lids. A chemical smell jabbed at the back of Sally's nose, making her dizzy. She glanced around.

"Where's your mummy?"

Eva squirted green goo into a shape without answering.

"What does your daddy do?"

Her friend shrugged. It felt strange. The flat was very big, made of white and grey rooms with wood and Formica furniture. Emptiness and silence filled the world. All she could see through the window at the far end of the room was a pale sky. It was as if Eva were the queen of her own kingdom, high above the clouds in a palace full of wonderful toys, with no parents to shout, swear, or tell her off.

Her friend finished filling the mould and put it on a plate on the electric stove. Sally stared as she turned it on and the chemical stink grew stronger. Whenever she went near any kitchen appliances her Mummy screamed at her and, more often than not, smacked her. Yet here was Eva using the cooker just like an adult, twisting the timer so it counted down.

"Hurry up," she said, pointing at Sally's centipede shape. Once it was finished and on the next ring, Sally looked around.

"Have you got a telephone? I should phone Mummy and tell her where I am." She suspected she'd been with Eva for more than half an hour. The other girl shook her head.

"Nobody has a telephone in the Blocko Tower."

That didn't sound right and it made Sally worry. The timer pinged. Eva used a big oven glove to put the two metal moulds to cool on the side.

"Let's play with the traffic game until they're ready."

Sally followed her friend into a pale, quiet living room. They sat down on the carpet next to a box that said *Driving Test Game*. Eva took the lid off to reveal a map with moulded houses in shades of red and brown. She took a control rod with a red ball at the end and screwed it into a hole in the corner. It looked like the gear stick in Mummy's yellow sports car. When Eva moved it back and forth, a plastic car drove along the streets. Sally recognised the place names. In the middle was the new Merrion Centre, Leeds Town Hall with its black lions that woke up at midnight and hunted down naughty children, Busby's Department Store and the Arcades. A street ran all the way around the outside in a circle. It had *Ring Road* stamped on its grey surface. Sally was surprised to see her own street in the upper right hand corner, with a house that had the number 5 on the door. That was her very own home. Beyond it, almost at the edge of the board, was a green wood and then the picture of a tower block. She leaned over and read the name.

"Backen... Backenforth Hei..., Hei..., Heights."

"That's what the Blocko Tower is called. It's named after the man who owns it."

"Who's that?"

"Professor Backenforth. He lives right at the top. I don't like him. He's a conjurer."

Some of her friends had conjurers at their birthday parties. They pulled rabbits out of hats and poured milk into the boy's ears so it came out of their elbows. Sally thought they were so exciting, and had asked if she could have one at hers. The answer had been a flat no. Mummy and Daddy seemed to think it was a kind of showing off.

"Does he go to children's parties?"

Eva shrugged.

"Why don't you like him?"

Another shrug. Her friend had her tongue stuck out as she tried to manoeuvre the tiny car past the railway station without touching the Queens Hotel. Sally had a go next. Eva held her hand until she could manage the movements by herself. It was fascinating. She loved the way the car drove as if by magic, down the streets and round the roundabouts. Finally, she could restrain herself no longer.

"Can I borrow it? Can I take it home to play with? I'll look after it very very carefully and be your best friend forever. You can ride my bicycle too."

Eva nodded, went into the kitchen and took a biro out of the drawer. She flipped the lid over and wrote her name on the cardboard.

Eva Benjamin.

"So you know it's mine."

"I should go home soon," Sally said. In truth, she wanted to play with the game all by herself. She was going to hide in her room and pretend she was driving her own magic car through Toy Town Leeds.

A bell tolled somewhere high above. Moments later there came a knock at the door.

"Eva?" It was a lady's voice, soft and friendly, like her own grandma's. "Eva? Are you going to the party?"

Her friend suddenly looked nervous, frightened even.

"Professor Backenforth is calling for all the children in the tower to come to his playground. He's going to let them climb inside the Mystery Planet."

Another knock, a little harder this time.

"I'm not allowed," Eva called out. She left the living room and returned with a wooden box. It was full of cards collected from packets of cigarette sweets. Sally recognised them straightaway.

Krazy Kreatures from Outer Space. She had a few herself, but some of them were too frightening. Their dead eyes and big alien grins hovered by her bed in her dreams. One, the Chernod from Planet Supor in the 7th Galaxy, had bothered her so much, with his blue skin, claws and old man's beard, that she'd flushed him down the lavatory. Eva picked out one of the less scary monsters, put it on the carpet beside her, replaced the lid, and carried on with the driving game.

"Oh come on Eva. Nobody will mind. Come up to Professor Backenforth's playground. All the other children are going too. Have you got a friend in there? She can have a turn as well."

"Don't you want to go?" Sally asked. She liked the idea of a party with a conjurer. Maybe she'd ask Mummy and Daddy if he could come to her party too, and this time they'd say yes. Another noise came from the corridor outside. It sounded like a crowd of children laughing and running towards the stairs, their Start-Rites clattering on the linoleum.

Eva shook her head.

"I hate Professor Backenforth. I don't want to go. You mustn't either."

Tap tap.

"Eee-va? Are you there?"

"Mummy says I can't open the door when she isn't here."

Her voice rose to an angry shout. She picked up the Krazy Kreature card and marched out into the hallway.

"If you don't open up, I'll break down the door with my wooden tail," the lady said. More rapping. This time it sounded like a stick. Sally suddenly felt scared. Eva held up the picture in her hand.

"If you do I'll ask the Wodaran to kill you with his raygun. You're a stupid Guessed a Poo. You marched my family into the woods and shot them and I hate you."

A long pause. Sally stared at her friend. Eva stood there like a soldier at attention with her arm high, holding the picture of the alien towards the door.

"Silly little girl. I was only teasing. Ah well, perhaps you'll go to Professor Backenforth's party next time. Give my love to your friend."

Silence. After a while Eva came back into the living room with an angry scowl on her face.

"We'll defeat them," she told the image on the cigarette card. Sally glanced at it. It wasn't the worst of the bunch, but still disturbing enough for her to look away, heart pounding. The Wodaran from Pluto wore white robes and had a head made out of an inverted parsnip. He looked extremely grumpy. Eva put him back in the box.

"She killed your family?" Sally asked, trying to imagine what that was like.

"A Guessed a Poo came to our house and took them away and shot them. That's why I came to live here. That's why I have the mezuzah - to keep the Guessed a Poo and the dybbuks away."

"I want to go home now."

Eva stared at her with those pretty brown eyes. They suddenly looked like a grown-up's, huge and full of kind sadness. She took a fork from the kitchen drawer and winkled Sally's centipede out of the mould.

"Here you are. I'll take you back. Be careful, we have to be very quiet."

Eva opened the door an inch, peered out, nodded and left the flat. Sally followed her, copying when the other girl put her finger to her lips and made big, exaggerated tip-toe steps. The corridor was silent and full of long shadows. It was getting near tea time, she guessed, which surprised her, as it didn't feel like she'd been here for more than a couple of half hours. The sound of the children had faded away and there was no sign of a lady, with or without a wooden tail. They crept to the lift. As it sank down through the building, Sally thought she saw a tall pointy-headed figure in white robes in the corner of her eye. She hoped she wouldn't have nightmares about the Wodaran from Pluto.

Trundling away from the Blocko Tower wasn't so bad, even though the wood was darker now and full of the wind. It rubbed the branches together so they made rustling noises deep in the shadows. For that reason, Sally kept her eyes down, only looking up when they arrived at the bottom of her street. To her surprise, Eva gave her a kiss on the cheek before turning and skipping off down the path. It was only after her friend had vanished that Sally realised she'd forgotten the driving game. She called out and almost started back through the woods, but Eva was nowhere to be seen. Perhaps she could go and get it tomorrow, or even persuade Daddy to drive over to the Blocko Tower to pick it up tonight.

Sally's old life ended the moment she stepped into the kitchen. Mummy fell on her in a raging storm of fists, shrieking and spittle.

"WHERE HAVE YOU BEEN? WHERE HAVE YOU BEEN?"

This wasn't a smacking across her bottom or bare calf. The brutal slaps rained down on her, making her fall backwards and bang her head against a chair leg. The plastic centipede from the Thingmaker set fell out of her hand and skittered under the fridge. Sally started to scream and wail, trying to hide beneath the table. Mummy dragged her out by her foot, grabbed her shoulders, and shook her hard. The room turned into a dark pit roofed over with an immense face full of hatred.

"WHERE HAVE YOU BEEN? YOU'VE BEEN GONE EIGHT HOURS. EIGHT FUCKING HOURS YOU STUPID WICKED LITTLE SHIT."

Sally wanted to say she'd been playing at Eva's, that she'd asked to use the phone but nobody in the Blocko Tower had one. It was impossible. The storm was inside her now, heaving the air in and out of her lungs. She tried to talk against it. All she could do was gasp and cry broken fragments of words as the world fell to pieces around her. Her mother pushed her away and Sally collapsed in a heap on her bottom. She struggled to her feet and staggered back, arms held out for a cuddle.

"Don't touch me," Mummy spat. "Have you any idea how much trouble you've caused?"

Dark shadows went past the window.

"The police are here," Mummy's voice turned flat and cold.

"You're going to say sorry."

"Noooooooo," Sally wailed. Mummy grabbed her arm and dragged her to the door.

Two policemen stood outside. They looked at Sally, frowned, glanced at her mother, then down again.

"Is she hurt?" asked the one on the right.

"She fell and banged her stupid head."

"Might want to get that seen to."

"Hello Sally. Where have you been?" said the one on the left. He had a big round face and was looking at her with the same disappointed smile Grandma sometimes gave her when she was rude or naughty. She couldn't speak. The hurricane in her chest kept pushing the air in and out of her lungs, drowning her voice.

"Your mummy has been very very worried," he continued. "Why did you run away like that? You've got a lovely house, and I bet you've lots of toys to play with, and your mummy and daddy love you very much."

Sally had only been gone for a few half hours, she knew that. And she'd been playing at her friend Eva's home. If only she could say the words properly then everything would be happy again. But it was impossible.

"You must do what Mummy and Daddy tell you," said the constable on the right. He looked older and had a moustache. "And what God tells you to as well. Remember what he told us. Honour thy father and mother."

Mummy poked her in the back of the head, where she'd hit it on the chair. It hurt.

"Say sorry."

Sally just about managed it.

"God and Baby Jesus will forgive you if you accept them into your heart," continued the second policeman. The first gave him a funny look. "Don't run off again."

They didn't arrest her and take her to prison, or shoot her like the Guessed a Poo shot Eva's family. Mummy sent her to bed where she curled up under the blankets and cried and cried and cried. Much later Daddy got home. He came up to her bedroom, yanked off the sheets, flipped her over onto her front, pulled her jim-jam trousers down, and smacked her twice on the bare bottom. He wasn't half as rough as Mummy had been but he'd never ever hit her before. That made it a million times worse.

"Done it," he called out as he left the room. "Happy now?"

Sally couldn't breathe, couldn't think. Her mind cannoned around, hunting for anything that might make sense. She hadn't done anything wrong, nothing so bad it would lead to this. It had to be her. She was a bad, wicked girl deep down inside, a wicked person - what other reason was there? She thought of the Wodaran, with his parsnip head and white cloak, and for some strange reason he didn't frighten her this time. Instead, he seemed to understand. He'd been there in the apartment, when the Guessed a Poo lady tried to persuade them to go to the party at the top of the Blocko Tower. He protected Eva, looked after little girls. He and Eva were the only ones left who knew the truth. Sally rocked back and forth in the damp, unhappy darkness of her bed, and sang herself to sleep.

"Wodaran... Wodaran... Wodaran."

CHAPTER TWO

It didn't end there. In fact, it never seemed to end. The new bicycle disappeared and there was no sixth birthday party. Eva must have been poorly too, for she wasn't at school for a while, leaving Sally feeling very sad and lonely. Perhaps Mummy had told her what a wicked little girl Sally was, and so her best friend didn't want to be her best friend anymore, and had met someone else to lend the driving game to.

Everything at home changed. One night, she went downstairs and found Mummy and Daddy sitting on the floor at opposite ends of the hallway. Mummy was crying so her mascara had run, and an empty bottle lay on the carpet beside her. She looked like a monster, like a Krazy Kreature from Outer Space.

"It's all your fault," she said, staring at Sally with the same red eyes as the Chernod from Planet Supor in the 7th Galaxy. "It's all your fault."

"Don't," said Daddy, in that weary, sad voice he sometimes used.

A few evenings later, she heard a big crash from the dining room, followed by the sound of a sports car roaring up the road. This time Sally was too scared to go downstairs. Instead, she peeked through the bannisters as Daddy picked up the broken plate of spaghetti and wiped the wall. When she felt brave enough, she crept down again to find him in front of the TV, drinking directly from another bottle. She stood by the chair and cried and said she was sorry, hoping that would make things right. He just ruffled her hair and sent her back to bed.

He took her to school the next morning. At home time Mummy appeared as if nothing had happened. Instead of getting into the car, Sally was marched into the headmaster's office. Mr Cooper plaited his hands and peered at her over the top of his big wooden desk. A nodding bird pecked at a glass of water on the edge. Sally watched it while the grownups talked - one fast and impatient, the other slow and irritated.

"Sally. Sally!"

She looked up at Mr Cooper.

"I told your mummy that we showed all the children a film about talking to strangers. I hope you paid attention. Do you remember what George did when that man offered him sweets?"

"He ran away and told the policeman."

"That's right." Mr Cooper nodded. "Never go off with someone you don't know, and always tell Mummy or a policeman."

"I didn't go with a stranger. I went to play with Eva in the Blocko Tower."

"Who?"

Mummy started to speak. Mr Cooper held up his hand. To Sally's surprise, Mummy shut up.

"Eva Benjamin. She's my best friend in all the world. I sit at the back of Mrs Ryan's class with her."

Mr Cooper frowned and wrote something down.

"Even if we go to play with friends, we must always tell Mummy where we are," he looked up. "I'll ask Mrs Ryan to show everyone the film again, and perhaps get someone from the police station to come and read them the riot act. We do all we can to din it into the little blighters, and to field any questions that might come up, especially if they see or hear any stories they shouldn't."

On the way home Sally asked Mummy what stories Mr Cooper meant, but got only silence in return.

At long last the atmosphere eased. There were still arguments at night and at weekends, but at least Mummy no longer looked at her with the face of an angry stranger. She even let her go to other children's parties again, which was how Sally first met

Professor Backenforth.

For Rosalind Samson's sixth, she invited everyone in the class. Her mummy was very, very pretty, and wore the same clothes as Twiggy - Mary Quant dresses covered in big black squares and circles. They were so short all the children sitting on the carpet could see her knickers. She didn't seem to care. She had white plastic bangles on her arms and smoked her cigarettes in a long holder. Sally thought that was ever so glamorous.

There was a film show, which all the kids loved, even though it had no sound. While Sally sat in the darkness, a hand touched hers. Looking round, she saw Eva cross-legged beside her.

"Hello."

"Hello."

She didn't know what to say. Was Eva still her best friend in all the world? She hadn't been at school for ages and Sally worried that Mummy might have told her how bad she'd been. The other little girl opened her fingers and showed her a plastic centipede sitting on her palm.

"I made you another one."

Sally took the Thingmaker bug, reached across and hugged her friend. Happiness washed over her. She was puzzled, though. How did Eva know that the first plastic centipede had ended up wedged under the fridge at home?

"Have you still got the driving game?"

"Come and play, and you can borrow it," Eva said.

"I don't know if Mummy will let me." Sally didn't want to tell her about the horrible sad things that had happened after her first visit. If Eva still thought she was a good girl then maybe their friendship would last.

They held hands in silence and watched the cartoon. Afterwards, she went to the table to get some food for the two of them.

"Hello Sally," said Mrs Samson, who was standing at the kitchen door. She had a long-stemmed glass in one hand and her cigarette holder in the other. "Enjoying yourself?"

"Yes. Thank you for having me."

"Not at all. Thank you for coming."

"I like being the token goy."

Mrs Samson went *sssspppppt*, and sprayed out a bit of red wine. Then she said a bad word and licked the drops off her wrist.

"Who on Earth told you that?" she laughed.

"Is this anything to do with you, Vick?" Mr Samson called from another room.

"What?" Mrs Samson peered through the kitchen window. "Oh, right. He's here. Show them a cartoon while he gets set up."

"We haven't any others."

"Well show them the same one again."

They watched the silent Felix the Cat from the beginning once more. When it finished, Mrs Samson came in and clapped her hands. She must have done it too hard because she was a bit wobbly on her feet.

"Children, pay attention! We've got a very special guest who's come here all the way from outer space. He's going to take you on the most wonderful journey you could ever imagine. Ready?"

She and her husband stood on either side of the curtains covering the French windows.

"Yes," everyone shouted.

"I can't hear you," Mr Samson said.

"YEEEESSSSS."

"Ta da!" Mrs Samson said, and the two grownups pulled back the drapes.

All the children went OOOOOH! Sally was momentarily distracted because Mrs Samson had stumbled as she stepped backwards in her high heels, and nearly ended up in a potted plant. When Sally turned to look outside, all the other kids were standing at the window, except for Eva. She stayed in the shadows by the television set, her eyes big and solemn.

The Samsons had a lawn that seemed as vast as the school's games pitch. It rose up in a gentle slope to a small apple orchard at the back. A red truck sat in the middle, towing a giant ball. The vehicle looked like something out of Toy Town. It only had three wheels and certainly didn't seem strong enough to pull the contraption behind it.

"How the hell did he squeeze that down the side of the house?" Mr Samson said. "I hope he's not buggering up the turf. Where on Earth did you find him?"

"Stop grumbling and fetch me a top-up." Mrs Samson rotated her husband on the spot and gave him a gentle push towards the kitchen.

The ball was as big as a Mini and painted to show a scene on another planet. The upper half was covered in stars and spaceships. The bottom showed a fantastic city of glass and jewels, sitting in the middle of a desert. Three people in white space suits and bubble helmets fired rayguns at a group of aliens. They had heads like starfishes with an eyeball at the end of each tentacle. Beneath the buildings, bright green words spelled out *Mystery Planet*. Somebody had propped a step ladder against the side so you could climb onto the top, which suddenly popped open in a spray of glitter. All the children gasped.

A thin figure jumped out of the ball and stood with his feet on either side of the hatch, arms flung to heaven. The afternoon sun was right behind him and it was hard make out any details.

"Really?" Mr Samson said, in a voice that suggested he thought his wife had done something very silly.

"Shush. The kids love him. Professor Backenforth comes highly recommended."

"By who?"

The man wore flared trousers, a jacket and a top hat. In the early evening light he resembled a clutch of curved sticks wrapped in black cellophane. Mrs Samson managed to open the French windows and the other children streamed out into the garden. Sally felt a tug. Eva was shaking her head and pulling on her arm, coaxing her back into the corner of the room, between the huge television set and the bookcases.

"Don't go out there," she whispered. "Don't climb inside."

The other children formed a crocodile, jiggling and screeching in excitement. The first one, a mass of freckles called Ian Millington, climbed up the ladder and disappeared into the

Mystery Planet. Professor Backenforth threw more glitter into the air and this time it exploded with pops and cracks, sending threads of smoke drifting over the garden. He rapped on the side of the ball and Ian Millington reappeared, his eyes and mouth big round Os. The lad must have seen something utterly wonderful. As soon as he told the others, the line broke into a crowd of excited boys and girls, all jumping up and down with their arms in the air, shrieking *me next, me, me, me*. Sally started forwards, caught up in the hysteria, but Eva held on tight.

She still couldn't see Professor Backenforth's face. Somewhere in the back of her mind she got the impression of a black beard and moustache, and bright eyes resembling two setting suns. It was more like something she'd find in a picture book or a cartoon, not in real life. The noise and chaos were overwhelming. With Eva's worried face beside her in the shadows, Sally started to feel frightened. The conjuror faced away from the house, guiding each child up and down the ladder. They tumbled out of the ball, one after the other, yelling in wonder, desperate to tell their friends what they'd seen inside, what adventures they'd been on. Even though each child only stayed in the Mystery Planet for a minute, they seemed to emerge with the most incredible tales. Some of them made whooshing shapes in the air with their hands, or waved and slinked about in imitation of odd dream creatures.

"Sally. Aren't you going to have a go?" Mrs Samson stood beside her. Eva's hand closed on hers so tightly it pinched. Sally shook her head.

"She's frightened of him. No bloody wonder," Mr Samson's voice came from somewhere behind his wife. Mrs Samson hunkered down and pushed her face into Sally's. Up close, she wasn't quite so pretty. She had lipstick on her teeth and her breath smelled of wine and cigarette smoke. There was an odd sadness in her eyes. It made her seem a lot older.

"Oh don't be silly, Sally. It's perfectly safe. Look how much fun all the others are having. Come on."

She reached forwards and gave Sally's wrist a tug. Sally suddenly felt like crying, and pulled away.

"Come on, Vick. Leave her alone, poor lass," Mr Samson said. "If she's scared of that nutter, don't force her."

A flash of disappointment crossed Mrs Samson's face and she made a funny shape with her lips. For a second, Sally thought she was going to shout at her.

"Suit yourself," she stood up unsteadily. "Silly Sally."

More than anything, Sally was terrified Professor Backenforth would turn towards the house and see her and Eva hiding inside. Once or twice he seemed to be looking into the room, as if hunting for someone. If he picked her out there'd be no stopping him, and all the other children would force her to climb the ladder too.

The doorbell rang. It was Sandra Gott's mummy, with another parent Sally didn't recognise standing behind her on the drive. One by one, the kids came in from the garden. They bustled in the hall for their goody bags and pieces of cake, reaching up for grownup hands to coax them outside and into waiting cars.

"Didn't see him go," Mr Samson said, herding the stragglers inside. "Did you pay him?"

"Think so," Mrs Samson shrugged. "I'll check later. Sally, here's your daddy."

She'd lost Eva in the crowd, which was a shame because she wanted Daddy to meet her friend so he'd understand she'd spent that awful day playing in the Blocko Tower and hadn't run away at all. Maybe Eva would be at school on Monday.

At home, Mummy took the goody bag and peered inside.

"Jesus Christ. Is that Fortnum and Mason's chocolate? And a book as well, as if she hasn't got enough already. Have a nice time?"

Sally shrugged.

"What did you do? I bet there was a conjuror."

"And a film show," Daddy said.

"Bloody hell. Don't get ideas," Mummy handed the bag back. "Eat it up, then clean your teeth and bed."

Later on, when she was trying to go to sleep, her bedroom door opened. It was Daddy, silhouetted against the landing light.

"Mrs Mendelssohn's on the phone. Was Anthony at the party?"

"Yes," Sally said. She'd watched him climb into Professor Backenforth's Mystery Planet.

"Did you see where he went? He wasn't there when she went to pick him up."

"No."

He shut the door and she lay back down. Professor Backenforth's shadow danced on the ceiling. She closed her eyes tight and pulled the blankets over her head. The phone rang an awful lot that evening, keeping her awake for ages. Eventually she fell asleep, only to wake up to find her door open again. This time two people stood in the passageway outside - Mummy and another woman.

"Sally, when did you last see Anthony Mendelssohn?"

"At the party."

She wanted to tell them about Professor Backenforth, but when she'd talked about it to Mummy before she'd been shouted at and smacked. That was when they thought she'd run away.

"You didn't see him leave with anyone?"

"No."

"Are you sure?"

"Yes."

Muttering in the hallway. The woman seemed worried, almost crying.

"She's pissed as a fart," she was saying. "How could you let yourself get into that state when you're supposed to be looking after twenty kids?"

"He must have gone home with one of the other parents," Mummy said.

"Nobody's seen him."

The woman's voice sounded broken and angry. They moved downstairs.

Sally tried to remember what had happened. When she sent her mind back to the party, to the moment Anthony Mendelssohn climbed that ladder, Professor Backenforth was standing at the bottom, staring back at her with a horrible grin. The shock kicked her out of the memory every time.

In the morning, two police officers knocked on the door. At first Sally thought they were going to tell her off again for running away, but these visitors were different. One was a woman with glossy brown hair tied back in a pony tail under her cap. She wore a tie like Daddy did for work, black tights, and shoes polished so brightly they reflected the whole room. The other was an old man with a bald head. He didn't wear a uniform.

"Hello Sally," the lady said. "I'm WPC Rhodes. You can call me Gill, and this is Detective Inspector Conway. Can we ask you a few questions about the party?"

"Don't worry, lass." The man had a voice so deep it made the floorboards rumble. "You're not in any trouble."

She wondered if he was going to talk about God, like the one who told her off on that horrible day.

"Now then poppet, did you see Anthony Mendelssohn at the party?" the man said.

She nodded.

"Was he still there when you left?" the policewoman asked.

Sally shook her head.

"Did you see him leave?" the detective said.

"No."

"This man, this magician, do you remember what he looked like?"

"He's Professor Backenforth. He has parties at the top of the Blocko Tower, where my friend Eva lives. He's a Guessed a Poo."

The two visitors swapped excited glances, as if she'd told them something really important. Happy to help, she opened her mouth but Daddy interrupted.

"Sally's got an imaginary friend she calls Eva. I wouldn't pay too much attention."

"She's not imaginary," Sally got cross. "She sits with me at the back of Mrs Ryan's class. I went to her flat in the Blocko Tower, on the other side of the woods, and we played with her driving game. You said I ran away. I didn't, I was playing at Eva's."

Mummy stared at her. For a second Sally thought she was going to shout and smack her for telling lies, but this time she looked sad for some reason, and when she spoke her voice was soft and kind.

"Sally, darling, Eva doesn't exist. Mrs Ryan says you sit on your own, and play on your own," she turned to the police. "She disappeared into the woods for eight hours, a few months back - said she'd been at a friend's in some tower block over Alwoodley way. It's all a fantasy."

The bald man blew a lot of air out of his mouth. It made him look like a hamster. The two visitors stood up.

"Is that it?" Daddy said.

"Thank you Sally, you've been very helpful." Gill reached down and ruffled her hair.

"Do you remember anything at all strange?" Mummy asked Sally. "Anything that might help?"

All she could do was shrug. She'd already told Mummy and Daddy what she knew. Professor Backenforth had probably taken Anthony to the top of the Blocko Tower. If they looked there they'd find him. Nobody believed her.

The grownups moved into the hallway. Mummy sounded like she was getting cross again.

"There's not a lot we can get from a bunch of six year olds. Twenty kids will come up with twenty different versions of what happened," the policewoman was saying. "At that age their heads are half in fairyland."

"What about Vicky Samson? Surely she knows where she hired the bloody pervert from in the first place."

"She's helping us with our enquiries. Here's a number to ring if you hear anything or see anything."

The door shut and two pairs of feet rapped their way down the drive.

"Anthony's at the top of the Blocko Tower on the other side of the woods," Sally said again, trying to be helpful.

"Right, I've had enough of this bloody nonsense," Mummy snapped. "Get your coat and wellies on."

They marched out of the house, down the street, and into the woods. Mummy was doing her usual fast walk so Sally had to keep running to stay close to her parents. The trees were silent and full of shadows. Sally kept her eyes down and waited for the dirt track to change into concrete. It never did. After a long time, the trees on either side turned into high privet hedges. The path came out onto a wide road stretching left to right. The homes opposite were identical to the ones on their street.

"There you go. Alwoodley Lane," Mummy announced. She gestured around her. "Where's your 'Blocko Tower' then?"

Sally looked up and down the street. Houses stretched away into the distance. This wasn't right. They must have gone down the wrong path. The Blocko Tower was here somewhere. She glanced back down the track and saw nothing more than a pale line disappearing into the gloomy wood. Mummy lit a Marlboro, shaking her head and muttering to herself.

"It's all in your bloody imagination," she poked her daughter hard on the forehead with the hand that held the cigarette. The smoke billowed around Sally's eyes and made them water.

"Let's not have any more talk about Eva and the Blocko Tower, eh?" Daddy asked, in that tired voice he used all the time these days.

"One more peep and, I swear to God, I'll whack the living daylights out of you," Mummy blew smoke out of her nose like a fierce dragon and stared at something beyond the rooftops of the houses opposite. "We've got to move, Doug. I'm going spare. I'm definitely not staying here if there's another bloody pervert murdering kids. What is it with you northerners? First the Moors Murders, now this."

In the following weeks a heavy silence descended on the neighbourhood. Sally wasn't allowed out by herself anymore and when she looked out of her bedroom window, she didn't see any other children playing in the street. In school assembly, Mr Cooper read everyone the riot act about going off with strange men. Halfway through, Mrs Ryan ran out of the hall crying. Miss Pritchard took over their class for the next few days.

Sally sat at the back and kept glancing at Eva's empty chair. How could she not be real? Her big brown eyes and curly black hair were so vivid in her mind. One of the buttons on her blue woollen coat was missing and her left shoe had a scuff mark. She remembered all of that, as well as the grey calm world of her apartment and the chemical reek from the Thingmaker. Maybe Professor Backenforth had her imprisoned too, at the top of the Blocko Tower or inside his Mystery Planet. Could Sally find her and set her free, and Anthony Mendelssohn? How?

On Sunday, there was a knock at the door. The man outside had a grey beard and a little black cap on the back of his head. She'd seen some of the boys in her class wear the same, on their way to the synagogue. He sat down on the sofa while Mummy and Daddy stared at him. It felt awkward and silent.

"Would you like some tea?" Mummy said eventually, in that tight voice she used when speaking to Grandad.

"That would be nice, thank you," the man turned to look at Sally. "Hello Sally. Do you know who I am?"

She shook her head.

"My name is Rabbi Jason Schemman. Do you know what a rabbi is?"

Mark Truman had once told her a rabbi was a special teacher. She said so.

"Clever girl. Kind of, yes. Christians have a church and a vicar. Jews have a synagogue and a rabbi - that's me."

"How can we help?" asked Mummy, pushing the tea under the man's nose. He smiled, took it, had a slurp, and set it on his knee.

"Obviously, in the light of what has happened, I felt it my duty to visit the community to offer what little help I can," he held his hand up. "I know, I know you're not of our faith. Nevertheless, you are part of this community, and so I wanted to come and speak with you too. As you can imagine, Victoria Samson is suffering such guilt over all this, and she specifically asked me to talk to every parent who had a child at the party."

"Ok," said Mummy. She sat down and stared at the visitor. "Go ahead."

The man turned to Sally.

"It is very important for you to understand that what

happened was nobody's fault."

Mummy went *humph*. The rabbi ignored her and smiled at Sally. He had big kind eyes like Eva's.

"You do realise that don't you?"

She nodded.

"Did you see the man the police are looking for, this Professor Backenforth?"

Sally nodded again.

"Did you go inside this Mystery Planet of his?"

"No."

"Oh. Why not?"

"My friend told me not to."

"Which friend was that?"

"Eva Benjamin."

"For Christ's sake," Mummy said.

"Eva Benjamin is her imaginary friend," Daddy said. "We've already spoken about this with the police. She only exists in Sally's head. No-one else has ever seen or heard of her."

"Really? What's this Eva Benjamin like?"

"Please don't encourage her," Mummy said.

"She lives in the Blocko Tower. It's called Backenforth Heights, and it's where Professor Backenforth lives too. Eva lives in a flat by herself. She has a mezuzah on the door to keep away the dybbuks and the Guessed a Poo."

The tea cup stopped halfway between the rabbi's knees and his lips.

"Where does she get all this bloody tripe from?" Mummy asked, of no-one in particular.

"The dybbuks and the who?" Rabbi Schemman said.

"The Guessed a Poo. They took her family away and shot them in the woods, so she became friends with the Wodaran from Pluto, and he protects her with his raygun."

"I'm sorry, she's talking rubbish again," Daddy said. Rabbi Schemman lifted up his hand and it had the same magic effect as when Mr Cooper did the same to Mummy. Both her parents fell silent.

"Guessed a Poo? Guessed a Poo, Guessed a Poo," the rabbi rolled the words around in his mouth as if he was trying to make sense of them. He shot a sudden look at Sally that made her jump. "Gestapo? The Gestapo executed her family? Are you sure? They existed a very long time ago. Way before you were born. Your friend Eva would have to be as old as me..."

"Right, that's it," Mummy said. She stood up and took the rabbi's cup and saucer. "Look, we all know what happened to you lot was awful and everything, but this is what you get when you constantly harp on about it in front of all the children. Sally now thinks she's best friends with Anne Frank's ghost. She doesn't need any more encouragement. My daughter's disturbed enough. For Christ's sake, can't you give it a rest? It was over twenty years ago. Isn't it time to move on?"

Rabbi Schemman smiled.

"Of course. Thank you for the tea," he stood up, looked down at Sally, winked, and headed for the door. Outside he paused and glanced back.

"Blessings be upon this house." He made a sign.

"Yes. Thanks. And you. Bye." said Mummy and shut the door. "Unbelievable. Honestly. Totally unbelievable. We've got to move. I told you, one more day in Moortown and I'm going to go mental."

Sally sensed another row starting and felt relieved when Daddy sent her to her bedroom. There she could hide under the covers and read the Tintin book Grandma had bought her while the storm rumbled below.

A few weeks later, Mummy took her to meet a woman in a big old house in Headingley. It was set behind high brick walls, and so far back from the road it was like walking through the woods again to reach the front door. The lady was tall, grey-haired, thin and scary-looking, but she had a kind smile, and gave her visitor a glass of lemon barley water, made precisely to the consistency she liked - nice and sweet and sticky.

Her name was Florence and she was a special doctor. She sat Sally down in an enormous chair in a room full of books and showed her some sheets of paper with black paint splashed on them. Florence asked her to say if she saw any shapes, like people or animals or things. She gave it her best shot - a tree, a cat, a Krazy Kreature from Outer Space. Florence wrote down a few words, and then wanted to know if she was happy and had lots of friends at school. Sally shrugged her way through most of the questions. When the woman asked about Eva, Sally told her about Backenforth Heights and her friend's fantastic toys. After half an hour the meeting was over and she was sent to play with a jigsaw in another room while Mummy and Florence talked.

They drove home in silence.

"Normal." Mummy tossed her car keys into the bowl by the front door.

"You sound disappointed," Daddy said.

"'An imaginative child, a bit young for her years, who just needs to make more real friends instead of made up ones'. Waste of bloody money. None of them know what they're talking about."

And that was that. Sally never saw Eva at school again, or anywhere else, for a very, very long time. Anthony Mendelssohn wasn't found, nor Professor Backenforth. Six months after the party, Vicky Samson got blind drunk and killed herself by wrapping her car around a tree on the A61. Two nights later, Sally had the nightmare for the first time.

She was pushing her new bicycle up the road, towards her home. Nobody else was about. All the houses were closed and silent, their windows echoing the heavy clouds that seemed low enough to touch. She'd almost reached the end of the drive when hands grabbed her from behind, thin and hard like branches. They started to drag her back down the street.

"Mummy help me," she screamed. "MUMMY MUMMY MUMMY."

The front of her home hinged down like a doll's house, falling with a crash across the lawn, crushing the laurel hedge. Instead of the lounge, hall and bedrooms, the entire interior was filled with Mummy's face, squashed into a giant square, as if her head had been rammed into a box that was way too small. Her mother's eyes, each as big as Sally, glared down. Her right one sat bang smack in the middle of the space where her bedroom should have been. Instead of her books and toys, all she could see was a bloodshot eye, red-ringed with wet muscle where the walls pulled back the skin at the side of the skull. The mouth was a downturned snarling garage door, with yellow teeth and a tongue as huge as a double bed. The reek of stale cigarettes saturated the air.

"WHERE HAVE YOU BEEN? YOU'VE BEEN GONE EIGHT HOURS. EIGHT FUCKING HOURS YOU STUPID WICKED LITTLE SHIT."

The voice thundered off the houses opposite and ricocheted down from the storm clouds, kicking up dried leaves. They clogged the air like birds. Unable to breathe, Sally tumbled backwards in slow motion, her heart bursting as she disappeared into a thicket of fingers as sharp as sea anemone spines.

CHAPTER THREE

Portslade, 1982

"Are you Bob?"

"Might be. Oo wants to know?"

"I'm here for the job you advertised in the window."

The owner of the junk shop near the cemetery resembled Asterix the Gaul's drug-addict grandad. He sat in the back room of the immense converted warehouse, wearing just a biker's waistcoat and bell bottoms. He had his bare feet on a desk and was halfway through rolling a dodgy-looking cigarette. A copy of *Tales from the Leather Nun* lay open on his lap. A consumptive sausage dog that looked too fat to move wheezed in front of a three bar electric fire. Bob stared at Sally, stroking his grey walrus moustache and goatee with yellowed fingers.

"Really? Fuck me." He glared at her a little longer. "How did you bust your nose?"

"Fighting."

"Who?"

"Yugoslavian kickboxer called Bogdan."

"Jesus Christ."

"He was a bit of a cunt," Sally acknowledged.

"'kin 'ell, 'kin Aida, 'kin arseholes, Lemmy," Bob addressed the dog. "We got a right little psycho here. What do you reck? Should I give her a chance?"

The dog didn't answer. Bob licked the paper in his hand with a tongue the colour of a portobello mushroom and sealed up his cigarette.

"20 a week."

"30."

"Fuck off. You're only a student. 22."

"25."

Bob lit his spliff, took a drag, and burst into a vicious fit of coughing.

"Done. And get a bra, for Christ's sake. Those chapel hat pegs are giving me a heart attack and frightening the dog."

"I haven't got a bra."

"There's a box of second hand knocker lockers over by the garage entrance. Take one of them. I don't want to spend my final days on Earth fending off a bunch of perverts from my new assistant, thank you very much. One flash of those baps and they'll have you over a packing crate."

Sally pulled her biker jacket closed and yanked up the zip.

"Happy now?"

Bob shook his head.

"You're trouble. I can feel it in my water. I've got a lorry load of tat from Worthing coming in at 7am tomorrow. Be here."

The job was as undemanding as it was boring, consisting of long days sorting crap out in the mahogany shadows of the warehouse. It had been partitioned with plasterboard walls into an immense maze. Most of the time Sally worked by herself, which suited her just fine. These days she was surrounded by an invisible wall, originally built to shut out Mummy's endless tantrums so they became nothing more than distant noise. Now the same barrier stood between her and everyone else. Once it had bugged her, especially when she'd longed for a boyfriend. After she'd hit her twenties, Sally found herself happy enough with her own company. As an added bonus, Bob left her well alone.

Once in a while, groups of men in donkey jackets brought in boxes of junk from the houses down by the beach. Those ancient buildings curved to and fro in their parades like scalloped coral.

When Sally wandered along the seafront on grey Sundays, eating chips out of newspaper, she caught glimpses of their inhabitants. Shadows sat bolt upright in their chairs, in the centre of vaulted rooms, surrounded by heavy furniture, and carpets liberally sprinkled with dried cat shit, watching for teatime visitors who never turned up.

When they died the men in donkey jackets gutted the house and brought the things they couldn't immediately sell to Bob. Later on, different men in different donkey jackets came and carted oddments away in unmarked vans. Sally wouldn't have been surprised to see the occasional mummified pensioner among the collections of dusty armchairs and cracked mirrors, still waiting and watching. All the while Bob sat with his feet propped up on a desk and read his comics through wreaths of smoke, studiously ignoring both her and his visitors.

One freezing Tuesday in March the rain poured off the Channel and hurled itself horizontally along the street. It was warmer at the back of the warehouse, where Bob stored the curtains and carpets, so Sally spent the afternoon rummaging through its musty corners. She came across a cardboard box full of old toys and carried it to the room next to the office so she could empty it out on the pool table.

Three broken Action Men with gripping hands and rotating eyeballs, a wind-up robot, a dusty ViewMaster with a reel still inside, and handfuls of Airfix plastic soldiers. When she came to the last box her hand flew to her mouth and she stepped back, heart pounding. It took her a good fifteen seconds to gather her thoughts and have another look.

Remote Control Driving Test Game - A Test of Skill, she read.

A boy in a blue jumper held a control stick at the bottom of a map. Behind him, red buses trundled up and down a busy road. She recognised it as the Old Steine in Brighton. Sally eased the box out, cleared a space for it on the patched felt, and took off the lid. Memories rushed back - of pale silence and the stink of chemicals. The lever lay across the board, next to a miniature Morris Minor and a BSA motorbike, a clumsily painted policeman with his arm up, a stop sign and a telephone booth. She screwed the control into place, set up the pieces at random, and put the yellow vehicle in the centre, between the moulded plastic houses. She wiggled the rod until the magnets clicked, and manoeuvred the car down the street.

Seven Dials, Church Road, Kemptown. Hang on a minute.

The game she remembered from her childhood was set in Leeds. This showed a stylised Brighton and Hove, with the Pavilion and the piers printed in badly offset colours. They must have done different editions for different cities, like the London and Chicago versions of Monopoly.

"What you got there?" Bob called out from his office.

"An old board game from the '60s."

"Has it got all its bits? Worth sod all without the bits."

"I think so."

Sally flipped over the lid and nearly dropped it. Near the edge she saw the words *Eva Benjamin* in a child's scrawl. Time had faded the letters to a pale blue but the pen had left an indent in the cardboard. Eva Benjamin, the girl she made up, who lived in the Blocko Tower. What was it called again? Backenforth Heights, owned by Professor Backenforth, the nonce who kidnapped that lad at the party all those years ago. Eva Benjamin, Professor Backenforth. The girl everyone told her didn't exist. The pervert they never found.

"Where's this from?"

She laid the lid on the green baize, put her hands either side to stop them shaking, and read the name again and again. The room around her boomed and rocked in time to the emotions thundering through her head.

"You what?"

"I said, where did you get this game from?"

"What game?"

She picked up the lid, marched into the office and stuck it under Bob's nose.

"This game. Where did it come from?"

"Alright, alright, cool your boots. Fucking 'ell, has rag week arrived early or something? What's the number on the box it was in?"

"479."

"479. 479." Bob flicked through his notebook. "An old arcade behind the concrete plant. Came in two weeks ago."

"I'm taking the rest of the afternoon off."

"Good. You're disturbing my idyll. Fuck off until the painters have left and you've learned how to be civil again, but don't expect me to pay you in the meantime."

Sally put the Driving Test Game back in its box and found a plastic bin bag to protect it from the lashing rain. Tucking the package under her arm, she shouldered her way out of the door and onto the deserted pavement. There was no barrier between the world and the inside of her head. The same freezing, salt-tainted tempest blew through her mind, sending waves crashing against its fragile walls. The box's sharp corner jabbed into her armpit as she crunched herself up as tight as possible against the ferocious downpour, and set off towards the concrete plant.

Grey rain on the long ribbon streets that wove through Portslade down to the sea like strands of an old woman's hair. They were all the same - flat dead tarmac flanked by rows of white-painted terrace houses, giving way to shops and takeaways closer to the front. Most were boarded up. The only thing that changed from street to street was the view at the end. Head down, hopping from one awning to the next when she could, ploughing on against the downpour when she couldn't, Sally used that patch of sea to get her bearings. As she did, the distant smudge changed, turning darker as if the world was dissolving. Gantries formed around the shadow, cranes reared up above it, their tops blurred by the torrent. One more junction and she turned to follow the road towards the shore, face down as the wind hammered the top of her skull and transformed her ragged mohican into a wet mane. No-one else was about. Nobody was that stupid.

Her thoughts began to reform around a kernel of bitter realisation. Eva the imaginary friend. Wasn't that what they'd said? It was so hard to push back in time, to when she was six, and piece together the fragments of memory. They shivered and bobbed like driftwood on the churning sea. Eva the imaginary friend. That's what they told her - her parents, her teacher, Mr Cooper the headmaster, the psychiatrist in her grand dame house at the end of a shadowed garden in Headingley. In the end, even she had convinced herself that the afternoon spent playing with the Thingmaker and the Driving Test Game in the Blocko Tower was nothing more than the fantasy of a lonely child.

Yet Eva turned over the box lid and wrote her name in biro, so I'd remember who it belonged to.

And here it was, jabbing into her armpit, the most real thing in the world while the rest of creation dissolved in the rain. They'd all lied to her. Why? After the party Sally never saw Eva again. Had something happened to the girl? Was everyone trying to protect little Sally from some awful truth, that her new playmate had also been abducted by that pervert, Professor Backenforth?

The street abruptly ended at the entrance to the cement works, a metal gate laced with bales of barbed wire. The perimeter fence stretched towards Hove to the east and west to Kingston, where it became a concrete wall after a quarter of a mile. Sally trudged along the narrow access road, pressing up against the low brick buildings. At the end, she spotted a sign over a shuttered warehouse. *Jimmy Corrigan Amusements*. She stopped and gawped. Here? In Portslade? There were plenty of these tired, seedy arcades on the Yorkshire coast. How many times had she blown all her holiday pocket money on the Penny Falls in Filey or Scarborough? But she'd never come across a Corrigans down here, on the South Coast, and why on earth stick it on an access road in these industrial wastelands, so far away from the beaches and the piers?

It was clearly deserted. In fact, it looked as if it had been abandoned for years. Maybe Bob had got his facts wrong and the game came from somewhere else. She doubted it. Despite the biker get-up and the weed, the old git's bookkeeping was ludicrously meticulous.

Even a crowbar wouldn't have shifted those padlocked shutters, but Sally wasn't going to give up that easily. An alleyway ran between the arcade and the last building. She climbed over the rusty gate without any problems, and squeezed her way through the high grass and rubble to a small window near the back. After making sure it wasn't overlooked, she picked up a brick, broke the glass and popped the latch. The rotten frame swung inwards, shedding tiny spiders and woodlice. Sally listened carefully. Nothing, and no lights inside. She balanced the game on the windowsill and pulled herself up and into the building.

She waited as her eyes adjusted to the gloom. Water dripped from her jacket and sodden jeans to puddle at her feet. It was cold in this shit-coloured murk. Shapes resolved themselves here and there, abandoned versions of the machines she'd played as a child, all smaller and pitifully tawdry, their badly drawn paintings of cowboys, castles and spaceships suspended over empty trays and broken mechanisms. Near the main entrance, where grey light and filthy water leaked under the shutters, Sally noticed a Claw Crane. It looked as if all the prizes had rotted long ago, turning into black sludge that coated the bottom half of the glass case. The rusted claw hung over the indistinct terrain like the hand of an angry god.

Now what? She retrieved the plastic bag containing the Driving Test Game and moved deeper into the building. Without any light it was hard to get a sense of the layout. A couple of doorways at the back emitted a faint radiance from hidden windows in the rooms beyond. It spread across the concrete in rippling fans.

"Hello?" she called out, not really expecting a reply. Whoever brought the toy box to Bob wasn't here. Probably another unknown man in a donkey-jacket. She imagined him and his mates moving through the cities and countryside like a flock of ravens, picking at random leavings from other people's lives. They'd have passed through here once or twice and moved on. None of them ever spoke more than a word to her when delivering their findings to the warehouse. None of them had ever tried to have her over a packing crate.

The door on the left led to a room with a single wooden table in the middle. It was covered in concrete dust and grime from the broken ceiling above. A row of high windows in the far wall let in a pale light. The next room was crammed full of shattered doors and chairs, making it impossible to enter. Not knowing what else to do, Sally returned to the table and opened the game on the tabletop, wiping as much muck off the wood as she could with her jacket sleeve. She wanted to reassure herself that she hadn't imagined Eva's name in faded biro. Yep, it was still there.

Bending over the board, she traced the streets. To her surprise Jimmy Corrigan's Amusement Arcade appeared down in the bottom left. Two children, barely more than a handful of screen printed dots, ran towards its entrance. A road curled around the building and ended at a tower block an inch further up. The picture was mis-set, half cut off by the edge of the board, along with its name. ...*enforth* ...*ights*.

For some inexplicable reason, Sally's eyes filled with tears. It was one of those odd moments when she seemed to split in two. One Sally was overtaken with an emotion whose roots she couldn't trace, the other watched herself dispassionately through a familiar glass wall. To compose herself, she walked to the end of the room and stood on tiptoe to try and see out of a window. It was too high up to show anything more than the lowering clouds, but that dark vertical rectangle in the distance, blurred by runnels of grubby water streaming down the pane, bothered her.

Eva's game had consisted of a simple map of Leeds, with Backenforth Heights to the north, near her old house. In this version of the Driving Test Game, with its comic-book pictures of Brighton Pavilion and Kemptown, it sat next to this amusement arcade. Was it some strange motif added to every map, like an artist's signature?

She rubbed her forehead and tried to remember. It was so hard to push back through time into the fuzzy mind of a six-year-old. So much was jumbled up and slathered over with the intervening years. Little Sally mixed up reality and fantasy, that's what they'd all said. Was she doing it again now? Was this all in her imagination, a symptom of something worse than infant loneliness? Her skin felt hot and there was a feverish hiss in her ears. Coming down with something after getting drenched. She wanted nothing more than to get back to her bedsit and bury herself under the duvet. Sally replaced the lid, wrapped up the game, and headed for the door.

And then Sally spotted something else in the shadows beyond the Claw Crane. She must have missed it before, distracted by the light from the back rooms. A sphere rested in the corner. It was about the same size as a Mini, tilted slightly on one side, with a hatch on top. On its surface bleached figures in faded space suits fought tentacled aliens, like an old cartoon straining to be seen on a misfiring television set. Two words ran round the middle.

Mystery Planet.

Heart pounding, she reached up and tried the hatch. It creaked open and fell back against the sphere with an almighty clang.

He stood on the top with the sun behind him and the children climbed in one by one. Eva held me back, told me not to go.

The pitch black hole rested at an angle, like the pupil of gouged-out eye. Sally did a quick recce around the base of the Mystery Planet but couldn't see a plug or a switch. Still wanting to understand what was inside after all these years, she pulled a stool out of the tangle in the backroom, set it beside the sphere, and clambered up for a better look. The opening smelled of metal and dust. There was an odd taste in her mouth, as if she'd licked a battery. She could make out shapes in there, angles and panels. Maybe it was supposed to be the interior of a spaceship. You sat in a chair and watched a cartoon that fooled you into thinking you were journeying through outer space. It wouldn't be anything fancy, especially if this was a hangover from the 1960s. Probably not even a movie, just a couple of shampoo bottles sprayed silver dangling on wires, a table tennis ball lit with a red bulb pretending to be Mars.

Sally found herself sitting inside, wrapped up in a warm fist made of shadows. How had that happened? Had she overbalanced and fallen, or climbed in of her own accord? She felt dizzy and the hissing in her ears was louder. No point in staying in this weird pit if it didn't have any power. She tried to heave herself back up. At that moment the hatch above closed with a dead thump and she was lost in total darkness.

CHAPTER FOUR

Sally tried to get up. An immense hand pressed her down into the seat. She was stuck in some kind of pilot's chair, almost on her back, with her knees up against her chest and her arms stretched out on either side, touching cold metal structures that felt like cobwebs knitted out of silver foil. All sense of direction had vanished the instant the hatch slammed shut, and now she couldn't even figure out which way was up. She guessed where the opening might be - a few feet away, opposite her face. She lifted her arm, it was so heavy, and reached into the darkness. Her fingertips met nothing and the effort exhausted her. Sally slumped down, the back of her skull thumping into a wad of musty cloth. It was as if the universe had dialled gravity up several notches.

From behind her glass wall she waited for the panic, the desperate fear. She'd locked herself in a disused ride in an abandoned amusement arcade in the middle of nowhere. The air was running out and she'd die screaming and gasping as she clawed her nails off against the hatch. Nothing. Her mind swam in an ocean of blank indifference, as if the sphere was full of frozen time in which every emotion foundered. Not even the slightest glimmer of urgency made her lift her hand again. Sally felt only a fatal lassitude as she sensed the curved walls race away in all directions, leaving her alone in a void.

The blackness still pressed against her face, but now Sally got the impression of other shapes within this new, vast nothing. An image formed in her mind, of a plain covered in spheres identical to the Mystery Planet. A hundred sat in a perfect ten by ten grid. The vision in her head became as clear as a photograph taken with an infra-red camera, and brought with it a precise geometry. Yet, at the same time, it had all the delirious grainy unreality of a picture slipping unbidden into her consciousness, through the thin gap between waking and a fever dream.

She was not alone. Another moved among the rows, a warden tended the spheres, gently touching each before moving onto the next. This being was at once recognisably human, although in perpetual silhouette so she could only glimpse its top hat and flared trousers, and at the same time formless and all-encompassing. The first shreds of emotion returned. A churning dread puddled in her stomach and lungs, swiftly replacing the dead emptiness. The edges of the creature bled out into this universe, became the cosmos itself. It wrapped long protean arms about Sally, arching above and around her to create a dark membrane in which a shapeless mouth and wet eyes slid, its expressions of idiot hunger endlessly dissolving and solidifying.

Fear and disgust dislodged something. Sally sensed her own sphere start to move backwards, drifting up and over the others. It was as if the vessel was trying to put as much distance as possible between herself and the creature. The entity did seem to be hunting for her now, peering under and around the spheres to find out where she was hiding.

And then the scene turned into something far stranger. The grid and spheres gave way to a landscape made entirely of iron. Sally sensed it was another realm, a world perhaps or even a universe, walled, floored and roofed with rusting plates as big as continents, and filled with an actinic radiance so bright it leached everything of colour. Four figures sat in high-back chairs. Etiolated and masked, they watched her retreat. In the next instant the vision switched off and the matrix of spheres continued to diminish as she drifted backwards. Her viewpoint rotated to face the direction of travel. As distance increased, her sense of dread faded, but she couldn't shake off the impression that the gardener was still searching for her, peering up into the darkness from between the rows of Mystery Planets.

After a while she noticed a glow ahead, as if a dawn were breaking on the featureless plain below. No star or sun appeared, just a dull red pulse below the horizon. At the same time, the landscape on either side began to bunch up, rising in mounds and hills like an untidy duvet, until she drifted between long ranges of slumped and half-melted mountains.

A structure appeared dead ahead, in the middle of a valley. Tall and thin, its top towered above the adjacent ridges. Sally recognised it instantly. The Blocko Tower. It looked exactly like any high rise block of flats, except this one stretched for miles into the featureless sky. A brush flick of shining dots marked its lighted windows. They rose from the entrance, which glowed with its own poisonous yellow. Sally's vessel dropped down to skim towards the glass doors. On the other side, she saw linoleum, concrete stairs and two stainless steel lifts.

A figure stepped in front of her before she could pass inside. The being stood taller than a human and wore a white robe. Its head looked like an inverted parsnip, a yellow, scabby cone rising to a lop-sided point. The Wodaran stared at her with its black button eyes and down-turned ink-slash mouth. A long arm, twisted and boneless, reached out from beneath its gown and arched up above her. The next second, blows rained down on Sally's face and shoulders and she heard her mother's voice screaming.

"EIGHT FUCKING HOURS YOU STUPID WICKED LITTLE SHIT!"

Sally woke up under white sheets. The same weight that had pressed her into the Mystery Planet pushed her into the mattress, barely leaving her with enough strength to lift her head. A tube full of clear liquid stretched from a needle in the back of her hand to an inverted bottle on a stand. Beyond her feet, a blue plastic curtain hid the rest of the room, except for a gap at the end. On the far side she saw another white-framed bed, and through the window above it, brick chimneys and a bright sky.

"Sally? Sally Aston?"

The doctor looked barely older than herself. His big National Health glasses drowned out his sallow face. The West Indian nurse next to him unhooked the notes from the end of the bed, handed it to her colleague, folded her arms and gave their patient a *What are we going to do with you then?* stare.

"I'm Doctor Gibson," the man tapped the report. "Pneumonia. You were found on the canal bank opposite the cement works on Albion Street, in the freezing rain. Somebody thought you were a dead body washed up on the shore. Lucky for you the police realised otherwise and brought you in. Did you fall in, or jump in?"

Sally ignored the question.

"How long have I been here?"

"Out like a light for three days, which has given us a chance to pump you full of antibiotics and get your fever down. Like I said, you're lucky. Anaemic, not unusual for a student living on booze and fags and not much else. Having said that, you're surprisingly fit, even if you don't eat properly. Aerobics?"

"Kickboxing."

"Well that explains a lot. Are you happy with the shape of your nose?"

"What?"

"The shape of your nose - are you happy with it?"

He sat on the bed and reached for her. She instinctively flinched, but he held her jaw ever so gently and turned her head this way and that. It wasn't a bad break. Bogdan's misplaced kick had hit the bridge side-on. He hadn't left her with a classic saddle nose but it was noticeable enough to make others wary when they first met her, which suited Sally just fine.

"It'd be a bugger to fix. We'd have to re-break it."

"Don't listen to him. I think it looks very sexy," the nurse said in a *he's talking bollocks* voice. It sounded like she used it a lot when trailing around after Doctor Gibson.

"I'm happy with the way it is, thanks."

The doctor eased his bottom off the sheets.

"Right, well, we contacted your parents and told them what happened. Seeing as how they're up in Yorkshire there's not a lot they can do. Absolutely no point them traipsing all the way down here if you're not at death's door. I spoke with the university. Somebody is going to come and see how you are and have a chat."

"How long have I got to stay here?"

"End of the week, I reckon. If your infection count's down by then, I might let you out."

They left Sally to her own thoughts and moved on down the ward. The nurse pulled her curtains apart, treating her to a view of the rest of the patients. They were mainly ancient women curled over or crumpled under the sheets like empty flour sacks. None of them showed the slightest interest in her. Even so, she still reached out and eased the blue sheet back along its runners to try and hide. They reminded her too much of the abandoned ghosts sitting in their lonely drawing rooms in those big old houses down by the front.

The drugs and pneumonia had scraped her insides out, leaving what was left hollow and breathless. Lying on the hospital bed, she watched the ceiling tiles pulse in time to her heart. This room felt as fragile as an eggshell. So did Sally. When she managed to lift her head to peer at the clear Brighton sky with its brick chimneys, it seemed merely an image projected onto grainy chaos.

Fragments of the past assembled themselves in her head. First the Driving Test Game in Bob's warehouse, then Jimmy Corrigan's by the cement factory. Inside the abandoned amusement arcade she'd climbed into Professor Backenforth's Mystery Planet and had some kind of fit or fugue. She'd imagined that she was flying through darkness over a landscape littered with spheres, towards the Blocko Tower. Fever did that, didn't it? The freezing downpour had ramped up whatever lurgy she'd caught, to the point where she'd started seeing things, pulling in nonsense from her childhood memories - toys, the pervert who'd kidnapped a kid from her primary school class, that alien from those sweet cigarette cards. What was it called? The Wodaran.

At what point had she fallen sick and started hallucinating? It must have been in that ratty warehouse where she'd found the driving game and convinced herself it had Eva's name in biro on the inside of the lid. Bob would remember. She'd stuck it under his nose and demanded to know where it came from.

The Head of English and American Studies and Sally's personal tutor came to visit her. It was odd talking to the two academics away from their pokey book-lined offices. They appeared so out of place in this world, hunched over with their hands on their knees as they stared at her intently, trying to ignore the illness surrounding them. She was behind on her essays, but that crime could be redeemed. Some of her tutors spoke well of her. The offer of a room on campus was still there, and it would be infinitely more sensible if she was within shouting distance of the medical centre, instead of by herself in some dingy bedsit in the middle of nowhere. She looked attentive and uttered noncommittal noises that seemed to satisfy them. After half an hour they grinned at each other in relief and made their hasty exits.

As they left, Sally thought she glimpsed a white robed figure with a head like an inverted parsnip, standing by the window watching her. When she looked directly at it, heart pounding, it was only one of the nurses, reaching up to draw the curtains against the fading light.

Doctor Gibson let her out on a Sunday, which meant nowhere was open and Portslade even more empty than usual. The rain had stopped but the town still seemed to be dissolving. The long street where she lived, with all its run-down shops and takeaways, continued to leach substance and meaning into the grey March sky.

When she stood in the middle of her bedsit she wondered what possessed her to live like this? It was dark and squalid, and stank of cat piss, and setting lotion from the hairdressers below. When Sally moved in there'd been a desiccated raven in the wardrobe and a hardcore German wank mag stuffed under the mattress. The only heating in the room came from a three bar electric fire. Had she imagined herself as some soulful romantic in a garret? Or was she punishing herself because, deep down, she knew she was nothing more than a stupid, wicked little shit who made things up? Sally stared at herself in the mirror. The Mohican was growing out. It looked like she'd covered her head in black Velcro and stuck a dead kitten on top. *Fuck this. You're not that child anymore.*

On Monday morning she stopped off at Bob's warehouse. It was locked. A card sellotaped to the window said *Closed Until Further Notice*. She cupped her hands against the daylight and peered inside. The doorway to the office stood open but it looked as if someone had cleared the place out long ago. No sign of the piles of underground comics, or the dog's filthy basket. Maybe the men in donkey jackets had finally carried Bob and Lemmy off to join the dead pensioners.

One last thing to do to put this all to rest. Sally navigated her way to the cement works and along the access road. She wanted to confirm her suspicions, that everything between finding the game and waking up on the ward was nothing more than a dream. The fever had fired her resentment and anger, dredging up flotsam from the ooze of her subconscious - Professor Backenforth, the Wodaran, Eva Benjamin.

She did find the amusement arcade, at the end of the low brick offices opposite the perimeter fence, but it had never been a Jimmy Corrigan's. Any signage had been pulled off years ago. The building was flanked with broken rubble and the wreckage of its contents. Broken machinery filled the alleyway down the side. There was no way she could have climbed over that lot. Sally stared at the fragments of pinball tables, penny falls and rides, piled up in the shadows and overgrown with weeds. No Mystery Planet and no way of getting inside to find the Driving Test Game, if it ever existed in the first place. Job done, she trudged back to the station.

On campus, Sally found a phone box and rang her parents. Her mother came on the line, her voice distant and querulous.

"You're better now?" she asked.

"Mum, do you remember when I was little and had an invisible friend called Eva?"

"I can't hear you properly, speak louder, Sally."

Her mother wasn't deaf, and yet every call ended with her daughter having to bellow into the receiver while those waiting for their turn on the phone sniggered and shuffled.

"My invisible friend. Called Eva. When I was little."

"You've got to talk to your father, Sally. He ignores me. I'm so lonely and he won't even have a conversation."

Sally could already feel the springs tightening in her gut, pulling on the wires that operated her jaw and fingers, filling them with a sick, grinding tension.

"I've always helped you when you needed it. You need to take more responsibility," the voice said. "I don't know what happened to you. You used to be such a sweet little girl, so helpful and happy. Why did you become so difficult? Dressing like that. Doing that stupid Kung Fu and breaking your nose and ruining your looks. Answering back. And the language. Why did you have to go to university at the other end of the country? Was it because you wanted to get away from us?"

Sally opened her mouth, and thought better of it. With age, she'd grown to realise that she, and everyone else her parents came across, were nothing more than characters in plays her mother invented in her head - endless dramas of victimhood, resentment and jealousy. The roles she ascribed to others bore no relationship to reality, and so conversations inevitably descended into bizarre jumbles of the actual and the imaginary. She took a deep breath and tried again.

"When I was little, a pervert abducted one of my classmates, at a children's party. Anthony Mendelssohn. There was a girl as well. You said I made her up. Eva Benjamin. Did he abduct her too? Were you trying to protect me by making me think she didn't exist?"

"Who?"

"Eva Benjamin."

"Was she Jewish?"

"Yes."

Silence. A queue had gathered outside the phone booth.

"You had lots of Jewish friends. You were the..."

"...token goy. I know. Were you lying to me? Was she real?"

"Was who real?"

"Eva Benjamin."

Silence.

"Tell your father he's got to talk to me. It's not fair. When are you coming up? I'm so lonely."

Sally replaced the receiver on its cradle and braced her hands on the glass to either side of the phone, breathing her anger back into its place. What did she expect? Sense? After all this time? What if her mother had said yes, Eva did exist? What did that even mean? It wouldn't have proved that her vision in Jimmy Corrigan's was real, merely that its roots lay in something altogether more cruel, a lie that had buried her best friend and made her doubt herself for over fifteen years. She pushed out of the phone booth. The expression on her face was enough to make the people waiting in line move back a couple of paces.

Sally left university with a 2:2 in English Literature and a Kickboxing black belt. She headed back to Yorkshire. Her parents had moved out of Leeds, selling their home to pay off her dad's business debts. They downsized to a cookie-cutter new-build on an estate in Guiseley. From what Sally could tell, they'd already started the long process of dying, isolated from the rest of the world and barely speaking to each other. She lasted all of four days before blagging space on a friend's couch while she looked for work. If she hadn't got away from that house, and her mother's interminable whinge-fests, she would have quite probably murdered someone. No point asking about Eva Benjamin. She'd already put the whole Portslade episode into a box labeled fever dream.

Even so, memories nagged. One day, Sally persuaded her dad to lend her his car, drove it over to Leeds and parked outside their old house. The hedge her parents had planted when she was little now towered a good ten feet high, obscuring the front from the road. When she walked to the end of the drive, she found herself looking at a dingy pebble-dashed semi-detached. Her bedroom window was filled with a grubby lace curtain sagging on a single wire. The garage roof had fallen in and the back garden was covered in weeds and bits of broken furniture. There were no hinges at the bottom of the house's facade, no danger of it falling down to reveal a giant screaming head.

Sally wandered along the road. Not only had the house shrunk, but everything else looked small. At one point she hunkered down, wondering if it was possible to recreate the point of view of a six-year-old girl with a head full of dreams. Getting closer to the cracked tarmac and dandelions made no difference. The street looked tired and forgotten. Turning left at the bottom of the road took her to the edge of the wood. The track where she'd learned to ride hadn't changed much, but the trees on the right were now fenced off. The path Eva had enticed her down lay on the other side of a padlocked gate topped with barbed wire. It bore the sign *PRIVATE PROPERTY - NO ENTRY*. She bristled at that. It was almost like a personal insult, and for a second she wondered if her mother had put it there - the final emphatic shutting down of all of that childish nonsense about a Blocko Tower. *One more peep and I swear to God...*

"You're getting as paranoid as she is," Sally muttered to herself. After a quick glance round, she pulled her leather jacket sleeves over her hands to protect them against the barbed wire, and hoisted herself up and over. The damp, quiet shadows of the woods enfolded her. Ahead, the path leading to Alwoodley Lane dwindled into a green, sunlight-dappled point. No doubt another locked gate prevented access at the other end. Sally decided to see how far she could get, and if there were any answers hiding among the shadows.

Ten minutes in, she noticed the house among the trees to her left. Had it always been there? She couldn't remember seeing it before, but age and neglect had made its roof and walls slump so it merged into the undergrowth. Intrigued, she moved away from the path and headed towards it. It looked long abandoned.

She found out how wrong she was a few moments later. A figure barged out of the sagging front door and thundered towards her, waving and yelling. It was some old git in shabby khaki gardening gear, carrying a spade in two hands like a weapon.

"FUCK OFF. FUCK OFF," he bellowed, stumbling over the mossy hummocks and bouncing off a sycamore trunk. At first, Sally assumed he was a gardener or a gamekeeper, but closer up he looked scrawny and wild eyed.

"Are you the twat who put that fence up?" she said.

The man kept coming. He lunged and took a swipe at her head. Instinct and training kicked in. She blocked his wrists, ducked under and turned, twisting them down and around in a quick spiral, so his momentum carried him headfirst into a tree. He dropped like a stone and rolled about in the muck and dead leaves, clutching his skull and crying. Sally threw the spade far into the wood.

"Try to touch me again and I'll break your arms," she said, starting to back away, fists up.

"Get out," the old dosser sobbed. He sounded Scottish. Sally realised he wasn't wearing gardening clothes. That was some kind of military jacket. "Get out, get out, get out."

"Alright, alright, I'm going. I'm sorry."

"I'll kill you. I've got a gun. I'll kill you," the man howled. Blood ran down his face from between his fingers.

Sally stumbled back, shaking as the adrenaline kicked in. She'd come here in search of childhood memories and ended up fighting a poor tramp in the middle of a breakdown. Angry, guilty, and desperate to get away, she ran back to the fence and vaulted over the gate.

CHAPTER FIVE

Four months later, Sally managed to land a part-time job in a record store in Otley. The owner ran a small press music and arts magazine on the side. She had a crack at writing a few articles, gaining enough confidence and pats on the head to start seriously thinking about becoming a journalist. But in the end there was already a Julie Burchill at the *New Musical Express*, and *Melody Maker* had Vivien Goldman, so Sally had to make do with the *Wharfedale Clarion* where she became a junior reporter. It paid enough for her to rent a flat.

The editor, George, bore a deep and abiding hatred for the main regional newspaper, the *Yorkshire Post*, after it fired him in 1974 for urinating on a rival reporter's desk after a heavy lunchtime session. He called it the Yorkshire Arse, and had dedicated his entire being to out-scooping them. Given the range and budget of the *Clarion*, it was never going to happen. That didn't stop him sending himself and Sally off on wild goose chases, desperately hunting for murders, scandals and political ructions more suited to *The Sun* or *Daily Mirror*. Somehow they always managed to pip the *Clarion* at the post, leaving the two of them to churn out endless articles about pet pythons, village fetes and the challenges of sheep farming in the Dales. George sat at the end of the office in his flamboyant and utterly out of date wing-collar jackets and lacy shirts. He resembled an overdressed Jabba the Hut, seething and burbling his resentments between whiskeys.

One day, he eased his not inconsiderable bulk into a chair opposite Sally, wheezing and squeaking like a deflating bouncy castle. He gave her a fleshy grin.

"Got the reprobates!"

"What?"

"Sally, my dear, I have the scallywags by the balls. Oh this is good. Squeeze, squeeze, squeezity squeeze." he rubbed his hands, "Oh this is very, very good. HOLMES!"

"HOLMES?"

"Home Office Large Major Enquiry System."

"You're kidding me."

"You know how after they finally nabbed the Yorkshire Ripper, it transpired that the police already had all the information they needed on millions and millions of index cards? Well some bright spark said 'If only we'd had a computer that would join all these dots we'd have got the bastard four years earlier.' Hence HOLMES. Now I have a very old friend in the West Yorkshire police whose job it is to install this HOLMES mega brain up here, and he's agreed to let you go and have a chat with him. None of those dimwits at the Arse have the slightest whiff. We'll grind their noses in horse plop for all eternity with this one."

"You want me to write an article about a computer?"

"It'll be full of the juiciest wonders and we'll dine out on them for months, years, while the hacks at the Arse gnash their teeth and wail."

"Isn't it all top secret?"

George winked.

"Harry is an old, old friend. I'm sure he'll give you plenty off the record. The Arse can't touch this. After they hauled the police over the coals for failing to spot the Ripper, none of the boys in blue will give their hacks so much as a whiff."

George leaned across and placed damp hands on top of hers.

"Go and talk to Harry and return post-haste with death and terror."

Her boss's unbridled enthusiasm led her to believe she'd be visiting West Yorkshire Police HQ in Leeds. Instead, she ended up in a converted Victorian Working Mens's Club in a forgotten corner of Keighley. Sally should have realised. Whoever this Harry was, it was unlikely he had access to anything juicy and she'd come all this way on another overblown fool's errand.

The constable on duty was a chunky short-arse with little angry eyes in a head fashioned out of millstone grit. He looked her up and down, twice.

"What do you want?"

"I'm here to see Sergeant Harry Mutherington."

"What for?"

She braced herself.

"I'm a reporter. Sally Aston."

He looked her up and down again, leaning over the counter to pay special attention to her bright red Dr. Martens boots.

"With?"

"*The Wharfedale Clarion.*"

"Never heard of it."

"Sergeant Mutherington is expecting me."

"Oh, is he indeed?"

For a moment Sally wondered if this was going to degenerate into a staring-down contest. PC short-arse disappeared into the back of the station.

"Sarge, there's some bird to see you," he yelled. "Says she's a reporter. Quite fit, apart from the bust conk."

He remerged and gestured at the door with a leer.

"Don't wear him out love. He's not long for this world. Upstairs at the end of the corridor."

Sally gave him a har-fucking-har smile in return, and climbed a narrow flight to the first floor.

It was clear from the moment she stepped into the room that Sergeant Mutherington was nothing more glamorous than a data entry clerk. He sat in front of a flickering green screen, touch-typing from a folder at his side. It was one of hundreds piled across the floor, radiating out to steel cabinets set against the walls. Between them, stacks of long wooden boxes that looked like library catalogue drawers reached almost to the ceiling.

"Did he offer you tea?" asked the sergeant without turning round.

"No."

"ALBERT. TEA!" he bellowed, eyes still fixed on the screen. Sally's ears rang. It was a wonder none of the stacks of wooden boxes collapsed.

"Yes Sarge," came the faint answer from downstairs.

"Pull up a seat, lass."

Sally found a stool and positioned it at the end of the desk.

"George sent you. How is the old puff?"

She studied Harry Mutherington from the side. He and her boss appeared to have been cast from the same die - hefty Yorkshiremen with pudding bowl haircuts, bright blue eyes and pink faces. They made her think of ice cream Vikings melting in the sun.

"He sends his regards."

"Still mithering on about the *Yorkshire Post*?"

"Yep."

"Well, let's see what we can give him, eh? How much do you weigh?"

"Excuse me?"

"How much do you weigh?"

He shuffled around in his seat and stared at her. She didn't know whether to tell him he was a sexist homophobic git, or let it go. For George's sake she bit her tongue.

"Bantamweight."

Eyebrows went up.

"Boxer? I thought lasses weren't allowed."

"Kickboxing."

"Is that how you got your nose bust?"

"Sort of."

The constable came up the stairs with two mugs of tea. He gave Sally a nod and a wink, and disappeared, chuckling to himself. Harry stared at the drinks, then swapped his for Sally's.

"Albert doesn't like reporters after all that shite printed about the Ripper running rings round the police. He's probably gobbed in yours." He took a sip and shrugged. "Perhaps not. The reason I asked about your weight is because we had to strengthen this floor during the investigation, on account of the number of boxes and cabinets, otherwise it would have collapsed. Just making sure it won't happen again. Having said that, soon this will all be gone thanks to this!" He gestured at the computer screen. "Everything fits into something no bigger than a single chest of drawers. As you can see, I am typing in records of crimes and open cases going back decades, in the full knowledge that the wonders of modern computing science will give us insights denied to our predecessors, leading to the swift apprehension of villains, no matter how many years have lapsed since their misdemeanours."

Sally stared at him as he beamed at her with evident pride. A very big penny dropped in her skull. Sergeant Mutherington was clearly on the edge of retirement, and had been given a quiet little clerk's job with the new computer system because none of the others wanted to do it. He now regarded himself as leading the vanguard of a new era in modern policing. If she wasn't careful, she'd be stuck here all afternoon, listening to him ramble on about floppy discs.

"I cannot describe the processes in detail, but there are four components to such a machine as this. Random Access Memory, or RAM, and ROM, which stands for..."

"Have you got any old cases you can tell me about?"

He stopped and pursed his lips at being interrupted.

"George wanted to know how it works with a case," Sally added. "To help the readers understand better."

"What kind of cases?"

"Child abduction in Moortown, 1966. Anthony Mendelssohn, Eva Benjamin."

He gave her a sideways glance.

"That's very specific."

"They were friends of mine who went missing," she didn't want to give too much away. It was more interesting to see what this supposedly amazing machine came up with. "Do the records go that far back?"

"Maybe. I started at both ends of the archive so there are some cases from the 60s already loaded. Are you sure George wants to write about bairns being carried off twenty years ago?"

She nodded at the monitor. Harry gave a great sigh.

"Spell those names."

He typed. From the end of the desk Sally watched green letters dissolve and reform across the screen. From this angle it was hard to see everything, and she didn't want to ask in case it set him off on another lecture.

He froze, fingers above the keyboard and eyes tracking back and forth as he read the words. Sally shifted to get a better look and he hit Return. The text vanished, but not before she'd spotted a name.

Backenforth.

"Not a sausage," Harry said.

"What do you mean?"

"Nothing in that case that's worth writing about."

His whole manner had changed. The pink, open friendliness had dissolved into wary irritation.

"Why not?"

"Listen, sunshine. I don't mind helping George out if he wants to write a piece about the new era in detective work, ushered in by the wonders of computer science, but I'm not raking up old tragedies for his entertainment."

"Did you find him?" she nodded at the screen.

"Who?"

"Professor Backenforth."

For a second he looked as if he was about to hit her. It was so unexpected she flinched.

"Eva Benjamin was my best friend," she said. "They pretended she didn't exist when that pervert abducted her. Made out I was going mental."

Harry studied his guest, expression softer. "What happened?"

"We were at a party. Professor Backenforth turned up with a magic ride and the other kids got inside it. Eva and me were too scared. Then Anthony disappeared, and everybody told me Eva didn't exist, said I'd made her up and the nonexistent tower block she and that scumbag pervert lived in. Backenforth Heights. I thought I'd visited it to play with her toys. I even went looking for it recently, but there's nothing there but woods and some mad tramp."

Harry's face shut down again.

"The case hit a dead end. Horrible business, kids being abducted. People want to forget, not read it about it in the papers. There's nowt for you or George in this," he gestured at the monitor. "Now do you want to talk about HOLMES, or not?"

Sally listened while he rabbited on about bits and bytes. In the end she succeeded in squeezing a gangland drug bust and a couple of murders out of him, enough to keep George's bloodlust satisfied. She found it hard to concentrate. Buried in that machine lay fragments of her past, both real and imaginary. Why had Harry refused to talk to her about Professor Backenforth? Did he simply not want another failure to be spread out for all the world to laugh at in the wake of the Ripper fiasco? But this was over twenty years ago, so hardly going to dent the already battered reputation of the West Yorkshire constabulary. Were there squalid and vile secrets that made this child abduction case particularly unpleasant? Did he view her as a sensitive lass who needed protecting? No, it had to be something else. Something he wasn't telling her. She hadn't a clue how to get it out of him.

The sergeant finished up and looked at her expectantly. Sally wanted to ask more about that brief word she'd spotted on his screen.

"I thought I visited my friend at the tower block, Backenforth Heights. Maybe I got the name wrong and it did exist, but not in Alwoodley. I just want to know what happened to Eva. One day she was there, the next she'd gone and they'd hauled me off to a child psychiatrist, pretending she never existed. Six years old. I wish I remembered my best friend. My only friend. Lots of shit happened in them days and it's hard to recall any of it properly."

Harry just looked at her, expression unreadable. She closed her notebook, stood up and stretched. What a waste of time. He wasn't going to tell her anything else.

"We never found him, or them," he said. She nodded, keeping herself bottled up, and headed down the stairs. Harry squeezed after her, shoulders rubbing the plaster on both sides of the narrow passageway. Albert had a great big grin on his face.

"A right seeing-to was it, Sarge?"

"Bugger off," Harry said, leading his guest to the door. She clambered into her Fiat 500 and rattled down the road. The last she saw of the sergeant was his round silhouette, framed against the station light.

Two murders and a heroin gang weren't thunderingly spectacular, but they'd have to do. George struggled to hide his disappointment as visions of next year's National Press Awards receded into the shadows once more. They ran a handful of articles about HOLMES but the *Yorkshire Post* kept outselling the *Wharfedale Clarion* by a factor of 10 to 1, and her boss continued to grumble his way through various whiskey brands.

A couple of months later, he perched himself on the corner of Sally's desk and leered down at her.

"What did you say to Sergeant Harry Mutherington?"

"I asked him about HOLMES, like you told me to."

"He wants to meet you again."

"Really?"

"The bugger's 58 with grown up kids. Old enough to be your grandad, and then some."

"So? I'm not going to shag him, if that's what he's after. What does he want?"

"I don't know. Get some more juice out of the cantankerous sod. Find out if any of the town councillors are taking bribes. Or even better, ask who's having it away with sheep on the side. I want a bit more than the thin gruel you came back with last time."

"Ok, I'll head over to Keighley again."

"He doesn't want to meet you at the station."

George handed her a scrap of paper with a phone number on it. Sally's heart sank. PC Albert's horrible little gloating prediction wasn't about to come true, was it? A dinner date followed by attempted tongues and fat fingers, until she broke Harry's arm and ended up in jail for assaulting a copper? She rang while George plaited his hands over his stomach and watched her carefully from under sleepy eyelids.

Five minutes later, she put the receiver back on its cradle.

"He wants to meet me for lunch at The Hermit."

"The Hermit? Bloody hell. That's about as romantic as a carthorse's cock sock."

The Hermit was a shepherd's pub on the edge of Ilkley Moor. Sally parked her Fiat and entered a dark box with just one window at the opposite end from the bar. Named pewter tankards hung from hooks screwed into the rafters. Half a dozen ancient men in wellies and flat caps sat against the walls and drank from theirs in silence. Sergeant Mutherington had a seat by the log fire, and two pints of Theakston's Old Peculier on the table in front of him. He was in civvies. Outside the rain rattled against the glass, turning the outer world into a blurry mess.

"You didn't remember me the other day, did you?" he said, as she plonked herself down on the stool opposite.

Sally shook her head and took a swig of her ale.

"Sally Aston. You went missing when you were little. We came round to your house after you turned up again. You're a lot different now. I recall you as a pretty wee thing, with a whopping bruise on your scalp from where your mam lamped you for running away from home."

"I grew up."

"So I see."

He might have been one of the policemen who'd come to the door. If so, twenty years had piled on the stress of coppering, changing him out of all recognition. She studied his face in the gloom, trying to see the younger man and match him to her memories. When her screaming mummy dragged Sally out from under the kitchen table by her ankle it had jangled them all into a complete mess.

"Did you tell me to honour my father and mother?"

He laughed.

"That were Bill Seddon. God botherer and a half he were. The daft bastard. That time you went missing - did you go to Backenforth Heights?"

"It never existed. There's nothing in Alwoodley, just woods and ordinary houses," Sally said.

Harry blew air through hamster cheeks and stared at the rain over Wharfedale. Sally placed her pint down on the table very slowly so as not to spill any. She sat on her hands to stop them shaking.

"It was real, wasn't it?"

"You tell me."

"What's that supposed to mean?"

"I had a couple of mates working the case. They ended up trying to track down that Professor Backenforth fella as he was the main suspect. If you hire a conjurer for a kid's party, where do you go first?"

"Yellow Pages."

"Right, but they found nothing there, not in any of them. When we asked the mother who'd hosted it, she couldn't remember where she'd found him. Didn't even recall what he looked like."

"She'd been necking wine all afternoon."

"Her husband hadn't, and he wasn't able to give us a description either. Kids are kids, so they hadn't a clue. We hunted everywhere, talked to every children's entertainer in West Yorkshire, tracked down all the travelling fun fairs. Nobody had ever heard of him, nobody had ever hired him. The other thing is this - if Professor Backenforth took the lad, when did he do it? How do you abduct a child from a party? If you pretend you're a friend of the family, collecting them at the end, you can try to carry them off, but don't forget this was just after the Moors Murders. Everyone was obsessed with kids being snatched, and watching out like hawks. A nonce trying his chances at a party, in front of all the other parents queuing up on the drive, wouldn't have got very far."

"Perhaps Anthony climbed into his Mystery Planet ride and

didn't get out again," Sally said, but the idea was ridiculous. Everyone had been desperate for a turn and would have noticed. Besides, Eva hadn't gone anywhere near Professor Backenforth and she'd disappeared too. Also fallen victim to the twisted fucker, no doubt. The thought turned her stomach.

"What about Backenforth Heights?" she asked.

"Never found. No leads, not a sausage."

"You said it was real."

"No I didn't. I asked you."

"How the bloody hell am I supposed to know?" Sally snapped. A couple of the shepherds looked up from their pints. "This is a waste of time. Why did you bring me here?"

"There is this. A couple of years later, one of the detectives on the case did see summat. A mate of mine, DI Conway."

The name rang faint bells, of a man with a ridiculously deep voice, sitting next to a pretty woman constable called Gill.

"He was at the Harrogate Cat Show in the Valley Gardens. Into his Siamese, old Gareth Conway. Anyhow, the way he told it was that a lass came up to him and asked if he'd walk her home. She was scared that a funny man wanted to make off with her. He reckoned she must have been about seven or eight. He wore mufti at the time, but he always carried himself like a copper. She must have sensed it."

"What did she look like?"

"A little Jewish lass, Gareth said, dressed a bit old fashioned like. Reminded him of the ones you see in photos of children being herded about by the Nazis."

Eva.

Harry had another sip of Theakstons and carried on.

"Soft bastard, he was, and dopey with it. Should have told one of the PCs on duty at the show. Instead, he said he'd look after her. She took him into the woods at the back of the gardens, above the mini golf course. Now, you've been to Harrogate a few times in your life. What's up there?"

"Harlow Carr Gardens."

"That's right. You go through Pine Woods, come out on Crag

Lane and there's the garden centre. At first he reckoned she might live in one of the old houses by the water tower, but no."

"She took him to the Blocko Tower," Sally said.

"The what?"

"Backenforth Heights."

Harry nodded.

"A bloody great block of flats," Harry continued. "In fact, the way he described it, the biggest tower block he'd seen in his life. He reckoned it rose up so high, you couldn't see the top for clouds. The lass took him inside - it were just like any other entrance - and into the lift. Up and up they rode, for hours, he said. He lost count of how many floors it had. When the doors opened they were on the roof, except it weren't no roof. It was a big field under a black sky, covered in giant balls."

CHAPTER SIX

Sally gripped the edge of her stool, half-hunched over the table, trying not to react, to cry out or start swearing. The interior of the pub suddenly felt as if it was dissolving in the rain, that the men in shadows were being absorbed into an oily chaos coating the inside and outside of this old stone building. The same dissolution she'd seen in Portslade on that stormy day invaded The Hermit. Harry was watching, measuring her reaction. When she trusted herself not to spill anything, she took a long draught of beer and set the glass back on its coaster with both hands.

"What happened?" she managed.

"That's all we ever got out of him. He hadn't reported it in. Gareth only told us in the pub one evening after getting totally plastered. Everyone fancied he'd gone mental, finally cracked. It happens. Pressures of the job and all that. At first it sounded like a sick joke, typical copper gallows humour. But you could see in his eyes that he completely believed it."

"Nobody else went to have a look?"

"Get out of it. There's no tower block at the back of the Valley Gardens. The only high rise in Harrogate is Park Place on the Stray and it's all of thirteen floors. This Backenforth Heights of yours had hundreds and hundreds, according to Conway."

"So what happened next?"

"As time went by he got worse and worse. Wouldn't go anywhere near a block of flats, which didn't help his coppering. In the end he 'resigned' from the force. Drank himself into a mental institute. Ended up drawing pictures of monsters on the walls of his room with his own shit. Eventually smashed a lightbulb when the nurses weren't looking, wrapped the bits up in toilet paper, and swallowed them. Took him a week and a half to die. Poor Gareth. God knows what he saw, or thought he saw. He was hard as nails, had come across stuff under the Arches or down by Leeds Canal that would really turn your stomach. Whatever happened to him that day must have either been a whole lot worse, or the straw that broke the camel's back."

"Why are you telling me all this now?"

Harry patted her on the knee.

"I've got two cracking lasses about your age. You remind me of them. You're bonny too, when you're not pulling a face like a bulldog chewing on a wasp. If there is something out there, stay away, well away. I saw Conway when he was dying. I wouldn't wish that on anyone. Especially someone like you."

She sat for an hour in the pub car park, staring across the valley. Harry had left ten minutes after she'd walked out without saying a word. He didn't spot her Fiat 500, his mind was no doubt on other things. He kept his face down as he plodded through the rain to a mud-spattered Land Rover. Sally watched his car disappear, and turned back to the view. Far away, the old radio mast at Lindley Moor scratched the clouds. It was one of those Dales days when the earth was lighter than the sky. The whole world looked about to fold up around her and come crashing down. She chewed the inside of her cheek to keep the angry tears at bay.

Backenforth Heights existed, but in different places. Moortown, Harrogate, Sally even thought she'd spotted it from the back of the amusement arcade in Portslade. Eva existed as well, a little Jewish girl trapped in the tower block, trying to coax people inside to rescue her from Professor Backenforth and his Mystery Planet. Detective Inspector Conway had said she reminded him of the schoolchildren herded into the camps by the Nazis. That triggered another echo in her head, a conversation years ago with a kind old man who'd asked her questions she couldn't remember. The absolute killer was the vast plain covered in black spheres that Harry's friend claimed he saw on the roof above the clouds. What else had Detective Inspector Conway found that drove him mad? A demon gardener tending those seeds, listening to their vile guts with a stethoscope? Checking whether the hideousness they incubated was ready to be hatched?

Her first instinct was go round to her parents and shout at them for lying to her all those years ago, robbing her of a burgeoning friendship she'd treasured as only a six-year-old could. Sense kicked in. She'd be arguing with a mother who didn't exist anymore. The querulous, self-centred bat who'd replaced her wouldn't understand what she was going on about.

Sally didn't bother returning to the office or calling George. Instead, she headed straight for Otley Army and Navy stores and bought the biggest hunting knife she could find. The woman behind the counter took one look at her and the weapon, and went into the storeroom to confer with her colleague. To make herself appear a wee bit more legit, Sally picked up a random selection of cheap camping equipment and an ordinance survey map of Leeds. She dumped the haul next to the register and stared back at the two faces peeking around the door. The shopkeeper sullenly ran everything through the till, clearly not wanting a confrontation with this scrawny broken-nosed yob in a biker jacket.

She drove over to Moortown, parked the car outside her old house, and wrestled the map open on the dashboard. It was the first time she'd ever bothered trying to locate all the landmarks of her childhood, but nothing important stood out. The woods were called Alwoodley Moss and bordered a golf course. That was probably owned by the rich bastards who'd fenced everything off, despite the dotted line marking the right of way. All the streets were filled with little orange rectangles denoting ordinary semis. No tower block in sight, to be honest she hadn't expected to find any.

She stuffed the map into the new backpack, left the Fiat, and made her way down to the woods, threading her belt through the knife sheath and pulling her jacket over it as she went. The trees and their shadows formed an olive-drab wall on the other side of the bright steel posts and barbed wire. She stared into the darkness and wondered why she was doing this, chasing ghosts from nearly twenty years ago. Sensible Sally, the one who'd taken her in hand after she'd collapsed in Portslade, thought she was off her chump. Since graduating, the battles with her mum had ceased to be nothing more than poisonous monologues inside her own head. Though her parent cast a heavy shadow, it was growing weaker and more frayed by the day. Even so, the discovery that Eva might have been real added toxic fuel to the smouldering resentment at being gaslighted as a child - forced to doubt her own thoughts, her sense of self-worth dependent on the moods of her frustrated and miserable mother. She really should just turn around, go back to the office, get on with her life, and abandon this decades-long rebellion.

But there was more, wasn't there? A lot more. Harry's detective friend found the Blocko Tower, went inside and saw the same vision from Sally's fever dream in Portslade. It drove him mad. Was that a reason to keep going, or to run away in the opposite direction and never return? Some deep grinding anger was driving her on, a visceral hatred of an unknown evil concentrating its attentions on the little Jewish girl who'd been her friend. She tightened the straps of the backpack and climbed over the fence.

A heavy silence lay on the woods. Sally heard the creak of branches and rustling of leaves. The sound had an odd grainy quality to it, as if it'd been recorded on a scratched '78. Shafts of light fell through the mote-speckled air, making the surroundings resemble an illustration of an enchanted forest from a book of Arthurian tales. Once in a while, she caught glimpses of long green corridors punctuated by bright glades receding like dropped coins. The geography seemed off. After a few hundred yards wouldn't she spot the golf course links through the trees? All she could see were endless colonnades of elm, ash and oak.

Sally eventually came across the house, nestled among the soft hummocks between the trees. Last time, the building had resembled a cottage slumped with the weight of ages. Now she realised that was an illusion, caused by the piled-up waves of blackberry and thorn around the walls. From this side it looked like a terrace house missing the rest of the street. It reminded her of one of the Victorian council houses down on Clay Pit Lane that had been bombed into isolation by the Luftwaffe during the war. The front had all but vanished into the shadow of an enormous chestnut tree whose uppermost branches pressed up against the dark windows of the second floor. Three stone steps led up to an open door at the back.

Today the wino wouldn't catch her by surprise, not that she was particularly worried if he did. When she'd fought him before it'd been easy to disarm the old bastard and throw him into a tree. She toyed with the idea of taking out the knife to frighten him, but that seemed pointlessly cruel. To be honest, she still felt guilty about braining him the first time round.

Sally climbed the steps and peered inside. To her surprise she found herself at the entrance to a narrow kitchen that looked as tidy, neat and old-fashioned as her grandma's. It was nothing like the filthy reeking pit she'd expected. There was the same heavy Butler sink, flanked by wooden countertops stacked with clean plates. No signs of any cans or bottles of cider, meths or lighter fuel.

Struggling to process her surroundings, Sally stepped through the kitchen into a room that appeared just as meticulous. Paper doilies sat on the table, in front of four chairs. Silver and heavy crystal glinted behind glass cabinet doors. An antimacassar lay across the back of a plum-coloured armchair by the fire. Even the grate was set ready for lighting, with lumps of coal, fragments of wood and twists of newspaper.

A Bakelite telephone sat on the sideboard. She picked the receiver up and listened to the gentle hiss. She didn't recall seeing any wires going into the house so why did it sound like an open line? On a whim she went to call George at the office. Something round, hard and cold pressed against the base of her skull.

"One false move, lassie, and I'll blow your head off."

A quick hand dipped under her jacket and relieved her of the knife. The man pushed her away. She banged into the glass cabinet, making all the silverware and glasses rattle, turned round, and found herself staring at the tramp she'd thrown into a tree.

He'd transformed. Instead of rags, he wore a heavy brown uniform with a canvas belt, army boots and a beret with a pom-pom on top. The outfit was threadbare in places and frayed around the cuffs, but everything had been polished and pressed. The long grey hair was gathered in a ponytail. He watched her with the marked calculation of a falcon about to swoop. Craggy to the point of gauntness, his mouth and eyes reminded her of pits and cracks in moorland rock. He looked extremely dangerous. It was also impossible to figure out his age - 40s? 50s? Perhaps the same as Bob the Warehouse Boss, but there was a darkness inside his pupils that appeared more ancient. Perhaps he was a Falklands vet who'd lost his marbles and decided to go full Rambo on the borders of Alwoodley Golf Course.

"You're the lassie who smacked me into that oak," he murmured. He was Scottish then. He lifted up the edge of his beret to show a red welt on his forehead. "And what were you planning on doing with this?" The soldier wiggled the hunting knife by the point.

"Defend myself."

Sally's mind settled into its own watchfulness. Her captor dropped the barrel of his automatic so it pointed at the floor, and placed the knife carefully on the sideboard next to the telephone. Was she fast enough to barge past him, into the kitchen and out through the woods? He wouldn't really shoot her, would he? He must have sensed her getting ready as he broke into a grin, showing teeth that looked like stone flagging.

"Oh aye? Defend yourself from who?" he whispered. Something in his face made her step back until her bottom thumped into the cabinet door again.

Three more people came through the kitchen in a clattering racket, and suddenly the room felt very crowded. More soldiers in uniform - two men and a woman. All stopped and stared at Sally.

"Who's the dame?" one of the men said. The guys wore identical outfits - similar to the Scotsman, though green instead of brown, and with helmets. More to the point, they each had a Tommy gun slung over their shoulders. The woman looked like a pirate. She had a tent-shaped cap with a red tassel perched on the side of her head, baggy blue pants and blouse, two bandoliers criss-crossing her chest, and a rifle across her back. She held a bottle of milk, popped the foil with her thumb, and gulped half of it down without taking her eyes off Sally. All three appeared gaunt and haunted, which made it impossible to calculate their age. She pegged the lass as not much older than herself, but that didn't sit right with the general air of brutalised weariness.

"This is the wee yin who thumped me the other day," the Scotsman said.

"What do you mean the other day? It was over two years ago," Sally said.

"Aye, time's a funny thing round here."

"No shit," the woman said, passing the bottle to one of the other newcomers. "Where you from?" Her accent sounded French, or Mediterranean.

"Moortown."

Safer to give her childhood address. Sally relaxed slightly, feeling marginally easier with another lass around. The four of them watched her with wary curiosity rather than malice. One of the men was grinning, probably at the Scotsman's confession that this scrawny little punk had bested him.

"Where's that?" the woman asked. Odd question. Sally nodded past them.

"Just over there, at the edge of the golf course."

"What city?" one of the other men said. Judging by the accent, her two companions were Americans.

"Leeds, obviously."

They all looked to the Scotsman.

"Big place in the north of England," he said.

"What are you talking about?" Sally said. "Moortown's five minutes that way." She pointed in the rough direction she'd arrived from. "Are you part of some weird re-enactment club or something?"

Everyone knew about the Sealed Knot dressing up as Cavaliers and Roundheads. Her parents had dragged her to Marston Moor one year to suffer through a completely tedious replay of that particular battle. At the Yorkshire Show, Sally had sometimes come across others who liked to dress up and pretend to be soldiers. This bunch seemed to be kitted out in World War II uniforms. A lot of people had lost their taste for wargames and military make-believe when the limbless and the dead started to ship back from the Falklands, but there were still a few bloodthirsty nutters around who hadn't grown up. Or maybe this lot were actors rehearsing for a film.

"What year?" the woman asked.

"Oh, come on," Sally replied.

"Answer the question, lassie," the Scotsman said, in a tone of voice that brought the temperature in the room down another couple of degrees.

"1985. Why, what year are you from?"

"1938," the woman said.

Sally glanced at the others, looking for the joke. Nobody was rolling their eyes or smirking. One of the American soldiers shrugged and heaved his machine gun onto the table.

"Mind me bloody doilies," the Scotsman said.

"Who are you lot, anyway?" Sally asked.

The soldier spoiling the decorations jabbed a thumb at his own chest.

"Sergeant Chisum. This dumb Polish bastard here is Corporal Szymanski. That's Pash," the woman gave a half nod. "And your boyfriend is Angus. We three are from Munich in 1946. She's from Barcelona. Me and Ziz are 45th US Infantry Division. Pash? She's some goddamn foul-mouthed communist ball breaker."

"Anarchist. *Mujeres Libres*," the woman protested.

"And I am with the Queens Own Cameron Highlanders," Angus said, giving a mock salute.

None of it made the slightest bit of sense to Sally. They were either all completely mad, or determined not to break character in some bloody-minded piece of method acting for whatever role-playing game this was.

"Why you here?" Pash said.

"I'm looking for a block of flats called Backenforth Heights. I think it's around here somewhere. I found it when I was a kid. A friend of mine called Eva lived there. Everyone told me I'd made it all up, that she was imaginary like the Blocko Tower. I reckon it exists but moves about. Or there's different versions in different places. I also saw it in Brighton, and a policeman told me his friend came across it in Harrogate. It drove him mad and he killed himself."

The others were swapping deadly serious glances. There was a recognition in their eyes that poured ice water into Sally's head.

"You've seen it too," she said.

Chisum nodded. Under his helmet he was all black bristles and teeth, like a shaved wolf.

"In Munich."

"And you?" Sally turned to Pash. In contrast to the others she looked untouched by war, until you caught her gaze.

"Barcelona."

Silence. None of them seemed to want to add anything else.

"So who the hell are you, anyway?" Sally tried.

"The shit on Satan's boots," Angus said. "He cannae winkle us out, we're that deep in the tread."

"What does that even mean?"

"Wherever the tower goes, we go with it," Chisum explained. "From the distant past to the distant future, to places that don't exist in our universe. It can't shake us off, and one day we'll bring the whole thing down around his ears." He pulled a battered pack of Chelsea cigarettes out of his tunic pocket, tapped three out, and handed them to his companions.

"This friend you spoke of?" the Spaniard asked, leaning hers into Chisum's Zippo flame. She held his wrist to stop the American's hand from shaking. "The one who lived inside the skyscraper."

Sally told them about Eva. At the end of her story they all exchanged more glances filled with a hidden conversation.

"You think?" Szymanski asked the others. His voice was so soft it sounded like little more than laboured breathing. He unbuckled his helmet and placed it on the table, running fingers over his sandpaper head. Angus shrugged.

"Maybe."

"Maybe what?" Sally said.

The general shuffling about and unhitching of weapons amid tired sighs suggested the danger had passed its peak. It didn't look like anyone was going to shoot her after all. Instead, her story about Eva seemed to have thrown them, as if it had rejigged strategies they'd worked on for years. They slumped down - the two Americans at the table, Pash in the armchair with her feet on top of the fireguard.

"Can someone actually tell me what the fuck this is about. What are you all doing hiding out in Alwoodley Golf Course? You're not IRA, are you?" she asked in a last attempt to link these four raggedy soldiers to anything approaching contemporary normality. Angus burst out laughing.

"Like the sarge explained, this isn't where you think it is," Szymanski said. "You are in the realm of the tower. It shifts from place to place and time to time and we go with it. In each place, the demon who dwells at the summit steals people like your little friend. We're trying to stop it."

Sally snorted. She couldn't help herself. It sounded like the plot of a cheap sci-fi video or some crap horror novel.

"A demon? I saw him. He was just some paedophile at a children's party, wearing a silly hat and prancing about on his Mystery Planet."

"Who lives in a block of flats that moves from place to place and age to age," Angus said, handing out more milk bottles. "How do you figure that out?"

Sally stared at the foil top he'd stuck under her nose and shook her head.

"You don't believe us?" Chisum said. "We found this today, on the thirty-second floor."

He fished into his breast pocket, pulled out a piece of card, and handed it to Sally. She looked at the crude painting of a black, blue-eyed spider with a giant brain. *Cerebra from Mercury*, claimed the reverse. *Inhabits the twilight zone between the hot and cold faces of the planet. Friendly and playful. Krazy Kreatures from Outer Space. Primrose Confectionery.*

"Your friend leaves these as calling cards, usually on the dead."

Sally swallowed. Her throat was full of sand and pain. She should've taken the milk bottle after all.

"The dead?" she managed.

"She's all grown up now," Pash said. "Like you, like us, but working on the inside. Fighting monsters. Sometimes she helps. We don't see her, but doors are unlocked, lift shafts cleared, escape routes opened up when we get stuck. In exchange we drop off weapons, ammunition and food."

Sally turned and ran.

CHAPTER SEVEN

Sally stood holding the car door handle, staring at her reflection in the driver's window. The glass sucked all light out of the street and flattened everything into a mud lake. Her own face floated in front of her like a dead woman's, filth silting up her eyes and turning her into a stranger's corpse. She'd become a soul anchored to this world by nothing more than a Fiat 500. If she let go, she'd float up into the sky, break through its grey eggshell, and drift helplessly through the starless abyss to the Blocko Tower and its hundred black spheres.

As soon as they started talking about Eva, the warrior running up and down stairwells machine-gunning monsters, she'd had a horrible suspicion they were all taking the piss. The very idea of a colossal cosmic joke with her as the butt was ridiculous. She was grown-up enough to know that not everything in this fucked-up universe was about Sally Aston. Yet the whole surreal masque of four World War II soldiers, surrounded by doilies and cheap silverware, banging on about demons in time-shifting towers, seemed nothing more than a continuation of all the lies fed to her from childhood. Memories of contempt, humiliation, and the slaps and blows bouncing off her head and shoulders, sent her stumbling through the trees and up to her old house.

Sally glanced along the street. She remembered the journey back from the woods, pushing her bicycle and full of happiness after playing with her new best friend, just before the world turned irrevocably to shit. Her nose prickled and the buildings blurred. Furious at her sudden weakness, she let go of the door and wiped the tears and snot away with her jacket sleeve, realising she didn't actually have a decision to make.

They were all sitting around the dining table, still in uniform. It looked like Angus had managed to rustle up a complete Sunday dinner in the last half hour. He paused in forking out Yorkshire puddings to each of his mates, but didn't seem surprised to see her. He'd mentioned time ran differently here, long enough for a roast at least. Her stomach rumbled.

"Lets you in and out pretty easily," Pash grinned.

It was true. Nobody had tried to stop her when she left and the mossy trails had taken her straight to the metal fence. Similarly, she'd found this crew once more with little trouble, though when she hesitated at the door and glanced around, all she could make out were endless corridors of ash, oak and elm. There were no signs of the houses or a golf course.

"Take me there."

"It's not for you, lassie," Angus said. "Go home, back to wherever it is you came from. It looks like whatever let you in here will let you out again."

"No. I want to see the Blocko Tower. All my life they told me I'd made it up, that Eva didn't exist, that she was some pathetic fantasy concocted in my brain because I was stupid or mental. They lied to me. I want to see the truth so I know it wasn't me."

Pash cocked her head to one side and studied Sally with a grin.

"Ever used a shotgun?"

"No way" Szymanski grumbled. "Not getting my balls blown off by some whiny runt."

"I can fight."

The Pole snorted and tore a Yorkshire pudding in two with his fingers.

"I've never fired a gun but I was trained to use a sword, and I have a black belt in Muay Thai."

"Is that some kind of Nip shit?" Chisum asked.

"I said I can fight."

"Not so well judging by that nose." Angus grabbed a plate out of the sideboard and piled on the food. Sally bristled.

"I fucked you over good enough."

"Oh, aye. Only 'cos I let me guard down on account of you being a wee slip of nothing. And on that note, here. You need feeding up."

He put the dinner on the table. Pash shuffled to one side and pulled over a fifth chair. She gave another grin, half mocking, half intrigued, as Sally squeezed in beside her.

"Ziz, haven't we got a Polish sabre from when your cavalry took on the fascist tanks and you got all your asses whupped? Give her that," the anarchist said.

"Go to hell, Pash. Not happening."

"Flailing around with a sword? This is room to room. Machine guns, grenades and satchel charges. Anything else is a dangerous waste of space," Chisum butted in. "What use is she to us?"

"Eva's your friend?" Angus asked. Sally nodded.

"I visited her flat when I was six."

"Do you remember where it is?" the Scotsman continued.

"She's not so stupid as to stay in one place all this time," the sergeant said. "We've not found her so far. Why should you?"

"You've never met her?" Sally asked.

"Eva's a ghost," Pash told her.

"Which is a wee pain when it comes to strategising," Angus explained. "She follows her own plans and we find out about it afterwards. But if you're with us, there's a chance she'll show her face. And if you lead us to her den, then there might be something there of benefit in our quest against Old Nick."

"Old Nick? What exactly are you fighting in there?"

They all swapped glances.

"Enemies," Pash said.

"People?"

"Sometimes."

The sardonic grin vanished. Trouble flickered in the woman's eyes. Angus started to collect the empty plates. The food hadn't been bad - mostly stodgy and boiled, like the meals her grandparents made when she'd stayed over as a child.

"There's normal humans in there as well. Maybe you can help them," Angus said. "Old Nick collects them as he sweeps from age to age. Most are never seen again, but some he doesn't bother with once they're inside. They live in the tower and no harm comes to them. Even so they should 'na be there. You might be able to persuade the poor buggers to escape."

"They need persuading?"

"It's a home to some who've lost theirs and have no reason to leave," Angus said.

Sally remembered the pale Formica and wool apartment where she'd made plastic bugs with Eva. Its soft, confident silence had contrasted with the endless tension and arguments in her parents' house. In the miserable months and years that followed her first visit, she'd often fantasised of living in Eva's flat with all those wonderful toys and no grownups to scream and shout at her. Instead, the Wodaran from Pluto, with its parsnip head and raygun, would look after the girls and together they'd play the days away.

By the time the squad finished dinner whatever sun looked over this forest had long set. From the dining room Sally noticed a long lawn divided into two by a rose bed. High sandstone walls soaked in soot enclosed it on three sides. There was even a garden shed in one of the bottom corners, its single window mercifully dark. Beyond the stones, more trees reached into the grey sky.

Angus scrubbed the plates in the trough-shaped sink. Nobody seemed to want to talk and Sally had run out of questions. She couldn't think of what to ask that would make sense of any of this. The reflections in the Fiat window had leached all meaning from her old world. The soldiers' red-brick house became even more dream-like as the shadows pushed in under the doors and around the casements. Chisum drew the curtains and switched on a couple of table lamps. They had heavy twisted cables resembling tree roots, and their dull light struggled against the thickening night.

Pash took Sally's hand as the men shuffled about in silence.

"Come. You need to sleep."

The Spaniard led her into the front room. It was stacked with guns and ammunition cases, piled around two more armchairs and a sofa. Most of the crates were stencilled with white stars. A few had a red hammer and sickle, and Sally noticed at least one swastika. A box was open and full of grenades. Pash turned Sally's hand over, palm up, and rubbed the callouses in the finger creases with her thumb.

"You work on farm? Factory?"

"They're from weightlifting and skipping."

"Skipping?"

Sally made the motions with her hands. The other woman laughed, looked around the room, and picked out a sawn-off double barrel shotgun and a pouch full of red shells. She nodded towards the kitchen.

"They are stupid men who say women fight bad. This is yours. I show you how to use it tomorrow."

It was surprisingly heavy. Pash watched her with an expression that suggested it would be a betrayal of all womankind if Sally handed it back. When she didn't, her guide led her up a narrow flight of stairs and into a backroom. She saw two beds pushed up against opposite walls, both heaped with blankets and eiderdowns. Pash pointed at one and sat down on the other. It had a smattering of old photos tacked to the wall by the headboard - men and women in grey and black uniforms against a white landscape of stone and scrub. Sally put the gun and ammunition under the bed and perched on her mattress.

"What's Pash short for?"

"My name is Rafaella Eliana Concepcion. 'Pash' is nothing to do with me. Chisum chose it. He called me after the Passionflower, Isidora Dolores Ibárruri Gómez. She was a famous communist, I'm anarchist. Communists are assholes. We are better street fighters. Don't they see that when they attack us in Barcelona they help the enemy? Not that it matters now. 'Pash' is ok I guess. Is easier for those idiots downstairs to pronounce."

"I don't know anything about the war in Spain. I heard

General Franco was a bit of a shit, though. Didn't he die recently?"

Pash shrugged.

"They never die. Mussolini, Franco, Hitler, whoever. They just shed their skin and come back in different suits and different hats. What's your name? Those rude bastards never asked."

"Sally."

Pash raised an eyebrow.

"...Aston."

"Sally Ass-Ton. Is that all?"

Sally had clearly been shortchanged by Spanish standards. The woman stripped down to a pair of faded pink granny bloomers and climbed into bed. She was even scrawnier than her new roommate - a skeleton wrapped up in tissue paper, arms glued on with two clumps of black armpit hair, tits flattened into muscle. A slightly podgy belly and stretch marks suggested children once. If so, what had happened to them? Pash also had a huge blue and brown bruise on her right shoulder blade, maybe a souvenir from the stairwells and passageways of the Blocko Tower. The anarchist pulled out a pack of cigarettes from under the pillow and shook it at Sally. When her guest refused, Pash lit one for herself and stared up at the ceiling, the back of her head cushioned on her hands.

"How did you end up here?" Sally asked. "Why are you fighting Professor Backenforth?"

"The devil, you mean?"

"Is that who you reckon he is?"

It was hard to figure out when the other woman was being serious. Her words were endlessly laced with a sardonic indifference that seemed to oscillate between bitterness and comedy.

"A lonely devil," Pash mumbled around the cigarette, making the smoke jitter. "People think God threw Satan out of heaven, with all the rebel angels, down into Hell together. Is not true. He is alone in his own universe. Nothing else, living or dead. No meaning or light or life, nada."

"You believe all that?"

The other woman turned onto her side and grinned at Sally.

"What you believe, Sally Ass-Ton?"

"I don't know."

"I'm anarchist," Pash said. "All religion is bullshit."

"But you're fighting the devil."

"The lonely devil. Yes. That's why he fly the tower here, there and everywhere, collecting lost spirits. He longs for company in his empty kingdom. He wants people to talk to, friends, souls to punish and reward, like he did in the olden times before the emperor of Rome imprison him in that building."

Sally felt herself beginning to lose it. The cynical war veteran pose was all very well, but she saw too much of her own snarky self in that grin to keep her patience any longer.

"Can you tell me what the hell all this is about. Properly, instead of all that crap about devils and souls and demons?"

Pash took a long drag of her cigarette and blew a cloud of smoke at the ceiling.

"I first looked at the tower when we fought in Barcelona. The bastard Communists tried to take over our telephone building in Plaça de Catalunya. They'd been trying to force us to join them. Said we wouldn't get their nice guns and bullets from Comrade Stalin if we didn't sign up to their armies. We told them to fuck off, and so we all ended up banging heads - Anarchists, Marxists, Communists, Syndicalists. The guards took over the ground floor. I am upstairs with the others. A lot of shooting and yelling. Smoke. I thought the building on fire, panicked and jumped out of window, scrambled up the outside to the next level. Angus says I am a 'wee gowk' who climb like a rat up a drainpipe," she grinned around her cigarette. "You'll see. Anyhow, trucks start arriving, so I kick in window and found stairs. I didn't understand they were our troops coming to throw out the guards, so I kept going. Up and up. At last it is all quiet, and I realise I am on fifteenth floor."

Pash paused as if expecting a reaction.

"The Telefonica only has nine floors," she said after blank looks from Sally.

"You were in the Blocko Tower."

"Si. I look out of window but all I can see is grey cloud above and grey cloud below, like I stand on top of mountain. I listen at the door and there is nothing. I go out into the corridor. Suddenly I'm in a very expensive hotel, like El Palace on Gran Via before the Sindicatos took it over. Beautiful carpets. Paintings. Chandeliers. Everywhere brass and wood. Doors and doors in corridors that are a kilometre long. I try a few, but all are locked. Then I hear noises behind one that..." Pash went quiet and still, although the smoke from her cigarette shuddered and twisted. To Sally's astonishment, the Spaniard rubbed at the corners of her eyes. Was she trying to hide tears?

"What was it?"

Pash smiled and shook her head, blinking.

"I knew an English boy," she continued after a few more silent moments. "I met him before Ebro. He was at our camp with the Brigadas Internacionales. Teddie Heath - he is student. Oxford University Conservador Association. Nice smile, funny voice. He last a minute under the stars of Catalonia and said sorry all the way through." Pash burst out laughing. "You know him?"

So much for the truth about the Blocko Tower.

"When was this?"

"Few months ago. Er, no," Pasha rubbed her forehead as if suddenly confused. "1938. June, perhaps."

"The only Ted Heath I've come across is the dozy joker Maggie Thatcher replaced. He was our Prime Minister. Everyone took the piss out of him. Sails yachts and plays the organ. Christ on a bike. You didn't fuck Ted Heath, did you?"

"Maybe. Time means nothing here. People who have died in your world are still alive in mine. The unborn of my Catalonia walk your streets. They are old now, I guess. Older than me. Perhaps I did fuck this Prime Minister of yours. Lots of foreigners came to help against Franco in the Brigadas Internacionales. I took a few as lovers. Crazy times. We were young and we were the *Mujeres Libres*. Women equal as women taking what we want for us, no longer in the shadow of men. There was a squad of Jews from Zimbergn, but not there to fight the fascists. They were after the tower and they told me what it really is."

"Which is?"

The Spaniard stubbed her cigarette out on the bedhead and dropped it into a cracked mug on the floor.

"If I tell you, you say I talk shit about devils."

"I won't."

Pash flicked her lighter open. In a room where the darkness beat the heavy electrics into submission it was a bright star.

"The tale they told me was thousands of years old. It came out of Persia, from the kingdom of Zarathustra. Two Gods. Light." She snapped the lid shut, snuffing the flame. "Dark. Fighting for eternity. Their battles make the universe. Where the sun, moon and stars consume the shadow, or the shadow crushes the fire, we living creatures come from the smoke and cinders. After Christ was born into the world, the emperor of Rome made a tower with the help of the Jews to trap the dark one in the land of Edom. But the god of the night stole the rabbis' wisdom and freed his prison in time and space. Now it belongs to him and he journeys here and there, collecting souls to take to his realm to keep him company."

"And the god of light?"

"Does nothing. Where was he when bombs fell on Guernica? When the Jews were gassed in their millions? When all the children cry out to him from their graves? He listens to the widow's prayer and the mother's screams, and is silent."

Light and Dark. Ancient magic wielded by creatures with daft names. The Jedi and the Force. On the one hand it sounded very familiar, yet totally ridiculous. One of Sally's neighbours at university had endlessly played some stupid fantasy game with little lead men he spent days painting. The twat tried to chat her up by showing off his collection. She suggested his money might be better invested in deodorant. He called her a bitch so she floored him, threatening to ram his entire metal army up his arse if he so much as looked at her again. He'd spouted the same nonsense about wizards in towers as Pash.

But tiredness and the heavy dinner had drained her of any more arguments. Pash flicked the lighter on and off, silently watching something unfold on the streets of 1930s Barcelona inside the flame. Whenever the wick caught again it seemed to make the room even darker, as if the heat thickened the air into a muddy soup. Exhausted by the effort of trying to understand, Sally closed her eyes and let herself drown.

She woke to a different world, one of dark blue silver-edged surfaces and a sharp mask staring down at her.

"Get up," Pash said, giving her a shake.

"What time is it?"

"5 am."

"Really?"

"You're in the army now. Get dressed and bring the gun."

Downstairs Angus was parcelling out bacon butties and tin mugs of sweet tea. Chisum and Szymanski stood at the table, bent over a battered notebook.

"What do you recall? What floor was Eva's apartment?" the Polish corporal asked.

"I don't remember. White corridor. Orange door with the number 239. If we get in a lift I could maybe guess by the amount of time it takes going up."

"Lifts are risky. Might be worth a go, though," Chisum said. "The inside of the tower changes but the room numbers seem to stay the same."

"Don't come near me with that thing," the corporal growled when he spotted the sawn-off shotgun. "Keep it broken and barrel down. I want her at the back," he added to Pash.

"You're coming because we think you can help reach out to Eva, persuade her to work more closely with us," Chisum said. "Pash'll keep you out of trouble. If it gets too hot in there, you two leave."

"I stay and fight," the anarchist said.

"If I tell you to take her out, you do it. That's an order."

"Go to hell."

Pash slapped her bicep and stuck her fist up, middle finger

pointing at the ceiling. Angus chuckled. Chisum growled something in his throat and went back to his notebook.

Outside, a pale light seeped through the trees. They trudged towards it in a line, Angus leading the way and Sally at the rear. She studied the back of Pash's head. The woman wore her tasselled cap and a bolt action rifle banged between her shoulder blades. The two Americans carried Tommy guns. Angus had what looked like a sniper rifle with a two-foot long scope. No birds sang and the air lay still. All was silent apart from the tramp and rattle of the soldiers trudging along the trail.

After a while Sally sensed a thickening in the sky, as if a great mass was gathering on the other side. It pressed against the grey dome like a thumb pushing on an eggshell. She didn't have to guess what was causing it. It carried the same awful weight as the black-spired church in Chapeltown, the one she'd screamed at from her pram until Grandad crossed the road. She was back in the realm of the Blocko Tower and somebody had turned gravity up a couple of notches. Instinctively she bent her head, concentrating on Pash's boots, trying to ignore the grinding tension in her stomach.

Grass and tree roots gave way to tarmac.

"This is new," Chisum said. "Any ideas?"

They stood on a square littered with weeds, staring at the back of a house. Identical buildings stretched into the haze on either side, each with a yard flanked by waist-high fences. There was something decidedly odd about the rear wall, with its bright red brickwork and four white-framed windows, two below and two above. In the centre the rows of bricks shifted out of alignment, as if somebody had taken separate halves of a building and carelessly glued them together. The others had noticed as well. Angus ran his hand up and down the fault. He dug in and pulled. The area of masonry in front of him peeled away like a patch of soggy wallpaper. Pash joined him and tugged at the other edge, tearing off a long strip that finished underneath a window.

"What is that?" Chisum asked, poking at the dark brown surface left behind. "Bakelite?"

Sally went and up and rubbed her fingers over the greasy patch.

"Plastic. It's a giant plastic box wrapped up in wallpaper. All fake."

The window frame was fashioned out of the same material. A jagged mould seam ran around the outside, rough and sharp enough to cut. The window itself seemed to be pressed out of thick cellophane and stuck on a blackboard, with a scrap of lace sandwiched between the layers. The only thing Sally could think of was a theatre flat or film set. She hopped over the nearest fence, also moulded out of plastic, and checked the adjacent house. It was identical, and the next, and the one after that. They were standing at the back of an entire row of phoney houses.

The rest of the squad caught up with her and trudged past. She fell in behind Pash again as they hunted for a break between the buildings. As far as Sally remembered, her journey to the Blocko Tower with Eva had been straightforward - grass to concrete to linoleum. But even so, a memory lurked in the back of her head. There was something familiar about this odd Potemkin village.

They finally came to an alleyway. It led onto a road with an identical set of houses on the opposite side. The fronts were all the same as the backs, apart from a bright red door replacing the bottom left window. Angus jogged down the garden path of one of the dwellings, but stopped a few feet away from the entrance. He looked suddenly hesitant.

"Leave it," Chisum growled. "We're wasting time."

He sounded strained, nervous. It wasn't surprising. This whole landscape possessed a watchful, brooding silence that was creeping Sally out. She had a brief vision of every single house crammed full of a purple angry face, the giant eyes scraping against the inside of the rough plastic boxes as they hunted for her.

Pash whistled, a piercing shriek from further down the street. The Spaniard stood in the middle of the road, looking at a big black mark at her feet. They joined her, Angus clearly relieved to get away from the houses. Sally angled her head and found herself staring at the letter *d*. To the left, where the tarmac gently curved into the distance, someone had stamped an *a*, then an *o*, each character about a yard in length. She carried on, the others trailing after her. Over the next ten yards they walked along two words painted on the pale asphalt.

Ring Road.

CHAPTER EIGHT

"Why would you put a road sign on the floor?" Szymanski said. "Only planes would spot it."

"You've never been here before?" Sally asked.

"It's usually a bombed-out precinct," Chisum replied. "Just like in Berlin."

"Or Barcelona," Pash added. "It change every time but only a little. Different streets, different buildings, but basically the same. Our cities all blown to pieces. We walk down them and eventually come to the tower. It always in the centre."

"So this is on you," Angus told Sally. "You're the only thing that's new around here."

She looked at the wallpaper and plastic houses, the oddly smooth road and giant letters. *Ring Road*. It felt so familiar, even though she'd never been anywhere as bizarre as this before. Maybe a dream once? She could sense monstrosity on the other side of those fake bricks, sliding in greasy dark channels, pressing against the corners, looking for any crack in the walls to bring her into view. Was this some old nightmare given form?

Their footfalls bounced off the surfaces like whip cracks. An odd smell hung between the buildings. It made her think of new carpets, cardboard and furniture polish. Sally closed her eyes and for a second it seemed as if she was sitting in a silent, white room full of leather upholstery and thick pile rugs. Something about the illusion was deeply unsettling. She walked past the letters. The road curved round to her right, flanked on both sides by the dark tenements. No, wait. A narrow break further on, another avenue leading off. She stopped at the corner and stared down it.

Absolutely no way.

A crossroads sat halfway along this street, with a single traffic light pointing in their direction. It was taller than the houses on either side and made entirely of what appeared to be more plastic. The three lights were marked by painted discs the size of cartwheels. Red, amber and green. Beyond the sign, and the rooftops beside it, she spotted an enormous hand, palm out, fingers pointed up at the sky. The cuff, bigger than a house chimney, alternated navy and white stripes. She looked down at the surface of the road and read the word leading up to the junction.

Headingley.

"Driving Test Game."

"What?" Pash asked. Sally put her hands on her knees and tried to focus, calming her heart with long shuddering gasps. The Spaniard rubbed her back, probably thinking she was about to throw up. She certainly wanted to.

"Driving Test Game. This is the board. We're inside it. I played it with Eva in her flat."

"What are you talking about?" Chisum said.

Sally pointed at the junction.

"That's the plastic traffic light from the game and that," she pointed at the hand, "...is the policeman. You have a control stick and you guide little magnetic cars around the map without knocking them over. There should be a phone box, a lollipop lady, and a couple of stop signs. There were two versions I saw. One was of Leeds and one was of Brighton. Both had Backenforth Heights on them. If this is Headingley we're in the Leeds' edition."

"What the hell are you talking about?" Szymanski said.

"We. Are. Inside. A. Kid's. Game."

Even as she snapped out the words, she knew what the response would be. He looked at her as if she was something he'd found under a rock.

"This is such horse shit," he finally said.

"Ok. Whatever this place is. One, do you know your way around? And two, are we in any immediate danger?" Chisum asked.

Sally forced herself to look beyond the traffic sign, the roofs and the giant policeman's hand. She thought she could just make out shadows in the mist but it was hard to tell.

"It was almost twenty years ago. I was only little. I think I can remember the layout. The end of this road should take us to the town hall. The Blocko Tower is north of that. As for danger. I don't know. It's a children's toy. Small parts might be a choking hazard?" The sarcasm bounced off everyone and died on the tarmac at her feet. She didn't want to mention what she'd imagined inside the houses.

Sally led them beyond the traffic light. She saw the policeman down one of the side streets. He had to be at least ten yards high, moulded in dark blue plastic. A giant toymaker had tried to give him a face, as well as patterned cuffs and silver buttons. Two eyes and a red smear of a mouth sat in the centre of a pink moon that bled into the seams of his collar. When he was an inch tall, and she was six, it'd been easy to overlook the ham-fisted paint job. Here it looked as if one of the creatures in the houses had escaped, smeared itself in pancake makeup, and decided to play the mime before devouring them, or worse. She hurried past while the rest of the squad trudged after her in morose silence, barely giving the colossus a glance.

The layout only bore a hazy similarity to the real Leeds. Headingley opened onto the main square. The town hall was a larger building with a crude tower at each corner, sitting beside a circle of painted grass. Two lions crouched on the perimeter, facing outwards. Their moulds were so poor they were nothing more than huge lumps of plastic with manes and muzzles. Scraps of flash jutted from their seams like broken fish scales.

When she was small, Grandad had told her of the one evening he was on the beat when he'd come across the lions prowling around the city. They'd been hunting for naughty little girls to eat and had asked him if he knew of any. Of course he said no because, at that time, Sally was nothing more than a twinkle in her father's eye. If he ever met them again, things might be different. He'd received a serious verbal kicking from Grandma after his granddaughter woke up screaming at 3am. She'd seen the real limestone statues many times since then, long since scoured clean of chimney soot and childhood horror. These grotesque plastic facsimiles brought all the nightmares back. She hurried on past, aiming for the street with *Scott Hall Road* printed on it. Memory of the game suggested this led to Moortown and beyond that, the edge of the board and the Blocko Tower.

But instead they hit the ring road again. More fake houses lined both sides of the avenue, packed closely together in curving rows. Thinking there might be another junction, Sally followed it round to the west. Nothing, apart from an angular jumble of treacle-coloured blocks as big as a cathedral. She stared at the structure, fighting the urge to run away screaming. The rest of the squad stood beside her. She sensed their growing impatience. They blamed her for this insane landscape and now they were angry with her for getting them lost.

"If we shoot you, will all this disappear?" Chisum asked. Angus snorted but Sally wondered if the sergeant was joking.

"We've wasted enough time already," the Pole said. "Bringing you here was a mistake."

"What is that?" Pash asked, putting her hand on Sally's shoulder.

"I think it's supposed to be the Merrion Centre. A big shopping mall. See that entrance at the top of the stairs? There's light. I bet it leads through to the rest of the map, in which case it'll take us to the Blocko Tower."

"Go on then lassie. Check it out and report. Not you Pash. The wee yin's expendable. You're not."

The anarchist took Sally's gun, loaded it, snapped the barrels shut and returned it.

"You find anything bad, come straight out."

Sally looked at the others. They glowered at her and she

scowled back. Pash was OK. The others could go fuck themselves. There was no way she was going to let them send her home with her tail between her legs.

Her boots struggled for purchase on the polystyrene stairs. The building had a greasy quality to it, the walls and roof of this crude structure barely one step away from congealed oil. The doorway leading into the shopping centre was nothing more than a big square hole, ringed by uneven, flash-caked edges. Beyond it, a passageway narrowed down to a smudge of light. The inside was littered with half-formed shapes. Maybe they were supposed to represent shopfronts stocked with toys and sweet jars. The badly cast crud made her think of a clogged artery. Sally tried to stay in the middle, desperate not to touch the walls or ceiling. It was no good, they closed in until she was wedged into a narrow crack. A few yards further on she saw another street and more houses but there was no way to struggle through. Unable to bear the touch of greasy plastic any longer, she fled back to the entrance.

"It's blocked."

Szymanski spat on the ground and swore in Polish. Pash took the shotgun from Sally and patted her on the shoulder.

"You say this is all in some kid's toy," Angus said. "If you go back to your world, can you find it in a shop so we can see the map before we set out? Otherwise we're just going round in circles."

"Maybe. If it's still on sale."

"Let's do that," Chisum said. "This place is creeping me out. I think we're being watched."

They returned the way they'd come. Sally trailed along at the back, battling with misery and a nausea she couldn't shake off since being wrapped up in the brown guts of that fake shopping centre. When they came to the words *Ring Road* again the three men stopped, guns ready.

"What is it?" she asked.

"Where's the place we came in?" Pash said. Sally walked past the soldiers, along the printed word, and looked around. There was no sign of the alleyway leading to the forest. She continued a little further. The houses on both sides still formed an unbroken double arc. Eventually she caught sight of another inner spoke on the left, leading to the city centre.

"It's gone."

Szymanski grabbed her by the throat, ran her backwards across the street, and pinned her up against a house front. She felt the brick wallpaper give at her back, as if it was covering flesh instead of plastic.

"Where have you brought us, you bitch?"

He fumbled with his holster. Maybe he thought he was going to shoot her or give her a pistol-whipping. His other fingers tightened around her throat, his face big and red and spitting anger. It looked like her own mother's filling the sky all those years ago, just before the world came raining down in blows on her head and shoulders.

"Hey! Cut it out!" Chisum yelled from down the street. Pash was running up the garden path towards them.

Sally lost it.

She pushed herself up on tiptoes, forcing Szymanski to loosen his grip on her neck, and grabbed his hand. She twisted left and right, bending his arm at the wrist and elbow so it resembled the crank handle of a classic car. Sally threw all her weight against the joints. He yelled out and collapsed at her feet, forearm trapped against her chest. She had him in a brutal lock and all he could do was bang the ground with his other fist.

"CUT IT OUT!" Chisum shouted. Sally twisted a little more and the Pole gasped in pain. Oh so tempting to break the wrist and elbow, or at least stick her boot into his face a few times. Someone pushed her sideways. She stumbled and fell to her knees. Chisum and Angus stood between her and her attacker. Pash helped her up.

"And that is 'Nip shit'," Sally spat. She shook off the other woman's grip and stalked into the road.

"Jesus Christ, lassie," the Scotsman said. "I don't feel so bad about losing to you anymore."

Chisum had his face in the corporal's, snarling words at him in the voice of a very angry Rottweiler. Szymanski kept his head down and nodded, massaging his wrist, occasionally casting wary glances her way.

"What is that?" Pash asked, unslinging her rifle.

Sally followed her gaze. A giant red plastic car sat at the next junction, facing in their direction. Its top was on a level with the first-floor windows of the houses, and there was barely any space between its wheels and the pavement on either side. From where she stood, Sally could see it was another crude toy. Memories of holding the tiny version in the palm of her hand popped into her head. It had an interior with badly moulded seats and a drooping steering wheel. The windows were spaces between the bent struts holding up the roof. Black discs formed the wheels, fixed in place by pins as thick as her arms.

Pash grabbed her and the pair of them dropped behind the nearest fence. The three men scattered, guns aimed at the vehicle, each taking cover in different gardens.

"What is that thing?" Angus yelled from a couple of houses down.

"The car from the game," Sally shouted back. The Spaniard cocked her weapon.

"Who's driving it?" she asked.

"It's empty." That was Szymanski from the opposite side of the street.

"So how did it get there?" Pash glanced across at Sally, her eyes wide with fear.

"There's a magnet under the board and one in the car. You make it move with a lever. That's the point of the game," Sally told her.

In her mind she remembered holding the round ball in her hand and ever-so-delicately nudging the stick to make the vehicle navigate its way through the streets. The trick was to be gentle enough to prevent it banging into the houses. You lost the game if you hit anything.

The car jerked forwards a dozen yards, coming to rest at an

angle. A brief spatter of gunfire. Sally saw dints appear between the red moulded headlights. Apart from that, the bullets seemed to have little effect.

"Hold your fire!" Chisum yelled. It must have been Angus shooting. Smoke hovered over his position.

"Lassie, who's making it move?" he shouted.

Sally looked up at the sky, wondering if she'd see the control lever towering up into the mist. She trawled through her memories, working out the orientation - where they'd sat when playing the game, how each tiny shift translated to the magnets.

The car jerked forwards again, left wheel banging into the end of one of the brown plastic fences.

No, silly, Eva's six-year-old voice warned in her head. *Back a bit and try again.*

The car reversed towards the junction in rapid magnetic shudders. It drove so quickly, anyone getting in its path would be instantly crushed. With no way of anticipating its movements, they were trapped. Except, hang on... Sally closed her eyes and held the control stick in her mind once more, imaginary hands clasped together to steady them. Ever so carefully, she nudged the lever so that the little car in her head moved slowly down the road an inch, straightening itself against the words printed on the tarmac.

She opened her eyes and looked again. There it sat, bang smack in the middle of the street name.

"I'm controlling it."

"What?" Chisum yelled.

"I'm moving it. Watch."

The trick was to focus her thoughts, breathe deeply, and not give way to panic. One slip might send it careening out of sight or smashing into them. Each time she recalled the tiny movements under her six-year-old palm, the giant red monstrosity responded.

"You're really doing that?" Pash said as the vehicle drew level with their position. It was hard to fine-tune its trajectory but somehow Sally managed to send it further down the road. The whole procedure was completely silent. If there was a giant magnet under their feet, it didn't make a sound. To her surprise, a side-street opened up to the south as the red car moved past the houses, the buildings folding inwards to make a space.

Slowly she backed the car into the junction to prevent the road closing again. Something fell over with a clatter. It sounded like she'd toppled a fence or two. Blanking her mind to stop any further movement, she walked towards the vehicle. Pash and the others followed. Beyond it, the houses ended at a low wall. It had a door in the centre, though at this distance it was difficult to make out if it was real or just painted on. The treetops rose into the pale sky on the other side.

"We can get over that," Angus said. "Come on."

"Wait," Sally said. After telling the others to stand well back, she coaxed the plastic toy back onto the ring road and sent it further on in jerks and starts, trotting after it to keep up.

"Hey, where are you going?" Chisum called after her. She ignored him. As expected, when the car reached the end of the visible curve another avenue opened up, angling to the north east. She sprinted over and read the words embossed on the tarmac.

Scott Hall Road.

"What the hell are you doing?" the sergeant snapped when she returned. "We're going back to the house and sending you home. No more bullshit toys. I don't care how big a buddy Eva was."

"I know how to reach the tower."

"What?" Szymanski growled. There was a touch of wary respect in his voice. Sally found it even more unsettling than his earlier contempt.

"The car will show me the way. It's opened up the street that leads to Moortown. If I send it in the right direction, I can take us to the Blocko Tower. Do you want to do this or do you want to fuck off back to your Yorkshire Puddings?"

Angus barked out a laugh.

"You're not suggesting we ride in that thing with a wee lassie like you driving?"

She was almost tempted to say yes, just to wind him up, but now was not the time. The angrier she got, the harder it was to concentrate. All her patience would be needed to coax the immense machine along the streets as they unfolded, without it getting stuck or running them over.

The red plastic car lurched on, roads opening up on either side as it moved ever northwards. Sally understood that they were walking through a child's version of Leeds, abstracted into a tangle of a dozen streets at most. She couldn't rely on the geography she remembered as an adult. Instead, she reached back in search of fragments of an infant's perception. What had mattered to her when she was six years old. What had she fixated on and what disregarded?

The bomb sites were here, of course - spaces the size of football fields with the outlines of shattered terraces printed on the floor. At this scale the mis-aligned coloured dots from the printing process were as big as her fist, and made it look as if the images were bleeding migraine-inducing cancerous bubbles from their edges. When they reached Chapeltown she saw the soot-coated church spire bending across the street under its own weight. That hadn't been in the original Driving Test Game. Something was reaching into her baby nightmares and adding them to the mix. That made her angry. The car slewed sideways and smacked into a couple of garden fences, uprooting them from their plastic lawns.

"What's up?" Pash asked. It was the first time any of the others had spoken for a while. Sally suspected her new power over the game made them wary. Maybe they thought she was leading them into a trap. If they tried to shoot her she'd command the car to grind them into the painted ground.

"You said you've got explosives. Can you bring that thing down?" she asked, nodding up at the spire. "Or burn it?"

"Charges or grenades won't work," Chisum told her. "You'd flood this place with molten plastic and poisonous fumes if you set fire to it. Why's it so important?"

Sally stared at the twisted spire.

"Doesn't matter."

Perhaps she wanted to send a message to those responsible for this unbidden dream, warning them not to conjure up anything else. She knew there were darker memories waiting for her between the church and the Blocko Tower.

Which was why she hesitated at the end of the last street, before the woods that led to Backenforth Heights. The red car had come to a halt halfway down and refused to shift, no matter how many times she moved the stick in her mind. She knew why. It was parked next to her old house.

"I think I can see the tower," Angus said. "Well done, lassie."

He offered her a swig out of a hip flask. Whiskey. Normally Sally thought it tasted like drain cleaner, but she needed this. She took a couple of swigs, forcing it down.

The squad walked past. Pash gave her a peck on the cheek and a big grin. Even Szymanski nodded approval. Sally had no idea how to react. Yes, the route was cleared for them, she could sense it, but what about her? The only way onwards lay between the car and the Toy Town version of her childhood home. Its shadow fell across the garden and the vehicle. At the edge of perception she sensed a screaming head, crammed inside, vast and angry.

Oh God, no. There's hinges at the bottom of the wall.

Any second now, the whole facade would come thudding down and she'd be mere feet away from that giant, crushed face. Sally forced herself to keep going. Creeping past the car, she stupidly glanced up at her old bedroom window. For an instant, she had the impression of a monstrous eye staring down at her, angry and bloodshot and full of hatred. Smoke poured from the chimney. It reeked of the Marlboros her parents used to smoke. The stink made her dizzy. Two voices echoed inside her head, one plaintive, one insane.

WHERE HAVE YOU BEEN?

I can't hear you properly, speak louder, Sally.

WHERE HAVE YOU BEEN? YOU'VE BEEN GONE EIGHT HOURS.

You've got to talk to your father, Sally. He ignores me.

EIGHT FUCKING HOURS, YOU STUPID WICKED LITTLE SHIT.

I've always helped you when you needed it. You need to take more responsibility.

By the time she'd managed to claw her way past the car, she was bawling her eyes out, slobbering the same word over and over as she staggered after the others.

"Wodaran, Wodaran..."

Pash held her until the sobs subsided, then stood at arm's length, hands still on her shoulders, and looked down at Sally's jeans. The men had turned away, muttering among themselves, occasionally casting awkward glances at the two women. Mortified, Sally realised she'd pissed herself.

CHAPTER NINE

A ngus had a regimental kilt in his pack. Sally pulled off her wet jeans and knickers, and wore that instead. Pash stood between her and the men so they wouldn't lech at her arse while she changed. She was lonely, humiliated and miserable, just like when she'd hidden under the conker tree at playtime all those years ago. Chisum had said their explosives and grenades wouldn't damage the plastic houses, but oh how she wanted to wipe out her old home, with its monstrous mother crushed inside, whining at her through clouds of cigarette smoke. She glowered tearfully at the distant building, wondering whether to smash the car into the front, again and again - a red polystyrene fist hammering all her hate into those paper bricks. Maybe it'd uproot the fences but she'd probably end up snapping off the wheels in the process. They needed the vehicle to find their way back.

"Suits you, lassie," Angus said. "You'd do well in the Queens Own Cameron Highlanders with those knees and those boots."

"What happened?" Corporal Szymanski asked. He kept glancing up the road, as if he sensed the hideous power locked up in Number 5. Sally shook her head, not trusting herself to speak.

"Come on," Pash said. "We're nearly there. I can smell the tower."

This version of the woods consisted of nothing more than the tops of trees painted onto the floor, with a trail between them leading north in the form of a heavy dotted line. As they walked along, the scale seemed to shift, the two dimensional forest growing out of all proportion to the rest of the Driving Test Game. The mist from the streets followed them, thickening until it completely surrounded the group. They trudged on in the centre of a circle of clear air bounded by pale emptiness. Here and there, in the spaces between the cartoon oaks and elms, the unknown artist had added Toy Town creatures - cute squirrels, dewy-eyed rabbits, robins and a Bambi-knockoff. They'd all been drawn side-on, rather than as seen from above. Sally thought it looked as if someone had flooded the glades with poison gas and left it littered with dinky animal corpses. The men ahead tramped over the image of a little girl wheeling her bicycle back down the path. Sally stopped and stared down at the picture.

"You OK?" Pash asked, after making sure her comrades were out of earshot.

"That's me."

The Spaniard looked down at the girl wearing a lovely blue coat and shiny buckled shoes on her feet. She had a red bicycle with white tyres, new by the looks of it. The infant was striding along with all the confidence of the rosy-cheeked heroine of the best story ever written, on her way home to warm milk and cuddles after playing in the woods with her new best friend.

"When I got back, my mother knocked me about for going missing. She called me a stupid little shit. Then the police rolled up," it took Sally a few deep breaths to stop her voice breaking. "Everything turned bad from then on."

She looked away, bent over, and blew her nose onto the ground. Snot and tears spattered the fairyland grass.

"Was that building back there something to do with it?" Pash asked.

"It was my old house. Mum was still there, just now. I could hear her as we went past. She was trying to drag me inside for another beating. This Sally's lucky," she tapped the girl with her boot. "Stuck forever in this happy moment before the crap starts."

For want of anything else, Sally quickly wiped her face dry with the edge of Angus's kilt.

"Chisum's worried about you," her friend said. "He doesn't know whose side you're on. He says he's gonna kill you if you mess us about. I won't let him, but they can't see you like this."

A piercing whistle came through the mist up ahead. The three men had stopped at a wall that cut across the woods. The path reached the base and carried on in the illustration painted on the barrier. Sally recognised it from the old Start-Rite shoe box.

Children's Shoes Have Far To Go.

"Now what?" Chisum said as the women approached. Sally pushed the wall.

"Cardboard."

Pash took out her bayonet and rammed it into the picture.

"Nothing on the other side."

She yanked the blade down to make a ragged gash. The five of them worked at it with their hands until they'd pulled open a space wide enough to squeeze through. Before anyone could stop her, Sally went first, desperate to get out of this insane place.

She found herself standing on a concrete plain, under a sky the colour of week-old porridge. The Blocko Tower stood about a mile away, a warped clone of one of the blocks of flats down in the centre of Leeds, except this one didn't end at eighteen floors. Its breeze-block and grimy glass facade rose up and up, darkening into a black slab set against the lowering clouds. She couldn't see the top. It disappeared into the churning murk. Compared to it, the twisted spire of Chapeltown church was a wilting daisy. Nausea and a pounding headache overwhelmed her, pasting her tongue to the roof of her mouth. Backenforth Heights was crashing down on her, or the ground was tilting up so she'd fall and roll all the way down into the lobby's steel and Formica trap. She closed her eyes. It made the vertigo worse. She opened them again and fixed her gaze on the grubby stone at her feet, fighting the terror.

"About time," the sergeant said.

It began to rain. Fat greasy drops thumped into the ground and stirred up the rainbows in the scattered puddles. Sally felt Pash's fingers on the back of her neck, massaging the pain out of her skull.

"Come on. This is worst. Inside gets easier. You don't see how huge everything is then."

Sally forced herself to keep walking, with the Spaniard's hand still pressed against her spine, as if she was a prisoner being led to the firing squad. She sensed broken walls and half-formed arches on either side, echoes of a Chirico wasteland built from memories of Barcelona, Munich, and God only knew where else. Long ago, scared to look up, she'd watched her scuffed Start-rites make their pigeon-toed way over the wet concrete. Now it was a pair of Doc Martens - black laces and blood-red leather over steel toecaps. They were the perfect metaphor for her own soul, heavy, hard combat boots wrapped around bonny little shoes that had once symbolised everything new, hopeful and adventurous.

A glass door opened inwards and Sally stepped through onto a filthy, threadbare mat edged with rubber. Instinctively she wiped her feet.

"I guess this is your world," Pash said. "Ain't nothing like El Palace on Gran Via."

Sally had assumed the lobby would appear smaller now she was all grown up. It was the opposite. She stood in a big box as large as a football pitch, with lemon yellow walls and a grubby white floor. Reflections lay across the glazed surfaces, random playing cards of orange and silver scattered from the neon tubes in the ceiling. None of it matched her memories. Twenty yards away two broken G-Plan sofas faced each other, mustard-coloured bricks with the stuffing falling out of their rotting seams. Beyond them, down the dwindling perspective, she saw another set, and another, repeating echoes in facing mirrors. Hidden speakers played 1960s airport Bossa Nova whose unseen choirs chanted meaningless lyrics on an endless loop. *Evoluon - ooh-wap ooh-waaah. Evoluon - ooh-wap ooh-waaah.* They seemed out of tune and desperate, the soundtrack to grainy films of miniskirts, black polo necks and National Health glasses. Sally could almost smell the Liebfraumilch and Steak Diane from long-abandoned wine bars.

"Is this what your world looks like? It's very empty. No soul." Pash said.

"This is the 1960s. By the mid '70s everything had turned to shit. Laura Ashley hippy bollocks, then the Bay City Rollers and shopping centres full of football hooligans. Thatcher was the cherry on the top."

"I have no idea what you just said."

Sally looked around at the echoes of dead people's dreams.

"We were promised a future we never got. By now we were supposed to be having holidays on the Moon. Instead we got dole queues, the Falklands War and AIDS."

The rest of the squad formed a cut-out silhouette by a row of lifts. Chisum waved the two of them over.

"Do you remember how long you rode up in the elevator? Roughly?" he asked.

"We can't risk using the lifts," Angus explained. "But we can work out Eva's floor if you tell us how long it took to get there."

"Half an hour." It was the first unit of time to pop into her head.

"Don't be stupid," Chisum said. "That would take you up hundreds of floors. You're telling me that's how long you rode in one of those?" he nodded at the steel doors. What was she going to tell him? Everything was half an hour when she was six. Half an hour or a random guess.

"I remember it was flat number 239."

"There's twenty apartments on each floor," Pash said. "So if you're right, we go for the eleventh."

"OK, let's head for base camp first," Chisum trudged over to the fire door leading to the stairwell and unhitched his Tommy gun.

"Base camp?" Sally asked.

"Third level. Up to that it's more or less safe," Angus said. "Though we should check on people in case anyone new has turned up."

Pash pulled the shotgun from Sally's backpack, opened it and plugged in a couple of shells. "Keep it broken and barrel down until I tell you. I'm right behind you."

Chisum eased open the door to the stairwell and used a hand mirror to see if the coast was clear. Once he was happy, the squad crept out onto the landing. Concrete steps rose into the gritty half-light. A metal railing ran along the edge, black enamel turned necrotic by patches of rust that had bubbled and burst through the plastic skin. Sally almost let the door bang shut behind her but Pash caught it and eased it back into the frame. She put a finger to her lips and winked. The two Americans sighted upwards with their Tommy guns while Angus and the anarchist aimed their rifles downwards over the railings, the Scotsman peering through the scope. That was weird. Why would he do that? Sally risked a peek. Vertigo slammed into her like a fist. She grabbed the bannister. It was so cold her fingers nearly stuck to the greasy steel. Pash took her elbow.

"Easy," she whispered.

"How far down does it go?"

"We don't know. Hundreds of floors, maybe thousands."

"Nothing down there," Angus said. "But we set trip mines on the stairs. Just in case something fancies following us from below."

Sally forced herself to look upwards. Once again it was like standing between filthy mirrors, watching the landscape iterate itself into darkness above and below. She couldn't tell if it was dizziness, the light, or the odd architecture that made the vortex overhead curve and twist into infinity. A freezing draft rose from the stairwell. It reeked of stagnant water, old drains and rotten meat. Endless kitchen bins perhaps, emptied down rubbish chutes as high as Everest. Sally had a horrible feeling it came from something far worse, piled strata-deep in those impossible depths.

Her companions made their way up the stairs. They didn't bother with the first floor, or the second, and Sally wasn't going to tarry long enough to glance through the wired glass, for fear she might see something as disturbing as that void beside her.

After six flights of concrete dust, cracked walls and scabby steel, Chisum led them through another fire door and onto a long corridor. It was coated in aluminium and Formica, painted with vast orange and white circles. All four paused. Szymanski glared at Sally, as if this sudden attack of Op Art was somehow her fault.

"What? I didn't build the place."

"We know that," Angus muttered. "It does this whenever someone new arrives. All this crap comes from your world, though. Any advice much appreciated."

She had no idea. Beyond his silhouette, white floor-to-ceiling windows at the far end of the passageway cast long geometries of light over the architecture.

"Definitely prefer El Palace on Gran Via," Pash picked a cigarette out of the pack with her teeth.

"Let's check on the folks," Chisum said. "Find out who's still here."

As with the lobby, dimensions inside the tower bore no relation to the outside. Fifty yards further on, the corridor turned ninety degrees to the left, but when Sally turned to look back the way they'd come, the passageway behind dwindled to a bright dot that seemed at least a mile away. Apartment doors punctuated both walls, some white, some orange, some a swirling bubble mixture of the two. Sally had no idea how she was going to find Eva's old flat. Half of these entrances could have been hers. The smell of rotting garbage from the stairwell had been replaced by ammonia, turpentine and fresh paint.

The soldiers paused at a door halfway between the stairs and the windows. Angus tapped a coded knock on the metal. A few moments later it opened. A scrawny old man in ragged pyjamas nodded up at them before drifting back into his apartment. They followed, Sally trailing behind.

The floor switched from linoleum to marble, the colours softening into pale cerise and gunmetal swirls. The hallway led to a square living room. A picture window in the far wall flooded the space with the same soft light as the corridor. The other three sides were painted in faded terracotta. Birds perched on vines that threaded upwards around columns and across broken walls, all rendered in muted watercolours. The man sat on a stone bench, hands between his knees, and stared at his guests with haunted, miserable eyes. Red pottery bowls lay at his feet, filled with scraps of fruit and what looked like porridge.

"Pash," Angus nodded at the anarchist. She plonked her backside on the seat beside the old man, shared out a cigarette apiece, lit them and started to speak to him in Spanish. It was an odd conversation, single words and phrases mixed up with a lot of gestures. The tenant seemed upset about something. At one point Pash put her arm across his shoulder as he wiped his eyes with the heel of his hand. Chisum walked to the window and stared out. Sally followed him. A pale, bright mist filled whatever world they now inhabited. She could see nothing beyond the tops of the windows of the floor below, and the bottom ledges of the ones above.

"Who is he?" she asked.

"Marcus? A Roman," Chisum said.

"What do you mean, 'Roman'?"

"He's one of the earliest," the sergeant gestured at the decor. "You never been to Italy? We were in Naples in '44 when the volcano blew up. Loads of ruins at Pompeii covered in these kind of paintings."

"He's Italian?"

She looked more closely at the apartment's owner. He resembled a handful of walnuts moulded into the passable imitation of a man in his early 50s. Dark curly hair turning to grey, skin stretched over the sharp bones of his arms and legs. Chisum gave her a perplexed grin, as if he was looking at the biggest idiot on the planet.

"No. He's Roman. Like in that movie *The Sign of the Cross*. He must have stumbled on this place in Jesus times. Have a look in his bedroom. You'll see what I mean."

The bedroom door was the first on the left. It had the same wall paintings and stone floor as the living room. A mattress leaking straw rested on a wooden bench. Two more statuettes stood on a shelf by the bedhead, illuminated by an Aladdin oil lamp. A spear stood propped against the far corner, next to an enormous rectangular shield showing four eagle wings and six lightning bolts in red and yellow.

"He says Proserpina took Magdalene," Pash was saying when Sally returned to the living room, trying to process what she'd just seen. Marcus still sat beside the Spaniard, her arm across his shoulders as he bent his face over the jade figurine he held in his knobbly hands.

Szymanski swore viciously in Polish and kicked the wall.

"Who's Proserpina?" Sally asked.

"Wife of Pluto," the anarchist said. "Queen of the underworld."

"We don't know what it is," Angus said. "Some creature that works for the devil in charge. She comes and smashes her way in, and carries people off if they're not protected, if Eva hasn't got to them yet."

If you don't open up I'll break down the door with my wooden tail. The words echoed down the years in Sally's head. Her friend had challenged whatever it was with the Wodaran from Pluto card, and the creature had slunk away.

"Magdalene was the last to arrive before you rolled up," Angus said. "Bonny wee lass from Malta, round about Napoleon times. Better head over and see if there's anything left to salvage."

Sally stared at Marcus. Was he really a Roman soldier who'd stumbled across the tower two thousand years ago? What had the anarchist told her? After Christ was born into the world, the emperor of Rome made a tower with the help of the Jews to trap the dark god in the land of Edom. This scrawny scatterling had been there at the start of it all.

Pash stood up.

"Nothing else to report, Sarge."

Szymanski pulled out three cans, put them on the bench next to Marcus and topped them with a fresh packet of cigarettes.

"You speak Latin?" Sally asked the Spaniard when they were out in the corridor.

"Catalan is close enough. We understand each other."

"He can't leave?"

"He could, but he won't," said Chisum who was leading the way again. "The ones the tower calls are stuck here. If they try and go outside they won't return to their own times, they'll get dumped somewhere else. So they hang on and try to make a life of it. We think they're supposed to head up to the top, either by themselves or carried by Proserpina. If Eva gets to them first she puts one of those Jew scrolls in the door frame, or a cigarette card with a monster on it. That seems to ward off the devil. It's screwed up, I know. But that's how it is."

"How does Marcus live? You've only given him three tins."

"The tower looks after you when you're here," the sergeant explained. "The coolers and the pantries have plenty of food in them. They fill up when you sleep. This dumb Polack just likes to hand out treats. He's soft that way. Here we are. Jesus Christ, this is completely TARFU."

It looked like somebody had taken a giant angle-grinder to the door, splitting it in two. The halves leaned out into the corridor, suspended by shards of stretched metal still connected to the hinges. Blood, and what looked suspiciously like shit, smeared the walls and floor. A long sinuous trail led across the wooden floorboards into the flat.

"Wait here," Pash said, all cockiness gone. The four soldiers switched into action mode, sighting down their guns and giving each other hand signals as they stepped past the wreckage and into the hall beyond. Maybe whatever had done this was still inside. Even so, Sally really didn't relish the idea of being left in the passageway all by herself. They'd walked a good hundred yards or more from the Roman soldier's refuge. The windows at the ends of the corridor were little more than dim postage stamps. Now she stood in semi-darkness. It fizzed with tiny motes, making her head spin. She flicked her gaze back and forth like a tennis spectator, heart pounding as she watched for some unholy wooden-tailed bulk to heave itself into view.

Her companions returned, grim faced.

"I wonder if your wee mate is losing it." Angus grumbled at Sally. "She should have been here sooner. It's carnage in there.

Doesn't look like there was a whole lot left for the devil to carry upstairs."

"Let's head for base camp," Chisum said.

The apartment they'd commandeered for themselves stood out like a sore thumb. The wooden door was a heavy mahogany monolith in a sea of bright abstract metal. It had a matchbox-sized brass frame at head height, designed for the occupant's name card. A pot-bellied Krazy Kreature alien in a green skin and white tunic looked out at them. Below the picture, someone had gouged the words *45th Thunderbirds - Semper Anticus* into the panelling with a knife. When Szymanski opened the door, Sally spotted a silver case nailed to the post, no bigger than her little finger and inscribed with Hebrew characters. Everybody touched it as they entered. Eva's voice came down to her through the years - *the word of God to protect our home against dybbuks and the Guessed-a-Poo*.

The camp was virtually identical to the front room of the house in the woods, although great cracks had torn through the wallpaper and punched lumps of plaster from the ceiling, exposing grey wooden slats. An old explosion had shattered the lintel over the kitchen door. The window ledges were piled up with sandbags and brown tape criss-crossed the glass.

As well as the stacks of ammunition boxes and ration crates, two dining tables and most of the walls were covered in maps - architectural diagrams scored in lines so thin they almost looked like cuts in the paper. An immense matrix rose up in the middle of every sheet, intersected with labelled arrows converging on multiple vanishing points. These cross-sections of the tower shattered outwards on all sides, twisting into planes, spirals, obliques, radials and composites. It was as if the artist had tried to capture the very framework of the universe itself in atom-fine perspective, only to discover new dimensions that had eventually driven them mad. Just looking at the charts gave Sally a headache. None of the others seemed bothered, though. They gathered around one of the posters and muttered and pointed, tracing different routes up through the floors. Pash took a pencil from her trouser pocket and scribbled a couple of marks near the bottom, most likely crossing off the wrecked apartment they'd just visited. Chisum tapped the centre of diagram and spoke to Sally over his shoulder.

"By your reckoning, Eva's place is somewhere here. I don't want to hang around any longer, especially if Proserpina's on the move. Grab whatever you need and let's keep going."

CHAPTER TEN

The destruction of Magdalene's flat rattled the squad. Nobody seemed interested in checking in on any of the other permanent residents. Instead, Chisum said they were heading straight for the eleventh floor.

They trudged along silent passageways, past hundreds of doors. Sally soon lost her bearings in the endless alternating light and gloom. At one point, she could have sworn she spotted the filigreed lines from the plans in the squad's base camp. They hung in the air, fine scored webs marked with tiny formulae, puncturing the walls, ceiling and long perspectives, reaching out into a white world beyond. Everything felt empty and their footsteps echoed like distant cymbals. If any other residents sat in their lonely rooms, it didn't matter to the soldiers. They just moved on by, forever sighting down their weapons at corners and shadows.

When they finally found Eva's flat, Chisum gently knocked on the door. No answer came so he tried the handle. It was open. They stepped into the hallway and locked themselves inside. As she'd expected, the place was empty. Faint echoes kicked off in her mind as she peered past the others into the quiet, monochrome interior. Yes it was vaguely familiar, yet something felt odd as soon as she walked into the kitchen. Everything looked the same, as if no-one had lived here for the last decade and a half. The apartment was a cold, 1960s time capsule. She struggled to sense what felt different. The utter silence perhaps, but hadn't it been the same when she was six? The soft, calm heaviness in the air had been so comforting after the endless tension and arguments at home. She went into the living room and stared at its white and charcoal walls and Formica furniture.

The penny dropped.

"It's the same size."

"And?" Szymanski said.

"It should be smaller because I'm three times bigger. The furniture's ok, but the rooms are huge."

"How is that relevant to anything?" Chisum grumbled.

"Don't ask me. I haven't been inside since I was little. You told me to bring you here, so here we are."

"What you remember?" Pash said.

"We played with some toys. That monster lady banged on the door and asked if we wanted to go to a party on the top floor. Eva told her to get lost, said the Wodaran would get her."

"The what?"

"The Wodaran from Pluto. It's one of those cards Eva leaves scattered about."

Angus snorted as he drifted through the kitchen, opening cupboards at random. Sally, angry that the others seemed to be blaming her for this massively anticlimactic waste of time, wandered into the main bedroom. She found an immaculately made bed, its bedspread that ubiquitous acid orange. The wardrobe and chest of drawers were empty. If Eva ever had parents they'd long moved on and taken all their crap with them.

The child's bedroom was more human, but barely just. She recognised the old dinosaur poster on the wall. A couple of boxes sat on the top shelf of the cupboard. She reached up and took one down. It contained a ViewMaster and dozens of cardboard reels with tiny transparencies around their edges. There was no sign of the Driving Test Game.

"What you got there?" Pash asked.

"It's called a ViewMaster. You stuck these discs in and saw 3D scenes, mainly from old movies."

Sally slotted a disc into the viewer and held it up to the light.

To her surprise, she found herself looking down a corridor almost identical to the ones in Backenforth Heights. She flicked a couple of slides along. They also showed various perspectives of tower block interiors, all 1960s chrome and linoleum. It was hard to think of a more boring toy.

"Let me look."

"Not much to see." Sally handed the ViewMaster over. The Spaniard took it and looked inside. She cried out and flung the toy away. It bounced off the wall and landed on Eva's old bed. Pash had one hand on her mouth, eyes full of tears while she flailed about with the other, as if trying to ward off invisible enemies.

"The hell's going on?" Szymanski stood at the door. Pash started screaming abuse at Sally in Spanish.

"Chris'sake, keep it down," the Pole said, making a grab for Pash. She pushed past him into the kitchen.

Sally picked up the ViewMaster from the coverlet. What had the other woman seen? It had to be something truly vile to rattle the anarchist. She didn't relish the idea of looking herself, but did so anyway. A landing with a pair of yellow lift doors and a white chair moulded out of a single curve of plastic. She flicked back and forth. More bland interior shots of the tower block. None of it made sense. Sally gave the machine to Szymanski.

"No idea. It's just flats, like this one."

The soldier looked through the viewer, gasped, dropped it on the floor and brought the heel of his boot down on top. He must have slipped because instead of smashing the toy he stumbled sideways, clutching his leg and cursing.

"Bitch!"

All the disgust and fury in Pash's eyes were echoed in Szymanski's and aimed right at her. Angus and Chisum squeezed into the room and all three glared at Sally. A sudden thought hit her.

"What did you see?" she asked the corporal.

Szymanski wouldn't answer. He just rubbed his shin and swore in Polish. Sally pointed at the ViewMaster.

"It changes depending on who looks at it. They're seeing something I'm not."

Chisum had a turn, holding the viewer up to the light and clicking through a couple of slides. When he lowered his hand it was trembling and his face was as grey as the carpet.

"Nobody saw what we did to them, nobody," he held up the ViewMaster again. "How could there be photos?"

"I dunno," Sally said. "It's just a kid's toy. Everyone else had them when I was little. They showed scenes from Disney films and stuff in 3D. I just see buildings."

Angus went next.

"Jesus Christ." He looked ready to throw up.

"Destroy it," Szymanski said, propping himself up against the doorframe and massaging his knee.

"Don't!" Sally shouted. Angus gave her a black look and smashed the toy against the wall. He swore and tried again.

"What the hell's this thing made of?"

So that was why Szymanski had almost broken his leg when he tried to stamp the ViewMaster flat. Angus spat an oath and tossed it to Sally. It felt like cheap plastic but despite the corporal's boot and Angus's blows she couldn't find a single scuff mark. She held it up and risked another peek. This time the corridor looked familiar. She recognised it as the one outside.

"It's the Blocko Tower."

"Not what I saw," Angus muttered. His voice shook.

Sally sat on the bed and scrabbled through the other reels in the shoe box. None were labelled. It was impossible to tell the subjects by holding the discs up to the light and squinting at the tiny swatches. She swapped in a new one, and this time nearly dropped the viewer herself.

It took her a second to understand what she was looking at. The scene was taken at night beneath a starless black sky. The scanty illumination came from a hidden source to the left, and marked out a field of cobalt-coloured slivers laid out in a geometric grid. Perspective shifted and she realised it was a plain covered in spheres barely outlined by the light. She clicked on to the next picture, hoping to get a better view. The shot looked the same, apart from a slight change in the outline of one of the objects in the middle distance. Once more, and a shape began to detach itself - a too-thin hand and part of a top hat. Sally cradled the ViewMaster in her lap and tried to breathe herself into some semblance of calm.

"It's showing me Professor Backenforth," she managed to say. She held out the toy to the others.

"No good giving it to us, lassie. We won't see the same thing."

"Any useful intel?" Chisum asked.

The ViewMaster suddenly felt so heavy and unbalanced when Sally lifted it up to her eye again, as if she was about to stove in her own face with a house brick. One more click, and the busy, hysterical motion made her pull away. Too many hands and arms and eyes, the film grain too feverish and full of the sick headaches of her childhood.

"Obviously not," the sergeant muttered.

After calming down a little Sally swapped in the first reel. Maybe she'd spot something of use in the empty architecture. Once again she found herself looking down the passageways of the eleventh floor. Their inhuman geometry and patchwork plastic, chrome and frosted glass pressed against her eyes like a cold flannel, easing away the nausea.

Somewhere a bell tolled, bright and clear. The others glanced at the ceiling. It came from further up, somewhere in the impossible heights of the Blocko Tower. A vague memory stirred in her head, bringing with it more unease verging on panic. The rest of the squad gathered up their weapons and moved towards the passageway. Sally went to stand behind Pash, who kneeled by the hob, rifle trained down the hall.

"I'm sorry about what happened back there. You OK?" Sally said.

The Spaniard nodded without looking around, but the muscles in her cheeks bunched and quivered. It was clear the ViewMaster had served up horrors from the soldiers' past. For the first time Sally realised that, for all their hard-nosed, ball-breaking cynicism, each member of the squad was a hair's breadth away from mental collapse. Angus, Chisum, Szymanski and Pash had dragged monstrous echoes from their former lives to the Blocko Tower, in the shadow of which nothing decent, healthy or holy would ever flourish. Teasing back its painted aluminium and clingfilm surfaces, they'd found the same blood, decay and madness that had stalked them in Barcelona and Munich. Rather than protect her, they were dragging her further into their collective nightmares.

Someone knocked on the door, a soft, kind rap-rap that exploded throughout the apartment like grenades going off.

"Sal-ly. Sal-ly, are you in there?"

"You hear that?" Sally whispered. Pash nodded. Nobody else answered.

"Sal-ly? Sal-ly? Are you off to the party? Professor Backenforth is calling for all the children in the tower to go to his playground. He'll let them climb inside his Mystery Planet. You missed all the fun last time. Anthony's there, and Rosalind Samson, and Ian Millington, and they told me to tell you how much they want you to come and join in all the games."

The tapping turned into scratching. Long nails slowly raked down the outside of the door.

"Do you remember the fun you had in Brighton? Do you remember the wonders you saw? That was only the start. That Mystery Planet didn't work anymore, but Professor Backenforth has made one just for you, and when you go inside you will see such delights. All the other children will be oh so envious. They can come too. Professor Backenforth's treats are for everyone."

Sally crouched behind the others in a sick puddle of frightened misery. Nobody had any words of reassurance or comfort. As the talons continued to hiss over the metal, tugging and plucking at the hinges and handle on the other side, she stared at the backs of the soldiers' heads. She knew they blamed her for this, for bringing them to Eva's flat. Now they were trapped by this thing, this Proserpina, wife of the devil, or whatever the hell it was.

"Silly Sally. Mummy won't mind. She told me herself. Come

up to Professor Backenforth's playground. All the other children are going too. Your friends can have a go as well."

At the mention of her mother, something cold and full of spikes formed in Sally's gut, sour anger congealing out of fear.

"Go away or I'll tell the Wodaran to shoot you with his raygun," the words tumbled out of her mouth, a childish threat from long ago. Chisum glared at her and made throat cutting gestures with the tips of his fingers against his neck. She didn't care, he could piss off as well. They all could. Something brought Sally to her feet to stride past the others and smack on the inside of the door with her fist. It rang like a bell. Pash yanked her back. The Spaniard's eyes were big fearful circles in the half-light.

"You hear me? Fuck off!" Sally yelled.

A few seconds' silence followed by laughter, low and terrible, but uncertain.

"The Wodaran, oh the Wodaran. Its raygun ran out of batteries and all the shops are shut. The picture is faded and torn and its power is no more. How disappointing. Hold the card in your hand, Sal-ly. How flimsy it looks after all these years. Primrose Confectionery, indeed. Did you really think a badly drawn monster from a box of sweeties would protect you, or the Chernod you flushed down the toilet because he was too frightening to look at, or the Krator, or the Fluss from the planet Gworg in the 3rd Galaxy? Little Eva realised they were useless and fled long ago. Where is she now? The rude and naughty girl said no to Professor Backenforth. Now she has nowhere to live except the cold darkness where there's no mummy to cuddle her or wipe her lonely tears. She's a skinny, dirty thing. Her lovely hair fell out, her arms and legs are stick thin. All her teeth have gone bad. They tattooed a number on her wrist, and now she can barely walk and stinks of her own shit. Nobody wants her. Eva's all alone. You came too late, all of you. Angus, William, Tomasz. It didn't matter how many Kraut guards you tortured to death, refusing to give them morphine when they cried like babies with the agony from their wounds, it brought none of their victims back. Not Eva, not Eva's daddy. Not one single filthy kike. Not one sin-gle fil-thy ki-ke," the voice sang.

The stench hit Sally like a hammer. The sickly reek of rotten meat poured into the corridor, borne on a freezing wind that seeped under the door and seemed to carry with it a desperate, bestial howling. Someone was stuffing her skull with barbed wire, wrapping it around her bones, and it was all she could do not to throw up with the sudden pain and nausea. Hands grabbed her waistband and dragged her back into the kitchen.

"I'm happy to wait here," the voice followed her. "I'll wait and wait for as long as it takes for you to learn some manners and some gratitude."

Sally sat on the floor with her head between her knees, breathing through her mouth. It did little to get rid of the stink of decay. The pain in her head eased a bit.

"It can't get in," she managed to gasp. "Eva's mezuzah will stop it."

She hoped to God she was right.

"So we're stuck in here," Angus said. He looked at Sally. For a horrible moment she thought he was going to suggest tossing her out into the corridor as a sacrificial decoy. "We can't take on Old Nick's missus. You've seen what she can do. This is your mate's flat, lassie. You'd better come up with something."

"And do it fast," Szymanski added.

Sally managed to stand up. Pash held out her canteen. She took a swig of water with a grateful nod and headed to the bedrooms. Rummaging through the wardrobes and drawers and checking under the beds yielded nothing.

Finally, Sally picked up the ViewMaster. Maybe the pictures of the tower's interior would help, if that's what it still served up to her. She put it to her eye, cried out, and dropped the toy onto the coverlet.

"What is it?" Chisum yelled from the kitchen.

"I can see outside, in the ViewMaster."

"And?"

She took half a dozen deep breaths to calm her nerves, long enough to take another look. Even then, it took all her courage to bring the lens right up to her face.

The silhouette of an old woman in a bonnet, but giant-sized. The monstrous head drooped down against the weight of the ceiling, and the dark, greasy clothes filled all the corridor. Long hands reached out to touch the door to Eva's flat. Too many fingers. A single pale disc glowed in the shadows of a hood as big as Sally's torso. The lens of a pair of giant spectacles, perhaps, or maybe even an eye. She could have sworn the light shimmered with obscene hunger.

Hands shaking, Sally held out the toy to the others.

"No good giving it here, lassie," Angus said. "It just shows us our own nightmares."

"I can see it outside the door."

"Anything to help?" Pash asked without looking round. The Spaniard crouched down, elbow on knee to steady her rifle.

"I don't know, I can't tell."

"Look again," Chisum hissed.

Another glance showed the same scene. Sally hurriedly clicked to the next image, praying it wouldn't be worse. It was, but she forced herself to keep moving through the ever-closer glimpses of their besieger. Glass eyes in a seething rot held together by rags. No matter how near the camera drew, none of it drifted out of focus. Instead, it blossomed into new fractal hells of putrescence so busy and detailed it seemed to seep out into the surrounding room. The walls of Eva's apartment dissolved into reeking chaos, the ViewMaster itself turning semi-liquid, like two fistfuls of decaying meat. Sally was on the verge of throwing up, when a single click carried her back into the clean simplicity of a 1960s kitchen. Hyperventilating to calm her heaving stomach, she felt nothing but hard plastic under her fingers, and smelled only the bleached air of a long-abandoned flat.

The ViewMaster showed the kitchen the squad crouched in. What use was that? She moved on to the next image, and this time saw an architectural diagram of the same space. Atom-thin perspective lines led up to the ceiling. They passed through it, disappearing into a mathematical landscape that appeared to exist in the interstices between floors. A whole universe of angles, grids and networks spiralled across her vision. Another push of the button superimposed the room and plan. Exhausted and sick at heart, she threw the toy onto the bed, looked up and froze.

A black line as thin as a spider thread ran down from the ceiling directly above Pash's head, ending a few inches above the anarchist. Symbols flickered at the periphery of Sally's vision. At first she assumed she was hallucinating, seeing the after-images from the ViewMaster reel, but when she stepped closer, the cord still floated in mid-air. She reached out and touched it. The space between Pash and the suspended tiles felt oddly elastic, as if an invisible block of jelly stretched from the woman up to the ceiling. Sally pinched the line between finger and thumb. The whole ceiling bellied down a couple of feet, opening a white mouth filled with spiralling planes and angles.

A crash from the doorway made her jump. It sounded as if the monster had attacked it with a pile driver. A convex dent appeared near the top. The metal door juddered on its hinges.

"Don't you dare, don't you dare," the voice hissed. It was the glutinous sound of iron boulders rolling through congealing blood.

"It's breaking in," Chisum stepped back. "Szymanski and Angus, set charges. Fall back to the kid's bedroom."

"No. Wait," Sally shouted. She had her fingers on the edge of the hole in the kitchen ceiling. She pulled it down a little more and words, scales and angles tumbled out around her.

Another shuddering blow, a second bulge in the door. The top left hinge pushed the heavy-set screws out half an inch. Concrete and plaster dust trickled down the edge. What about Eva's mezuzah? Had its power waned after all these years, like the Wodaran's, or had Sally somehow breached its protective shell by opening a gateway in the kitchen ceiling?

A slow scratching of claws on metal, writing curses on the other side of the door.

"She never wanted you in the first place. You do know that, don't you? She never wanted you in the first place."

"Yeah, I know," Sally called out. Hope had made her brave.

"Ruined her life, you little shit. You were an accident, and you ruined her life."

The low mutter was as much inside her skull as from the corridor. Could the others hear it? Szymanski and Angus were fussing over what looked like a school satchel. Chisum kept his Tommy gun trained on the door. Something leaned against it with enough pressure to pop a hinge screw completely out. Angus swore, covering his nose and mouth with one hand while he struggled with a wire in the other. The stench of drains and decay rolled down the hallway.

Pash looked up and swore in Catalan. Sally hadn't just pulled down a bunch of tiles to reveal the roof space. The line she held in her fist distorted the entire upper half of the kitchen, as if it were a thread holding everything together.

"Get me the ViewMaster," Sally said. She didn't want to let go in case the rift closed again or the apartment fell to pieces. Pash grabbed the toy from the bedroom and pushed it into her hand. The anarchist followed it up with a stack of reels, which she shoved inside Sally's shirt. Sally held the toy up to the hole, looked into the eyepiece, and clicked. Doors and corridors blossomed around the white void on the other side of the gap.

"Up here, we can get out," she said.

Sally hunkered down so the Spaniard could use her thigh and shoulders as steps. Pash pulled herself into the opening. As soon as the anarchist slithered between the polystyrene tiles, she shrank, tumbling down a long invisible slope to end up a good thirty yards away. Pash turned and stuck her arm out. It thrust at Sally's face and she almost fell backwards and lost her grip. Her friend looked like a reflection in a funfair mirror - huge fingers at the end of a tiny arm and body.

"Hey," Sally yelled, grabbing Pash's hand to lever herself up. "We've got an exit."

CHAPTER ELEVEN

Proserpina, wife of Pluto, broke down the door just as they hauled Angus up into the mathematical space between the floors of the Blocko Tower. Sally heard the brittle shriek of metal being ripped in half like paper, followed by the slithering noise of wet, filthy calico dragged across the walls, floor and ceiling. The creature tripped the satchel charge and the blast caught Szymanski as he turned to flee. Fire, rubble and an ear-bursting thump clamped mufflers on Sally's head. In the ringing silence she saw the Pole hurled past the rent. He must have smacked into the far wall and rebounded. His legs jerked into view and lay there, blood seeping through the tattered khaki and staining the concrete dust that settled on the kitchen tiles. For some reason nothing came through the gap. The flame and smoke stayed in the room below, as if seen through plate glass.

GO GO GO! Angus mouthed into her face. Someone else hauled her back into the great white world. Beyond the Scotsman something black, thin and jointed shot through the hole. It looked like a spider's leg trailing tattered lace. A hand made of iron knitting needles, scissors and rusty scalpels planted itself between Angus's legs, and began to lever the rest of the creature through the rent. The Scotsman rested his rifle between his feet and fired it point-blank. Whichever part he hit - head, shoulder, it was impossible to tell - didn't even twitch. The endless busy swirls simply swallowed the bullet. Angus crab-crawled backwards as Chisum took over, moving to Sally's side and emptying the Tommy gun's magazine at Proserpina. Maybe the creature paused a little. It was hard to make out. If a satchel full of high explosives had failed to damage her, small arms stood no chance.

Sally glanced up and saw the tangle of draftsman's lines spreading throughout the void above. On an impulse she reached up, grabbed the nearest and yanked it down like the bell pull on an old-fashioned tram. The opening snapped shut, severing the arm just above the elbow. The talons splayed out in agony, faded to white, and melted into the paper. They left a greasy stain spreadeagled amongst the floating diagrams.

Chisum pushed her hard in the chest. She fell onto her arse. He whipped out an automatic and pointed it at her head.

"You led us into a trap, you bitch," his voice sounded squeaky and distant, as if she was listening to him on a tin can telephone.

"Back off!" Pash yelled, knocking his arm away. He went to backhand her but she ducked and thrust upwards with a black-bladed dagger that stopped half an inch from the sergeant's Adam's apple.

"This knife come out the top of your head if you touch her again."

"She led us into a trap," Chisum repeated. "Took us to that apartment and summoned up that monster. That was never Eva's place."

"It was!" Sally scrambled to her feet, looking for an opportunity to smack the bastard as hard as she could, right in the middle of his fat nose.

"Pack it in," Angus got to his feet, face almost the same colour as the paper world. "I said, pack it in the lot of youse!" His hands shook as he cranked the spent cartridge out of his sniper rifle.

"She saved our lives," Pash said. Chisum's cheeks writhed as he stared at Sally. She willed him to make another move so she could pound him into the ground.

"That thing wouldn't have come after us if it wasn't for her." He holstered his automatic and stepped back with his hands up. Chisum blamed her for Szymanski's death, that much was obvious. Pash put her dagger away but kept her eye on the sergeant. That told Sally the bastard would probably try again at a later stage, unless she did something spectacularly in their favour. God only knew what.

"Now where?" Angus said. Sally's hearing was coming back. As she looked around, a soft wind made the atom-thin drawings vibrate with an odd music of their own. When she tried to follow their perspectives they vanished into the distance, leaving no suggestion of a way out.

"Perhaps that toy will help again," the Scotsman prompted.

Sally stepped away, just in case Chisum decided to have another pop while her attention was elsewhere, and held up the ViewMaster. She wasn't quick enough to click past the image of the creature feeding on Szymanski. It burned an after-image in her mind that made her jerk back and almost drop the toy. Swallowing hard, Sally checked the next picture. The lines in the slide matched the web surrounding them. She saw the outline of what looked like a sliding door, about ten yards beyond and to the right. Sally ran past the others and reached out to where she thought the edge might lie. Her fingers met glass. She felt her way to the frame, found the handle, and slid the heavy door aside. It opened onto a meeting room. A smoked perspex table sat on tubular steel legs in the middle of the carpet, surrounded by high-backed leather chairs. To her right, floor to ceiling windows showed the tops of pale clouds. Another door with a spy hole sat in the corner of the opposite wall.

Pash, Chisum and Angus followed her. Behind them the infinite perspectives of an architectural universe stretched away on all sides. The anarchist dragged the sliding window shut, clipping off the view. She pulled a chair out from under the table, slumped herself down in it, clanked her muddy heels onto the perspex and buried her face in her hands. Sally had no idea whether she was sleeping or crying.

Angus stalked to the end of the corridor, checked the spy hole, and opened the door. After reading the number and swearing, he came back into the meeting room and gave Sally a long, hard stare.

"What?"

"14009."

"The hell?" Chisum said. "That's impossible."

"You've taken us three times higher than we've ever been before," Angus said. Pash took her hands from her face. Her cheeks were dry but her eyes were rimmed with bruises.

"So how far is the top from here?" she asked.

"You tell me," Chisum nodded at the ViewMaster. "What does that thing say?"

More rooms and corridors, all long vistas of brutalist 1960s concrete mixed with semi-abstract interiors. Endless G-Plan furniture in white plastic, Formica and nylon. The landscapes of her childhood transformed into inhuman geometry. The more she gazed into those tiny 3D worlds, the more she felt her own identity strung out along faint Rotring diagrams, dissolving into dead, empty memories.

"Doesn't say."

"Can we get back using that?" Angus said.

What could she do but shrug? When she looked around there were none of the fine lines hanging down from the suspended ceiling, or slicing in through the walls and windows. The ViewMaster just showed her completely different spaces in other as-yet untouched levels.

"Stairs then," Angus said. He dumped his pack in the middle of the table and had a scrabble inside, pulling out half a dozen flat tins.

"Not sure how long our supplies are going to last. Water's never an issue here, but we might get bloody hungry before we're through. Sometimes we can pilfer the larders of those still alive on the lower floors. Christ only knows what's up here, or what they eat. Szymanski was a mug, handing out rations to Marcus like that."

Sally stared at him. The Pole had just been killed by a bomb and his corpse turned into food for some awful demon. Hadn't he been Chisum and Angus's mate in Germany or wherever? Now the Scotsman talked about him as if he were some idiot they'd once met in passing, years ago. She looked at her three companions in turn. Everyone had tightened up, gone colder, retreated into brutal stares and tired impatience. She wondered how many other friends her companions had watched die in front of them - shot or blown up or drowned or burned alive.

"What was your plan, when you eventually reached the top?" she asked. "When you finally got to Professor Backenforth, what were you going to do?"

"Stop him," Chisum said. He sat down on the carpet with his back to the wall, trying to light a cigarette with shaking hands.

"Stop him? You're mental, the lot of you. You saw what just happened."

"Easy lassie," Angus said. Chisum was staring through her at some other landscape.

"We never battle Proserpina face to face before," Pash clicked her fingers at the American. He tossed her the cigarettes and his Zippo. "That's what Eva does. Clears the path. Keeps them back. She has weapons we don't have. Stuff from future."

"The worst things we've come across are nothing compared to that beastie," Angus explained.

"Professor Backenforth will be a thousand times stronger. Guns and grenades won't hack it," Sally said.

"She's right," Chisum said. "Whatever she brought down on us is way out of our league."

"Bit late now," the Scotsman grumbled. He pulled the lid off a tin and spooned the contents into his mouth with his index finger. It looked and smelled like cat food.

"I say we go back to the house." The sergeant sucked his cigarette down to the filter in one go and flicked the stub across the floor. It smouldered on the nylon carpet. Sally gazed around the room again. This was some kind of 1960s office. Everyone smoked like chimneys back then. No sprinklers.

"Come on, Chisum. This is the highest we've ever been," Pash said.

"If we're going any further up, we need more people and more ordnance. A bazooka, maybe," the sergeant said.

"I don't want to retreat now," Sally said.

They all stared at her.

"You just told us we'd no chance by ourselves," Angus pointed out. "You saw what happened. We're a man down."

She wouldn't go back, not after all they'd come through, not past the picture of the little girl on the plastic forest floor or that house filled with Mummy's head. If she did make it back, then what? A lifetime not knowing if she was insane or not, whether she'd made all of this up? In her gut, Sally knew this was her only chance to find the truth, but she was on the edge. Bravery and bloody mindedness dissolved all too easily in this insane building. Take a step backwards and what was left of her courage would vanish.

There are forces in this building that to want to help you.

Eva, perhaps. The Wodaran? Proserpina had said its powers were spent. Apart from faded tatty cards, they'd found no evidence of the creature, if it even existed outside her imagination. Maybe this was all an elaborate trap. The ViewMaster was giving her the false hope of escape, only to drag her closer to the top of the building and whatever waited for her there. She stared down at her Doc Marts. It didn't matter. She couldn't give up.

"I'm going on," she said.

Chisum snorted and gestured at the ceiling.

"Be my guest. You're poison. A magnet for all sorts of shit," he nodded at the ViewMaster. "I hope you find what you're looking for."

"Seriously?" Pash said. "You let her go upstairs alone?"

"I'm heading out, down the stairwell. If this is room 14009 I reckon we're what? 700 floors up? That's three to four hours to the lobby," Chisum said.

He stood up and loaded another magazine into his machine gun.

"You're not really abandoning her?" Angus said.

"Let's move out."

The Scotsman pushed a couple of tins across the table towards Sally. He unhitched four grenades from his belt and put them beside the rations.

"Sorry lassie. Good luck an' all that."

"I'm staying," Pash said.

The Spaniard stood next to Sally and grabbed her hand.

"No you're not," the sergeant growled.

"You don't give me orders."

The American took a step towards the Spaniard. She walked up to him and stuck her nose an inch away from his chin, hands on hips, fingers of the right curled around her dagger hilt. They glared into each other's eyes forever and an age.

"What you gonna do, Gringo? Shoot me?"

Chisum swore, spat to the side and stalked out. Pash sent him on his way by simultaneously slapping her bicep and giving him the finger.

"You're a pair of bloody wee idiots," Angus hoisted his rifle onto his shoulder and followed the other man out into the corridor. Boots receded down the hall. Sally heard the grinding clang of a fire door opening and closing.

"Thanks," she said to the Spaniard. The other woman looked her up and down, still with those hard, exhausted eyes.

"So, now what?"

"This is Eva's toy," Sally held up the ViewMaster. "It showed me how to get away from that monster. Eva knows secret paths through the Blocko Tower, right? I reckon that's where we went. This opened a door into some weird space behind the walls that brought us here. Maybe it'll help locate her, if she's still alive."

"OK. Go ahead," Pash said.

"It's not showing me a route out of this office. We'll have to find the way onwards ourselves."

Pash glared at Sally, *now you tell me* written all over her face.

"Where to?"

Sally checked the photos. The third one showed an open space full of pillars and cracked lumps of concrete. Iron rods twisted out of the shadows like the hands of fossilised golems. Between their crystallised fingers she saw the perspective lines. They converged on the darkness at the far end of the hall, turning into threads of shimmering ash where the light faded. Someone had stencilled the number 15120 on the wall, in packing-case letters as tall as her.

"Looks like an underground carpark but it's way higher up."

Sally described what she saw. When she looked up, Pash's eyes had turned into white rings around black holes. The anarchist stared at the office exit. Judging by the dancing muscles in her cheeks she was having some kind of internal argument. Sally had the horrible suspicion the other woman was deciding whether to run after Chisum and Angus, leaving her completely by herself.

"What do you know about that place?" Sally said. Pash glared at her.

"If it above us, I never been. But there are other levels like it further down. Bad places, where the devil and his friends come to dance. I don't think even Eva risks going there."

"But this says it's important." She held up the toy.

"You sure about that?"

No I'm not.

But she was sick of hanging back, letting the fear swill up around her ankles like freezing sewage. She snapped the shotgun shut and stuck three of Angus's tins in her pocket. No more walking in the rear with her weapon broken, playing the family simpleton who couldn't be trusted to wipe her own arse. Pash took the grenades, slotted a pair into her own belt, and shoved two into Sally's. She jerked her head at the door. Sally led her out into the corridor.

The passageways on the seven hundredth floor were identical to those at the bottom of Backenforth Heights. Bleak, aluminium corridors that seemed to stretch for miles, studded on both sides with closed doors. It made Sally think of a stupid philosophy question her first boyfriend had asked her at university, right after their initial fuck.

If you have an infinite hotel with infinite rooms, and you put a guest in every odd-numbered room, how many guests?

An infinite number.

And if you then put a guest in every even numbered room as well, is that infinity times two?

In the warm swamp of the tiny camp bed she'd stared at him, realising she'd just surrendered her virtue to a total bell-end.

She yanked herself out of the memory as Pash eased the fire door open. The Spaniard nodded at the railings. Sally peered down into the shaft while the other woman covered the floors above with her rifle. There was no sign of Chisum or Angus, just a set of grubby squares, one inside the other, falling into microscopic infinity. She listened for the clatter of boots on concrete but heard nothing. The sergeant had said it would take them four hours to reach the bottom. How many miles up were they and how many still lay above? Ten? A hundred? She leaned away from the gulf, breathing hard to fight against the vertigo. For an instant the whole tower twisted around her so she could see both up and down at the same time. Giant faces filled the void at both ends. They had bloodshot eyes and down-turned mouths littered with yellow teeth as big as sideboards. Each stared at its mirror image through countless leagues of rancid cigarette smoke. The vision only lasted a fraction of a second before the stairwell straightened out again.

Sally pulled herself together and followed the other woman as she climbed. How many more floors did they have to go to reach 15120? She did the maths in her head. Based on the progress so far she reckoned, what? Sixty? Sally was exhausted. She hadn't slept since that uneasy night in the squad's house. Lack of sleep had you hallucinating, didn't it? Without any release, your dreams and nightmares stacked up in the mind's green room until there was no space left. Then they tumbled out into the real world. That had to be why she'd seen Mummy's face book-ending the Blocko Tower, why the stairs and railings felt spongy beneath her feet and hands.

She paused, pressing the sole of a Doc Mart against the dusty concrete. It looked firm enough but she could have sworn the stone gave under her boot. She squeezed the scabby metal rail and that too squashed under her fingers, the texture filling with greasy rot. Sally snatched her hand away and stared at her palm before wiping it on Angus's kilt.

"You OK?"

Pash was looking down at her from a landing two flights up.

"I don't know. Everything's weird."

And now she was down on one knee, scrabbling for balance on stairs that had turned to foam rubber. As the ground sank under her, the stench of rotten rubbish chutes and blocked drains filled her nostrils, making her retch.

Hands under her armpits hauled Sally upwards. She ended up sitting with her back to the wall beside a door. Pash unstoppered a water flask and handed it over. Sally managed to gulp down a couple of mouthfuls. It tasted of swimming pools.

"I need rest. I'm hallucinating."

"No you're not."

The other woman stood over her, hands propped against the doorframe, forming a protective arch with her body. She kept looking through the wired glass into the corridor beyond, ducking back, then glancing again, muttering to herself in Catalan.

"Give me shotgun. Better up close than a rifle."

Sally handed it up to her.

"This high, the building screw with your head," Pash whispered. "We gotta move on."

Sally pushed herself up the wall. The anarchist steered her with one hand to keep her away from the door. A glimpse through the window showed a passageway. It was full of spiny people with heads that wobbled like nodding dogs on a car's dash. They skipped and danced around each other at a ridiculously high speed, jerking this way and that, flinging out too many arms and long-fingered hands. It resembled a Balinese puppet show on acid, or the rubber-hose animals bouncing and twitching to crazy jazz from the old Betty Boop cartoons. Pash grabbed her hand and squeezed hard.

"You feel that? I'm real. I'm human. Don't think about all that shit. Focus on me and we get through it."

The anarchist turned and clambered on. Sally fixed her gaze on the other woman's arse and kept moving, trying to forget the rotting sponge under her feet. Neither woman looked at the fire doors as they ascended, although Pash always held the shotgun pointed towards the wall. Sally felt very exposed without a weapon. Maybe Pash didn't want an armed crazy woman behind her.

When they reached the 750th floor, Sally checked the ViewMaster again. It served up a couple of rooms choked with what looked like corpses, then a photograph of the landings above them. There, barely visible against the concrete, a sheaf of fine lines radiating out of a fire door eight levels above them. She told Pash.

"OK. Nice and slow," her friend said. "Last time we in such a place the devil's wife paid us a visit. That hall you showed me, we don't want to stay there any longer than we have to."

They took the final landings as if storming a bunker, crouched down, Pash leading the ascent. She used hand signals rather than speaking. A fist for stop, a flat hand chopping in the next direction, a thumbs up or a thumbs down as they approached each door. Sally didn't risk a glance through the windows until they reached the 758th floor. Looking through the fire door for the first time, Sally realised there was no corridor on the other side. Glass the colour of a fish tank looked out onto a vast space. Far away, on the opposite wall, she read the number 15120.

CHAPTER TWELVE

Pash held the door open while Sally checked the ViewMaster once more. All the perspective guides were there but something was wrong with the image.

In Eva's flat she'd seen the kitchen embedded in a mathematical labyrinth, the webs leading to safety through endless Rotring pathways and diminishing colonnades. This time the architectural world squeezed down to a jagged gash in the far corner, as if a rat had chewed an escape hole in a shoebox. All the delicate diagrams led to that point, the weight of the concrete and shadows crushing them into confusing tangles. It seemed to Sally that the fine lines frayed and bowed from the unholy pressure of their surroundings. On this level the darkness was winning in the struggle between universes. In the fuzzy 3D swatch inside the ViewMaster, the walls, floor and ceiling appeared oddly porous. At first she thought it was just poor resolution, but the more she squinted into the lens, the more it looked as if the room was made of grey sponge, as swollen and soft to the touch as the stairs outside.

"This doesn't look good," she told Pash.

"What else you got in there?"

The rest of the reel showed the same landscape. Sally swapped in another disc, and freezing water flooded into her from the boots upwards.

A little picture book girl walked through a wood, rosy-cheeked with shining new Start-Rites and a bright red bicycle.

Cartoon animals sat on branches and huddled at the bases of shady oak trees, watching her as she scampered by. How happy she looked. Going home for warm milk, cuddles and a story before bed. Without thinking she pushed down the button and the cardboard disk jerked to the next image.

Now little Sally was in Toy Town, striding purposefully between the red-brick houses, their gardens full of sunflowers. Fat robins perched on TV aerials and wooden fences. There was a phone box at the end of the road. Someone was making a call but she could only see a hunched shape painted in grubby brown. The artist must have got bored because the paint puddled at the bottom, staining the inside of the glass panels as if the speaker stood ankle deep in sewage.

"You ok?" Pash asked.

Click.

She was still in Toy Town, walking in front of the primary coloured facade of a shopping centre full of sweetshops.

Click.

The policeman from the Driving Test Game stood between the lions outside Leeds Town Hall. The artist had given them all red eyes. The traffic officer's upraised fingers curled into a claw and his nails were far too long and sharp. Little Sally had better mind her Kerb Drill. He looked very stern and cross - hungry even, with his pink tongue lolling out like that.

"Sally!"

Someone tugged on her arm but she really wanted to see where the girl was walking.

Hang on just a sec, will you?

Children's Shoes Have Far To Go.

The bomb sites along Kirkstall Road now, the houses tumbled down or boarded up. Thin faces with dark circles for eyes stared out from a couple of broken windows. As Sally strode on, a boy peered round a corner to watch her pass by, long bony fingers holding onto the shattered bricks. He looked sick in his stripy pyjamas, trying to hold himself upright. Maybe she'd stop and help him, find out where his mummy and daddy had gone. She knew the ViewMaster couldn't play sound but it seemed as if someone was yelling at her in a language she didn't understand.

No time to stop, Sally, hurry along now.

Click.

More houses. New buildings replacing the bombed-out ones. They all looked dark and unfriendly except one, right at the end. It was bright and cheerful with its pebble dash front, high laurel hedge and very own conker tree. Home at last, so why had Sally stopped at the other end of the street? Why were her eyes big and round? Why did she have her hand to her mouth? And her wet socks and the puddle at her feet? Mrs Ryan told her off because she hadn't said she needed the toilet. And why were there two huge hinges underneath the lounge window?

Click.

She didn't think she'd pressed the button that time.

Click.

The front of the house started to swing down.

Click, click, click.

Oh what big eyes you've got Mummy.

Sally fell backwards in dreamtime slow motion. Something hit her on the side of the head and the cartoon world span away into the gloom. A hand grabbed her lapels. Another slapped her once, then twice. She thumped on her arse onto a spongy floor. A dojo mat? Had Bogdan kicked her in the face again? She touched her nose. No blood this time.

"Sally, Sally. Snap out of it!" Pash stood over her, fists clenched, breathing hard, eyes white-circled with fear.

"I'm ok, I'm ok," Sally managed as the remnants of the nightmare washed through her. They were inside room 15120. It was as big as an underground carpark, stretching away on all sides with concrete monotony, ceiling supported by square pillars. She tried to get her bearings.

Another twisted vision, brought on by however many days without sleep. Or had something taken over the ViewMaster and used it to feed her terrors in the same way it'd served up trauma for Pash, Chisum and Szymanski?

The toy lay on the stone a good way off. Pash must have smacked it out of her hands when she began to hallucinate. The other woman stared into her eyes, as if looking for someone else. She had one hand on her dagger hilt. Whatever the anarchist saw in her face seemed to satisfy her. She relaxed and looked around.

"Where's the door gone?"

Sally got to her feet. When she put her palm on the floor to push herself up, she thought she felt squirming movement. Glancing down told her nothing. Between her boots there was only pitted concrete. She followed Pash's gaze. Four identical walls, each with the number 15120 stencilled from ground to head height. No sign of the exit, either on the wall behind them or the other three. Their featureless concrete surfaces faded into the grainy shadows. The one opposite looked almost a mile away. Maybe Sally had lost her bearings, wandering off in a daze during the nightmare fairy tale. No, it was worse than that. Clearly, this high up, Professor Backenforth had the power to shift stone, steel and glass, twisting the Blocko Tower into an unholy maze. Trying not to panic, Sally searched for the corner with the ragged hole that led into the great white world beyond the walls.

"We can't stay," Pash said.

Maybe the ViewMaster could still help. When she'd swapped in the new reel, Sally had stuffed the one that showed the photos of room 15120 into her jacket pocket with the others. She held each disc in the half-light, trying to figure out which was correct.

This one.

She swopped the discs but saw nothing in the viewfinder but a pitch black square. She clicked again, and again, and again. No luck. The toy itself appeared undamaged. It was tough enough to survive Szymanski's boot and Angus smashing it repeatedly into a wall. Dropping it on the floor should have had no effect. She tried two more reels without any luck. Maybe it was too gloomy in here.

"Give me your lighter."

Pash handed over the Zippo. The flame curdled the darkness, as if cooking the air into a gritty soup. Sally held it up to the toy, first the left hand window, then the right. Nothing. The blackness didn't seem to be down to a lack of light or something blocking the lenses. It was more like peering into a sunless emptiness, a door into a void stretching on forever. Out there, in the impossible distance, she sensed a faint presence, so tiny and so delicate, and yet filled with such desperate loneliness that the unyielding gulf quickly became unbearable. Sally gave the Spaniard her lighter. The other woman used it to examine the ground.

"You got to find us a way out." Pash's voice grew tighter, scared. She edged backwards. The floor moved between her boots. The pits in the concrete had widened into scores of tiny mouths, as if the room really had transformed into a giant grey sponge. Black insects wriggled out - odd tubular bugs like stubby worms, but with round heads and spiny limbs, tumbling over each other as they struggled for purchase. Sally's gorge rose. She turned, chose a corner at random, and ran.

The horrible things were everywhere, popping out of the ground and carpeting it with endless writhing movement. She crushed them with her Doc Marts, leaving black footprints. They stank of burnt rubber and quickly disappeared as more insects filled the gaps. Disgust made her try to sprint on tiptoe, like a ballerina. Pash did the same, stumbled, and fell full length. Bugs burst beneath and around her. Were they bigger now? At first glance they'd seemed no larger than her little finger. The ones seething next to the anarchist were the size of butcher's sausages.

Pash howled and jumped to her feet, shedding more of the things as she slapped at her arms and torso. Sally tried to grab her hand. Instead, the other woman pointed the shotgun diagonally at the ground and fired. The blasts cleared broad fans which immediately closed over. Swearing, the anarchist reloaded and pulled the trigger again, and again, moving forwards with Sally following, trying not to lose her footing in the greasy mess.

They were halfway across the room. The space between the two women and the corner quivered with insects grown as big as rotting courgettes. Now they stood on end and curled and writhed against each other, their round heads bobbing back and forth to some unseen orchestra. They squirmed against Sally's calves as the women pushed forward. The bugs didn't bite or sting, but the busy, twitching touch of their slick bodies was unbearable. Ten more steps and they both waded in a waist-high, churning mass. Crying with disgust, Sally held her arms up, desperate to keep as little of her body in contact with them as possible. Pash had stopped shooting, falling back as she struggled to keep going. When Sally risked a glance behind her, she saw the Spaniard's face tilted at the ceiling, mouth stretched down in a hideous grimace, tendons taut in her neck.

Unable to bear the sight, Sally aimed for the corner, closed her eyes and staggered on. In the oddly silent darkness all she sensed was the writhing tide about her. It reached her armpits. She instinctively snatched her arms in as the swarm poured over her shoulders. They were going to smother her. She'd suffocate with a mouth, nose and ears full of twitching insects.

"SALLY."

It was Pash, behind her, screaming, mad and desperate.

"SALLY WHERE ARE YOU?"

She opened her eyes and found herself walled in by giants. The bugs had grown beyond human size. They towered above her in gently swaying columns, dark and slimy. Their bodies pressed against hers so she couldn't move. Somewhere in the darkness above, round heads bobbed, jerked and chittered to each other. She was a child again, lost in a crowd of grownups. She heard explosions way in the distance, then two more, followed by screaming in Spanish.

The yelling switched from words to howls. Whether they were from fear or agony, it was impossible to tell. She wanted her Mummy, but Mummy would yell at her like she always did. Sally started to cry, trying to do it quietly, so none of these giant strangers would notice. Her arms were squashed against her side, trapped in a shifting cocoon that stank of burning plastic. She tried to wriggle some space around her, frantic to get away from the pressure and endless susurration. Her fingers touched metal at her waist. The adult, crushed into a corner of a terrified child's mind, remembered the grenades hanging from her belt. She grabbed one and eased it out. Perhaps it would clear a path. Maybe it was her way out of this, of everything, forever. But how did it work? She vaguely recalled seeing actors in movies pulling out pins. By twisting her hand, and sticking her thumb into the ring, she might be able to gain enough leverage to tease it free. Would she try and push it as far away as possible, between the giant creatures, or would it make more sense to yank it in and hold it close to her heart, or under her chin? God only knew what had happened to Pash. The anarchist had stopped shrieking ages ago.

She worked her arm sideways so it was sandwiched between the carapaces of these strange, indifferent monsters. Their hideous bodies touched her bare skin. Sometimes they felt like greasy Bakelite, sometimes like the patterned damask covering her grandma's sofa - heavy damp cloth and decaying nylon, the stuff of long abandoned rubbish tips. A horrible concoction of fear and homesickness swept over her again. She started to pull the grenade in towards her. None of the round bobbing heads near the ceiling looked down. Either they hadn't noticed what she was trying to do, or they simply didn't care.

Fingers closed over hers. She lost hold of the grenade. Had she pulled the pin? She didn't even know. The sensation of a warm, human grip was overwhelming. Pash, it had to be Pash. She was still alive. Sally lunged towards her. The other woman seized her wrist and yanked hard. As she squeezed between the bugs, face scraping filth and grease from their bodies, the insistent tugging almost dislocated her arm. She tried to cry out, to tell the anarchist to take it easy, but the pressure from the creatures on all sides forced the air out of her lungs. Something cracked and a sharp pain spiked under her left breast. Idiot had broken her rib. Sally struggled to speak. As the darkness poured into her skull all she could manage was a whisper.

"Stop, stop, please stop…"

And then the pressure vanished and the universe dissolved into white light scored with hairline scribbles. Sally fell to the ground, curled up whimpering and tried to breathe against the pain in her chest.

"Get up," a woman's voice.

A foot nudged her. She opened her eyes and saw a grey boot. It resembled a metal welly covered in glowing, golden letters in a script she didn't recognise. They flowed over the gunmetal like leaves in a stream.

"Get..." a hand under her armpit. "...up!"

Sally was yanked to her feet. The fractured rib flared. She yelled and struck out. Her fist hit something painfully hard. She swore and doubled over, massaging her side.

At which point Sally realised it wasn't Pash.

The stranger wore a weird leotard made out of metal plates moulded to her body. The writing covered the entire surface, rolling up over sculpted abdomen, breasts, shoulders, arms and neck. The only place it didn't touch was the head. That was protected by what looked like the top half of a big steel fig, with a horsetail hanging from the point, and chainmail flaps on either side of the face. Her rescuer held two long cords in her other hand. They ended in an empty hand-sized pouch swinging down by her ankles. Large brown eyes watched Sally, the woman's face screwed up in an angry frown.

Sally's mind was a dropped jigsaw. She tried to separate the pieces and push them back together.

"Pash," she managed, looking around at the white grids, graphs and schematics enfolding the two of them.

"Gone."

"We have to save her."

"Too late. Professor Backenforth's got her now."

The woman stuck her fingers in the air, hooked them into an invisible corner and pulled down. Reality peeled open a couple of feet to show the inside of Room 15120. It was completely empty. No insects, no Pash, nothing more than a slate-coloured cavern with square pillars and a green fire door set in the middle of the far wall.

"She could have escaped, got back to the stairs," Sally said.

"No."

"Then we have to rescue her."

Sally made for the gap but the woman let go. It rolled up and disappeared.

"You bitch! Open it, now!"

The soldier stared at her, saying nothing. Her eyes were black gems, hollowed out into unfathomable spaces. Sally wondered what they'd looked upon, for they brought a whole weight of angry power to bear on her and the urge to hit out and swear evaporated. There was something else, too, in that face. Surely not?

"Eva?"

"We can't stay here," the woman turned and walked away. Sally grabbed her arm. The letters squirmed under her fingers, reminding her of the sea of bugs. She let go with a yelp.

"Eva. Is it really you?"

"How did you break your nose?"

The gaze flicked up and down Sally, who suddenly felt uncomfortable. Doc Martens, tartan skirt, leather jacket.

"I learned Kickboxing."

"You'll need more than that here."

Sally took Eva's hand and revelled in its warm reality.

"I found you. You're real. They said I'd invented you, tried to tell me I was nuts," her nose prickled and the lines hanging in the air around them blurred. "You really were my best friend. I didn't make you up."

Eva pursed her lips.

"Come on. We can't stay here."

She turned and walked into the paper universe. The graphs and formulae shimmering around her engaged in an unholy dialogue with the words on her armour. Sally stared after Eva, trying to process what was happening, to believe that it was all true and real, no matter how strange.

"Is there nothing we can do about Pash?" she called.

"She's gone."

Empty and miserable again, Sally followed her rescuer who

strode on without once glancing back. The landscape flickered and shifted around them. New perspectives rolled into view on all sides, flattened and disappeared. A gunmetal rectangle tumbled out of the sky. As the shape landed upright on one corner, Eva stepped into it. Frightened she'd be left behind, Sally ran after and found herself struggling against a cold wind blowing out of a misty world full of concrete planes. She pushed through and ended up on a ledge.

To her right, a cliff face of stone and glass stretched up into the fog, hundreds of windows reflecting the empty clouds. On the other side, the howling gale poured upwards from a void. Even though the shelf on which Sally stood was a good two yards wide, the vertigo hit her like a hammer and she collapsed to her knees against the wall, hands clamped to the aluminium sill of a window as unyielding as a mirror.

We're on the outside of the tower, miles up.

Eva stopped a little way further on. Staring upwards, she took something out her belt, put it in the pouch with the ridiculously long drawstrings, and started to whirl it around in lazy circles. Faster and faster it sped until Eva flicked her arm skyward. Whatever was in the sling sped up the front of the Blocko Tower with a shriek. A few seconds later Sally saw an orange fireball high up in the mist. The dull thud came a few moments after. A dark, many-tentacled shape as big as a St Bernard fell out of the sky, hit the edge of the shelf and plummeted into the gulf. It made a noise like a sack of coat hangers when it smashed into the lip, mingled with what she could have sworn were human words gasped out in pain and fear. Eva was already twirling the next missile round and round.

"Better get a move on," she called in that sing-song voice exasperated parents sometimes used with slow children.

Staying out here would let terror and exhaustion take over, glueing Sally to the wet concrete. Eva seemed confident enough flinging those whistling bombs at whatever lay above, but who knew how many there were. Another muffled bang and some of the faint shadows shifted position. Nothing fell this time. Sally pushed herself off her knees and clawed along the ledge as quickly as she could.

Two more missiles. One brought a creature down on the spot where Sally had crouched moments ago, with the rattle and crash of a kitchen cupboard coming off a wall. She daren't look behind. The bugs in Room 15120 had almost driven her mad last time. Eva jammed her fingers under the frame of the nearest window and heaved it open.

"In."

Sally pulled herself over the sill and fell onto a wooden floor, crying out with the pain from her bust rib. The other woman followed, letting the casement drop and cutting off the gale. Dusty silence enveloped the two of them.

"What were those things?" Sally gasped.

"Plobboes."

"What?"

"Plobboes. They're from *Des Knaben Wunderhorn*, a book of children's songs and fairy tales."

Sally stood up, wincing, and looked around the empty room. It had the appearance of an unfurnished apartment in an old city mansion. Floorboards, plaster walls with grubby cobwebs anchored to the dado rail, and a boarded-up fireplace.

"Is every monster in this place from a kid's book or a cheap plastic toy?"

"Perhaps for you," Eva said. "Some come to me from playthings and stories, others from things I saw and did. This tower pulls it out of our fears and hopes. They're different for everyone who passes through."

"Hopes?"

"Not everything here is out to get you."

"Like the Wodaran."

Now it was her companion's turn to look puzzled.

"The Wodaran from Pluto? Remember? The sweet cigarette cards you've been using to protect people."

Eva grinned for the first time. For a moment Sally saw the happy, kind six year old who'd wanted to be her kitten under the conker tree all those years ago. She struggled to keep it together, wiping her eyes with the palm of her hand. It still stank of bug grease.

"The Plobboes were friendly," Eva said. "They helped the blind shoemaker finish the silver boots for the Mayor of Lübeck. Here you never know what 'friendly' will involve. Those insects were being friendly to you."

Sally shuddered at the memory, how she'd felt like a little girl again, tangled up in the legs of adults in a frightening crowd. Was Eva telling the truth? As revolting as the bugs had been, they hadn't actually harmed her. But what had they done to Pash to make her scream so?

"Of course I remember the Wodaran," Eva said. "He's retired and lives in my attic. Do you want to meet him?"

CHAPTER THIRTEEN

Eva's house sat in the centre of a much larger room, an empty space with more wooden floorboards, white walls and a plaster ceiling a good twenty yards above their heads. Her friend's base reminded Sally of Angus's in the woods - a terrace building pulled out of a bombed street like a rotten tooth and dumped in the middle of the floor. Its windows were boarded up. The door had a yellow star daubed over it and someone had painted *Nāve ebrejiem!* across the planks nailed to the downstairs window frame.

"What's that say?" Sally asked.

"Death to the Jews," Eva said.

"This is your real home?"

"Yep."

"Where from?"

"Riga."

"Where's that?"

"Latvia."

Somewhere in Europe, Sally guessed, maybe on the other side of the Iron Curtain. She found it hard to concentrate. The pounding ache in her ribs made her want to throw up. As they approached the house everything began to dissolve in whirling motes of light. Eva tried to prop her up with a shoulder but it hurt too much. By the time they made the front door Sally was practically on her knees.

Once inside, Eva got her sat up against the wall and removed

Sally's jacket and shirt, wrinkling her nose. Sally realised she must stink to high heaven. She hadn't showered since the day she met Harry Mutherington in The Hermit. She couldn't smell anything. All her senses had lumped together into a grainy brown clod, telling her very little about her surroundings. Bare boards in the hallway, torn wallpaper over plaster that had fallen away in patches to reveal more wooden slats. What looked like scorch marks and smoke damage on the ceiling by the entrance. It was a house from a war zone, graffitied and firebombed by Nazi vermin.

"You've fractured a rib."

No. You bust it by pulling too hard.

A multicoloured bruise spread from Sally's belt to her armpit. Looking at Eva, she felt oddly sad and angry. In the half light her best friend turned into a cloud of grey and silver through which golden letters swirled and tumbled.

"What's all that say?"

"It's the Torah. It protects me."

"Like the mezuzah."

Eva looked at her, puzzled. At some point she'd probably grown into a pleasant-looking young woman, but the anger and violence visited on her in these corridors, stairwells and rooms over the years had hardened those eyes and pinched the mouth into dismissive impatience, maybe even cruelty. It felt like a betrayal.

"They told me you didn't exist. That I'd made you up," Sally said.

"Can you stand?"

Sally managed to push herself up the wall.

"You are really Eva, aren't you? Eva Benjamin from Moortown Infants School? You're not some horrible monster conjured out of a kid's shit toy from 1968, or a Star Wars figure, or something?"

"I'm really Eva. Bath and sleep. Then we'll talk."

So much for gentle silence in pale grey Formica, wool pile carpets and G-plan furniture. This building bore all the heavy closeness of a world built from brick, cast iron and chintz. Eva showed Sally to the bathroom on the second floor and left her to it. The taps filled the deep enamelled bath with warm water the colour of diluted piss. It took Sally forever to ease out of her clothes, wincing and whimpering all the while from her cracked rib. The water came up to her sternum and she sat on what felt like fine grit. Perhaps it was rust from the tub itself, or crystallised gunk channelled through the endless plumbing of Backenforth Heights. Pipes towered over her like jungle lianas and the toilet chain looked thick enough to shackle a murderer. A lump of coal tar soap loosened most of the crud on her skin and in her hair. It hurt to wash. Whenever she paused, the lukewarm suds started to pull her under, threatening sleep, drowning and oblivion. Sally did the best she could, wrapped herself up in a threadbare towel, and went in search of Eva.

Three steps along the corridor and the shakes hit her so hard she almost fell over. Sally managed to grab a door frame and use it to catapult herself across the next room along and onto a bed. She sat and stared at her hands. They spasmed uncontrollably. Her lungs worked like demented bellows, the air whistling in and out, each panting breath sending shards of agony ricocheting back and forth inside her chest.

Shock. I'm in shock.

Interlacing her fingers slowed the trembling enough for her to look around and try to get her bearings.

A child's bedroom, by the look of things. A huge pile of blankets on an iron bedstead, a china potty, and floorboards covered in a dusty rug. An oil lamp sat on a round table beside a stack of books. Sally stumbled through their titles. *Des Knaben Wunderhorn*, and, she guessed, Franz Kafka's *The Trial* and Thomas Mann's *The Magic Mountain* translated into Latvian. Two dolls watched her from a green wooden chair in the corner, next to a wardrobe where a blue wool coat hung from the handle. It had a big yellow star on the back. Eva's room. No Thingmaker, ViewMaster, or Driving Test Game.

A little Jewish lass dressed a bit old fashioned like. Children being herded about by Nazis.

Angus, William, Tomasz. It didn't matter how many Kraut guards you tortured to death, refusing to give them morphine when they cried like babies with the agony from their wounds, it brought none of their victims back.

Sally really didn't want to lie down on that bed. It was piled thick with sheets, blankets, an eiderdown and a bed cover. She'd slept in similar at Grandma's when she was little, or in the house in the woods while Pash stared at the ceiling through cigarette smoke, talking about having sex with Ted Heath under the stars of Catalonia. Here, in this place, anything could happen. She might sink into a fusty wool pit full of bugs, or jitterbugging cartoon animals, or the blood and guts of millions dead turned into greasy plastic bricks to build the houses of Toy Town. Yet in the end it was no good. The only way she could control the shuddering was by lying on the counterpane. As soon as she did that, the blankets folded over her and dragged her down into darkness.

Sally didn't dream at all, though waking up seemed to involve a long climb up a pit lined with cotton wool soaked in petrol and soot. She emerged back in Eva's bedroom, tried to sit up, and swore very loudly on the first and second tries. Eva must have attempted first aid while she was asleep. Her friend had wrapped Sally's torso up in tight yellow gauze which dug under her breasts. She finally got out from under the covers by rolling over onto the floorboards on her hands and knees and using the bedstead to haul herself onto her feet. Someone had left a pair of Levis, knickers and a t-shirt on the chair with the dolls. They looked completely out of place. Sally managed to put them on without too much wincing and yelping.

Eva sat downstairs, eating soup and crusty bread out of a rations tin with her fingers. She went to the cast iron pan rattling on a black stove, slopped some out into a bowl for Sally, and passed it over. Buttery potatoes with lumps of spicy sausage filled a grumbling belly and soothed away the ache in her ribs. It was unbelievably delicious.

Her childhood friend had shucked off her armour, with all its glowing words, and wore what appeared to be a leotard threaded with silver wire. She resembled an extra in a David Bowie video. Without the helmet her black curly hair came halfway down her back. Those eyes were still big and pretty, despite the angry patina of age and suffering. Eva watched Sally eat, breaking off a lump of her own bread and dipping it into the tin. Sally glanced around at the cracked plaster and the inside of the boards nailed to the window.

"You were only six when I met you, but you weren't born in '61 like me," she said.

"1934."

Sally did the sums in her head. Eva looked early 30s at most.

"How old are you now?" Sally asked.

"I've no idea. The tower hops about so I lost track of the years."

"What happened to you? How did you end up in Backenforth Heights?"

"We lived in Riga. This is my old house. When the Nazis arrived they burned the synagogues and moved all of us into a ghetto. In the winter of 1941 the Latvian SS carted people off in batches to Rumbula Woods and herded them into big pits to be shot, a thousand at a time. We were marching through the eastern part of the ghetto, on our way to the killing grounds. Some Nazi bastard started firing his Luger into the column at random. People were screaming and running, tripping over the dead. In the panic Papa pushed me away, out of the line, and told me to run and not look back. I was little so they didn't spot me escaping through the streets, hunting desperately for somewhere to hide. I came across this tower at the end of an alleyway and sneaked inside. After they'd finished the massacre, they made an even smaller ghetto for the ones left behind, a few thousand men and women the Nazis claimed were still fit enough to work."

Eva drew two concentric circles with her soup on the tabletop. She pointed at the space between the inner and outer circumferences.

"I was trapped in the tower here, in the old section. I never saw my parents again. Later I heard the Nazis forced them to climb on top of the corpses of those they'd already murdered, and shot them in the back of the head."

Sally had no idea what to say. When she was little, World War II consisted of *Dad's Army* and endless reruns of *The Bridge over the River Kwai* on Saturday afternoon telly. Her parents had dutifully watched ITV's *The World at War*, and she'd caught five minutes of the episode about the Jews - gaunt and frightened children next to men with helmets and machine guns. In her family it had all been a bit of a joke, wrapped up in her mother's envious nonsense about their wealthier and more successful neighbours. She vaguely remembered someone wondering aloud why 'that lot' couldn't just drop it all now, seeing as how it had happened decades before.

Forgive and forget for pity's sake, stop harping on about the bloody camps.

Nobody taught her anything about the Holocaust at school. Punks sometimes wore swastikas and other SS paraphernalia, to rub 'boring old farts' up the wrong way. She'd toyed with the notion herself, until somebody's nan had started crying and screaming at a girl sporting a swastika armband in Brighton Station. The tiny old lady clawed at her own face before collapsing into a hysterical puddle, while the gaggle of spotty wankers in safety pins and bondage trousers sniggered uncertainly. Now the memory made her feel sick and ashamed.

Eva was staring at her.

"How did you survive?" was all Sally could manage.

The other woman shrugged.

"The tower looks after you until the time comes for you to go to the roof." Eva nodded at Sally's bowl. "Farmer's Breakfast. I feasted on it every day. The poor bastards in the Small Ghetto survived on 200 grams of rotten fish and stale bread, if they were lucky. I wanted to bring everyone who'd survived here. I knew the Nazis wouldn't be able to get to them inside the tower. But we were too late."

"We?"

"I wasn't the only refugee hiding in here. There was a rabbi studying this place - how it worked, the magic behind it. He was an alchemist who'd learned the spells and incantations needed to ward off the demon who sails the tower from age to age. He taught me how to use the Torah for protection against the things it sends to defend itself. Rabbi Löwy had a plan to negotiate with the lord of all this, your Professor Backenforth. He was going to persuade it to rescue the Jews in the ghetto, but the rituals were too difficult, the powers too hard to master."

"Magic?" Sally knew how scornful she sounded and mentally kicked herself. None of the forces operating in this world had anything to do with normality. Her friend didn't even bother responding.

"That's how you can move about in this place," Sally continued. "And stick those mezuzah on the doors to keep the dybbuks away."

That got her an odd look.

"Your own words. The mezuzah and the Wodaran keep away the dybbuks and the Gestapo."

"Did I say that?" Eva shook her head and gave a weary grin. She had the same lovely smile of yesteryear, though without the gaps of a six year old. Any second now, she'd lift up her hands to make paws and suggest they play Mummy Cats and Kittens. Sally hastily wiped her eyes on her sleeve.

"Where's the rabbi now?" she asked.

"Went back into the real world. No doubt captured and shot. Buried in a mass grave in Rumbula forest with all the rest."

"So why me? Why turn up at Moortown Primary in 1967 and invite me to this place?"

"When Rabbi Löwy left to try and save everyone I was on my own. Shortly after, the tower jumped to the 1960s. The old man had fashioned enough magic to protect me, and had taught me how to use some of it. I was lonely and wanted a playmate. I found you."

"Why didn't you escape into our world?" Sally said. "Plenty of people would have helped. Moortown has a big Jewish community. Someone would have taken care of you,"

Eva gave her a hard stare. Sally couldn't tell if she'd asked a stupid question, or her friend was struggling to piece together an answer in her own head. The other woman gestured around her.

"I had everything I needed here. This is my home. The outside was full of death and terror. Even when I walked to school through Moortown I sensed it waiting, just over the horizon, biding its time. It's always there - the horror behind the world, the poisonous creeds of hatred and resentment that prey on me and mine. You goyim don't see it. We do. It never dies, only rests and waits until the next opportunity comes along." Eva shrugged. "I hoped you'd live with me and be my friend, that we'd grow up together and use Rabbi Löwy's magic to defeat Professor Backenforth. But I was only six and as soon as he'd got his victim from your time we jumped again."

"Anthony Mendelssohn?"

Eva nodded.

"What happened to him?"

"He ended up on the roof like all the rest."

The other woman stood up, took the ration tin and bowl, and dumped them in the sink.

"I have to go out for a while. Things to do. You can stay in the house. Don't leave. There's food in the pantry, books and stuff. The radio doesn't work."

Had Sally said something wrong? She stared at the back of Eva's head, feeling sad and resentful.

"If you're bored being by yourself, go and have a chat with the Wodaran. It's in the attic. I won't be long. We'll talk again when I return."

And with that Eva left. After clattering about elsewhere, she reappeared at the kitchen door in full armour. Verses skittered over her body as she tied up her hair with a scrunchy and put the helmet on. She hesitated a moment.

"You'll be ok?" Sally said.

"I'll be fine."

And after a curt nod, the front door slammed, leaving Sally alone with the grainy silence.

Half of Sally fell to bits. It sat and bawled its heart out while the other half watched the process through glass, like studying rain running down the outside of a window. Trying to make sense of it all proved impossible. Everything lay in fragments. All the paths, roads and stairways she'd followed to this place were supposed to lead her to the truth - that Eva wasn't a figment of an unhappy six-year-old's fantasy, a phantom conjured out of loneliness and her parent's indifference. When Mummy sneered that she had an imaginary friend, was best mates with Anne Frank's ghost, Sally had felt so wretched and worthless. The memory of the two of them playing together in that calm silence long ago had become a fragment of warm light she'd treasured through the years. She'd used it to remind herself that not everything in the universe had to be so impatient and dismissive.

Finding out from Harry Mutherington that others had encountered a Jewish lass from the Blocko Tower had filled Sally with angry hope. It had pushed her through deranged and wicked landscapes, past monsters and death, to here. To what? What resolution had she expected? She and Eva would fetch down the games from the top of the cupboard, squirt chemical goo into tin moulds, and put them on the stove to make Creeple Peeple and plastic centipedes? Of course not, but was this it? Eva wasn't interested in her, seemed to view her as an irritation, one more thing to have to deal with. Sally's bust nose, Doc Martens and foul mouth meant she wasn't the winsome infant from Mrs Ryan's class anymore. Was that the cause of her friend's indifference?

She let out a great sigh, rubbed the tears and snot away with her hands, wiped them on a tea towel, and went for a wander. Maybe this was it, the grand climax nothing more than the confirmation that she hadn't imagined Eva, something to stick in her mother's face and say *Ner, ner, told you so.* Perhaps all she needed to do now was descend all those stairs to the lobby, make her way to 1980s Leeds, and get on with her life.

She nosed around the rooms for an hour. They offered little in the way of explanation or interest. As with Angus's base in the woods, Eva's home reminded Sally of her grandparent's council house in Chapeltown. Heavy, solid furniture on floorboards scattered here and there with thick rugs. Most of the windows on the ground floor were broken and boarded up. It didn't take much imagination to understand why. One thing that struck her was the absence of any family photos or portraits. She guessed they'd be far too painful to have on display. Even when she rooted through sideboards and chests of drawers, nothing turned up - no diaries, no images of murdered fathers or mothers buried under surprisingly modern t-shirts and underwear.

Sally reckoned she'd woken up in Eva's childhood room. At some point her friend had moved into her parents' and set up camp on a brass bed covered in little more than a stripy mattress and a handful of blankets. Military kit lay neatly stacked against the walls and in the corners. Most were the same as the squad's - machine guns, rifles, a crate of grenades, and what looked like five giant metal tadpoles with German writing along the sides. A box of ball bearings as big as her fist sat beside a dressing table. Sally recognised them as the missiles from Eva's sling.

And then it got weird. A silver oval, a yard high and a foot across, enclosed a sheet of shimmering air. When she reached out to touch it, the frame began to hum and the space inside turned milky white. An angular biker's full-face helmet rested on a stool next to the artefact. It also started glowing, the light resolving itself into rivers of tiny words flowing around the interior. She gave it all a wide berth. They were clearly weapons as well but God only knew from where and when.

A radio sat on a polished oak sideboard in the dining room. At some point in the past a fight had broken out in here. There were long scars gouged into the tabletop and bullet holes in the wall above the fireplace. Judging by the stains on the wallpaper and carpet, not all of Eva's family had made it to the forest murder pits. The set had a wooden case, four black knobs, a window with a printed card full of station names she didn't recognise, and *VEF SUPER* embossed on the side. She fiddled around with the controls, not expecting much, and belted the top of the cabinet with the flat of her hand for good measure, like Grandad used to do with the telly when she was small. The window lit up and the speaker crackled. *Shit.* Had she just fixed it or was Eva lying when she said it wasn't working?

Sally found the frequency dial and went in search of a signal. Tantalising ghosts of voices made her concentrate, putting an ear close to the patterned fabric in the middle of the box to try and pick anything up. The subsequent burst of music almost punctured her eardrum. A man singing in Spanish to the sound of a classical guitar.

Voy a la cárcel de Oviedo
A ver a los pacifistas
Que los tienen prisioneros
Esa canalla fascista...

His voice had the querulous timbre of an old recording. When the unseen chorus clapped along to the ballad they sounded like broken castanets. Sally kept going through the spectrum - something in German, then more music, a jolly oompah band with saxophone, violin and tambourines. The next song made her jerk back from the set as if it had turned radioactive.

Marina, Aqua Marina,

What are these strange enchantments that start whenever you're near?

Marina, Aqua Marina,

Why can't you whisper the words my heart is longing to hear?

Memories of grotesque giant-headed puppets bouncing across the TV on strings surged through her head, followed by one of herself sitting in a couple of inches of lukewarm water, while brusque hands massaged shampoo into her scalp and she pressed a flannel to her eyes to stop the suds getting in. *The only way I'd let you wash my hair was if you sang Aqua Marina from Stingray. God you even resented doing that.*

The big band orchestration swept over her. Sally inside the glass was about to start crying again from loss and regret when she heard a noise upstairs. A few seconds of panicky fiddling to turn the radio off, and the house lapsed once more into emptiness and solitude.

No. Wait. There it was again. A thump in the attic.

Wishing she'd picked up a weapon, Sally stepped out onto the landing and looked up the staircase at the top floor. The hatch to the attic hung open.

If you're bored go and have a chat with the Wodaran.

Surely not. Eva had to be joking.

A stepladder leaned against the wall below the opening. Had it been like that before? She couldn't remember. A quick scamper into the master bedroom to grab the nearest gun. It had a pistol grip and a long rectangular magazine sticking downwards under the barrel. Sally hadn't a clue how to fire the thing. There was a metal knob ratcheted into a slot above the trigger which no doubt did something, but she hoped the appearance of the weapon would be enough.

Sally positioned the step ladder under the trapdoor. Watery light picked out unvarnished beams in the pitched roof, suggesting skylights. She'd stick her head through the opening first, just to check. At a glance it looked empty, a long Toblerone-shaped space with none of the boxes, crates or abandoned knick-knacks you'd expect. The windows dropped silver discs onto the floorboards like street lamps stretching into the gloom.

"Hello?"

Nothing. Sally pushed the machine gun through the dust and clambered into the loft, wincing all the while from the pain in her ribs. There was something else in here after all, a shaped piled up against the far wall. Was it a tailor's dummy covered in a white sheet, with an odd lampshade perched on top? She paced slowly forwards - light, shadow, light, shadow - until she was close enough to resolve the detail. The Wodaran, fully eight feet tall, stared down at her with glittering currant eyes at the bottom of its shrivelled parsnip head.

CHAPTER FOURTEEN

To grown-up Sally, the Wodaran in real life possessed none of the uncanny terrors that had disturbed her six-year-old imagination. Even though she only came to its shoulder, the Krazy Kreature looked ridiculous. It reminded her of the cat-eyed alien from *Star Trek* that terrified her as a child. Watching the episode as an adult she'd seen nothing but a cheap dummy head with a hidden operator rotating its wooden eyeballs. This creature trailed a faint smell of ammonia and plastic glue. It made Sally think of the top shelf in her parent's garage where they kept the paint brushes.

"Can you speak? Do you understand me?"

The mouth creaked open, showing two rows of shiny black fangs, and the alien spoke silent words that meant nothing. Sally saw a desperate urgency in its raisin eyes. Its head truly did resemble a parsnip, the twisted point lost somewhere in the shadows of the rafters. Short orange bristles stuck out of the creases at random points. Designed to fill children's heads with uncanny mystery and dread, the only impression it made on Sally was one of mild disappointment.

The monster Proserpina had a point. What possible protection could this stiff heap of cloth and vegetable matter give against the creature that had murdered and eaten Szymanski? It was nothing more than a big toy, left up in an attic for nostalgia's sake. Staring back into its face merely reinforced Sally's forlorn mood.

A three-fingered spider-jointed hand emerged from the folds

of its gown, holding a raygun shaped like red pear. An aerial stuck out of the narrow end, encompassed by a little radar dish. The ribbed plastic handle had one button. For a second, Sally wondered if it was going to shoot her. Instead, the alien turned the weapon upside down, so the grip stuck upwards, and pushed it against her stomach. The movements had all the fluid grace of a malfunctioning toy crane in a Jimmy Corrigan arcade. She took it, noting how light it seemed compared to the machine gun. The bottom of the handle flipped open to reveal two empty tubes with brass contact points at the bottom.

"Jesus, really?"

The Wodaran, oh the Wodaran. Its raygun ran out of batteries and all the shops are shut.

"Can't help you," Sally said. "The nearest newsagents is miles away. Sorry."

The front door slammed and distant footsteps echoed through the lower floors. Eva's voice floated up through the trapdoor, calling her name. The Wodaran's claw retracted into its robes. The creature continued to stare at her, all energy gone, as if expecting her to feed another 10p into whatever mechanism brought it to life.

Sally gingerly climbed down from the loft with the two weapons. Her friend was putting her helmet on the kitchen table and teasing the scrunchy out of her ponytail. Her calves were splattered with what seemed to be whitewash, mixed with streaks of blood. Sally hoped Eva wouldn't notice her own red eyes from the earlier meltdown. She kept her distance, watching her old friend with wary resentment, determined to meet the other woman's apparent indifference with matter-of-fact bluntness.

Eva put the ViewMaster on the table.

"You got it back," Sally said.

"A lot of work went into setting that up," Eva stacked the picture discs beside it. "I reckon you'd find it if I left it with the other toys."

"It was supposed to show us the way into that white world

behind the walls?"

Eva nodded.

"There was also a load of horrible shit in there as well," Sally said. "Chisum and Szymanski saw stuff from the war. I saw a nightmare fairy tale about me."

"It uses the same power source as Professor Backenforth, like a wire tap. His evil leaks into it, hunting for your dreams and memories to turn into reality. I'm sorry but it was the only way I could think of to get you here as quickly as possible."

Sally looked at the toy and remembered Pash knocking it out of her hands, just before the bugs turned up and killed the anarchist.

"What power source?"

Eva shook her head.

"It's best you don't know."

Sally kept her temper with difficulty. Her childhood playmate had turned into a right condescending shit.

"Why have you taken an MP 40 from the stash, and what's with the plastic pistol?" Eva said.

Sally counted to five in her head.

"I met the Wodaran. Went upstairs for a chat like you suggested. The machine gun was in case it got arsey. Complete waste of time in the end. Is that all it does now, stand in the loft saying nowt?"

"Pretty much. Its time has passed."

"And all the other Krazy Kreatures from Outer Space?"

A shrug.

"They never manifested themselves, at least none that I ever saw."

When Eva was an ordinary little girl there'd been nothing odd in her boasting that she'd collected all of the scary alien cards. Now Sally couldn't help wondering why a refugee from a Nazi ghetto had ever been interested in the playthings of a different generation. Thingmakers and ViewMasters were the must-have toys of the Swinging Sixties, not the 1940s.

She did it to entice you here.

"The raygun needs batteries. Double-As by the look of it."

That got Sally a puzzled stare.

"The Wodaran actually gave it to you. Why would he do that?"

She expected her friend to laugh. Instead, Eva pulled open a drawer, rummaged around inside, took out four AAs and stacked them on the side.

"Seriously?" Sally said.

She picked them up, dropped them in the handle, and pointed the pistol at the cooker. Before she had a chance to press the button, Eva grabbed her arm and snatched it out of her hand.

"I've seen what this does."

"It's only a toy." Sally massaged her wrist where the glowing Torah fingers had dug in.

Bitch.

"No it isn't."

"Proserpina said the Wodaran had run out of batteries, that he couldn't protect us anymore. She also broke her way past your mezuzah in the old flat where we played as kids. Does that mean all your magic is getting weaker?"

Eva dropped the raygun into the batteries drawer and pushed it shut.

"Who?"

"Proserpina. That evil mountain of squirmy rot that knocked on your door and invited us to play in Professor Backenforth's Mystery Planet, remember? Marcus the ancient Roman called her that. He said she was the wife of the king of the dead. Afterwards, we found another apartment she'd broken open, and then she attacked us in your old place and ended up eating Szymanski. We barely got away."

Her friend took a bowl of cold Farmer's Breakfast and dumped herself at the table. She pulled her gloves off and stuffed the food into her mouth with her fingers. Whatever she'd been doing had given her an appetite along with a mild case of the shakes.

"She's not anybody's wife. That monster was the first of his mistakes," she mumbled around the sausages and potatoes.

"What do you mean?"

Eva swallowed and grimaced, as if the last mouthful had too many corners.

"He stole a girl from the late 1880s, in England, but pulled her out of a mental asylum by mistake. Charlotte Baird. Only ten but she'd been stuffed with laudanum and sexually abused by her uncle for years. In the end she went insane and her family had her committed."

"Jesus Christ." Sally felt sick.

"That creature was formed out of her memories, some fairy story like the Plobboes from *Des Knaben Wunderhorn* but filled with all the horrors of her own personal hell. I've no clue what it was called originally. The poor child died soon after arriving here, but that thing sucked in a lot of power before Professor Backenforth could stop it. Now it wanders through the corridors, pretending to be his herald, summoning people up to the roof in his name. I'm not sure he sees it that way."

"His first mistake?"

"The second was when the tower journeyed too far into the future and I found out what he really is, and why he's here."

Eva gathered up the last of the potatoes and sausage and pushed them into her mouth. She sucked each finger clean in turn, finishing with her thumb.

"He picked up a scientist, Angharad. She came from a time when humanity understands how universes are fashioned - ones that work, ones that don't, ones that are good, and those that aren't. The poor woman didn't last long. He saw to that. I tried to protect her and failed, but not before she'd told me what she knew. That was the last time he journeyed anywhere that threatened to reveal his secrets."

"And they are?"

Eva placed her hand flat on the table with fingers spread wide. The knuckles were bruised and bloody, as if she'd been punching a wall.

"Angharad explained to me that five numbers make the whole of creation. If they're all correct you get a stable reality, like the cosmos we live in. If one or two are too strong, or too weak, then a universe never starts, collapses too soon or is totally empty. Professor Backenforth is the god of a parallel reality with nothing in it, no planets, suns or galaxies, only eternal emptiness and him. Maybe gravity was too low," Eva wiggled her little finger. "That meant stars never formed. Perhaps the force that binds atoms was wrong," her forefinger tapped on the wood. "So the bits that make a nucleus flew apart. In any case he was completely by himself, lonely and miserable, desperate for worshippers or just any intelligence to share his eternity with. That's what he's looking for. Companions."

"Companions? Is that why the bastard's stealing people? To be his mates?"

It sounded like a sick joke, on a par with a space gun that ran on AA batteries. She thought of Vicky Samson drinking herself stupid before driving her car into a tree after Antony Mendelssohn went missing at her party, of Detective Conway chewing on a light bulb to rid himself of the memory of whatever he'd seen amid those spheres on the roof, of the mad girl's storybook monster with a wooden tail and its face buried in Szymanski's guts. It was a hell of a way to win friends and influence people.

"It's not as simple as that," Eva said.

"Really?" Sally struggled to keep the sarcasm out of her voice.

"Rabbi Löwy reckoned Professor Backenforth is trying to make a pact with other gods. He said that each one of those balls on the roof is a link to another reality, a method of reaching out for help in exchange for sacrifices. He can move through an infinity of parallel creations. He's asked the deities who rule some of them for help."

Realisation hit Sally like a hammer.

"So the bastard's not kidnapping people to be his friends. He's using them as bribes, to get monsters from other universes to keep him company. Why doesn't he just find one that's already full of people and planets and settle down there?"

"He's a god," Eva said. "He wants a universe of his own, fashioned to his own purpose. But he needs friends to make it all come true, so he collects people to hand out in return for favours."

After Eva vanished, all those years ago, Sally stole money from Mummy's purse to buy sweets to give to the other kids, until she was found out and dealt a right walloping. *I'll let you have some Jelly Babies if you'll be my friend. You can come and play with my Thingmaker and I'll lend you my Driving Test Game, if you like. You can have the soul of a six year old boy, but you've got to keep me company in my empty universe. We're all the same - me, Eva and Professor Backenforth.*

"Don't feel sorry for him." Eva was staring at her again, hard-faced. Sally bristled. The woman was a mind reader as well.

"He's got a hundred altars to aliens, monsters and demons up there, a hundred pots to cook up treats for whatever godawful creatures he's going to populate his sad life with," Eva looked down at her empty bowl and pushed it to one side. "Professor Backenforth's filling them one by one with victims - boys, girls, men and women, the innocent, the lost, the broken and the helpless. Each one's a unique dish tailored to the appetites of his targets."

"How many has he done so far?" Sally asked.

"Nearly all of them. There's less than ten to go, maybe only two or three. Once everybody inside the tower has been gathered to the roof, he'll enact the last rituals and that'll be that. This place will vanish back into his universe and the lonely god will have friends to keep him company until it collapses in on itself, or fades away to nothingness."

Eva drew invisible hieroglyphs on the tabletop with her finger.

"I've tried to stop the bastard, or at least slow him down," she said.

"All those deaths aren't your fault."

For a brief moment, Sally was tempted to ask why they didn't just let Professor Backenforth get on with it. If his victims were already here - broken sods like Marcus the Roman, out of time and with nothing left to live for - surely all they needed to do was allow the ceremonies to finish, and then the Blocko Tower and all its nightmares would disappear into another cosmos forever.

Then she remembered Eva's description of the Jews in Riga marching through the forest to the pits, and the irritation and impatience with which her own parents had dismissed all mentions of the Holocaust.

"The people in those spheres aren't dead," Eva said.

It was Sally's turn to stare.

"I'm not sure, but something's happening to them. It's part of the final ritual. It won't be complete until every ball is filled and sealed. Until then they're all alive, though God knows what they're going through."

"You took a Yorkshire policeman all the way to the top, fifteen years ago. In Harrogate," Sally said.

Eva managed a grin.

"I remember. I thought he'd arrest Professor Backenforth. I was eight or nine."

"The poor bastard killed himself in a mental asylum. What did he see?"

The finger drew more shapes on the wood.

"We arrived at the top. There was no sign of Professor Backenforth. I assumed he was hiding from the policeman. Then the man said he could hear a child crying inside one of the spheres. It was still open so he climbed into it. I remember he was all lit up, like the ball was full of twinkling lights. I must have waited an hour for him to return. He came back empty handed and told me he was going to get help. I took him back down to the ground. Never saw him again. Sorry he died."

Sally remembered floating backwards across the plain as the unholy gardener slipped among his crop, listening and searching.

"How are you going to defeat Professor Backenforth?"

She'd asked Chisum the same question, and realised very quickly that the squad hadn't an ice cube's chance in hell. All they had to drive them on were bitter regrets and guilt, some desperate need to atone for all they'd seen and done in the war. Eva was on the same suicide mission, fighting monsters to try to forget the family she thought she'd abandoned, planning to go out in one last blaze of heroic failure.

"We can rescue the ones he's already captured, though we won't be able to get them all. That might just delay everything until he makes up the numbers again," Eva said. "A better way would be to take out one of the spheres. Rabbi Löwy said they're unique and can't be replaced. There has to be precisely a hundred or none of the sacrifices will work."

"And how, exactly, do we do that?"

"Explosives and the Torah. One of us goes inside an empty sphere and plants the charge. The other one transfers these scriptures to the shell itself," Eva held her arms out. The Hebrew verses ran back and forth across her body like deranged tickertape.

"You want me to climb into a Mystery Planet and plant a bomb while you scribble graffiti all over the outside?" Sally said. "And what will Professor Backenforth be doing while all this is going on?"

"I'll deal with him."

The whole idea was ridiculous. More and more, Sally was thinking she shouldn't be here. The passion and desperation that had driven her in search of her friend had dissipated. Yes, she wasn't deranged, hadn't made Eva up. She only needed to reach across and take the other woman's hand to prove to all of them how wrong they'd been. The Blocko Tower existed and its ruler hopped to and fro through time and space to steal children like a perverted Dr Who. All the vindication she'd looked for was here, and it was proving to be a massive, draining anticlimax.

Let Eva fight her battles with the monsters. Professor Backenforth could finish the last of his unholy rituals, and the lot of them could fuck off to Universe X, leaving her to return to the *Wharfedale Clarion* and get on with her life.

Eva must have taken her silence for agreement. She pushed herself upright and threw the bowl into the sink.

"We can't stay here for much longer. I think your presence has changed something, shifted the forces within this tower. If the monster mother broke into the flat so easily, she might be able to do the same here. I need to rest, though. So do you with that bust rib. I'll give it a couple of days and then we'll head up."

Sally sat on the bed in Eva's childhood room, leafing through *Des Knaben Wunderhorn*. It was illustrated with heavy-lined grotesques. What she'd once found cute made her uneasy. The over-bright polished apple cheeks and twisted puppet arms and legs of the children, as they scampered through toy landscapes, were the stuff of nightmares. The tale about the plobboes and the shoemaker showed a fuzzy picture of creatures in the shape of shiny blue starfish, hopping around the sleeping cobbler's workshop, sewing and hammering away with big fairy-tale eyes and grins. They looked nothing like the beasts Eva had brought down with her sling. Sally shut the book, dropped it onto the nearest chair, and headed back down to the kitchen.

The building lay silent. Her friend was somewhere upstairs, resting, sleeping or planning their next moves over ancient alchemical tomes from her rabbi mate. Sally fished out the Wodaran's raygun from the drawer and stuck it in her belt. Rummaging through a few cupboards turned up a stack of ration tins. She pocketed two. Eva must have put the machine gun back with all the other weapons. Sally didn't want to risk trying to get it, especially with all the creaky floorboards in the house. It wouldn't have been much use anyway. Hefting it made her ribs hurt. Somehow it was easier to trust in the plastic pistol from the Wodaran. There was an odd affinity between them, both were echoes of an earlier age when brave Eva had stood up to Proserpina with her Krazy Kreature card. Sally remembered calling on it for comfort all those years ago, in the depths of her bed at the end of that horrible day.

She eased herself out of the front door, closing it with a gentle click. Inside the bigger room, Eva's home resembled a broken doll's house left behind by removal men. The main windows were all shut, which was a relief. No point in starting her trek with a laser battle with monsters on a ledge miles up. She hoped the central stairs reached all the way to here. Pash and the others had said they went to the top of the building. Sally hadn't found out what level this was. Chisum thought it'd take four hours from the

700th floor to the lobby. If she was twice as high again, that was more or less a day climbing back down. She'd have to find somewhere to rest en route. Her plan was to locate the stairwell and cane it downstairs for as long as she could before exhaustion set in. Perhaps if she kept away from the corridors and rooms she could move fast and silent enough to make it in one go. After that there was only the driving game map to navigate.

The corridor leading into the room looked like the inside of a brothel. She stood at the start of a long blood-red passageway. Doors ran along the left side and pus-coloured windows shone high up on the wall opposite. More light came from globe lanterns as big as footballs, dyed the colour of fresh pigs' hearts. Hyper-ventilating to stop herself screaming, Sally headed for the door at the far end. It opened onto another length of giant intestine, coated in flock wallpaper and punctuated by heavy oak doors. The handles were at the same height as her head. Like an idiot Sally had been so excited at leaving Eva's, she'd forgotten where she'd exited and all the doors appeared identical.

Where was the stairwell? Sally pulled out the Wodaran's raygun and trotted along the passageway. It was cold and damp, and the carpet squished under her boots, reminding her of Room 15120 before the bugs turned up. She was about to turn back and hunt for the room containing Eva's house, when she spotted stairs through a small glass window. Desperate with relief, she threw herself out onto the landing.

The stench of garbage and rot hit her like a tyre iron. The walls ran with green and brown stains, disappearing into the darkness above and below. It was as if she stood inside a colossal drain. Breathing through her mouth, Sally clattered down the steps. She slipped a few times, almost going over on her ankle. The thought of crippling herself in this place made her more cautious, but she still wanted to reach the lobby as fast as possible.

Eventually the glistening runnels dried and faded into the walls. The stairs felt marginally less spongy, and once or twice she managed to touch the metal rail without retching. Sally paused on a landing to catch her breath, and made the mistake of glancing through the fire window at the passageway beyond. A figure stood on the other side, cast in silhouette by a distant light. Its head seemed to be dissolving into a pale cloud. She brought up the raygun and aimed it at the thing's face, even as it eased open the door. The roar of the hinges echoed up and down the surrounding shaft.

CHAPTER FIFTEEN

"I need someone to operate the camera and there's nobody else about."

The woman appeared to be in her late fifties. The cloud was nothing more than a mushroom of frizzy brown hair with grey roots. She wore a long navy dress spattered in random sequins. It resembled a children's storybook night sky. Sally had no idea whether she was looking at a human, or another dream creature about to dissolve into a heap of slime or bugs. The face was awfully familiar though.

"Please. Be a darling. It's just so I can record my latest video. An hour of your time. If that."

"Who are you?"

The old lady's shoulders sagged. The woebegone expression was a tad overdone, a little too theatrical, but Sally saw real sadness behind it.

"I'm Hannah Able."

Nothing registered.

"*Dark Lady Winter*?" Sadder, more desperate.

Holy shit.

Dark Lady Winter was number one on Top of the Pops for an entire week in 1982, sandwiched between Dexy's Midnight Runners and *Eye of the Tiger*. Hannah Able, barefoot and dressed in black chiffon, had wafted around the BBC studio to pan pipes and tubular bells, looking and sounding like a Woolworth's bargain-bin Kate Bush, before disappearing out of sight and mind forever. Everyone had heard of the infinitely more successful brother, Simon Able, whose magnum opus *Beacon* ended up on various film soundtracks and in countless elevators. Hannah had been consigned to history as a one-hit wonder. This wasn't a monster, just another lost soul who thought she'd found a home in the Blocko Tower.

Sally put the raygun back into her belt and looked into the corridor beyond. Functional and nondescript, more boxy than the one with Eva's old flat. Metal doors stretched into the distance, reflected in the polished floor and ceiling.

"You shouldn't be here," Sally said. "You need to get out of Backenforth Heights."

Hannah Able had already turned away. Sally knew she ought to leave this relic to it, but curiosity and guilt sent her down the passageway. The singer's voice echoed off their surroundings.

"Simon's a condescending shit. Dangling pathetic lifebelts on condition I sing for free on his crap albums. He says 'I want to help you because you're my sister.' Well I was his sister when *Beacon* went platinum. I was his sister self-harming in a Putney bedsit when he bought his villa in Spain. I was my fucking sister when Kyle Patterson dropped me from the fucking label at the same time he was organising Simon's fucking world tour."

Hannah Able heaved open a door that'd been left on its latch. Sally followed her into rooms heavy with cheap incense and shapeless furniture slumping under its own weight. Sure enough, a huge poster advertising *Dark Lady Winter* dominated the space above the sofa. A much younger version of the woman in front of her bowed her face over cupped hands filled with snow. Behind her, fractal mountains rose up into a pale sky.

"I never knew you did an album."

"Eight of them. I moved to Germany permanently because nobody in England gave a shit anymore and Simon didn't care. They'd jammed his head so far up his arse in therapy he'd gone blind and deaf. Totally ignored me when I was the one who forced him into it in the first place, because he was a whinging little druggy driving us all insane. It wasn't my fault he was a fucking head-case. Or Mum's, God rest her soul."

Sally spotted a lump of masonry in the corner of the room. A couple of floating candles sat in a bowl beside it, illuminating graffiti on the bricks - *Nomad Minds* and a heart in bleeding red spray paint. Hannah nodded at the wreckage.

"A lovely young woman from the Landespolizei brought that back to my old flat on Erdmannstrasse. Said she was a big fan. Maybe I should sell it. Probably worth thousands now but it's a piece of history and I'd be sad to let it go."

"What is it?"

"Part of the Berlin Wall. Got that the day after it came down."

"The Berlin Wall fell?"

Hannah Able gave her a very strange look.

"When?" Sally asked. She looked around the room. There were other posters hanging from blobs of Blu-Tack, advertising more albums. The art got progressively worse. The Pre-Raphaelite elegance of *Dark Lady Winter* was gradually replaced by cheap-looking collages of dolphins and Native Americans floating through badly painted galactic backdrops. It was the kind of music you'd find next to the tills in garden centres. All but two were in German. The last one said *LIEDER DER KOSMISCHEN MUTTER* in shiny foil, and had the date *Oktober 1996* in big letters under a photograph of a much older Hannah. This time she wore a silver circlet and hovered above Stonehenge holding what appeared to be a stuffed dove in each fist.

She's from eleven years in the future.

"9 November 1989. Midnight. Christ, don't they teach anything in English schools any more?"

Sally wanted to ask if there'd been a war, whether America and Russia had finally had it out and the Soviets somehow lost without setting the world on fire. Hannah Able had disappeared into a bedroom.

"I helped Simon. I saved his fucking life! And here I am in a cupboard," her voice floated into the lounge. "Can't even make videos anymore because there's nobody to operate the camera. I could do an entire album with the change down the back of that arsehole's sofa, a double LP even."

Sally joined her. The space was indeed small enough for a cupboard. One wall was taken up with a keyboard, surrounded by knobs and sliders and a tiny cream-coloured TV with a rainbow apple stamped on the front. A recording mic and pop shield sat on a tripod in the middle of the carpet, and another stand sported a video camera, sandwiched between a drying rack laden with damp knickers and a broken chest of drawers.

Hannah Able trickled tobacco along a cigarette paper with shaking fingers.

"It's that grasping two-faced wanker Kyle's fault Simon ended up like he did. Where's my bloody lighter? I put it down here somewhere. Where is the fucking thing?"

Sally found it next to a big flat button at the end of a wire extending from the back of the television. She handed it over. The singer lit up and blew furious smoke at the ceiling. The smell of weed was overpowering.

"Just wait till this concert. They'll all be there, the ones that believed in me, still believe in me. The Professor said so."

"Concert?"

But Hannah Able had already stuck a pair of studio headphones on her ears and was fiddling with the mixing desk. She hadn't heard the question.

"What's your name?" she asked, lifting up one rubber shell from the side of her head.

"Sally."

"Right, Sally. When I count to three I want you to start the camera. We'll shoot it static against the wall to begin with. It should already be framed so you can't see the thermostat or that ugly crack. When I'm singing, not a peep, or we'll have to do the whole thing again from scratch. These Neumann microphones are ridiculously sensitive. They'll pick up a baby's fart from a mile away."

She grabbed a long-stemmed glass from the desk and took a swig.

"Lordy, where are my manners? Wine? You can get yourself a

glass from the kitchen if you want some."

"No thanks. You can't stay in this flat. It's dangerous. I'll get you to safety."

But Hannah had the headphones back on and was gesturing at the camera. Sally reached round and pressed the record button. One take and she was out of here.

All the music was piped through the cans. Lights and dials flickered as the singer held the headphones close and belted her heart out. Without the overproduced mush that accompanied her on Top of the Pops in 1982, the voice was resonant and beautiful, despite the naff lyrics about angels, shamans and a phoenix in the core of every star. Sally remembered poor Hannah Able on TV at the height of punk, lost in time and space on a BBC that only saw her as a gloriously cheesy throwback.

"Right. Next I want you to zoom in on my face when I sing 'And the children shall play in the astral void'. I'm doing the harmony so it might sound a bit weird."

"Please listen to me. You have got to get out of this flat, out of this whole building."

"Hmmm?" the old woman said over the lip of her glass. "Why?"

"You know where you are, right? This isn't Berlin. You are the prisoner of a... someone who wants to hurt you, badly. There's no concert. He'll find you and take you to the top of the Blocko Tower, and that'll be it. Come with me now, back to the world."

"You mean Professor Backenforth? He's set up the most wonderful stadium for me. I've seen all the plans. It'll be bigger than Bowie's Glass Spider tour, and Simon and Kyle can kiss my arse."

Was she drunk? Stoned? Going batty? The hand slopping out another glass-full from the bottle still trembled.

"You. Cannot. Stay. Here," Sally said.

"Where else will I go?" Hannah's eyes filled with tears and she shrugged. "They all dumped me in the end. My own brother, Kyle, then Spektrum, then Gunther Mende, and even Candy DeRouge for Christ's sake. Why do you think I'm doing this all by myself? I was flat broke when he invited me here and gave me all this kit. No way could I afford any of it myself. I know where I am. I'm not stupid. I realise this isn't Berlin, but it's all I have left. One more take. Just the harmony, ok? Please? And afterwards you can fuck off if you're so desperate."

Just one more take.

Hannah showed her where the zoom button was, fiddled with the controls behind her, and counted back in. This time it sounded as if she'd dropped at least two octaves. She really had the most astonishing voice.

"Through shades of starlight, eternal wings aflame... Oh for fuck's sake!" She yanked the headphones off. "There's someone outside the door."

Ice congealed in Sally's stomach. She hadn't heard a thing.

"The Neumann picked it up. Be a love and go and see what they want while I reset."

Sally left Hannah to her mixing desk and cat-paced through the lounge, drawing the Wodaran's raygun as she went. This apartment had a fish eye security peephole. She risked a glance and found herself peering into total darkness. With a shock she realised it was the same void that had filled the ViewMaster before the insects turned up. A nail scraped across metal on the other side, close to her cheek. Sally jerked away so violently she almost ended up on her arse.

"Sally, Sally, Sal-ly. There you are. Found you at last. I've been looking all over for you."

She hit the inside of the door with her fist and hissed back at the creature.

"I've got the Wodaran's raygun and Eva's alive. She didn't end up in a Nazi camp with a tattoo on her wrist. She's here in the tower, tooled up and waiting, and she gave me all the batteries I need to blow you to hell, you miserable heap of shit."

A pause, more scraping and then that unmistakable stink of rot oozing into the flat.

"Who is it?" Hannah called from her studio.

Sally almost said Proserpina but another name popped into

her head.

"Charlotte Baird."

"Who?" the singer asked.

The scratching stopped and a heavy silence fell, so thick with dread and hatred the air turned to glue around her.

"Charlotte Baird. A Victorian lass who was raped by her uncle. They locked her up in a mental institution. Said it was all her fault. Didn't they?"

The memory of the creature's gloating lies, when she and the squad were trapped in Eva's flat, drove Sally back to the door. What had she said? *You were an accident and you ruined her life.* Except that wasn't a lie, was it?

"Is that what happened? Nobody believed a child, did they?" Sally hissed. "It was all in her imagination - made up. He would never do such a thing. What a wicked, wicked little shit she was, to fib about her own uncle so. Charlotte Baird."

"Stop it."

Grating, foul and sludgy. For the first time, Sally heard fear in the voice.

"She created you from her druggy nightmares. You're the filth dredged from cruelty, rape and madness, not a fairy tale at all. You're him, aren't you? The uncle. That disgusting pedo, turned into a monster in a battered child's nightmares and then made real by Professor Backenforth."

"No. You're wrong."

The stench of rot poured around the door and almost made Sally faint.

"What's that godawful stink? For God's sake what's happening?" Hannah cried out. Sally didn't dare take her eyes off the door to look behind her. She heard the singer throwing up.

"I'm her new mother," the voice from the corridor whined. "I protect her. He won't touch her, not when she's in this state."

The metal bulged inwards, the hinges popping. Any second it would give away and they'd either drown in filth or be torn apart and eaten. Trying not to throw up herself, Sally pressed the button on the Wodaran's raygun.

Expanding ovals of white light drifted slowly towards the door, trailing rainbow sparkles. The first touched the surface, passed through, and a shock wave thundered sideways into the walls, shattering the stonework into molten fragments. Sally felt nothing. All the power surged outwards in a cone of destruction that punched a trench across the corridor, through the far wall and into rooms beyond. Ceilings and furniture exploded, metal instantly slumping into puddles of slag. She stopped firing, appalled by the carnage, and searched for anything left of Proserpina.

The beast must have possessed enough power to deflect much of the destruction into the surrounding architecture. Its body lay slumped on a fragment of floor, itself rising out of an island of steel and concrete chewed out of the passageway. A massive corona of what looked suspiciously like cooked shit had baked onto the wall around the collapsed mannequin - a wooden articulated creature in the smouldering fragments of a Victorian governess's dress, all black lace and spikes. One bony claw clutched at the handle of a Gladstone bag, the other arm had been severed at the elbow. The broken end of a tail half reduced to glowing ash smouldered beside the carved feet. It smelled of cedar incense.

"I can't stop him now. You made me too clean," the entity whispered. Sally approached, scrambling down into a rubble-filled trench and up again. It sounded like Hannah was having hysterics somewhere in the flat behind her.

Maybe the blast had left some kind of face under that hood, but she really didn't want to see it. A cold, sick guilt fell on Sally. It was as if two voices spoke to her at once, the wooden cogs of the puppet and the desperate whimpers of a child. Beyond the shattered fragment of corridor, the raygun had carved a void in the fabric of Backenforth Heights. It resembled a cutaway diagram of a building. Rooms upon rooms, stacked on top of each other and stuffed with clutter from a million cities over a thousand ages - sofas, divans, tables, cookers, baths of all shapes and sizes, strange sculptures flickering and twisting, lights of every hue. It seemed to Sally that the inhabitants stood and peered back at her, an audience of tiny silhouettes, some human, some monstrous. None of them moved, only watched and judged.

"Too clean. Too clean," the monster hissed.

Sally reached out to touch the dress. It crumbled to ash, the dissolution spreading as swiftly as sugar dissolving in water. In a second the crushed marionette vanished. In its place lay a girl coiled up in the dust. Her skin was as white as the torn shift she wore, except where scratches and scars wrote horrible words on her arms and legs. Most of her hair had been pulled out.

"God, you're alive. Charlotte?"

The lass curled tighter, whimpering, as Sally hunkered down.

"Hannah, help me." Between them, she and the singer could get the child down to the lobby, away from this place and into the hands of people who'd look after her properly.

"Your uncle's long dead. You're safe now," Sally said.

Silence.

All the lights went out.

Sally scrabbled for the raygun in total blackness. She was still in the corridor, but it had abstracted itself into a collection of cold planes, angles and surfaces. She patted the floor around her, hunting for Charlotte in the hope she could gather the child into her arms. If she could get her inside the flat, it'd be easier to defend them all. Nothing, just freezing metal. All the damage had been wicked away and now the passageway seemed to be at once a confining prison, yet at the same time infinite, like the field of spheres at the top of the tower.

Footsteps coming closer, leisurely and confident. Calm soft breathing. Stale tobacco smoke and cheap aftershave uncurled about her, the same putrid Old Spice her first boyfriend had slathered on top of his BO. Sally pointed the Wodaran's pistol in what she thought was the right direction and pressed the button. Nothing happened.

"You're alive, Charlotte. I didn't realise. I'm so sorry."

He had a lounge lizard voice. Sally wanted to cry out *leave her alone*, but the weight of the infinite space pushed her flat against the floor and stopped the air in her lungs. She'd had night terrors before. They were nothing compared to this.

Rustling, as of someone picking a child up for a cuddle.

"She befouled herself to stop him raping her, scarred her beautiful body and pulled her lovely hair out by the fistful. Because of that and the laudanum he used on her, she ended up strapped to a bed in Hanwell Asylum. But it's all in the past now, centuries ago, and she can finally heal," he said. "Hannah, do you mind taking hold of my coat tails? My hands are full. From today onwards everything will be perfect for her, for you, for Eva and Sally, for everyone. Darling, are your songs ready? They're preparing the sound check. Shall we go?"

Footsteps receded, leaving Sally crushed against the ground. The pressure eased and she managed to sit up.

All the lights came back on.

It was if nothing had happened. The neon tubes, tinking away behind frosted glass in the ceiling, revealed none of the damage from the Wodaran's raygun. The walls and floor were all in place, immaculate and untouched. Hannah's door stood half-open. Even the stink had vanished, replaced by the all-pervasive hint of bleach and furniture polish. It could have been an empty corridor anywhere in the tower - steel, Formica, plaster and a window in the distance looking out onto white fog.

Sally got to her feet and made her way back into the apartment, holding onto the walls.

"Hannah?"

An untenanted flat that hadn't been lived in for years. The couch still sagged in the half-light but everything else had gone, even the fragment of the Berlin Wall. At first Sally thought she'd wandered into the wrong apartment. Then she spotted Blu-tack stains on the wallpaper, marking the corners and sides of posters taken down and binned long ago. A single wine glass sat on a shelf in a dusty kitchen cupboard. It carried the faint hint of cheap Chardonnay. She found nothing else, apart from the empty drying rack in the closet studio and the edge of a shiny disk poking out from under the broken chest of drawers. She picked it up and read Hannah's loopy handwriting.

The Phoenix of the Heart Master 4 May 1998

Eva was standing in the lounge, dressed in full armour. Echoes of the Torah span over the walls like reflections from a cheap disco ball.

"I killed that creature with the Wodaran's raygun. It was Charlotte Baird herself," Sally said.

The other woman looked around at the pristine flat and the corridor beyond. Sally suspected she didn't believe her, that she'd made it up as an excuse for doing a runner. But Eva didn't yell at her. Instead she stared into space, chewing the inside of her cheek.

"I detected a massive burst of power down here, bigger than anything I've come across before," she tapped her breastplate. "It almost fried the sensors. What happened?"

Sally told her.

"Charlotte was alive?" Eva asked.

She nodded.

"It wasn't a monster. It was Charlotte all along. She made herself hideous and hid inside a ton of squirming rot to keep her uncle's filthy hands away. Professor Backenforth's got her now, and Hannah Able."

"Not good. He may have enough victims to finish the rituals. We need to get up there fast, unless you want to run off again."

Sally bit her lip, not trusting herself to reply. The thought of the lord of the Blocko Tower carrying that poor, sick little girl up to his lair reminded her of Anthony Mendelssohn, and killed any notions she had of leaving.

"He said a weird thing, that everything would be perfect for us in the end - you, me, Hannah and Charlotte."

"I know all about monsters trying to build their so-called perfect worlds on the corpses of the innocent. They've fed on me and mine since the beginning of time," Eva said.

She reached into her suit and pulled out a handful of batteries, along with a brown ribbed bottle of aspirin.

"My home isn't safe anymore. This is all I could retrieve for you. The pills are for your rib. Reckon you're fit enough to make it to the top?"

Sally took the tablets and the AAs. She worked her shoulder against the pain. It was bad but bearable, as long as she kept her arms close to her sides.

"We'll get as far as we can in white space. There's something about you that's changing things, turning you into a kind of beacon. He's tracking you. That must have been how Charlotte knew where you were. I've no idea why he didn't take you here and now. Maybe he thinks you'll lead him to me," Eva shrugged. "Good, but I want to make sure we reach the top first. It'll involve travelling through parts of the tower I'd rather avoid. He won't expect that."

She walked over to the wall and rubbed the surface with her finger, up and down, left to right. Sally realised her friend was tracing the outlines of a brick, pressing into the mortar. Once the grooves were nail-deep she dug in and pulled it out in a shower of cement. There was no apartment on the other side, only white space scored with the faintest of lines. Sally joined Eva and helped as best she could with one hand. The gap widened easily and in a few moments they'd made it big enough to step through.

CHAPTER SIXTEEN

"Rabbi Löwy discovered the white space beyond the walls. Angharad helped him map it and learn how to force openings in and out."

They walked a chalk path delimited by two thin black lines. Sally sensed immense geometric forms rotating in the void. She couldn't see them directly but some of their facets carried diagrams of rooms and corridors that swung into view as the mountain-sized polyhedra shifted and turned. She remembered the intricate schema on Chisum's base camp wall, Pash crossing off locations that had fallen to Charlotte the monster.

"Did you give the maps to Angus and the others?" Sally asked.

"Yes. I left them lying around in obvious places, and changed the charts to keep them away from the dangerous zones."

No doubt she meant the very country she and Sally were traipsing through, the final region before they came to the roof itself. She wondered how far they had to go. A few floors? Hundreds of yards? Miles? Eva had said the fabric of this realm was changing, adapting itself to some purpose that held Sally at its centre.

The first step back into the tower found them at the side of a swimming pool as big as a football field. Green tiling lined the walls, floor and ceiling. Black mould transformed the grouting into an immense cancerous net. The long-gone attendants had saturated the water with so much chlorine it made Sally's eyes water and her nose run. The cavern was sealed with no visible exits. Eva walked to the wide steps at the shallow end and started to descend. For a horrible moment, Sally thought they'd be crawling to the next location along a secret airless tunnel. The second her friend's toe touched the surface the entire ground rose up 90 degrees, thousands of gallons of rancid liquid hanging in front of them. Eva twisted right, and they emerged in the white space once more. Sally glanced behind to see a pale olive rectangle tumble into the distance like a playing card in a gale.

Eva marched on and Sally trotted after. Neither spoke. She simply couldn't think of what to say. There was so much unspoken between them. She could also sense a third presence, an invisible intelligence tracking their progress as if the two women were insects crawling across the pages of an immense book of mathematics, the reader waiting for the right moment to slam the covers shut.

Her friend stopped, squatted down and tore a hole in the floor, dropping into a pit filled with amber twilight. Sally hurried after, relieved to get out of a space that no longer felt quite so safe.

"Angharad's home. We'll rest a while before the final stage."

They stood in a low-ceilinged hallway made out of wood. Three oval rooms radiated from this central hub, each with a wall-high window looking out across sterile terrain - a snowfield under a purple sky, a desert at night, a lake as flat as a mirror. How could a room so far up look on landscapes? She walked towards the dunes and realised she was staring into one of three immense TV screens, their images so crisp and clear they'd fooled her into thinking they were real.

"Skies," Eva had fallen back onto a low sofa. She had her hands over her face as if trying to rub the exhaustion away. "Angharad loved skies because there weren't any where she came from."

"What do you mean?"

"She was from Earth a hundred years from now. In the middle of the next century the entire planet is trapped within an immense machine. The sky becomes metal. Everything falls apart, everything in the world stops working. She explained it all to me. Most of it didn't make any sense."

Sally looked around. Besides the fake windows nothing spoke of the future.

"You had a glowing shield and a helmet filled with lights in your old house. If it all collapses in Angharad's time, where did that technology come from?"

"Inside the sky. Whatever engine encased the world was so big it trapped most of the other planets too. But it was riddled with spaces - rooms and corridors with air and gravity. Angharad was a poacher in the tunnels between the Earth and the Moon. That's where she discovered the tower. She rode in it for a while, up and down the time stream, hoping it would jump to a future where the solar system was free again. But Professor Backenforth tracked her down.

"Before Angharad disappeared, she told me and Rabbi Löwy what she knew. The old man stayed here with her for a while, trying to understand all her science and combine it with his own knowledge. After she died I salvaged what I could and took it to my house, thinking we'd carry on there, but the rabbi said my home reminded him too much of the ghetto. It made him realise he needed to be back in the real world fighting the Nazis. That's when he left me and returned to Riga."

"Pash claimed the rabbis helped the Roman Emperor build this tower to try and trap Professor Backenforth. He broke their spell, took it over and flew away."

"Maybe," Eva said from behind her fingers. "There's an old Jewish folktale about a fallen angel imprisoned in a tower."

She lapsed into silence. Sally got the impression Eva didn't want to move, that she'd be perfectly happy to spend the rest of her days on a sofa, looking out on other worlds. Was she scared despite all her triumphs, armour and weaponry? Afraid to chance the final approach to the field of spheres? Sally let the woman be and went in search of any other wonders that might remain in this apartment from the future.

"I'm sorry I haven't been kinder," Eva called after her.

It took a few moments of staring across the snowfield, and wondering where all the stars were in that clear sky, for Sally to clock what she'd said.

"I know finding me was important to you," her friend continued. "Me too. I longed for your friendship as time went by. I was so lonely. Rabbi Löwy was company after a fashion, but he was an old man wrapped up in his books, with little interest in a child. I wish you'd been here all those years ago."

"Why me? Weren't there any others?"

It was odd, watching Eva talk to the fake window from the sofa, more like hearing a confession than reminiscing with a childhood classmate.

"No. You were always going to be my greatest friend. Don't forget, I came from a world filled with suspicion, then hatred, then mass murder. That makes you wary of anyone and everyone. As I grew older I realised how much danger I'd put you in for my own selfish reasons. When the tower returned to your era, I reached out a couple more times until Professor Backenforth noticed and I had to stop."

"The game and the amusement arcade in Portslade. That was you again," Sally said.

Eva nodded.

"Professor Backenforth didn't seem so monstrous when he came for Charlotte Baird," Sally said. "He sounded genuinely concerned, slimy as fuck, but not some foul demon bent on torment."

"He's a genial Nazi. There's plenty of them about and they're the most dangerous," Eva said. "They're all smiles and courtesy and apologetic concern, right up to the point they turn on the gas. Don't be fooled."

Eva heaved herself out of the seat.

"This building's architecture feeds off the dreams and nightmares of those who live in it. From here on in its power will grow, using what's in our heads. The older the memories and fears, the deeper they'll be embedded. It'll draw on those most of all, so be ready. You might come across things torn out of your worst fears and darkest secrets. Don't react unless I tell you to."

They stepped out of the apartment into a passageway walled

in red brick.

"Aren't we using the white space anymore?" Sally asked, trying to make sense of the posters littering the damp stone underfoot. They were the torn fragments of the same image. More tattered remains dotted the length of the corridor wall, as if somebody had recently come by and tried to rip them down. They showed the back of a charcoal soldier wielding a rifle in a red cloud with the words *ROKAS NOST NO LATVIJAS*. Someone had daubed a black swastika on one.

"Angharad and the rabbi failed to pin down the mathematics for the last ten floors. We might end up getting lost or fall into one of the professor's traps. This way's easier. Trust me."

Sally followed Eva. What else was there to do? She still wasn't sure what to make of Eva's apology in Angharad's apartment. It didn't seem right. Was it supposed to be an attempt at reconciliation? It sounded more like a speech excusing things yet to come. It occurred to Sally that the only weapon she had was the Wodaran's plastic raygun and a spare pair of batteries. Maybe that would be enough, that and the kickboxing.

The ceiling rose higher and higher until it vanished into darkness. She noticed a few lighted windows way above in the gloom. Faint noises tumbled around her. At first they sounded like the ambient chaos of any apartment block - a baby crying, music playing, arguments and laughter. But she also heard screaming, desperate horrible shrieks that told of tortures in concrete rooms far beyond the cold boundaries of hope.

After a while, the trench turned right. Eva stopped. There was barely enough room for them to stand side by side. The freezing brick pressed against Sally's shoulder. Her rib was hurting again. The other woman nodded ahead without speaking. In the distance Sally saw people huddled in the gloom, shuffling away from them in a slow, miserable crowd. Light from a couple of windows high above picked out the edge of skull here, wisps of hair falling on bony shoulders there. A man started laughing. He'd flung up one of the casements and was leaning on the windowsill in shirt sleeves, looking down and smoking a pipe.

"Stand back," Eva hissed. Sally stepped away as her friend loaded up the sling and began to spin it faster and faster. With a hoarse scream she let the bullet fly. Seconds later the window exploded in fire, glass and shards of brick. A wet, ragged shape tumbled onto the crowd far below. When the smoked cleared, the distant shadows looked empty, though Sally thought she heard the sound of something being dragged into darkness.

"Shouldn't have done that. Stupid," Eva muttered through her teeth. "I remember him. He was the doctor who lived opposite. He delivered my sisters and brother, but when the Nazis came he signed up, boasting how they'd finally rid the neighbourhood of Jewish scum. That's what he did when they marched us off, leaned out of the window and waved goodbye with a big grin on his face. Now do you see what I mean? The tower's using memories to make itself. Haven't you got anything in your head? I'm sick of mine."

Sally's turn came soon enough. A narrow flight of stairs took the pair of them back into the 1960s, and a series of rooms filled with Parker Knoll furniture, huge sprays of pampas grass in white vases and thick carpets. In a far-off room at the end of a corridor, a little boy sobbed on his hands and knees, trying to scrub spilled Heinz spaghetti out of the wool pile while an obscenely fat woman, dressed as Bob's leather nun, beat him with a flint-studded cricket bat. His blood mingled with the acid-red tomato sauce. One eye dangled from the lad's socket on a pale thread as he cried and scrubbed, cried and scrubbed. In the next hallway, all plate glass and potted ferns, Sally threw up across a pile of bean bags. She had no idea where that particular horror had come from.

And so it continued, a neat alternation between the two of them as they walked, ran, climbed, and scrambled through increasingly chaotic architecture. Eva's rooms mingled brick, steel, blood and burning remnants with hysterical imagery from fairy tales and stories Sally didn't recognise. Everything was cloying, heavy and sinister, even the puddingy characters from the folk tales. They wore fake medieval clothes and page boy haircuts and swore, fought, sang and sweated in dungeons, feasting halls, and on crenellated battlements.

They came across whole buildings inside entire rooms, exactly like dolls' houses but swollen to actual size or bigger. Tenements, shops, a building she guessed was a synagogue - all damaged or broken in one way or another, every window boarded up, stars of David scrawled in paint or blood, and endless ragged words in German and Latvian - *Jews Out, Death to Jews*. She didn't need any translation. In a couple of chambers the walls were pitted concrete and steel. Immense shadows bent over the buildings - grownups condescending to take an interest in a child's toys, hands on knees, doctors' coats or military jackets open to reveal more darkness filled with thousands of red hungry eyes. At first Eva took it all in her stride, though she occasionally hurled more exploding bullets at shapes and silhouettes at the end of dark alleyways. Finally, on stepping out into yet another corridor, she broke down, sobbing into her fists. Sally put her arm around the woman's shoulders. Her friend was locked deep in her sorrow and it was like trying to comfort a boulder.

At last they came to a narrow flight of iron steps that opened out into an immense room full of people, all sitting silently in armchairs. Windows on four sides looked out on the ever-present grey clouds.

This high up, Backenforth Heights appeared to have contracted to the width of an ordinary tower block. They paused at the entrance, waiting for some response from the crowd. Nobody moved or even glanced their way. It was hard to see into the space. Someone had shaded over reality with a 6B pencil, so the pale light illuminating the first few rows soon petered out, replaced by dusty gloom. Eva entered, lazily swinging the sling over and over. Nobody reacted.

Sally approached a figure sitting ramrod straight in an old leather-backed chair. An odd quality in the air turned the man into a silhouette, even though he sat in front of the nearest window. No matter where she stood, he appeared to be little more than a clutch of shadows. Was he dead? He wasn't breathing but his posture suggested expectation, a crisis about to happen. He reminded her of the abandoned pensioners in their Portslade flats, staring at the endless rain, waiting to see who'd turn up next - disinterested relatives or death. So this was where the men in donkey jackets had brought them, to the top of the Blocko Tower.

She looked around at the others. This one wore a t-shirt and jeans. The woman in the next chair along was dressed in a shawl and heavy coat. On her far side sat a trawler fisherman, net piled up on his lap, motionless fish glittering in its folds.

"They're not dead," Eva said, her voice coming out of the darkness in the centre of the room. "Their time is frozen."

"How do you know?"

"My armour tells me."

"So why are they here?"

"This last floor's a vestibule. They came by their own free will, thinking Professor Backenforth was going to save them from the world, their lives. I guess they're waiting to be taken with the others to the roof."

"They wanted to be sacrificed to other gods?" Sally said.

"It's not such a strange desire. Whole religions have been founded on it. They'll never get their wish though. He chose who he wanted a long time ago and the rituals are almost complete."

"So all these poor buggers will stay like this forever?"

Eva didn't answer. She'd moved further on into the room. Sally hurried after and found her friend standing at the foot of a stepladder. Insulation foam and what looked like asbestos matting hung down in shreds from a hole in the tiles above.

"That way," Eva said. "I'll go first."

She disappeared into the space. Sally followed and ended up crammed between Eva and a network of piping, balancing on the frame of the suspended ceiling. Her companion reached up and started to pull away the fibreglass above their heads. Sally helped. The crystal fibres dug into her fingers and made her skin itch. There seemed no end to it. The two of them burrowed further and further upwards into a sweaty, chemical darkness that quickly became unbearable. No longer able to breathe, Sally fought against the panic that stuck in her throat like a hot rock. She didn't even know whether Eva was still with her, or had been swallowed up and suffocated in these candy floss clouds.

Her fingers touched plasterboard and she pushed. Another hand appeared beside hers and together they heaved again. The sheet broke in two with a gunshot crack and they scrambled out onto flat rock under a seething bloody sky. A cold wind scoured Sally's face and lungs clean. For a moment she was happy to lie there and watch the grey and red clots swarming over each other miles above. The sense of space intoxicated her. How long had her thoughts, her mind, her life, been encompassed by walls and floors, carpets and partitions, kitchens and bathrooms, Formica, wood polish and chintz? For the first time in what seemed like eternity she sprawled outside, heaving bucketfuls of air into her chest and laughing with the relief of it.

"Get up," Eva said.

Sally rolled onto her hands and knees and looked around. If there was another entrance, it was hidden beyond the spheres. They lay in the distance, a perfectly spaced row of identical Mystery Planets. It was hard to work out the scale. She thought the nearest stood about fifty yards off, but the endlessly shifting geometry of the Blocko Tower had fried Sally's brain. They might have been as vast as mountains and hundreds of miles away, or no bigger than tennis balls and within grabbing distance.

Eva tried to haul her upright. Sally pushed her off, remembering the pain in her injured rib from the last time her friend yanked her around. She stood up and rotated on the spot. Here they were, on the roof of Backenforth Heights, in the realm of the creature who'd stolen Anthony and all the others. It was empty apart from the spheres. Nothing else disturbed the landscape, which stretched in flat uniformity into the distance. No mountains, no demon castle or villain's lair, only the immaculate symmetry of one hundred sacrificial urns in a precise ten by ten matrix. Maybe the smug bastard thought nobody would ever make it this far. Then she remembered the visions she'd had before, in Portslade and through the ViewMaster, of the dark gardener who tended these monstrous seeds, rising out of blackness, extended claws curling over their slick skins as he hunted for her.

"Here," Eva handed her a packet. It looked like three jumbo chocolate bars taped together. "That's the charge. It can't explode until I tell it to. We need to find one of the last empty crucibles so you can stick that inside while I transfer the rabbi's incantations to its shell."

"Where is he then?"

"I don't know. He might not realise we're here yet, but that won't last long. We can't hang around."

She set off towards the rows at a jog. Sally pushed her fear away and followed. As they approached, she saw more shapes beyond. Each orb stood at the beginning of a line of ten, stretching back over the plain in perfect alignment. Glancing down to watch her step, she tried to work out what the ground was made of. It looked like wet slate but gave slightly underfoot. More plastic, perhaps.

The spheres were fashioned from smooth metal. Up close, they were slathered in pictures, words and diagrams like the ones she'd seen in Vicky Samson's garden and the amusement arcade. The first she came to was covered in paintings of fruit and flowers, the colours faded into dark shades barely distinguishable from the chipped cadmium undercoat. Craning her neck allowed her to see the edge of the hatch wheel on top. The trap was shut and sealed. Some poor bugger was inside, probably alive. She didn't want to press her ear against the shell for a listen. Something about the entire mechanism repelled her. What if she clambered up there and tried to free the prisoner? No, no time. They had to find an open ball and blow it up.

All the Mystery Planets in the first few rows were closed. Sally walked past bleached and worn pictures of mountain landscapes, complex machinery, the interior of a castle, and at least three seascapes. One surface was entirely covered with mathematical equations, another with a poem in a language she didn't recognise.

The deeper they went, the greater the silence, until each breath Sally drew sounded like a waterfall. The red and charcoal clouds high above continued to race by at hurricane speed. Glances upwards brought a churning surge of vertigo. The air felt heavier as well. It was as if she really did stand among worlds, and each had a toxic atmosphere leaking out. They spread and mingled, filling the gaps between the spheres, making her head swim.

"He's here," Eva muttered, pausing next to a painting of an eyeless baby on a serving dish, surrounded by bunches of grapes. God only knew what that was supposed to mean, and who was stuck inside.

They padded onwards, instinctively hunkering down against the underside of each sphere. Eva stopped suddenly and held her finger to her lips. Sally mouthed *Where?*, and her friend pointed down the next side alley. They crouched tight beneath the underbelly and Sally risked a glance. Thin legs in flared trousers, platform boots, all in black paper cut-out. Four rows away, walking with high steps in the opposite direction. Those might have been the ends of claws, or twisted fingernails, dangling just below the curve of another sphere. The gardener with his monstrous seeds, Professor Backenforth. He seemed in no hurry, strolling along without the slightest hint of urgency. He either hadn't realised he had company or didn't give a shit.

Eva tugged Sally across the space to the next row. They moved away from the creature, picking up as much speed as they could, silently checking the tops of the Mystery Planets for an opening. Sally stopped suddenly. There, to the right, three spheres beyond. The hatch was thrown back and something stood propped against the shell.

It was a bolt-action rifle. Sally examined the faded images on the curving wall. Abstract men and women holding guns, torches and banners aloft, all in reds and yellows. *UNIDAD SINDICAL. ¡NO PASARAN! POR ESPAÑA.*

"Pash! She's alive. That's her gun. I can get her out," she whispered.

"No. We need to find an empty one. The charge won't work if

there's a victim inside."

"I'm not leaving her. Help me up."

"No," The woman grabbed her arm but Sally ducked under and broke free. The rifle clattered to the ground and went off with a loud crack. A spark on a distant sphere, followed by the whine of the ricochet echoing on and on throughout the matrix. Eva spat out a curse and unfurled her sling. Sally seized the moment, stepped back until metal pressed between her shoulder blades, and ran for Pash's prison.

"Sally! Stop!" Eva hissed. Sally jumped, barely managed to hook her fingers around the edge of the opening, and heaved herself upwards. She'd forgotten her own strength. Her momentum carried her over the rim and she tumbled down into soft grey clouds full of coloured light.

CHAPTER SEVENTEEN

Sally opened her eyes to find herself standing on a ridge, overlooking a stony valley scattered with orchards. The land rose to a second line of hills and, beyond those, a topaz sea dusted with mist. Three tall ships followed each other to the horizon. Delicate tangles of white canvas and wood rose out of hulls that resembled cupped hands. Gulls scribbled calligraphy in the sky above their wakes.

She stood at the junction of two cart tracks. One ran along the ridge towards distant mountains on her left and continued to a broad plain on her right. The other trail wound down the slope and among fields and groves. White houses joined by dry stone walls began apart, then moved closer together until a small town sprawled up the far side of the valley. Tiny shadows and shapes flitted back and forth in the crevasses between the buildings. Sally could have sworn the hint of singing and laughter came to her on a wind filled with oleander and jasmine. A few threads of colour dangled from high windows and the single church steeple - banners, perhaps?

She'd had an odd dream - of darkness and spheres and a tall tower ruled by the devil who'd been imprisoned in its uppermost levels by the King of Edom, thousands of years before she was born. It was an image from a fairy story told to her long ago by her new mother. She glanced down at herself and saw she was wearing leather sandals, baggy cream slacks and a muslin shirt. Something lay tight about her temples. She reached up to unwind the bandanna and felt the bright sun on her scalp. Red, black and white batik with the words *Revolution and War are Inseparable*, flanking a crudely printed chimney and a cannon. Revolution and war in blood-coloured dye. And yet there were no signs of either in this landscape. It looked so happy and peaceful, the sky and land filled with an open friendliness, tugging her down towards the settlement. She tied the scarf in the shape of a garrison cap and bundled her hair back up inside. From what she could tell from where she stood, people were singing and dancing in the distant streets. She walked down the path, kicking flints and pebbles aside as she followed well-worn cart ruts.

The orchards lay heavy with olives, apples, pears and oranges. She caught sight of women and men dressed like herself sauntering easily up and down between the rows of trees and vines, carrying wide straw baskets. One or two waved to her and she lifted her hand. A bracelet flashed bright on her wrist - pure gold etched with words. A woman at the top of a ladder tossed her an orange. It flew through the air like a daytime moon. She snatched it out of the sky, and peeled and broke the fruit into segments as long as her thumb.

It tasted unbelievably good.

Everything will be perfect from now on.

A man's words echoed in her memory, low and gentle, full of seductive warmth, the breath of a lover under the stars of Catalonia a hundred thousand years ago.

Darling, are your songs ready? They're preparing the sound check.

On entering the town she heard a man playing a guitar and singing. The voice was practically identical to the one in her memory.

"Tell me where you're going, my pretty brunette,
I'm going to Oviedo prison
To see the pacifists
They have locked up there
Those fascist bastards…"

An old favourite she'd once heard on the radio. Shielding her eyes against the sun, she looked up to find the guitarist on a balcony, his bare feet resting on the iron rails. It was hard to make him out against the fierce white stone - thin, rangy, a handlebar moustache, an old fashioned top hat.

"Such a sad song for such a beautiful day," she called.

"Just one more time, Senyoreta. I was imprisoned in Oviedo too and it reminds me of my comrades who perished in that place."

"But we won in the end."

"Indeed, we won. Salut!"

He hefted up a jug, balanced it on his forearm and took a swig. "Join me?"

"I'm heading into town," Sally said.

"Ah, yes. Rafaella will be very happy to see you."

She left him to his song and walked up the white cobbles, searching through her memories for a Rafaella. Short ragged hair and a filthy laugh were all she could dredge up.

The street led to a wider boulevard that eventually opened onto the main square. Up close, the scraps of cloth that had looked so tiny from the ridge became long banners and gonfalons covered in slogans and acronyms.

They shall not pass! We shall pass!

C.N.T, F.A.I, P.O.U.M.

For a free humanity! For anarchy!

Clusters of men and women stood chatting and smoking in entranceways and on the pavement, easy and smiling. Several greeted Sally as she passed by. One of the younger girls, who wore a hibiscus flower in her hair, jumped down from a doorstep, planted a kiss on her cheek and gave her a friendly push.

"Don't keep Rafaella waiting."

Sally wanted to stop and ask who she meant, but the woman and her friends were shooing her along, good natured and laughing as they pointed at the town square.

Long trestle tables covered in blue checkered cloth stretched from the shadows at one end of the plaza to the bottom of the church steps at the far side. A dozen citizens passed up and down between them, preparing for the coming feast. They disappeared and reappeared from the rough-edged doorways and cafe porticos with baskets, tureens, bowls, jugs and barrels. Men filled pitchers from the fountain and emptied them into three brass cauldrons resting above olive-wood fires. At the far corner, beneath the biggest banner, four hogs and two cows turned on spits. Sally had to dodge out of the way more than once. As she came close to a bench groaning with earthenware dishes, an old man with an eyepatch slopped a wedge of tapenade as rich and thick as blood-soaked mud onto a flatbread, folded it over, and passed it to her.

"Welcome to our new world of Arcadia, Senyoreta. Comrade Rafaella is in the church. I think they're cutting the priest's balls off for the Potatoes Riojana."

He roared with laughter as Sally bit into the bread.

It tasted unbelievably good.

Everything will be perfect from now on.

The townsfolk started lighting lanterns as twilight fell. Sally walked up the steps and pushed open the iron-bound church door. Inside it was already cool and dark. Clusters of candles on altars and on top of high candelabras illuminated the aisle, pews and, at the far end, a knot of people around a table. Some of these men and women leant on rifles, their silhouettes turned into saint's statues by an oil lamp resting between the two seated figures. Everyone stared inwards in calm silence, ignoring Sally until she came up to the ones at the back of the crowd. They quietly stepped aside to let her pass.

A woman wearing the same slacks and muslin shirt as Sally sat opposite a priest whose gaze was fixed on his hands. They were clasped together on the splintered table top, the wrists bound with rope. The woman had one knee up, heel on the edge of her seat, fingers plaited around her shin, and a laconic grin on her face. She glanced up as Sally appeared at the inner circle and barked out a laugh.

"Sally Ass-Ton. What the hell are you doing in Arcadia?"

"Pash?"

"And you're speaking Catalan. Holy shit. I thought you died

in the room of bugs."

Echoes of memories tumbled uncertainly through Sally's mind, some wild story from long ago with her as the heroine. When she tried to piece together the narrative it kept slipping away.

"Comrades this is my friend. Hell of a soldier. I saw her finish off a Nazi cavalry officer." She winked at Sally. "Giant he was and carried a sabre as big as my leg. She broke his neck with her bare hands. Bastard bust her nose but she showed that filthy fascist how a real woman can fight."

A few people applauded.

"Didn't they kill you?" Sally felt she ought to say.

"The worms? Me?" Pash gestured around her. "Nope. They brought me here, to the truth. To truth and beauty forever and ever. To Arcadia."

"What is this place?"

"Anarchist paradise and this old bastard is the icing on the cake." She pushed the table with her foot so the far edge jabbed the priest in the stomach. He winced, but said nothing.

"Father Agustí, he gave you to me for a purpose, so what are we going to do with you?"

"Four thousand priests and two and half thousand monks murdered. Three hundred nuns raped and slaughtered. Some of them you beheaded, some you burned to death with gasoline." The priest spoke for the first time. His voice was soft and weary, reasonable.

"Yeah, yeah. Well we won, didn't we? So tough shit. And your Father Vicente massacred half my family."

Pash fished a battered pack of cigarettes out of her breast pocket and lit one from the oil lamp in the centre of the table. She pushed the rest across to the prisoner. Despite his tied hands he managed to manoeuvre another into his mouth. A soldier standing behind struck a match for him.

"So, priest, what are we going to do with you?" Pash repeated to the vault above her head, the cigarette wiggling between her teeth and sending twisted smoke signals to the rafters. "OK. I sentence you to death, but not today. Today you go free, do whatever you want, live your life, talk shit from the pulpit, come and eat and drink with us this evening. One day in the future, a week, a year, ten years, a hundred years from now, someone will walk up behind you in the street in broad daylight and put a bullet in your skull, but not today."

She gestured to the comrade with the lighter. He pulled out a dagger and cut the priest's bonds. The old man massaged his wrists, watching Pash all the while.

"We're done here, comrades." Pash pushed her chair back and stood up. She grinned at the door and jerked her head.

"Come on Sally Ass-Ton, let's talk. I want to hear you speak perfect Catalan again. It's so funny."

When they were close enough, Pash swept her up in a brutal hug and planted a smacker on each cheek.

"Really good to see you, though I don't know why you're here. Haven't you got your own world? Never mind, let's grab some wine."

They descended into the courtyard and a few shouted greetings echoed from stone to stone.

"Rafaella, Rafaella!"

The anarchist grabbed a bottle and two glasses from one of the tables. She waved them in the air to general applause before heading up a set of open stairs on the side of a cafe to a balcony at the back, overlooking more orchards. Twilight turned the trees into puddles of frozen iron scattered across grey rock and scrub. They sat down on a stone bench and Pash slopped out the wine.

"Rafaella Eliana Concepcion?" Sally asked.

"Wow. Good memory."

"Not really."

Pash put her hand on Sally's head, holding up her fringe with her thumb as she peered into her eyes, shifting this way and that as if looking for something.

"Your brain is messed up somehow?"

"I remember some things. There were three others."

"Chisum, Szymanski and Angus. Do you recall Proserpina

attacking us? The Pole died, then the other two cowardly men ran away."

"She wasn't a monster."

Pash gave her a sideways grin of wary disbelief. It looked very familiar.

"Her real name was Charlotte Baird," Sally said. "She turned herself into a heap of evil shit to stop her uncle raping her."

"Fuck," her friend muttered from inside the wine glass.

A voice echoed in Sally's mind.

Everything will be perfect from now on.

She'd heard it again, recently.

"There was a guitarist on the edge of town, playing *Tell Me Where You're Going*.."

"Professor d'Aquícapallà? I didn't know he was here tonight. He comes and goes, hence the name. He likes to visit all his friends."

Pash pointed at the sky. Sally looked up and almost fell off the bench. Six stars stretched up from the horizon in a perfect line, so precise it could have been drawn with a ruler. Beyond them, more stars faded into the night, set in regular rows one above the other, no more than a finger width apart. It was like looking at a mathematical lattice made of identical suns, into which this world had been placed like a tiny opal. Other than this bizarre grid, the cloudless vault above them was utterly black and empty.

"What is this place? Where am I?" Sally asked. She'd reached out for Pash's hand, grabbing and holding on, terrified that even gravity might come apart in this insane cosmos and send her tumbling into the void.

"You climbed into my Mystery Planet, no?"

"Did I?"

"A hundred worlds for a new universe made by Professor d'Aquícapallà."

"I remember now. He was stealing people and imprisoning them in those spheres, ready to sacrifice them to demons from other realities, and in return they'd give him companionship. That's why he was kidnapping children and lonely losers like

Marcus the Roman and Hannah Able. Eva said that once he had everybody the rituals would begin."

The memories were returning thick and fast now, though they still felt unreal - muddy pictures on the other side of heavy perspex. With them came a growing dread.

Pash laughed and poured some more wine into her own glass.

"We were wrong. So wrong," she said.

"Where am I, Pash? What is this place?"

A ball as big as a land rover covered in slogans in Spanish and Catalan. The hatch still open, leaking a faint glow into the black mist. Jumping up the side, wanting to rescue her friend. Falling in and passing out.

"He's not kidnapping people to sacrifice them to anyone. He's giving them new perfect worlds where everything they want and hope for will become real. Tell me Sally, in Spain in your time who won the war between the Nationalists and the Republicans?"

She'd no idea.

"That bastard Franco, yes? You said so when we first met. And after our defeat came the bigger war between the fascists and everybody else. Each filthy cruelty those Nazi pieces of shit learned and practiced in my Catalonia, they visited on the rest of humanity - on the Jews, on the Soviets. But not here," Pash gestured around her. "In Arcadia we won. The anarchists. Not the communists, not POUM or CNT, us. This is our world where everyone will be free and equal, and nobody shall have power over anyone. And once in a while Professor d'Aquícapallà will visit us and break bread and drink wine, and play a guitar and dance before he heads up there," she gestured at the stars. "A boy, a girl, a soldier, a singer, a painter, a poet, a farmer, a fisherman," she pointed at each star in turn. "One hundred different worlds created from the dreams of each of his new friends. All perfect. All beautiful."

She grinned at Sally, reached up and ruffled her hair.

"I bet there's one waiting for you. That's why you came to the tower."

"I was searching for my friend Eva."

"You found her?"

"Yes. She was real, not made up like everybody said."

"Good to know. I remember her helping me and the guys, clearing the way to get to the top. I wonder what happened to those stupid bastards, Chisum and the others. Are they up there, each in their own paradise?" She nodded at the sky. "Or are they still sitting in that silly house in the woods, eating that dreadful food? Angus couldn't cook for shit."

Sally looked at the matrix. At the edge of her vision she caught glimpses of fine threads stretching away from the stars into the empty universe beyond.

"What are those glowing lines?"

"The suns draw their power from other universes. They're like electricity wires hooked up to dynamos on the other side of the sky," Pash said. "There's nothing in this cosmos, so everything has to be convoyed in. He's smart, the being who created all this. Shame I don't believe in God."

"So what is he?"

Pash shrugged. Sally tried the wine. She hadn't a clue whether it was any good or not, but she drained the glass in one. Her friend filled it again. Sally nodded behind her at the shouting and laughter coming up from the town square.

"So all these anarchists of yours were captured by Professor Backenforth as well. How come we never saw them?"

"Some I know from the war, most are new to me. The tower's a big place."

"But it's one person for each sphere, each different, like you said. This is your planet they're living on. They don't each get their own?"

The other woman studied the lit end of a fresh cigarette, as if looking for an answer in the grainy heat.

"And the priest? How does that fit in with your anarchist utopia?" Sally continued. "He sounded like he was your enemy."

"Father Augustí? Yeah. He was. Funny him being here. Professor d'Aquícapallà left him. Perhaps it's something to do with forgiveness."

"Are you really going to shoot him?"

"You're asking a lot of questions." That old sideways grin again. Maybe she was, but Sally's head was still full of mush and she wanted to try to stitch all this into a tale that made some sense. The rich wine didn't help.

"Just accept it for what it is, Sally Ass-Ton. I'm so happy you're here and that you can be a guest in my perfect world. Enjoy the evening. Stay as long as you like, and when you're ready, go and find your own Arcadia in this brand new universe."

Her own Arcadia. An entire planet in a new universe. Which was it? From here they could see maybe sixty or so suns, which meant the other forty were hidden by the curve of the horizon. It could be any of them. And Hannah Able's? Was she running through her sound check before the biggest audience ever seen, full of eager record executives waiting to sign her on? Was Anthony Mendelssohn playing a wonderful space game on his unique world?

"What would Sally Ass-Ton's perfect paradise be like?" Pash asked.

She had no idea. One where her parents were actually interested in her, cared for her even? Perhaps she wouldn't have a broken nose and her first boyfriend wouldn't have turned out to be such a complete bell-end. She'd be writing for *NME* or *Sounds*, not some chip-paper rag in the Thatcherite wastelands of the West Riding.

Thinking about it, her ambitions were all pretty lame. Pash had the great political ideals of anarchy and had fought in a bloody, brutal war against fascism on its behalf. There was real meat on the bones of this Arcadia, hard-won and thought through in depth, well deserving of a feast with wine, hog roast and tapenade. Did Sally have anything comparable - a vision of a perfect world worth celebrating with something a bit more lavish than a pint of Theakstons and a bag of warmed-over batter scraps?

"You look sad," Pash said. "Let's go and have a party."

When they emerged at the top of the stairs leading down into the plaza, a huge cheer rose up from the crowd now assembled by the tables.

"Rafaella, Rafaella, Rafaella!"

As soon as Pash reached the bottom step they grabbed her and hoisted her up onto the tallest man's shoulders, leaving Sally behind to watch. He carried the anarchist into the throng, dancing all the while as Pash swayed and conducted the people around her. A bottle appeared in one hand, a revolver in the other. She took a swig and fired three shots into the air. Sally jumped, as did several others. Two older women held Sally's hands, guiding her after her friend. The wine hit her hard now and it took all her concentration not to fall over in the shifting, singing mass. All other thoughts ended up forced to the back of her mind. Her last realisation, before she lost herself in food, booze and laughter, was that she understood every single word of every song, slogan and bellowed conversation.

I can speak fluent Catalan.

When a boy barely into his teens shoved another bottle at her, she lifted it to the sky.

To Professor Backenforth.

The rest of the night fell into hot, crazy fragments, like the coals that fell from the fires and rattled over the cobbles, hissing in spilled wine and among discarded bones and peel, until the morning started to turn everything grey and rusty. Sally found herself tipped back on a bench with her bare feet resting on a table. Pash slept on the seat beside her, using her lap as a pillow and snoring and dribbling over Sally's slacks. When Sally stirred, her friend lifted herself up with an almighty effort, still trailing drool, and looked around with bleary eyes at the various semi-conscious party-goers.

"Wassup? Time is it?"

"Morning," Sally said, astonished at her own lack of a hangover. God only knew how much she'd consumed in the crazy long hours, but all she felt now was tired and stiff from the hard bench.

Pash grunted, pushed her hair back, and peered across the

square. Father Agustí staggered towards the church steps. He'd ended up as pissed everyone else, even joining in with several anarchist songs, much to everyone's delight as he seemed to know all the lyrics.

"Esteban," Pash clicked her fingers at the fat cook stacking dishes a couple of tables away. He looked up as she approached him to mutter in his ear. When she stepped beyond, heading towards the priest, Sally saw he'd given her a revolver. Her friend trundled over to the old cleric and shot him in the back of the head. Father Agustí fell forwards, his blood tracing a thin line from the gun's muzzle to his skull. Pash peered at him, nudged his leg with her boot, grunted, and fired again.

Sally got up from the table and walked out of the square. She headed down the path she'd first followed, finding her way to the edge of town. The balcony where Professor Backenforth had played his guitar and sung *Tell Me Where You're Going..* was deserted. She trudged along the track, past the men and women still gathering fruit in their wide baskets. When they called out their morning greetings she ignored them.

At the top of the ridge she turned back to look across the valley. There was no sign of the lattice of stars in the bright air, though Pash's own Arcadian sun hung warm and crisp above the mountains to her left. Out at sea three tall ships sailed towards the horizon. Were they the same ones she'd seen yesterday, or did this coast generate an endless supply of eager voyagers, seeking to build more anarchist communes on fresh shores on the far side of the planet?

Sally looked about her. Now what? Where was the exit to this place? Unbroken sand, rock and scrub undulated in all directions from the ocean. She glanced up at the fathomless sky and noticed a little speck floating down towards her. She thought it might be a bird, the first she'd seen in this land, but when it came closer, she realised it was a plastic raygun in the shape of a pear with a handle. An antenna stuck out of the narrow end. She picked it out of the sky, feeling the heft of the batteries, pointed it towards the dawn, and pressed the trigger. Lazy ovals drifted away, leaving trails of sparks. A couple of yards further on they seemed to hit something. The air pulsed and peeled back in a ragged circle, revealing a sheet of dark metal curving inwards. Sally reached out, stepped through the rent, and hauled herself up and out of Rafaella's Mystery Planet.

CHAPTER EIGHTEEN

A wave of dizziness hit Sally when she climbed out. As her face rose above the rim, a storm of words rolled out of her head into oblivion and a new storm of words rolled in. With it came a sharpening of memories and another identity, off-centred and out of phase. As she clung to the upper surface of the ball, trying hard not to fall onto the ground below, it felt as if someone was attempting to put her on like an ill-fitting jumpsuit, pushing hands, feet and head into awkward spaces with mis-aligned seams.

Tell me where you're going, my pretty brunette,
Voy a la cárcel de Oviedo
A ver a los pacifistas

Sally sat up, lost her grip, and slid off Pash's Mystery Planet, landing in a painful tangle on the wet rock. Briefly winded, she stared at the upside-down revolutionary slogans on the underside.

Once I could speak fluent Catalan and danced and feasted at our victory.

Not anymore.

Where was Eva? There was no sign. She'd tried to stop Sally climbing inside. Was she hiding somewhere, or been captured or killed by Professor Backenforth? Sally cursed herself for an idiot, and then spotted the Wodaran's raygun lying in the darkness under the belly of the sphere. She had a vague recollection of it drifting down into her hand from a porcelain blue sky. If Eva ran off as soon as Sally had tumbled into the ball, who'd thrown the pistol in after her? Without it she'd still be stuck on the stony ridge, watching ships sail endlessly towards the horizon, thinking about the thin arc of a priest's blood as he fell across the steps of his church.

She picked up the toy and tried to get her bearings. Two rows of five balls stretched away to her left, opening onto the endless grey plain and its burning cotton wool sky. Two more sets of four sat on her right. Eva must have gone searching for the last open planets. They could be anywhere. Maybe she'd even given Sally up for dead and was trying to defeat the lord of the tower by herself. Forcing panic down, Sally crept from sphere to sphere, staying as far under the curves as possible, hoping the shadows would keep her concealed. This close to the metal skins she heard the hissing wind conjure soft harmonics from a hundred worlds. Nothing moved in the long geometric perspectives.

Fragments from her encounter in the Catalan city continued to resurface. They had the hazy plasticity of remembered dreams. Pash's perfect utopia. All her fantasies come true. Franco defeated. No more fascism. An anarchist paradise. None of it suggested unholy and tormented sacrifice.

What did her friend say as they sat and drank wine and looked up at that bizarre matrix of stars, each with its own ribbon joining it to yet another creation? The words were vague, difficult to grasp, as if clumsily translated from a language she once knew long ago.

He doesn't stealing people to give them to others. He make them each paradise for their own. For you too.

Or something like that.

A paradise where the anarchist shot a defenceless priest in the back of the head. Sally had never seen someone murdered in cold blood before. Fighting monsters in the corridors of the Blocko Tower was one thing. She was perfectly happy for Pash and the others to machine-gun or blow up as many warped creatures from her nightmares as they fancied. Killing an old man for no apparent reason was totally different. What did she expect? They were soldiers in brutal wars. That's what they did. But the memory of it, as muted as it seemed, turned her stomach.

She paused beside a sphere decorated with a dancing chain of boys and girls in long flowing gowns and ornate headdresses. They held hands as they skipped, alternately bowing and arching their backs. Stylised lemon eyes and red-lipped smiles mingled with curving horns and bright mantillas. Dogs played at their feet and birds of paradise framed the procession with their curling lacework tails. Another perfect world for someone plucked from history, but that wasn't what made her catch her breath and step away. It was the contrast with the Mystery Planet directly opposite.

It sucked the pale light out of the surrounding landscape with a gravity so strong, Sally swore it pulled at her as well. Some odd optical effect made it appear like one of those alternating convex and concave illusions. She found herself looking into a dark bowl, then a hemisphere, then a circular void as vast as the night sky. It had decorations, more sensed than seen, and they also seemed to shift and change. Four tall thin figures, three in masks. An accident of some kind - steam, blood and oil spread across wreckage. A broken body in a dress covered in black and white squares. Sally could bear it no longer. She turned and ran down the next passage, not caring whether anyone or anything spotted her, just desperate to get away from the images crowding in. She couldn't tell if they were projected onto the surface of the Mystery Planet or the inside of her own skull. The sphere had already been sealed. So what in the name of holy fuck lived within? And what was its perfect world?

Sense took over from fear. She stopped, hands on knees to calm herself, trying to refocus on the rock under her feet. Where the hell was Eva? Should she keep looking, try to get back to the tower entrance and escape, or seek some way of destroying Professor Backenforth herself? She straightened up and some force snatched the Wodaran's raygun out of her hand. It tumbled up towards the clouds, but swift claws plucked the toy out of the air before it passed the apex of the sphere opposite.

"Now do you understand?" said that voice.

He sat on the top, boots crossed at the ankles. The Mystery Planet was the one from the children's party all those years ago. Bubble-helmeted space men and women fired ray guns at star-headed aliens. Their weapons emitted circles of light that trailed rainbow sparkles, exactly like the Wodaran's pistol.

"Is Anthony in there?" Sally found enough courage to ask.

Professor Backenforth tapped the metal under his backside. "Yes he is." Lounge lizard once more, words oily and way too enticing. She could smell the cheap aftershave and BO from here, even though he was only a silhouette. How far away was he? Four strides? If Sally crossed the space and reached up, she'd touch his boots. Yet the creature still defied all light, enshrouded in his own grainy shadows. It was like trying to make out an image on a misfiring TV screen smeared with dried blood. He resembled a tangle of broken letters - twisted Ws and Ms topped with a ridiculous hat, huge tapered collars and laced shirt cuffs. Sally found it hard to tell if she was scared of him, repelled, or incapable of any useful emotion at all in the face of something so absurd and yet so fundamentally alien.

"He had leukaemia, though they didn't know it at the time of Rosalind Samson's birthday party. Poor lad would have died in a couple of months. Now Master Mendelssohn is healthy and happy, and has an entire world full of all the things he loves. He's king of the greatest land, a realm soaked in enchantment and mystery that will never be exhausted. Narnia has nothing on Anthony's planet."

"How did you steal him without anyone noticing?"

"Fogging minds is easy enough."

"Is that what happened to me in Pash's sphere?"

"Yes. It's to make sure you enjoy yourself all the more, by stripping away any doubts, worries or fears that might get in the way."

"You brainwash your victims."

Professor Backenforth chuckled.

"Sally, Sally, Sally. You're determined to find the worst motives in everything I do. What did you see in the city by the sea?"

"A world where Pash and her anarchist friends win and they all live happily ever after. That was you on the balcony, wasn't it? Playing the guitar."

"Exactly. Whatever you were told by my enemies simply isn't true. I'm not stealing people to sacrifice them to alien deities, or unspeakable entities from beyond time and space, in exchange for fellowship. I have no interest in other gods. They're all so boring for a start, so high and mighty. When I came into being in a barren universe, unutterably desolate and desperate for any scrap of affection, or even mere attention, they laughed at me. So what? they said. Throughout the multiverse, countless creations appear and disappear each millisecond. Some are full of life and worship, some are empty, some have lonely gods like poor Professor Backenforth, some have celestial beings for whom every second of a trillion, trillion eons is utter agony. You're not special, they told me. Why should we be your friends?

"At first I attempted to curry favour by spending countless lifetimes making wonders to entertain them. Some had grown tired and jaded for their worshippers had abandoned them. I thought I'd reintroduce amusement and a little spice back into their lives. Of course it didn't work. I became nothing more than their jester, their toy maker. Then I fashioned a plaything for myself, my greatest artifice." He unfurled disturbingly long hands, fingers tapering into threads. Sally had the impression they carried on extending into microscopic filaments, a subatomic weave spreading out over this entire realm.

"I give the lost, the broken and the defeated their perfect worlds. In my universe there shall be one hundred realities matched in perfection to the needs and hopes of those I have chosen. Anthony has his Narnia, his Middle-Earth. Hannah Able will inhabit a planet where her music and creative vision informs every landscape, relationship and thought. She's no longer drinking herself to death in a tiny flat in Berlin, dreading the waking hours because of the fight she has to face every day, between what meagre hope is left and the sweet promise of those sleeping pills stashed in her bathroom cabinet. Her art flies free like the phoenix. In your real world, Rafaella's friends lose and are forced to endure Franco and his fascists for the rest of their lives. In the sphere you visited all her dreams come true."

"She shot a priest in the back of the head. I saw her. Where does that fit in with your idea of a perfect planet?"

"I build utopias from the minds of those I want to serve, to make them happy in my universe. That man fulfilled a need."

"For murder and revenge."

"And what will you have in your ideal world, Sally Aston? I wonder. There are plenty of creatures like Father Agustí in your dreams and nightmares, all warranting retribution. Pash shot him once, got it out of her system, and now she's free to enjoy a guiltless eternity in Arcadia. I shall arrange the same for you, sweet girl."

One more peep and, I swear to God, I'll whack the living daylights out of you.

Who would she seek to punish? That sad stupid woman who didn't even know her anymore? The wasters, the users and the bullies endlessly pestering her for a shag? Bogdan the kickboxer for breaking her nose?

"I don't want one of your worlds. I want you to set all these people free and send them and me back to reality. All of your Mystery Planets are built out of fantasies and lies. This is nothing but utter poison, you sick bastard."

"But you are one of the very last, Sally. We're all waiting for you. There are two more to finish and when the pair of you are safely inside, my creation will be complete. You shall live in a beautiful world made just for you, without anyone to sneer or dismiss or hate you. Everything shall be exactly as it should be, and most of all, you will be wanted, by me and all these others who form the lattice of divine stars served and stewarded by myself."

"Which two are left? Me and Eva?"

"Yes," Eva said, stepping out from between the spheres to her right. She held the pack of explosives. Sally realised she must have dropped them when she jumped into Pash's sphere.

"Look out," Sally yelled, "He's got the raygun!"

But her friend merely leaned against Anthony's Mystery Planet and watched her with an odd expression, as if seeing her for the first time and trying to figure out who or what she was. Why wasn't Eva running, or hurling her sling bullets at the demonic bastard sitting there right above her? Sally sensed a big grin among the shadows under Professor Backenforth's hat. In the silence that followed she kept looking from him to Eva and back again as hope drained away.

"What are you doing?" she managed to ask. Churning nausea grew in her gut, making her legs unsteady.

"There's a planet prepared for you," Eva said. "Once you're inside it I can activate mine and the new universe will be complete, ready and waiting."

"For what?"

"Redemption."

The bastard had cast a spell on her childhood friend. The monster must have ambushed the other woman and messed with her head while Sally was partying with Pash in her Arcadia.

"Eva, please. That bastard's done something to you. You and I are here to stop him, to free all these people."

"No we're not," Eva said. "And no, he hasn't taken over my mind. Sorry Sally, I lied to you. I'm not here to destroy Professor Backenforth or the Blocko Tower. He's not evil. The perfect planets he's created in this new universe offer us hope and a refuge."

Sally wanted to throw up. She had to run, but the bile lay so heavy on her stomach her legs no longer had the strength to carry her. They barely kept her upright. She had to lean back against the metal skin of the Mystery Planet to stop from falling over.

"Why?" was all she could manage.

"Why do you think? When the rabbis built Backenforth Heights for him, it wasn't intended to be a prison. They made a pact. He wants company in his empty universe. We want safety and redemption. Professor Backenforth offers us a promised land of universal peace and spiritual regeneration, free from persecution and hatred. Those scholars set his fortress free so he can move back and forth through history. Once the planets are complete, I will journey with him through the ages, gathering up my people to bring them to a new cosmos."

"You're completely insane."

"Use your brain, Sally. I can rescue all those who perished in Rumbula Woods before the Nazis even get their hands on them. All the Jews wiped out by their filthy fascist creed, none of them have to die. I have the power to go anywhere and any place - the pogroms in Russia, the massacres in France and Germany, even the time of the Pharaohs. Nobody will suffer. There'll be no vengeance, no hatred. I won't kill unless I have to. But I intend to save my people, my family and anyone else I can."

Eva gasped, eyes suddenly glistening, and turned her face away. Sally stood and watched the other woman, surrounded by her own horrible emptiness, unable to master a single idea. As she sank into an ocean of misery, only two words bumped together in her head. Betrayal and hatred.

"Why me?"

"Why not?" The baffled contempt in Eva's voice came as a slap to the face. "What are you compared to the millions upon millions who will die, have died, if I don't intervene?"

"That's unkind," Professor Backenforth murmured. Sally stared at him. They really were messing with her head this time, making her doubt who was the villain and who the friend.

"You were chosen because you were unhappy," he continued. "Perhaps a lonely child who's suffered little more than disinterested parents and the spiritual wasteland of her age is not as deserving as others, but I believe that even that makes you a worthy choice. I like you, so does Eva. Hence you won the lottery."

"You total and utter fucking cunt. I didn't fall into this by chance," Sally spat at Eva. "You picked me out, fooled me into thinking I had a friend, and made me a target for all this bastard's lies."

Anger and hatred had flushed out the sickness. Sally finally had the strength to stay upright unaided. She pushed herself away from the sphere at her back and hunched, balling her fists. Just one chance, that's all she wanted.

"You're going to rescue the Jews and stick them on a perfect planet in this insane universe, and everything will be fine and dandy?" she told Eva. "I've seen an example of this prick's utopias. It's not so bloody wonderful, is it?"

Professor Backenforth studied her in silence. Sally jabbed her finger at Eva.

"There's still murder and hatred. I saw my mate Pash, my real friend, shoot a defenceless priest in the back of the skull for revenge, gun the poor shit down in cold blood. What are you going to do in your new world, Eva? Torture Nazi children as payback for the ones they experimented on?"

Eva strode up to Sally and slapped her hard. Sally's head smacked into the metal behind her and her mouth filled with wet iron. Instinctively she threw a punch. The other woman caught her wrist in one hand and thumped her on the cracked rib with the other. Sally yelled and fell to her knees, forehead on cold rock. Glittering words ran over her attacker's boots inches in front of her face. If she'd had the energy Sally would have yanked Eva's feet from under her, but the pain had sucked all air out of her lungs.

"Fucking bitch," she managed to gasp.

"How dare you," Eva spat, so angry her voice felt like handfuls of razor blades rubbed into Sally's ears. "You and your kind have absolutely no idea what suffering is, what we have endured. I saw your world with all its pretence, lies and evasion. Just twenty years later, and the excuses and the forgetting had already started. I chose you because I wanted your friendship, and to give you this gift. Maybe I should dump you back in that shithole city of yours."

"Go on then," Sally muttered into the ground. "I don't want any part of this. Send me back."

"Please. Children," Professor Backenforth said. "This petty

squabbling doesn't help. Sally, nobody has to kill or torture or hurt anyone. Pash asked for Father Agustí to try to purge the hatred poisoning her own heart and so I indulged her. Eva wants nothing like that in the last world of my universe. I offered and she told me no."

"How very noble," Sally said, rolling onto her arse and trying to work out if her rib had cracked again.

"And you shall have whatever you want in your utopia. If you wish for revenge, to spite all those who sneered at you, then it can be arranged."

"I'll have this fucking liar for a start," she growled. Eva shook her head, sad faced all of a sudden, and went to help her to her feet. A snarl drove her back. It took a while but Sally managed to stand by herself.

"So you fooled me into thinking you were my best friend, that together we'd destroy this smug bastard and free everyone. But you were in it from the very start, helping him kidnap Anthony, luring me with all your lovely toys. When those insects captured Pash was that your doing also? It did seem a bit of a coincidence, you rolling up and saving me at the last minute. It's all been one big lie, hasn't it, from the first time you spoke to me in the playground? And I fell for it. Poor, pathetic, stupid Sally, a mug to think you cared. Mum was right. It was all in my bloody imagination wasn't it?"

Eva looked oddly hurt. She stood a little way back, between Anthony Mendelssohn's Mystery Planet and a ball decorated with landscapes straight out of a Constable painting. She shook her head ever so slightly, eyes suggesting that she wanted to say something more to Sally.

"Don't bother. I'm not interested in your excuses, or your pity."

Sally turned and ran. Her chest hurt like buggery and she almost tripped over her own feet as more nausea and dizziness welled up inside her head. With one hand clamped to her side and the other flailing at the spheres to stop herself colliding with those cold metal surfaces, she lurched towards the end of the row. Dodging sideways into the maze would buy her time but Sally was past caring. All she wanted to do was flee this place, get as far away from the cruelty and betrayal as possible.

"Sally, wait!" Eva shouted.

Let her go.

She didn't know if Professor Backenforth had said those words or she'd only heard them in her mind. The Mystery Planets fell away on either side. She kept running across the shining rock. *Don't stop, don't look back.* The plain swallowed her up and she became nothing more than a tiny insect fleeing in unending desperation beneath the ash and blood sky. *Don't stop because if you do, you'll think, and remember, and understand precisely how little you mattered to anyone in the end.*

Eventually her legs and lungs gave out. Glancing over her shoulder, she spotted the spheres. They were no bigger than a cluster of pinheads sticking out of the ground. Sally kept walking. The pain in her ribcage had settled into a dull ache. If she started crying or screaming it'd hurt. She had no desire to do either. In fact, she had no desire to do anything other than trudge into oblivion.

The ground ahead changed. A black slash in the rock became a square mouth. Sally found herself on the edge of a shaft several yards across. It dropped into darkness. A metal staircase spiralled down the walls and she thought she saw a couple of pale lights far below. It had to be the stairwell. It certainly looked like it. The faint smell of rot wafted up on a cold current of air. Hundreds of miles down to the lobby, she reckoned, and then beyond that into unfathomable depths. She remembered Angus pointing his rifle downwards, telling her they'd put tripwires and mines on the steps, just in case those that lived in the basement levels fancied their chances higher up.

It had to be the main route up through the Blocko Tower. If she wanted to leave this place she had two choices - the slow climb past level after level, flanked by nightmares and monsters, or the quick and easy method. Sally sat on the edge of the shaft, legs dangling in the void. Could she be bothered to descend all that way? Even if she made the lobby there'd still be the driving game map and then the real world. The Fiat 500 was outside her old house. Christ knew where the keys were, probably dropped during some fight or scramble to safety. She'd have to get the bus into the city centre, change at least twice, and then out again to Wharfedale, but she had no money either. Find a phone box, reverse the charges, and beg her mum and dad for a lift?

Tell your father he's got to talk to me. It's not fair. When are you coming up? I'm so lonely.

Screw that. The easy way then. She stood up, took a few steps back to give herself a run-up, closed her eyes, and jumped into the shaft.

Something grabbed her around the waist, clamping down on her chest so she yelled out at the pain from her rib. She looked down and saw claws the colour of midnight. A vast hand bore her up into the air. She screamed and struggled to be free, but the talons lifted her in front of Professor Backenforth's face, still in shadow, but as big as a mountain. It had an expression of bemused disappointment, the same indulgent smile Grandma wore when her favourite little girl had been naughty. The head span away and creation turned upside down. A row of spheres appeared above her, all closed save two. Their tiny mouths swelled as she raced towards them. The demon's grip shifted to one ankle. Suspended by her leg, Sally thrashed and screamed, her cries lost beneath the churning heavens. Ever so carefully, Professor Backenforth lowered her into a Mystery Planet. She tried to grab the lip but her hands slipped and she fell into new clouds full of coloured lights. The hatch clanged shut and Professor Backenforth's spells tore her mind to pieces.

CHAPTER NINETEEN

Moortown, Leeds, 1967

One day Sally wet herself in the playground. She begged the others not to tell the teacher, promising each of them in turn that she'd be their best friend forever. It didn't work. They pointed and went AAAAAHHH, all round-eyed and round-mouthed, and told on her. Mrs Ryan came outside, shouted at them for being wicked and locked them inside the cages. She told the crying Creeple Peeple that the funny men would come for them as punishment for being so mean to someone who'd just had a simple accident. They shook the bars and said they were so sorry. Mrs Ryan was very firm and told them that for the rest of the day only Sally would be allowed to take part in the lessons. Those that were still alive at home time might, just might, be permitted to come back inside tomorrow, but only if they promised to be on their best behaviour.

Mrs Ryan changed Sally into a spare set of knickers and a dress from the class cupboard, and told her not to be sad. The new clothes were designed by Mary Quant. They were covered in black and white squares and circles, just like her teacher's. Sally felt ever so glamorous. At first it was hard to concentrate on her colouring-in because of all the shouting and screaming from outside, but that soon died down. At 11 o'clock she fetched her own bottle of milk from the crate and sipped it under the dinosaur poster, trying to work out how to pronounce all the names.

At lunchtime Sally stood in the far corner of the playground and looked at the broken cages, wondering if any of the Creeple Peeple had escaped the funny men. It made her feel a little bit sad but at least nobody was there to tease her.

Her new mother was very happy to let Sally make her own way home, seeing as how she was such a big girl now. Mr Cooper, Mrs Ryan and Miss Pritchard gathered in the playground to wave her off. They told her what an excellent pupil she'd been and stuck a gold star on the Mary Quant dress. She was to go home straight away. They also warned her to keep in mind her Kerb Drill just in case Gareth the Policeman was about. She didn't want to get eaten up, did she? Sally said of course not and set off down the path, waving at the teachers who smiled and waved back.

All the houses were closed, their windows full of darkness. A soft breeze ruffled Sally's hair. It smelled faintly of wood polish, carpets and some odd chemical. She recognised it as the scent of the Creeple Peeple, though she knew none of them would dare to be outside after what had happened in the playground.

There was a secret route that avoided the shops where the funny men and strange men might be waiting with bags of sweets and promises of puppies. It took her round the back of the garages and straight through to Nursery Lane. When Sally reached the zebra crossing a soldier made her stop and wait. A long line of people were walking slowly and sadly towards the woods next to the main road. Men, women and children in dark clothes shuffled past in a column. None of them looked happy and nobody glanced at her. They all fixed their gaze on the heels of the ones in front and trudged solemnly along. On either side of the street the men in uniforms stood and watched. Many of them had guns. Those that hadn't rested their fists on their hips or hooked thumbs into belts and peered down their noses at the passersby. Nobody spoke, not even the man who'd stuck his hand out to prevent Sally from trying to cross. He didn't bother to glance down at her from under his heavy grey helmet. The people took forever. When the last of them had gone, the soldier waved

Sally on and she skipped over the crossing, turned left and headed down the tree-lined avenue.

She was halfway along when she spotted Gareth the Policeman rising high above the houses at the far end. He looked as if he was standing at the edge of the wasteland, where it stretched down the hill to the woods and the golf course. He had his back to her, one arm by his side and the other raised in the halt gesture, palm out, long nails translucent against the pale grey sky. She told herself she didn't need to worry. She knew the Kerb Drill inside out. *At the Kerb, Stop! Look Right. Then Left. Then Right again. If All Is Clear Walk Quickly to the Other Side.* She'd easily answer his questions but still wasn't keen on having his big head loom over her, with those smeary eyes and that slimy pink tongue. She sneaked down a side street using giant tip-toe steps. It led to a cul-de-sac. In the garden of Number 12, Vicky Samson sunned herself on a blue plastic lounger. She wore a yellow polka dot bikini and alternately took a swig from the wine bottle in her right hand and a drag on the cigarette holder in her left.

"Don't dilly dally Sally," she sang, not unkindly, and waved her on.

"Thank you, Mrs Samson." Sally said and ran quickly down their drive, past the wrecked car and the shattered tree, and into the orchard at the back of the garden. She scooched through the gap in the Samson's fence, scampered across a lawn and out onto another street. That led straight home without her having to go past Gareth the Policeman. He was still standing among the tall grasses and red hot pokers in the empty field way over to her left, rotating slowly on the spot, watching out for anyone who didn't know their Kerb Drill.

When Sally arrived home, Charlotte, her new mother, was busy preparing tea in the kitchen. It was a bit of a squeeze. Her bonnet scraped against the ceiling and her wooden tail stretched out into the hall, scratching the purple polystyrene floorboards. Whatever she was cooking smelled delicious and made Sally's tummy rumble.

"There are presents for you in the lounge," Charlotte called out. "Someone's a very lucky girl."

A huge parcel sat on the sofa, with a smaller package on top. The little one had her address in loopy writing. The stamp said *SELLO EDITORIAL* and showed a woman's head with the name *Rafaella Concepcion* underneath. The portrait rang a faint bell but Sally couldn't remember where she'd seen the lady before. The big box was far more interesting and exciting. She put the padded envelope to one side and tore apart the brown paper and string. This present had no stamps on it. She wondered who it was from.

Several boxes fell out. *Sally Aston Play Set*. Wow. A toy named after her and it looked so fab. It reminded her of Action Man, which had always seemed far more interesting than the dolls and Barbies. This was clearly for a very grown-up girl. The Sally Aston doll came in a narrow cardboard box with a picture of a pretty young woman in a plaid skirt, red boots and leather jacket.

The other containers were larger and had clear plastic windows so you could see inside. *Sally Aston Kickboxer*, *Sally Aston Student*, *Sally Aston Ace Reporter*. They included other figurines and various pieces of equipment and clothes for Sally to wear, all fastened to the backing card with yellow thread. She'd need to be very careful with scissors to get them out without breaking anything. By squinting and holding the packages up to the light she could read the names of the characters on the labels inside - *Bogdan the Bit of a Cunt, Gary the Total Bell-end, Bob the Pot-Head* - he came with a comic called *Leather Nun*, a little three-bar electric fire and a fat dog whose name was Lemmy. You had to cut open the boxes to make panoramas - a grubby warehouse office, or a wrestling ring like the one on Saturday afternoon telly.

Heart thumping with excitement, she opened the Sally Aston box and pulled the doll out. Wow and triple Wow. It was exactly like an Action Man with jointed legs and arms and real hair in a raggedy brown mop. Sally glanced at the kitchen. Charlotte was fiddling with the cooker and had her back to the lounge. Sally peeked inside the t-shirt and skirt. All the boys had joked about Action Man not having a willy but this figurine had realistic plastic boobs with sharp red nipples, and a patch of black felt between her thighs. Sally hurriedly re-arranged its clothes and stared into its face, feeling weird. Pale blue eyes just like her own, though the nose looked a bit odd - ever so slightly skew-whiff with a small bump on the arch.

Sally studied the doll, then the rest of play sets. She felt tearful and overwhelmed. All these wonderful things and it wasn't even her birthday.

"Let me see," Charlotte came creaking into the room. She gently took the figure from Sally with her wooden fingers and brought it up to her bonnet, near the glass eyes that gave off a pale radiance and picked out the edge of her sharp iron nose. She turned her head this way and that.

"What a lovely doll."

"She's Big Sally."

"Big Sally? And you're Little Sally. That is funny."

Charlotte held the toy up, as if comparing the heights of her and her daughter. Sally giggled. But it was true. She was Little Sally because she was six, whereas the grown-up doll came with boobs, and hair on her foofoo and under her armpits, just like she would have one day. Hence 'Big Sally'.

"I think you got this as a special present for being so good at school today. Mr Cooper, Mrs Ryan and Miss Pritchard phoned to tell me, so well done you. Now come and have tea and you can play with all these lovely new toys afterwards."

She had sausages and Heinz Beans and chips. Afterwards, she watched *Betty Boop* on the telly and then it was time for bed. Charlotte had carried all her presents up to her room. After warm milk, cuddles and another chapter from *The Phantom Tollbooth*, her new mother left her to her own devices before lights out at 9 o'clock sharp.

She spotted the other package lying on the carpet. It must have fallen off the pile. It was tightly wrapped with parcel tape. Eventually she managed to open the thick envelope and empty the contents onto the counterpane - a ViewMaster reel inside a piece of paper folded in half to protect it. Sally read the message.

Dear Sally. I am sorry you went away. I know you think what I did was wrong, but the priest was a bad man and hurt a lot of my comrades. We had a nice time at the party, so please come again, and let's be best friends. Rafaella.

Rafaella Concepcion. She looked at the stamp with its tiny portrait. The name Pash popped into her head. Wasn't that the name of one of the stars in the sky? Sally fetched her ViewMaster from the top shelf and slotted in the new disc.

She saw lots of scenes of a town full of white buildings under a bright blue sky, with smiling men and women dancing and eating at long tables outside cafes. It looked fun. Later on the images showed two women at night-time, sitting side by side and looking up at the stars, their heads touching. The one on the left looked awfully like her new Big Sally doll.

Her Batman clock told her it was 9 already. She moved all the toy boxes onto the floor and turned out the light. She kept Big Sally to hand. The doll could sleep with her tonight. Before snuggling under the covers, she knee-walked along the mattress to the window and looked out between the curtains at the night sky.

The bright matrix of stars spread away into the darkness. She picked up her toy binoculars from the windowsill and tried to get a closer look. She knew the names of three - *Anthony, Marcus, Hannah*. Some of the others were called after people's jobs or a type of person - *Sailor, Poetess, Old Man, Shepherd*. She knew that each one had its own planet, even though the binoculars weren't strong enough to show her. Charlotte had told her that the world they lived on was called *Sally*. Her own planet, full of lovely things and kind friends. A shadow moved in the street below. She glanced down and saw the shape of a lion stretched out over the tarmac, huge and languid. The beast paced slowly by, looking for naughty girls not yet asleep. Sally jumped into bed and squeezed up next to Big Sally, comforted by the sharp knobs of the doll's plastic elbows pressed against her cheek.

Next morning, she was so excited to play with her new action figure that she got up at daybreak and carefully unpacked the *Kickboxer Play Set*, dressing the toy woman in white pyjamas with a black belt. According to the story book tucked into the back of the box, Bogdan the Bit of A Cunt broke Sally's nose by accidentally kicking her in the face, at which point she threw him to the floor and started pounding the living shit out of him, until the instructor pulled her off, said she was a fucking psycho head case, and made her sit at the edge of the ring until she'd calmed down. All great fun.

It was Saturday so after breakfast she asked Charlotte if she could play outside for a while. Her new mother said yes, warned her about the funny men and remembering the Kerb Drill, and pushed her out into the garden. Sally skipped down the road towards the woods, her Start-Rites tapping on the pavement where the town hall lion had walked the night before. There was no sign of Gareth the Policeman rising above the rooftops. When Sally got to the bottom of the street, she followed the track that ran between the edge of the woods and the wasteland. Tall grass and red hot pokers waved in the breeze on both sides. Later on she'd make a maze by stamping her way through the high weeds.

Something seemed odd about the trees today. Usually she didn't go inside because they bothered her. The forest path formed a bright ribbon dwindling away to the north. The spaces between the trunks were full of darkness. It was so gloomy and dense it looked like water, as if she stood outside a dirty aquarium. Sally never stepped between the oaks and elms because she'd end up trapped on the other side of the glass, among the shapeless ones that twisted and slid over the hummocks and between the bushes and lichen. The feeling was stronger this morning, much stronger, as if someone studied her from deep within. Maybe she didn't want to make a maze after all. It'd be fun, and feel a lot safer, to head back home and try out the *Student Play Set* with Gary the Total Bell-End.

"Hello? Sally?"

She glanced around. A lady stood just on the edge of the forest. She was tall and pretty with black curly hair and big brown eyes, but a stern expression. She wore strange grey clothes covered in glowing letters. The yellow symbols drifted over her arms, legs and chest.

"Sally. Is that you?"

"Yes."

The woman looked worried and sad. She glanced around and bit her lip.

"This? This is your perfect world?"

"Yes."

The way the newcomer said it made Sally a little cross. What was the matter with it? It was lovely.

"It's not supposed to be as bad as this. I didn't realise the virus would have such an impact. How old are you?"

"Six."

"Oy vey! Do you know who I am?"

Sally shook her head. The lady pointed at herself.

"Eva. I'm Eva. Remember?"

Sally shook her head.

Eva came forward and Sally took a step back, wishing she could run away or call out to Charlotte. What would Big Sally do? Throw this horrible grownup to the floor and pound the living shit out of her, that's what she'd do. Eva hunkered down and grabbed Sally's hand in her cold fingers. She tried to pull back. The woman held on tight, peering into Sally's eyes.

"Are you in there, Sally? It's me. Eva. You're inside the Mystery Planet, the last one Professor Backenforth needed. He doesn't know I'm here. I need to you do something for me."

Sally didn't want to do anything for her. The way she said it made it sound as if she was going to be asked to be naughty and not tell anyone. She knew what happened to people who did that. The Creeple Peeple had found out yesterday afternoon after they were mean to her for wetting herself.

"You'll get a special visitor soon. I want you to say to her..."

Sally yanked her hand free, turned and ran.

"Sally! SALLY!" Eva called after her. "Come back!"

She was terrified the stranger would chase after her, grab her and carry her off. She glanced over her shoulder but the woman still stood just inside the trees, as if there really was a sheet of dirty aquarium glass stopping her from following. Even so, Sally didn't slow down until she reached home, anxiously hopping up and down outside until the front of the building swung down and she could run into Charlotte's wooden arms.

When Sally told her what had happened, her new mother headed outside. The smell coming through the letterbox told her Charlotte was very angry and looking to fight whatever had upset her daughter. Sally went upstairs and got the bath ready, adding half a box of Radox. It turned the water fluorescent purple and the perfume nearly knocked her out. Next Sally found her new doll, still in the kickboxer clothes, and propped her up on the windowsill facing outwards. She knelt beside and peered down the street and waited.

Some time later she heard the sound of the hosepipe in the garden. She'd just got to the part in the *Sally Aston Student Play Set* story where Big Sally had finished doing rudey-dudies with Gary the Total Bell-End in the toy bed, and had realised he was a complete nob for asking stupid questions about a hotel. She opened her bedroom window and pinched her nose while Charlotte went into the bathroom. After fifteen minutes of splashing her new mother went back downstairs. By that time a slightly embarrassed Sally had dressed her action figure and returned Gary and the rest of the bits to the box.

Charlotte was unusually quiet at lunchtime. Sally munched her ham and cheese doorstep sandwich while her new mother watched with her pale glass eyes.

"Did you see the woman?" Sally finally had the courage to ask.

"Yes. I had a word with her. She didn't mean any harm, but won't bother you any more." Silence. When her daughter had finished eating, Charlotte gave her a Fondant Fancy as a special treat and an empty tumbler, which was odd. The doorbell rang. Sally jumped, thinking it might be the woman who called herself Eva. When Charlotte answered the door she heard a different voice.

A tall thin lady, with grey hair tied back in a bun and National Health spectacles, stood in the kitchen doorway and smiled at her. Sally thought she looked a bit stern and scary.

"Hi Sally," she held up a bottle of lemon barley water, not Robinsons but some other type she hadn't come across before. While her new mother poured some into the glass and topped it up from the tap, the woman sat down opposite and reached into her bag to pull out a set of cards.

"My name is Florence and I'm a special kind of doctor for very clever children. I want to play a game with you. Your mummy said yes, I could. Is that OK with you?"

Charlotte put the drink on the table and gave her daughter's shoulder a squeeze with her wooden hand. Florence had a nice smile. Sally nodded and looked expectantly at the cards lying face down on the Formica top. The visitor turned the first one over.

"This is the Nabik from the planet Veela in the 2nd Galaxy."

Sally stared at the picture. The monster had a head like a dried cherry and stood in front of a green city. It wore a blue coat but didn't seem to have any arms. The alien glowered back with button eyes set inside deep wrinkles. It made her feel uncomfortable and she squirmed on her seat.

"And this is the Klopan from Pargos in the 6th Galaxy." The eyes were bigger now, like frogspawn, the clothes bright yellow and red. "They are hard and cruel, difficult to befriend and they mistrust Earthmen."

She wished she had Big Sally with her. She'd throw this frightening monster to the floor and pound the living shit out of it. Florence studied her carefully but not unkindly.

"Why don't you have some lemon barley water?" she said.

Sally took a couple of mouthfuls. It was made precisely to the sweet and sticky consistency she liked. When she looked again at the freaky alien it didn't seem quite so frightening. She giggled a little at its face and clothes.

"Last one," Florence said, flipping over the final card. Sally gasped and jumped half out of the chair, almost knocking the glass onto the kitchen floor. Charlotte gave her shoulder another squeeze.

"Alright, it's only a picture," she said.

Florence tapped the image.

"The Chernod from the Planet Cupor in the 7th Galaxy is very mischievous but friendly."

Her new mother filled the tumbler again and handed it to Sally. She drank it slowly, the rim hiding the red eyes and long blond hair, the black claws and tubby blue body. She peeked, ducked down to sip a little more, and looked again. Actually, now she thought of it, the Chernod was almost as daft as the Klopan, and perhaps that burning gaze was friendly after all.

"So if you met any of these, would you be worried?" Florence asked.

Sally shrugged.

"Are they real?"

Florence ignored the question.

"When we're frightened of something it's important to face it and not run away or hide our eyes," she said. "That way we will come to understand that our scariest nightmares are not all that bad. Even Queen Death herself can seem a friend if we shake her hand."

Sally looked at Florence.

"Queen Death?"

The woman gave her a kind smile.

"Queen Death and her companions are our closest allies."

What an odd thing to say.

"What's an ally?"

"Someone who fights on your side," Florence said.

"People were scared of me once, because of how I look," Charlotte chipped in. "When they came to know me, and to understand why I'm like this, they realised I wasn't horrible and scary at all. Do you think I'm frightening?"

Sally shook her head.

"Of course not. You're my new mother."

Florence gathered up the cards and handed them to Sally. At first she hesitated, but the faces of the Nabik, the Klopan and the Chernod no longer made her gut churn and her heart thump.

"Take them. Introduce them to your new doll," the doctor

stood up. "You've been a model pupil. Such a bright child." She stroked Sally's hair. "For being so co-operative I reckon your mummy will let you have one last glass of my special lemon barley water before bedtime."

"I'm sure we can make exception this once," Charlotte said, showing their visitor to the front door.

CHAPTER TWENTY

Sally had a very odd dream that night. She was walking down her street towards the lane that ran between the wasteland and the woods, wheeling a red bicycle with white tyres. Everywhere looked peculiar. Instead of bright paper and coloured plastic, the houses were dull and oddly textured, as if they'd been formed out of lots of pieces of rough stone, painted wood and, in some cases, thousands of pebbles stuck in dried clay on the fronts and sides. Even the road was different - grainy and black. The sky was heavy with cloud. A cold wind blew between the buildings, stirring litter in the gutters. Normally the town hall lions made sure everything outside was kept neat and tidy.

The trees looked different too. Usually the thick gloom came right up to the edge of the woods. This morning, despite the overcast sky, the daylight stretched between the trunks, turning the darkness into corridors filled with a thousand shades of green, punctuated with dusty columns of sunlight. The path no longer looked like a white thread stitched through black velvet. Instead, Sally found herself staring down a tube lined with fluttering leaves and flickers of dust kicked up from the sandy trail.

"Hello Sally."

A girl the same age as her stood at the entrance. She had dark curly hair, a blue coat that had seen better days, and scuffed Start-Rites. The newcomer watched her with big serious eyes the colour of acorns.

"My name's Eva. Do you want to come and play with my toys?"

"Yes please"

"But first we need to get you out of here."

Eva turned and skipped down the path. She had a big yellow star sewn onto her coat. The sky beyond the treetops grew black. Sally glanced up and saw an immense shadow rising up into the clouds, which parted as if frightened of its touch. All those windows, all that darkness, all ready to fall on her. Fingers as sharp as knives grabbed her wrists. Terrified, she looked down, straight into the face of a woman she didn't recognise - vast and filled with hatred, spit-laced words bursting out between nicotine-stained teeth.

"EIGHT FUCKING HOURS, YOU STUPID WICKED LITTLE SHIT."

Sally cried out and sat up in bed, back in the soft silence of her room. The walls were still made of polystyrene. She could see the mould seams around the door and the wire connecting the ceiling light bulb to the battery in the attic. Charlotte's voice floated up the stairs. She was talking to someone on the telephone and hadn't heard her daughter. Sally grabbed the Big Sally Action Figure and hugged it tight. She'd left it sitting on top of the cards Florence had given her, just in case she decided that the aliens were too scary after all. Pressing the bony doll to her face, she picked the top one up. It was the Chernod and her stomach flipped briefly, but in reality he did look a bit daft. Big Sally would give him what for.

After the bad dream she was still anxious for some grownup comfort, so she padded onto the landing. Charlotte filled the hallway downstairs, bonnet angled down as she held the receiver in her claw.

"I'll give her some more at breakfast," she was saying. "There's no sign of the policeman. I think it moved down towards Briggate. We'll check again but unless you hear from me assume that everything's fine. You can land on the field at the back, by the woods."

Charlotte hung up and saw Sally at the top of the stairs.

"Come on slug-a-bed. Skates on."

A full glass of lemon barley water sat next to her bowl of Rice Krispies.

"Won't that make my teeth bad?"

"Not if you give them a good brush afterwards."

She wondered whether to tell her new mother about the nightmare, but decided not to. In the light of the morning it didn't have the same hold over her, especially with the Big Sally doll sitting on the seat next to hers.

"Did you have a think about what Florence said, how we shouldn't be frightened of strange things like those Krazy Kreatures from Outer Space she showed you?"

Sally nodded.

"And our scariest nightmares are not all that bad, not even Queen Death and her companions. If you ever met her, what would you do?"

A couple of glugs of the sticky drink gave her a moment to think her answer through. What had the doctor said yesterday?

"I'd take her hand."

"Attagirl. Finish up, clean your teeth, and then you can play outside with your new toy. Shame to waste such a lovely Sunday by staying indoors."

She took the *Sally Aston Student Play Set* onto the front lawn, this time with Bob and his dog in the grubby warehouse. Big Sally was going to tell him off for reading his comic, *Tales from the Leather Nun*. Sally herself had tried to make out the tiny pictures and words, first with a magnifying glass, then her toy microscope. A few pages in, she decided not to persist. The story was very odd. Most of the characters didn't have any clothes on and the whole thing made her tummy feel deeply weird.

After half an hour or thereabouts, Charlotte came outside with another drink and a couple of biscuits. Truth be told, Sally was getting sick of the same squash all the time and was about to ask for milk instead, when her new mother looked up at the sky, shielding her glass eyes.

"Hello, what's this?" she said in that exaggerated tone grownups sometimes used when they were only pretending to be surprised. "Look. There! See?"

A dot hovered in the void, black against the rich aquamarine sky. Sally realised it was a disc descending towards the houses.

"A flying saucer," Charlotte exclaimed. "How exciting. Whoever can it be?"

The spaceship drifted over the roofs. It looked like two Mexican hats glued together at the rims and painted with concentric rings in white, red and yellow. A glass dome rose from the upper half and three legs poked down from the bottom. The craft hummed for a few moments over the house before moving down towards the end of the road. It angled left and disappeared behind the buildings.

"It must have landed. Let's go and see."

The arrival of the flying saucer suggested something exciting, but scary too. Charlotte held out her hand and Sally took it, carrying her new doll in the other, safe in the knowledge that both would protect her. Bob and Lemmy the dog could wait.

The craft had landed among the red hot pokers and high meadow grasses, just at the edge of the lane that ran past the woods. Darkness filled the spaces between the trees, rich and brown like the turtle soup her new mother sometimes made. No sign of the long corridors of light in the dream, or the tower that had threatened to crush her.

A ramp angled down from the bottom of the ship. Three figures waited beside it - the Chernod, the Nabik and the Klopan. Sally juddered to a halt without thinking, pulling Charlotte back. The new mother turned and hunkered down to look into her eyes. Her riveted iron and glass face smiled into hers, sharp copper teeth sparkling in the morning light. It was much friendlier than the nightmare woman and her horrible shouting.

"Florence and I prepared a special treat for you. A trip into outer space! But we knew you might find our alien friends scary, which is why she came and visited you last night and showed you their pictures first. The lemon barley water had special medicine inside to get your body ready for the journey."

Sally leaned sideways to look past Charlotte at the Chernod. She remembered how, as she'd sipped her drink, his red gaze softened and his tubby blue body appeared more ridiculous than alarming.

"Are you coming too, Mummy?"

"I'm afraid I'm far too heavy," Charlotte said. "If I went on board the flying saucer it would never take off again. Besides, you're a big girl now, who can walk home from school by herself. You don't need a mummy to come with you anymore, do you?"

Sally supposed not. Charlotte stood up and stepped back.

"She's all yours."

The Chernod waddled up and took Sally's hand. His black-tipped fingers were made from soft rubber and he smelled like a bag of sweets. He even had a seam. It ran down from under his beard, between his legs, and up the middle of his back.

The Klopan turned and floated up the ramp, followed by the Nabik. Sally allowed herself to be led inside. Three seats faced outwards towards the edge of the glass-domed cabin, with a fourth raised on a plinth in the middle, angled so whoever sat in it would have a perfect view. Sally was still apprehensive, but Charlotte had said everything would be ok and she trusted her new mother. All her fears of the creatures dissipated with the overpowering smell of bubble gum and memories of lemon barley water.

The Chernod guided her to the centre couch, holding her hand like a prince helping a princess into her carriage, and fastened a seat belt over her chest and around her tummy. He made sure that Big Sally was tucked inside the straps as well. He patted the two of them on their shoulders, doll's and girl's, and joined his companions down at the controls. As the flying saucer lifted into the sky, Sally saw her new mother making her way back up the street towards home.

The vessel tilted forwards and aimed for the horizon, which started to curve as they rose higher into the cloudless blue. The streets and buildings of Leeds clumped together and flattened into an immense square. Far away to the right, on the other side of the River Ouse, Sally saw a thin column ending in a bright sphere rise out of the cityscape, taller even than the blocks of flats on the old bomb sites. As the ship accelerated, more squares appeared in the distance, set in the green and brown wastelands of Yorkshire, each with its own ball and rod sticking into the air. She guessed they were other cities like York, Bradford and Harrogate.

Although Sally couldn't feel the changes of direction and speed, her head fooled her into thinking she was riding a roller-coaster. She was so busy concentrating on catching her breath whenever her stomach flipped, she didn't notice the exact point at which the sky turned from blue to black. In an instant, the vessel was floating into a night void. The only illumination inside the cabin came from the dials and screens. She found it hard to make out her three companions. As she watched, the vessel tilted again, and the matrix of stars swung into view.

She gasped. Outside the toytown landscape, without an atmosphere to deaden the effect, the suns burned with a steady fury. Each looked identical, as if dropped from the same jeweller's mould and soldered into an invisible mathematical net. She picked out the fine chords stretching from each into the blackness. With all frames of reference removed, there was no way of telling which star was which. She guessed her own world lay somewhere behind her, but with all those dips and turns the ship might have been facing in any direction. If one of those suns below was hers, it was impossible to tell.

She shifted in her seat and stared at the backs of the Krazy Kreatures.

"Where are we going?"

No answer. They seemed about as alive as silhouettes made out of smoky glass. Like the Wodaran in Eva's attic. That brought her up with a start. Why these three and not the creature who'd appeared to her when she was little?

When I was little.

Sally examined her hands, front and back. Callouses on her

knuckles from endlessly punching makiwara boards, and in the creases of her palm from weight lifting when she'd gone a bit mental with the combat training in her second year at university.

She pulled the doll out from under the strap around her stomach. Nauseatingly cute, with a bright red coat and shiny shoes, all wide-eyed and innocent, off to play with the squirrels and pixies in the wood. *Little Sally*. Memories of a smaller, simpler mind bounced through her skull. The sphere had screwed with her brain as soon as she'd climbed inside. This time, instead of a Catalan-speaking anarchist, she'd returned to her six-year-old self in some weird Betty Boop cartoon version of an infant's dreams, living in a plastic house in a giant driving game with - Jesus H. Christ - Charlotte the rotting monster as her mother. What had Eva said?

"This? This is your perfect world?"

All her friend's treachery spilled into her head, curdling her gut and making her twist against the restraints. That lying bitch had sold her out to Professor Backenforth. From the very first time she'd come up to her in the playground, invited her to play in the flat with all those cool toys, yanked her out of the room full of bugs, it'd been part of a grand betrayal. Conning silly Sally, pathetic Sally, no, fucking moronic Sally, into thinking she'd always had a best friend just out of reach, waiting to be found again. Kid her into some great quest against evil, bring her to the plain of spheres, and stuff her inside the last but one. Eva wanted to save the Jews, gather them up from throughout all of history, and give them sanctuary on a magic planet in this fake universe, free from persecution and extermination. Very noble and all that, but Sally was the sacrifice. Why? Why pick on her? Couldn't Eva have chosen some blond-haired blue-eyed Nazi brat instead, the sprog of one of those bastards who'd murdered her family? Because Sally's miserable childhood made her a prime candidate, that's why, a venomous combination of loneliness and desperation to find Eva, and thereby prove to her bitch of a mother she'd told the truth on that horrible day.

So where was this now? The ship couldn't be inside the sphere

247

anymore because she'd changed back into her real self. Judging by the lattice of stars, the flying saucer still flew through Professor Backenforth's universe. They hadn't returned to Sally's own space and time, or the realm of the tower.

Bugger caution. She unhitched herself from the seat and stepped down into the cabin, momentarily surprised when she didn't start floating around like an astronaut. The bridge was empty apart from herself. Perhaps those faded afterimages in the corner of her eye were the shadowy echoes of the three Krazy Kreatures. The controls still glowed. When she came closer, they turned out to be screen-printed fluorescent decals, clumsily stuck onto the plastic consoles.

She peered through the badly moulded perspex canopy. Now she could see the sun from her own perfect world off to the right, as large as an orange. The vessel changed course, aiming for the pale thread running from its boiling surface into the darkness. What had Pash said? The stars drew their power from dynamos in other universes. Was that where they were heading, to the energy source for her own star. Why? To turn it off?

There was nothing to do, no-one to speak to, and no working controls to try and commandeer. Sally hadn't a clue how long the journey would take - hours, days, centuries? Was she going to end up a skeleton floating through empty space in a plastic flying saucer? Logic said she ought to be frightened but exhaustion and anger had numbed everything to the point of indifference. When was the last time she'd enjoyed anything approaching normality, stood in a place that didn't mess with her head? She'd have given her right arm for a pint of Theakstons and a bag of scraps from the local chippy. No chance, far too normal for a cosmos seemingly fuelled by lemon barley water and bubble gum.

Sally climbed back into the couch and stared up at nothing. After a while she dozed off. A weight vanished from her hand and something thumped onto the cabin floor. *Little Sally*. She didn't bother retrieving the doll.

The first couple of times she opened her eyes it looked as though the ship had left the star grid way behind. The canopy was full of midnight, save for a faint ribbon stretching ahead like a misty road. The third time, Sally jackknifed out of the chair. She hadn't bothered to refasten the harness so she slid off the seat and landed painfully on her arse at the foot of the pedestal.

The saucer appeared to be rapidly descending down an immense iron pipe. Segments flashed by, clamped to each other with rivets she suspected were as big as a planet. There was no visible entrance above. The seams dwindled into an infinity of receding circles. Sally hadn't a clue how long she'd been here. Maybe she'd slept a few hours at most. The translucent power line had also vanished. Was this another universe, the one that supplied her star with energy, or somewhere altogether different? She hoped to God it didn't consist of yet more bizarre confections from someone's dreams, full of twisted toys fashioned in service to a lunatic's idea of utopia.

The walls vanished and the ship continued to drop down through an immense landscape. Beneath a honey-coloured sky, sharp mountains stretched away on all sides. Valleys and cliffs rose up around her, some paint-flecked with lights that might have been cities spread over their endless fractal surfaces. A second later, she was back in the shaft.

After a few moments, the scene repeated itself. She emerged from the pipe above a ragged terrain of what appeared to be black sandstone broken into ravines and escarpments. The saucer fell like a stone into the cracked depths and back into another shaft. And again, this time the scenery seemed softer with miles-high crags muted by endless forests. Sally thought she caught sight of an ocean in the distance, reflecting the dull amber sky. She noticed more lights, bundled together in immense clusters joined by tenuous threads. Vast cities, perhaps, though these weren't coloured with bright neon or yellow sodium, but duller ochres, purples and greens. They carried with them the disturbing hint of luminescent decay.

As more and more of these vistas swept past, punctuated by thousands of miles of dull iron, Sally tried to get a sense of where she was. It was almost as if the vessel was descending the Blocko

Tower stairwell, but instead of corridors and rooms on each floor, this insane place had entire worlds. Did that mean she'd eventually hit the basement? The vessel was accelerating. Now each realm only appeared for few seconds, then an instant, until finally they were nothing but flickering bands of light punctuating the inside of the pipe.

Sally sat in the reclining chair, letting the rhythm lull her into malevolent reveries, chiefly to do with finding and killing Eva. If she eventually got out of this and had the chance, she'd hunt the bitch down and kick her head in for betraying every scrap of hope she'd ever had. Best friend, imaginary friend - her arse. The first and last user in a long line of users - Gary the Nob, George at the *Clarion*, Pash. All pretending to be her biggest pals, all simply out for what they could get, whether it was a meek and compliant fuck, the scoop of the century, or a new route to the top of Backenforth Heights. Sally didn't give a tin shit how noble the cause might be. Burning, sickening anger was all she had left. It was that, or the fearful knowledge she was probably going to die inside this cheap plastic toy in the middle of endless nowheres.

She couldn't even remember how she'd ended up here. On being dropped into the Mystery Planet by Professor Backenforth her brain had reverted to a six-year-old's. Whatever she'd seen and heard before boarding this ship was as clear as any other thought in a clueless infant's head. Half-images and words, coloured by childish obsessions. Eva had been there, she remembered that much, dressed in her scriptural armour and coming up with a load of gobbledygook about Sally's world and its visitors. Then there was something involving glass after glass of nauseatingly sweet lemon barley water. Christ, nothing of any use whatsoever.

Clutching at memories pushed her once more into sleepiness. She closed her eyes and dozed, and dreamed that she lay curled up on cold iron, the same material as the shaft walls. Its smell and taste filled her senses like old blood.

She opened her eyes and found herself in a vast room filled with ramps and platforms rising up into darkness. A soft wind made her shiver and she realised she was naked.

"God's sake. Now what?"

She lay on her side, looking at her hand. It seemed weird somehow - blotchy grey on top, bruised where it lay on the rusted metal. And what was that stink?

"Quickly," the voice was like two red hot knitting needles driven simultaneously into her ears. She clapped her palms to the side of her head. The skin of her temples was fever-hot and moved oddly, like thin tissue paper laid across jelly.

Impossibly long fingers, sheathed in a fine lacework glove of gold and silver, appeared in front of her face. Sally flinched back and lifted her own hand to her face because her nose felt like it was running. She wiped it and stared at the back of her wrist. Two thread-like worms writhed in a pool of snot, streaked with clotted blood and yellow pus. The smell grew worse.

"What's wrong with me? What's happening?"

Things broke in her mouth. A tooth, more than one, chalky and brittle, falling from her gums to dissolve on her tongue like rancid sweets.

"Quickly," the voice called out. A woman's, but odd, musical, echoing.

That pain again. Sally screamed. The hand grabbed her wrist and yanked her onto her feet. Her skin tore and along her forearm she saw white bone nestling in grey and purple meat. Someone snatched her other arm and she found herself yanked out into a human cross. She kicked and struggled, but the grinding in her knees and hips, and the splits opening up on her thighs, made her freeze in sick horror.

A tall, impossibly thin woman walked towards her, dressed in pale grey and black robes, wearing a gold filigree mask that covered her entire face. It curved over and around her head. Sally saw delicate white hair spilling through the spirals and curlicues at the sides.

"Please, please, bleeze, bler.." Sally begged as her mouth and jaw crumbled inside the flesh wrappings covering what was left of her skull. The newcomer set down a galvanised bucket with a clang. It was full of what looked like rotting mince mixed with lava, so hot that even at this distance the skin on her shins began to smoke and blacken. The woman scooped up a palmful, hand undamaged by the liquid. Sally drew on the last shreds of energy to pull away, to beg, to shriek for pity, but it was no good. The woman slapped the dripping magma on her breasts.

The agony was beyond thought. There was acid within the glowing sludge that chewed through Sally's skin and flesh, working in towards the bone. It hissed and popped. The fumes filled her eyes. She went insane. The hands moved swiftly over her torso, arms and legs, and she became nothing but unthinking pain and madness. Sharp fingers like broken branches covered in thorns stuffed the acid up her cunt and arse, working it around inside. They invaded her mouth. The creature held up a black, rotten tooth, dipped it in the mixture puddling in her palm, and pushed back into Sally's jaw. The poison was rammed so far into each ear she felt it curdle and destroy everything behind her eyes. Finally her attacker poked one globule up each nostril with her little finger, scratching around her sinuses as if trying to dislodge an intransigent bogey. The fragments of her broken nose grated against each other like shards of glass.

The hands let ago and Sally fell to the iron. Somewhere somebody was tearing a donkey to pieces. The poor animal wouldn't stop its braying even as they ripped it limb from limb. Sally clamped her hands over her mouth and the din stopped. Silence fell.

CHAPTER TWENTY-ONE

Shadows moved, climbed stairs and sat down. Sally scrabbled frantically away, banging up against a wall. She wrapped her arms around her knees and rocked backwards and forwards, singing all the while, the words mixing with the spittle running down her chin.

"Wodaran, Wodaran, Wodaran..."

How long did she sit there? Hours? Days? Years? The fear and madness glued her arse to the iron while she waited for the next torment, the next violation at the hands of these monstrous torturers. It never came. The hideous decay of her own body had stopped. Where were the splits in her thighs and arms? She unclenched her hands and looked at them, front and back. All normal. She ran her tongue around her teeth. No gaps, no stink. When she wiped the snot and dribble from her face, it was clear and maggot free.

Sally found the courage to look around.

"Sally Aston," a soft and gentle greeting. "Welcome. I am sorry for the terror and the pain. We had to move quickly to temper your flesh against my universe in order to keep you alive."

Narrow steps rose up to four chairs placed in a semi-circle on a platform at the other end of the immense room. A woman sat in each, all dressed like her tormentor. The only difference lay in their faces. Three wore masks - gold, silver and ebony. The one directly opposite was bare faced, but there was something about her expression, as beautiful as it appeared, that made Sally gasp and look away, terrified to sickness.

"What is this place and who are you?" she managed to ask.

"This is my realm and I am its queen. We brought you here to help us."

"I was in a spaceship. Where's it gone? I want to go home."

The woman plaited her hands at her waist and cocked her head slightly, like a teacher might express mild disapproval at a gobby pupil.

"Your realm?" Sally said eventually. A vague memory of faces carved on the surface of a jet black sphere nagged at the back of her tortured mind.

"Yes. I'm queen of this creation and these are my three companions - Bright, Gracious and Sweet." She gestured towards each.

The one called Bright unfurled languid fingers at a low table that had appeared at the foot of the steps.

"If you wish, you can dress yourself, and please eat."

A neatly laundered pile of clothes sat next to a pair of red boots. A full beer glass stood beside them, along with a newspaper packet spotted with grease.

"No way. I'm not touching it."

More silence. None of the figures moved. Maybe it was months later when Sally finally got to her feet, looking for an exit. The room had blank iron walls with no visible way in or out. At last she approached the clothes. Levis, jacket, M&S knickers, *Frankie Says Relax* t-shirt and a pair of socks. They still had the shop labels on them. It was ridiculous, but knowing she'd feel less vulnerable with her kit on, she quickly dressed.

"You're hungry," the queen said.

"I told you, I'm not eating any of that."

"If I wanted to kill you I wouldn't need poison. I simply had to leave you to rot," the queen said. "I know some say that if you eat at my table, you become my creature for all eternity. You are all my creatures anyway, so the point is moot."

Sally unpeeled the newspaper and a fierce hunger gripped her stomach. *The Wharfedale Clarion, 23rd October 1985*, she read,

Drunken Yobs Set Fire to Station Bin. Inside, not just scraps but a wedge of fish and hot chips, slathered with salt and vinegar. Not caring whether they were laced with rat poison or LSD or weapons-grade plutonium, she stuffed three into her mouth and blinked. The idea of one of these creatures being served by Fat Kevin from Otley chippy was just too funny for words, though she had no energy to laugh. The beer gave her some of her old courage back.

"Are all the worlds in this universe as uninspiring as this?"

"Worlds?" the queen asked.

"This rusty Death Star's a world. Isn't it?"

"My creation is different to all the others. The forces that power it are of a singularly unique nature. That's one of the reasons why it has neither stars nor planets. It is fashioned from infinite layers, each bigger than the next, all converging down to this centre."

"Same as the infinity hotel?"

Silence.

"Never mind," Sally said. "How did you get to be queen of this place, or are you another god cut from the same cloth as Backenforth?"

"Our queen is nothing like that rascal, nor any of the other gods," Bright said, sitting on her high-backed chair with all the demure knees-together elegance of a 1950s *Vogue* model.

"The being you call Professor Backenforth reached out to one hundred universes to draw power for his new worlds," Gracious continued. Her voice was so low Sally thought she heard the iron walls vibrate in harmony. "He mistakenly chose this realm as one of them. That will cause ramifications throughout the Multiverse and upset the balance of life and death."

To Sally's ears Gracious and Bright's explanations sounded like the sleeve notes from the back of one of Hannah Able's later albums, knocked out by herself in a cupboard in Berlin.

"We asked him to stop and he refused. We threatened him with what is to come at the end of all things," Gracious gestured about her. "But he still refused. He is as arrogant as he is clever and cunning."

Sally finished the last of the chips and screwed up the paper.

"So why am I here?"

There was something very strange about this room. It wasn't just the beer talking. She sensed heat on the other side of those iron walls, as if the chamber floated through an ocean of acidic lava, the same stuff they'd smeared over her, inside and out.

"You shall help me put a stop to the creature stealing energy from my universe," the queen was saying.

"How?" Sally took another swig of beer.

"We'll set up a trap in your perfect world. Your task is to entice him inside."

"My perfect world? You mean that horrible nightmare I flew here from? The one where my brain gets fried and I end up a stupid six-year-old again? No thanks."

The four creatures watched her - the queen, Bright, Gracious and Sweet. They didn't speak or move. Sally wondered if they were trying to stare her into compliance. Nobody threatened. What would happen if she just refused to help them?

"Nothing," Sweet said. *She read my thoughts.* "You're free to leave this room. There are doors everywhere. I will show you how to open them."

"Ok, take me back to Earth in 1985," she gestured at the screwed up page from *The Wharfedale Clarion*. "So I can get on with my life."

"If you help plant a trap for Professor Backenforth in your perfect world, you'll be returned to your real home, or wherever you choose to go. Once we have him," Bright said.

"Or?"

"Or remain here," Gracious said. "You can try to find your own way back by yourself. We are at the centre of a creation of infinite layers and your only means of transport are those we allow you. It'll take you a while."

"Enough, all of you," the queen said. "Don't toy with our guest. It's cruel."

"Guest?" Sally laughed. "Fuck off if this is how you treat

guests. I have no choice, do I?"

Silence.

"Why me?"

Silence.

"Ok. What's the plan?"

"In your perfect world there is someone you know. She has become a messenger from this realm. When you go back, she'll explain the nature of the trap we've set," the queen said.

"You mean Charlotte?" Sally said.

"No."

"Who then? That treacherous bitch Eva? Turns out she was in league with the bastard all along."

"We can't tell you," Gracious said. "She'll make contact when you're a child again."

"Oh for Christ's sake."

"Once the trap is set, your task is to make sure Professor Backenforth enters it," Sweet said. "We shall create a mighty spell to cloud his mind, to make him forget where he is, but he's very powerful and even we can't maintain the illusion for long."

"And when you've got him, what happens next?" Sally asked.

"We'll sever all the links between his and the other universes," Bright said.

"What'll happen to the perfect worlds? Pash's Arcadia?"

"First the suns will go nova," Sweet answered. "Then the bonds within the false atoms will dissolve. The reality Professor Backenforth created shall dissipate, as its final photons evaporate."

"Those planets have got people on them - my friends. Rafaella, Hannah Able, Anthony. There're others too, living in their utopias."

"The destruction of the parasite cosmos will occur at light speed," Gracious said. "They won't feel anything."

"No. I'm not helping you kill them all."

"If we don't prevent it, that arrogant fool's pocket universe will destroy a hundred creations," Bright said. "Those realities only exist and support life because they are precisely balanced.

Professor Backenforth shattered that equilibrium the instant he pulled energy into his playground. If we stop him, the other universes still have a chance to continue. If not, every living creature and their deities are doomed to perish through his capricious selfishness."

"There must be some way to save them. You took me out of that universe and brought me here. Can't you do the same with those planets?"

"Bring whole worlds to this realm? No," Gracious said. "There is no point. They will all end up here anyway."

What is this place?

"Anywhere then. Stick them in mine, give them stars that don't need to feed on others to keep going. I won't help you if you won't even try."

The masked creatures glanced at each other, invisible messages passing between them. She watched the queen. The woman might have been smiling pleasantly enough at her, but for a fraction of a second Sally glimpsed a churning, fractal infinity in those features that made her heart pound. A wild panic set in and she tensed, desperate to flee. She doubted she'd get very far.

"We will think on your words. There may be a solution," Bright said. "But you must still help us."

"If that bastard's wrecking whole creations why aren't all the other gods having a go at him? Why is it down to me?"

"He's placed barriers to intercept anything coming into his realm. However, the singular nature of my kingdom," the queen gestured about her. "Means I'm able to circumvent them in ways he doesn't expect. But nobody must see me intervene. I cannot appear to take sides in anything to do with a single soul, let alone entire universes. We need someone who is already embedded within his stratagems, who has experience of the symbolic language he draws upon, so they can entice him with his own words. You have been chosen."

"Are you going to give me anything to help? Guns? Armour? His bitch Eva has a whole load of kit from the future and I'll have to deal with her as well."

"No. No weapons from here can pass into his cosmos. Leave Eva Benjamin to us."

"So what do I do to get him?"

"There's no point in telling you now," Gracious said. "When you re-enter the planet Professor Backenforth built for you, you'll be a six-year-old once more. All of this will be the echo of a nightmare you once had. Our discourse will be transformed into dream murmurs without substance, of no use to you whatsoever. We will, however, give you a gift to take to our agent, who will tell you the next steps."

"You're kidding me, right?"

Sally looked around the inside of the iron room and at its terrifying inhabitants.

"Are you sending me back in that uncomfortable plastic toy?"

Stupid question. Of course they were. No doubt it waited outside, still smelling of penny chews and sherbet dips.

"If I do this for you, will you set me free of all this bullshit? I want an ordinary life with normal friends, not users, or treacherous liars. I know my real family is shot to hell, and really don't want to revisit that unholy mess, but a couple of mates and a job, and some peace, or anything approaching normality?"

The crack in her voice made her furious with herself. She stood up and coughed into her fist to disguise it.

"That's no longer possible," the queen said. "We have tempered you to withstand the powers of this universe, which is the most destructive and poisonous of all, and that will have ramifications."

"I just want to go home," Sally whispered.

The ruler of this realm suddenly stood before her, towering over Sally by a good yard.

"Take my hand."

The fingers were as white and cold as ice. The second Sally touched them, the room vanished, popping like a rusty soap bubble. Sally found herself on an iron platform in darkness. The red, yellow and white saucer stood in the centre on its spindly legs, the access ramp down. Bright, Gracious and Sweet stood in a line at the edge of the metal sheet, all clasping their hands in front of their waists in identical poses. Sally wondered how easy it would be to push them over the edge.

"How will I recognise your agent in my world?" she asked.

"She knows you," Gracious said.

"How? The queen said she returned from here, from your realm. How could I possibly know anyone from this place when I've never been here in my life?"

Sweet opened her hand. A red metal ball rested on the palm.

"She will ask for this. Give it to her and then do as she bids," Bright said.

"What is it?"

"A sphere," Sweet said.

Sally picked it up and examined it between finger and thumb. It looked like a model of one of Professor Backenforth's Mystery Planets, though without any pictures or words on the outside, just a uniform scarlet enamel. It was very heavy. She put it in her jacket pocket.

The three creatures stared at her, silver, black and gold, like a set of Art Deco bronzes. Tired of their enigmatic pronouncements, Sally trudged up the ramp and into the cabin. The doll sat on the couch. For a second she was tempted to chuck it out of the ship, or at least hurl it against the wall. Instead she merely dropped the toy onto the floor. On a whim she arranged the figure so it was sitting up with its hands in its lap. She wedged the metal ball between the marionette's forearms.

"You're the poor wee sod who's going to have to do all this crap, so there you go."

Sally heaved herself into the seat and waited for liftoff. It came soon enough. The initial slow ascent gave her momentary glimpses of the bottom two dozen levels within the queen's infinite sphere. They bore no resemblance to the mountainous worlds of the first regions. One looked as if it was stuffed with quivering hair. It made her think of the contents of a vacuum cleaner bag, still populated with twitching and wriggling insects yanked out of some unholy carpet weave. The next was filled with an ocean of bright orange liquid. Sally had no idea how deep it was, how large the buzzing clouds of rainbow oil swirling in its depths, but sensed they would have swallowed entire stars.

The visions grew briefer as the vessel sped up. Instead of feeling relieved, Sally found herself watching intently. She clung on to each scene, wondering how monstrously bizarre the next would be - silhouettes of immense cranes, inverted hands threaded with continent-sized clouds. Eyes - Christ, those eyes. An odd hunger replaced the fear and exhausting misery caused by this endless shunting from one surreal encounter to another. She began to question if she actually wanted normal friends, a decent job as a music journalist, a relationship with somebody who wasn't an utter twat, the final opportunity to step out of the long shadow cast by her mother.

What if that wasn't it at all? What if, instead, she embraced all this? She voyaged through a multiverse inhabited by bored and lonely gods. They drained energy from infinite realities to feed their desperate need for companionship. Professor Backenforth could build worlds out of dreams and nightmares, the twisted bricolage of her own six-year-old mind, and of others, for her to wander through. Did she really want to go back and plonk her arse behind a desk, opposite George in the *Clarion* offices? Neck Theakstons and listen to obscure indie bands, sitting on the worn carpet in a friend's flat? What if she changed the game? Her perfect world came from inside her own head. Surely she'd know it better than anyone else. Would that let her engineer her own way out? And if she did manage to kill Eva, it'd give her the chance to get her hands on all those future weapons. Maybe home didn't appeal after all. The queen had changed her, called it 'tempering' so she'd withstand the vile radiation of her particular hell. Did that give her the power to withstand other energies, in other universes? Was it responsible for this new hunger inside her mind? What if she asked the queen and her three companions for her own spaceship - not this plastic toy, but a real one with the power to voyage between endless realities?

By now the levels had merged into a flicker. It quickly blurred into soft ochre, the light from countless skies blending with the iron walls of the pipe. Time to fall asleep soon and she might not wake up until the ship arrived in her perfect world. She'd be an infant again, her thoughts and ambitions contracted into simple primary-coloured bubbles. Was there some way of sending herself a message?

She patted her pockets. Nothing. Then she remembered the studs in her ears, but were the pins sharp enough?

"Sally? Sally! Wake up, sleepyhead."

She unpeeled her cheek from the table and blinked up at Mrs Ryan.

"I expect you had wonderful adventures in the flying saucer that brought you to school this morning. Nevertheless, I think Mummy needs to be a little bit more careful about tiring you out before lessons." She looked through the window. "And it is a hot day and very stuffy in here. Let me see your colouring-in."

She teased the open book from under Sally's hands.

"Excellent, excellent work. Even when you're tired you keep inside the lines and don't scribble. A silver star today."

"Aw," Sally felt cheated, especially as she was still the only one in the class.

"Silver stars for sleepy heads. Gold stars for children who are as bright as buttons. Early bed tonight, OK?"

"Yes, Mrs Ryan."

"Good girl, off you go. And don't forget your satchel. I bet it's full of exciting things from your adventures. Is the flying saucer taking you home?"

Sally shrugged. She hadn't a clue.

"Well in case it doesn't, remember the Kerb Drill for when you run into Gareth the Policeman."

Sally pulled the satchel off her peg and peeped inside, trying to recall any of the wonderful events Mrs Ryan had talked about. She remembered sitting in a flying saucer while the Chernod, the Nabik and the Klopan piloted it past the stars, but the memories were fuzzy. Had they landed on any planets? Didn't she end up in a room with some grownups - old ladies who chatted on about things she was too young to understand? Had they given her anything? All she found in the bag was her Big Sally Action Figure and a metal ball painted bright red. It had no openings or buttons and felt heavy. Disappointed, she trudged out of the cloakroom, waved goodbye to Mr Cooper and the other teachers, and set off for home.

The world seemed strange this afternoon. It was normal for the streets to be quiet and deserted, but not this silent, or so filled with expectation. As Sally dawdled her way along the pavements, feet clumsy through lack of energy, she sensed eyes watching from behind the thick windows, watchful faces buried deep in the far shadows of plastic lounges and polystyrene bedrooms.

Nursery Lane was empty. The crowd shuffling by under the gaze of the soldiers had disappeared. There were a few signs of their passing next to the zebra crossing. A battered leather suitcase lay open on the pavement, its handle smeared red. A smashed pair of wireframe glasses poked out of a drain cover. *They must have all gone into the woods.* She glanced at the trees clustered at the end, where the street joined the main road. There was something important about the place, hidden in the shadows near the water tower that bulked above the branches.

Gareth the Policeman stood at the top of the wasteland, head towering above the roofs, so Sally took the shortcut again. When she reached the driveway of Number 12, Vicky Samson called to her from her sun lounger.

"Hey Sally. Come over here."

She dutifully wandered across the grass. It was dry and sounded crisp under her shoes, although the shadow under the blue plastic strips of the fold-out chair looked wet. Mrs Samson heaved herself up onto her elbows. It seemed to be an effort. Her arms made crackling noises and a drop of blood leaked out of her nose. She muttered a bad word and wiped it away with her palm.

"I heard you've got a present for me from outer space," she said. Sally always thought Mrs Samson was ever so glamorous, especially in that yellow bikini with the big rings at the side. Today, standing this close to the grownup made her feel weird. At first Sally assumed it was because Mrs Samson was practically in her nothings and her foofoo hair was visible, stretching up in a line from the edge of her pants to her tummy button. No, something else bugged her. The cigarette smoke and wine fumes didn't completely hide an odd, sickly smell, and the woman's arms and legs looked lumpy and bruised in places.

"What have you brought me then?" Vicky Samson reached out and teased her fingers under the satchel flap. Sally suddenly had the urge to push them away. Yellow gunk was leaking out from under the nails and she didn't want her new doll getting dirty.

"Is that what I think it is?" The woman's hand dipped in and out in a flash and held up the red sphere. "Just what I always wanted. How thoughtful. Clever Sally." Vicky Samson kissed the souvenir. "Now run along Sally, don't dilly dally."

Glad to get away, Sally skipped past the car and the broken tree, and through the garden leading to the Crescent. She wasn't sorry to be rid of the ball. If it was a gift from outer space it was pretty rubbish. At first she was worried her new mother might be cross because she hadn't given it to her as a present. In fact, Charlotte seemed pleased when she told her what had happened.

"And you gave it to Vicky Samson? Excellent, well done you," she said as she handed over the plate of spaghetti on toast. "I'm glad you had such a good time in the flying saucer."

Sally braced herself for the inevitable questions about her adventures. To her surprise, none came. Perhaps it was because her new mother realised she was tired. She guessed Mrs Ryan had phoned up to tell her, in which case it'd be an early bath and bed. After shovelling her way through tea, she allowed herself to be led upstairs. Charlotte added a few squirts of Fairy Liquid under the taps, but her daughter didn't have the energy to build castles in the foam. Her new mother washed her hair instead, singing the Sally's favourite song in her clockwork voice.

Marina, Aqua Marina,
Why can't you whisper the words my heart is longing to hear?

Everything still seemed oddly flat, the house quiet, her mother's voice muted. The street waited and watched, like the audience at a circus preparing to witness the last spectacular act.

"Sleep tight, beauty girl," Charlotte said, blessing her with an iron kiss on the forehead. "Tomorrow's Saturday again. Busy day."

CHAPTER TWENTY-TWO

The morning started badly. Sally woke up early and decided to play with her new doll. She hadn't tried the *Ace Reporter Play Set* yet, but it looked very interesting. Part of the story took place in a police station and involved Big Sally giving one of the officers a right proper seeing to, whatever that meant. She removed the clothes her doll had worn on the spaceship, ready to dress her in jeans, t-shirt and boots, and stopped. There were marks on the figure's tummy. She rubbed them with her thumb but they didn't go away. Instead, she felt tiny scratches. They looked like writing when she held them up to the light. Sally struggled to make out the letters. She got out her magnifying glass and found herself looking at cuts in the plastic, tinged red as if they'd made Big Sally bleed.

Lie.

Somebody had spoiled her new toy, scribbled on it with a sharp pin by the look of things. She'd barely had it for any length of time at all. What a cruel and horrible thing to do. Tears welling up, she rubbed and rubbed at the words. The colour faded a little so the damage wasn't quite so obvious, but she still noticed it under her fingers. In her anger and disappointment the scratches felt like spikes digging into her own skin. Who? Who would be so mean? She'd been very careful, even when taking her doll into the flying saucer. Had one of the Krazy Kreatures done it when she wasn't looking or while she was asleep? The Chernod, the Nabik or the Klopan? Why?

Sally laid the figure down on the bed and cried. After a few moments she gave Big Sally a cuddle, took her into the bathroom, and stuck the biggest Elastoplast she could find on the toy's stomach. Perhaps that would help. She knew it was make-believe but it made her feel a little better. To be fair, she'd only see the marks when swopping the doll's clothes. It was still a rotten thing to happen.

She didn't want to tell Charlotte. Her mother might get cross with her for not looking after her toys properly. After tucking the doll ever so carefully up in bed to make sure nothing else happened to it, she made her way down for breakfast. Charlotte was chatting away on the phone so Sally helped herself. She was halfway through a bowl of Rice Krispies when Charlotte put the receiver down and shuffled into the kitchen.

"How nice. Vicky Samson has invited you to a party today. There'll be a film show and, would you believe it, an actual conjuror! That's what happens to little girls who are thoughtful and kind. They get all sorts of lovely treats."

A glass of lemon barley water appeared by the side of her bowl. Sally stared at it. She wasn't going to say anything about the damaged doll now. If she did, Charlotte would probably tell her she couldn't go to the Samson's for being so careless with her things.

"I bet there'll be a goody bag too, with books and diamonds and chocolates from Fortnum and Masons. Drink up and finish your cereal, and let's get you into your party dress."

Sally cheered up. She liked Vicky Samson, even if the woman had seemed a little unwell the day before. She hoped she'd be better today. Charlotte got her done up to the nines. She even gave her a squirt of her own favourite perfume. It was called *Fleurs de Bulgarie by Creed* and was so strong it made Sally's eyes water. After fussing with her daughter's hair, her new mother declared herself content and sent her on her way.

The door to the Samson's was on the latch. When Sally rang the bell, Vicky called out for her to come in. Party food covered the kitchen table and a cine projector pointed at the lounge wall.

The curtains were drawn to keep out the light and hide the garden. Mrs Samson sat on a chair in the corner between the TV and the bookshelf, where the shadows lay deepest. She had a bottle of wine on the top of the telly, a glass in her right hand, and her cigarette holder in the left. In the gloom it was hard to make her out. It looked as though she wore a Mary Quant dress just like the one Mrs Ryan had given Sally the day she wet herself.

"That's a lovely perfume," Vicky Samson said. The woman sounded hoarse, as if struggling to say the words. Maybe it was the wine or perhaps she still felt poorly. "Help yourself to cake and pop and we'll watch the film together, and then I have a special guest, just for you."

After loading up a paper plate, Sally parked herself on the carpet with her back to the projector. She glanced towards the other end of the room. The boys had always said that from certain angles you could see Vicky Samson's knickers because her dresses were that short. Sally didn't look for long. The woman's legs still appeared odd, the bruises darker in the shadows. Some of the stains on her thighs were wet, and patches had transferred onto the upholstery under her bottom.

The projector flicked on. A grainy square of light blossomed on the wall.

"There's no sound but I'll tell you what's happening."

A cartoon started. Sally loved those, especially Betty Boop or Felix the Cat. This didn't look familiar at all, though. It told the story of a woman who'd lost another mother's little boy. The tale began with a monster from beyond the sky bringing a giant ball to the lady's garden.

"The police said it wasn't my fault, but what did that even mean? I'd invited him into my house, this dybbuk who feeds on the innocent," Vicky Samson said. "And all the other mothers? Well, day in, day out, the stares, the insinuations, no more invitations to their cocktail parties. The phone silent for weeks on end. Joseph Bergman actually spat in my face outside the Post Office. Somebody pushed dog shit through the letterbox. God in heaven, we'd do that to our own? After all that happened? That was the last straw. I'd just lost my grandmother, the only one of her sisters and brothers to survive Dachau. You goyim don't realise what it was like. Every single family crushed by those people, broken and cast into the wind, generation upon generation, millions and millions. You lot wanted to sweep it all under the carpet, act as if it never happened, or say that we were whining about nothing, like we always do. I hope you kids won't be so desperate to pretend that humans aren't capable of such evil. If there's any lesson to be learned from what I'm telling you, let it be that."

A little girl ran down a broken street, away from a line of people trudging between burning houses. *Run, Eva, Run. Don't look back.*

The sound of another cigarette, another glass filled, and someone trying to shuffle into a more comfortable position despite the crackling of fractured bones. Did Vicky Samson want some cake? Sally'd be happy to fetch her a piece if it'd make her feel better, but she also wanted to know what happened next in the story.

"I drank a bottle of vodka, climbed into the MG and set off for Harrogate."

A rubber car on rubber wheels skipped along a road, cotton wool smoke popping out of the exhaust. The cows in the field and birds in the sky all bounced up and down on their rubber hosepipe legs and watched, mouths perfect black circles.

"Look out Vicky! Look out! Look out! Crash! Bang! Wallop!" Vicky Samson slurred explosion noises.

The driver of the car floated out of the shattered windscreen, trailing drops of cartoon blood. In the next scene she drifted down and down a pipe surrounded by darkness, into an iron room where four thin women in gowns and masks danced to the same silent rhythm as the farm animals who'd witnessed the crash. The picture disappeared, numbers ran sideways up the screen, and the end of the film clattered in the reel.

"Well? What did you think? Was it fun?" Vicky Samson asked. Sally glanced her way. All she could see was the burning tip of a cigarette. She nodded. The cartoon was interesting, if weird.

"I'll be glad when this is all over," the woman said, with such sadness in her voice that Sally wanted to run over and give her a hug. Something about the darkness in the corner stopped her.

"Anthony's alive," she found herself saying. "He lives on a planet in the sky. You can see his star at night."

"I know already, but thank you. You're a sweet kid." Mrs Samson seemed to rally herself, leaning forwards into the light. What Sally saw made her look away with a gasp.

"More cake? More pop? There's loads to eat and only the two of us. I won't be able to finish what you leave. I've no appetite anymore."

Sally shook her head.

"Well... Today we've a very special guest, all the way from outer space. He's going to take you on the most wonderful journey imaginable. Ready?"

"Yes."

"I can't hear you. Ready?"

"YEEEESSSS!" Sally shouted at the top of her voice.

Invisible hands pulled the drapes aside and Sally gasped. A red sphere as big as an ice-cream van sat in the middle of Mrs Samson's lawn, a step ladder propped against it and the hatch open. The French Windows were ajar and the tap tap of someone's shoes echoed down the side of the house, coming closer.

"Make sure he gets inside with you. He'll be trapped in a feedback loop," Vicky Samson's voice was suddenly by her ear, hissing urgently. It sounded full of broken teeth. Sally was too scared to turn round and kept her gaze fixed on the red sphere. "Tell him it's gone wrong, that you need his help. Go." Something wet and soft pushed her in the small of her back. Desperate to get out of that dark room, Sally ran into the garden. The French Windows banged shut behind her.

The sky was so bright it was hard to see the figure who rose up above her. He stood on the top of the sphere, arms gesturing at heaven with all the elegant mannerisms of a ballet dancer. A tall hat, dark hair down to his shoulders, a curled moustache, and a precisely clipped goatee.

"A Mystery Planet for a mysterious girl. Who is this inquisitive child seeking adventure and wonders among new stars? Is she brave enough to climb inside? Is she ready for all her wishes to come true?"

The voice slid over the grass like soft oil, tumbled from the sky like warm summer rain. When Sally heard it, thoughts broke into her head from outside, a bigger, richer mind that enveloped her own. Professor Backenforth's words tasted of wine and chocolate, Theakstons Old Peculier and a bag of scraps from the chippy slathered in vinegar, the one good fuck she'd had from that bloke whose name she didn't remember. They reminded her of David Bowie singing *Ashes to Ashes*, rain on the moors, the sheer physical joy of a faultless kata.

Everything will be perfect from now on.

Of course she was going to climb inside. Sally stuck her hand up and shouted, "Me Me Me!".

She scrambled up the step ladder and balanced on the top. Professor Backenforth took her fingers in his own and guided her to the hatchway. His hand felt like dry bones wrapped in silver foil. Even up close it was impossible to focus on his face or clothes, but who cared? Giggling with excitement, Sally teetered on the edge and looked down at the cloudy darkness inside the ball. Lights of all colours flashed in the depths, like fireworks shrouded in smoke.

"Mind how you go, Sally dear, don't fall."

Lie.

Sally stepped down and found herself at the top of a narrow flight of stairs leading into the flickering mist. The first step was a fraction wider than the hatch, just enough for her to stand with her feet pressed together. She descended a little further and the steps rapidly widened, the fog rising to her shoulders. The inside of the sphere looked much bigger than the outside. She still held Professor Backenforth's fingers. More thoughts broke through from the larger mind surrounding her own.

Lie.

The skin of her stomach itched. It felt sore, as if she'd scratched it or stung it with nettles.

Don't let go of the bastard. As long as you've got hold of him he can't close the hatch.

Now there was a tightness around her middle, as if it was wrapped in a big bandage. She glanced down and saw that the grainy darkness made her legs look different, somehow longer. The Start-Rites had turned into heavy red boots. She dipped down and the vapours closed over her head, turning the circle of daylight into a fuzzy disc.

The queen has fooled him into thinking he made this sphere, but the spell won't last.

"There's something wrong," she called out, but her voice was a grownup's. *Shit.* She climbed up a step and her face emerged into clear air again. Millions of words faded from her consciousness, thoughts unstringing. She wished she could grab them before they vanished. They were full of grownup wisdom and would tell her what to do.

"What did you say, poppet?" the voice sounded uncertain.

"I don't like it in here. It's frightening."

"Not for a brave girl such as yourself. Everything's perfect in there. Everything's made exactly how clever Sally would wish it."

"There's someone else down here, a scary woman."

"Is there? You know what? I thought I heard a voice."

Professor Backenforth's face appeared at the hatch. The brim of his hat cut a precise circle within the daylight, as if a giant eye stared down at her.

"If there is anyone else with you, they're a friend, a playmate. I fill all these Mystery Planets with companions for you to have fun with, for ever and ever."

"Don't let go, please."

"Don't worry. I'm still here. Take your time."

Sally crouched down, still holding on. The second her head went under the fog the adult poured back. She checked her right hand. It too had grown larger, lumpier from callouses and fractured knuckles. Professor Backenforth held the left one and if it changed as well he'd realise what was happening. She had to keep that arm above the smoke. Sally glanced down. Beyond her Doc Marts, the stairs fell into an impossible void. Huge forms swam to and fro a hundred miles, a million miles, a trillion light years below. Despite the eternity at her feet, Sally sensed four minds waiting in hungry expectation at the very bottom, sitting in the last iron room of the Infinity Hotel.

Above her the mist swirled and pulsed in time to the lights exploding all around. Professor Backenforth had leaned in up to his waist, fingers still interlaced with Sally's, the other arm planted against the curving wall to steady himself.

"This isn't right. What are you doing?" he said.

Sally moved into action. She dropped down to the next step, bringing her free hand up out of the mist to grab his wrist while, at the same time, pulling down hard. She almost lost hold. Both hands were those of a six-year-old again, with none of her adult strength.

"Careful sweetie, I've got you."

The fool had assumed she'd tripped on the stairs and was trying to steady herself, but he was also glancing around, baffled.

"I'M SCARED," Sally yelled at the top of her voice and yanked again, putting all her weight behind it. Professor Backenforth fell into the sphere like a bag of sticks. His body seemed to have no coherence. It tumbled about her in a cascade of cloth, cheap aftershave and spikes. She lost her footing and ended up on her back, sliding down the stairs head-first, the circle of light receding above her.

Something grabbed her ankle. At the same time, claws buried themselves in her scalp. The joint-wrenching stop knocked the breath out of her lungs.

"What are you doing? What are you doing? What are you doing?"

Beyond the sharp agonising pain in her head, Professor Backenforth's voice jabbered away, repeating the same phrase with all the mechanical hysteria of a broken cassette player.

Feedback loop.

"WHATAREYOUDOINGWHATAREYOUDOINGWHATARE YOUDOING..."

Sally tried to push herself back up the stairs one-handed, using the other to dislodge whatever clung to her skull. The grip on her ankle slackened and she bumped down half a dozen steps. Professor Backenforth was going to drag her down with him. Glowing letters filled the mist above, hiding the exit. Something whirled round and round, scattering the words. The fog hissed, and a second later the pit below erupted in a thundering detonation. The pain in her scalp vanished. Hands grabbed her by the ankles and dragged her up the staircase, through the vapour, and into the light. She tumbled out of the red sphere, thumping onto Vicky Samson's lawn. A silhouette stood on top of the ball.

We failed. He got out.

But instead of leaping down to attack her, the figure slammed the hatch, spinning the wheel to seal it. Eva dropped onto the grass beside Sally and heaved her upright.

"You're fine. He didn't hurt you. We have to go, now," she said.

"Bitch."

Sally hit Eva on the jaw. The other woman's head snapped sideways and she collapsed down on one knee. Sally went for a kick to the throat. Eva grabbed her foot and used Sally's leg to slam her into the side of the sphere. Winded, she bounced off and ended up on her knees, agony radiating out from her armpit. Felt like Eva had smacked her on the damaged rib, again.

"Idiot. We don't have time for this." Eva rubbed blood away from her mouth.

"You betrayed me," Sally snarled.

"I just saved your life."

"Go," came a voice from the Samson's lounge. It sounded full of agony. The doors slid open once more. Something lay on the carpet just inside, barely moving. Sally thought she saw three slender shadows converge on it from the corners of the room.

The ground shook, causing the red sphere to wobble. The roof of Vicky Samson's house sagged inwards, losing shape as if the plastic was beginning to melt.

"This world is falling apart," Eva said.

Sally got to her feet and stared down at herself. She wasn't six anymore.

"I'm all grown up."

"Your Mystery Planet is dying. We planted a virus in it," Eva said.

"You did what?"

"You have to get us out of your world, now!"

The sky churned, red and yellow veins threading through the clouds. It reminded Sally of the inside of her eye when she closed it in front of a bright light. More buildings were collapsing as if they'd been stuck in an oven. A shadow loomed above them. At first she thought it might be the tower, but this had arms, legs and a policeman's helmet.

"I used the Wodaran's raygun to leave Pash's Arcadia. You took it from me, remember? When you sold me down the river to that bastard."

Eva swore and scrabbled in one of the pouches hanging from her belt. She pulled out the toy and threw it to Sally, who pointed it into the sky and pressed the button. Nothing happened. She fired again. No response. She opened the handle and almost dropped the weapon. The batteries had decayed. She shook the cancerous lumps onto the grass and shoved the toy into her jacket pocket. The lawn smoked from the spilled acid.

"There must be other ways out of this place. Think." Eva said. She kept glancing nervously at the French Windows.

What if they headed down to the trees and the golf course? That would take them back to the Blocko Tower. Maybe they could use that as a gateway back to reality. Right now they were in the corner of the Driving Test Game. If they went the other way and made it through Toy Town Leeds, they'd come to the woods where Angus and the rest had their house, just on the border between the actual world and this nightmare.

Eva grabbed her arm and dragged her down the side of the

building. The wall bellied out, red plastic bursting through the brick-patterned paper. If it hadn't been for the shattered tree and wrecked car, they'd have been trapped in the garden. The polystyrene from the melting house pushed up against the torn MG, scraping it across the drive. It left fresh smears of blood and oil over the tarmac. Eva and Sally barely managed to jump free in time.

"Down to the woods. You came through there from the tower." Sally pushed Eva along the pavement in front of her. They'd only got a few yards when feet as big as cars planted themselves at the end of the road. Everything went dark. Looking up, Sally found herself staring into a smeared face of peeling enamel, applied with a cack-handed brush to Gareth the Policeman's lumpen head. The mouth split the cheeks in two, revealing jagged teeth interlaced with shredded brown thickets of cellophane. The eyes were blue fried eggs hurled against a pink boulder.

"Children. To attention! Kerb drill."

The creature's hand came down across the street, sealing the way forward behind a flesh-coloured wall. On either side, discoloured and shapeless faces appeared above the collapsed roofs and next to the wilting chimneys.

Creeple Peeple.

What was that nonsense they'd dinned into her as a child? How often had Mr Cooper made the whole school chant out the litany in morning assembly, teachers and kids repeating and repeating until it was carved in their brains? She barely remembered any of it. Six-year-old Sally would have known, but she was bugger all use now.

"Stop at the Kerb, Look Right..."

"Not you," the voice sounded like spit-drenched music from a broken flute. "Her first."

A giant fingernail, edged with flash as sharp as a razor, hovered above Eva's head. She froze, one hand close to her sling. Sally knew that if the other woman tried anything, she'd be ground into pulp before either of them could react. Eva glanced her way. For the first time there was panic in her eyes. Of course she hadn't a clue.

"Stop at the Kerb," she managed, copying Sally.

Look Right...

But before Eva had a chance to continue, Gareth the Policeman belched and attempted to straighten up.

"What's that stink, Sally?" he roared. "Something smells like it has gone off. Have you soiled yourself as well as pissed your knickers?"

Christ, what was it? A thick stench of decay rolled up the street, pouring between the policeman's legs. Sally started breathing through her mouth but it didn't help.

Gareth the Policeman managed to stand up. Four iron spikes curled out of his stomach, arching back from the centre to pierce his uniform, tearing gouges in the tattered paint to reveal the plastic underneath. They flattened and suddenly pulled inwards, ripping a hole from his abdomen to his back. Through the gap, Sally saw the top of a mountain of roiling decay.

Charlotte.

The toy policeman staggered round and flailed out. Sally's new mother, swollen to monstrous size, brought another claw down on his shoulder. It tore apart the greasy polystyrene so his arm dangled from a handful of threads.

"Run," Sally screamed, and headed for the end of the street. Eva's boots clattered on the pavement behind her. The officer's voice rose in a cacophony of discordant shrieks and whistles, overlain with a metallic howling that might have been claws on plastic, or Charlotte's own words transformed into inhuman rage. As the women sprinted into Nursery Lane, Sally ahead and aiming for the secret route through the garages, something vast rolled across the road behind them, fetching up against a fence on the opposite side. Sally glanced over her shoulder. The policeman's head came to a stop. Half the face was missing, the matter underneath ripped into ugly chaos. The rest was smeared with slime and blood. Silence fell, punctuated only by the occasional soft thud of a melting house as it collapsed.

CHAPTER TWENTY-THREE

Eva stared at the blood-stained suitcase. She'd already fished the spectacles out of the drain.

"I remember a crowd of people walking along here, heading towards those woods, herded by soldiers in Nazi uniforms," Sally said. "Wasn't anything from my childhood."

"I know." Eva nodded at the water tower. "What's over that way?"

"In real life? I don't remember. Harrogate Road is on the other side, and Roundhay Park beyond that. Hey, I thought you wanted to get out of this place."

Eva strode on past the zebra crossing, aiming for the trees. A sudden realisation hit Sally.

"You said you'd done something to my world. Was that parade of people anything to do with it?"

Nursery Lane sat on a ridge above Moortown. The buildings beyond didn't look as damaged as those closer to home, but their outlines had already started to soften. Busy hissing shadows flickered in the streets and gardens around the primary school. Sally suspected they'd need to move fast if they were to make it to the ring road and the place where she and the soldiers had found their way in.

Eva didn't answer. She climbed the bank on the south side of the street. The water tower stood on a narrow strip of grass at the edge of the woods. Its plastic legs had buckled, making it tilt over. Sally saw cartoon footprints painted on the ground, a path leading into the shadows.

She's looking for her family. There's pits among the trees, full of thousands of corpses.

This whole place was supposed to be Sally's perfect world. Somehow it had ended up with the worst evil in human history smeared into the paintwork, a cruelty and hatred utterly beyond any reason. Here monsters and their real horrors hovered on the borderland of a childhood fantasy, with its sweets, toys and cartoons. It'd always been there, hadn't it? The memories, the darkness ignored by the smug and the indifferent who were all too happy to relegate the war to the tea-cosy safety of *Dad's Army*. Sally's mother's voice echoed in her mind.

For Christ's sake can't you lot give it a rest? It was over twenty years ago. Isn't it time to move on?

Sally followed Eva into the trees. A dark shape loomed at the end of long colonnades of sunlit oak and ash. What hideous form waited at the intersection of a six-year-old's nightmares and mass murder? Then she remembered the sign. She'd walked past it on the days when she'd taken a different route home from school.

"It's a synagogue. All my friends came here on a Saturday. I used to see them traipsing along, the boys in their little black caps. A rabbi visited our house after Antony Mendelssohn went missing. He pissed my mum off by talking about the Holocaust. I think he worked here. I don't remember anything like this, though."

Pale sandstone walls set with high mullioned windows gave way to a steep terracotta roof. Not a whiff of polystyrene in any of it. The building looked fortified, as if designed to withstand a medieval siege.

"That's because the Maharal's fortress synagogue was built for the descendants of those who fought the Philistines, slew giants and walked with Nephilim." Eva stood with her fists on her hips, staring up at the temple. She had that beautiful grin again and tears in her eyes.

"Maharal?"

"Rabbi Löwy, the Maharal of Prague," Eva said. "This is where he created his famous golem and sent him to the moon, before he came to the tower and took me under his wing. Together he and I made contact with the queen in the iron hell, and she helped us plant the virus that destabilised your perfect planet."

"What do you mean a 'virus'?"

Eva stared at her.

"In your future all the computers on Earth are linked together. Criminals and rebels make programmes that take over other peoples' machines. They're called viruses. The one we wrote drew upon the nightmares of a little girl and mixed them up with other horrors concocted by the queen. Putting you inside triggered the routines, switched control of this sphere to her and her companions, and allowed us to trap the Professor Backenforth in a perpetual loop - a Mystery Planet within a Mystery Planet."

"So I was the sacrifice after all." Sally felt like punching the bitch again.

"We're both sacrifices."

"Oh really? How so?"

"My reward for doing this was another five minutes. That's all the queen would give me, and only after Gracious had pleaded my case for a hundred and one days."

"Another five minutes with who? For what?"

"Who do you think? To say I was sorry for running off and abandoning them to those dogs." The smile had gone and the tears spilled down Eva's cheeks. "Saving you took that chance away. I couldn't leave you trapped with Professor Backenforth."

"What happened to your perfect planet? You were going to rescue all the Jews and take them into outer space."

"And give those who hate my people exactly what they wanted? Pluck us from history? Banish us to another universe so we never sully your world again? We who gave you so much? Every Jew wiped from every age of the Earth as if we'd never existed. Seriously?"

"So you won't even get those five minutes because you rescued me," Sally said.

"I've no idea how to reach the queen now. I was supposed to

go with her companions when they collected Vicky Samson but I wasn't going to leave you behind like I did the others. Besides, what use is five more minutes anyway? It would only prolong things. There'd be no closure. There never will be for the ones who survived."

Eva sniffed, bent over and blew her nose onto the plastic grass, one finger on her nostril, rugby player style.

"We could barricade ourselves in the Maharal's fortress," she continued. "Rabbi Löwy was the greatest alchemist who ever lived. He walked with Noah and self-fashioning Thoth at the very dawn of the world. Nothing can touch the magic within."

"I don't want to stay here," Sally said. "I hate this place. I never want to come here ever again. Everything shit about my childhood is here in plastic and bubblegum. If we don't shift our arses it'll kill us or trap us forever."

She could see Eva itching to barricade herself inside her teacher's magic castle. Fine. If that's what she wanted the woman was welcome to it. Sally would make her own way home. She wondered what other repulsive nightmares waited for her down in Leeds, dredged up from childish fevers by the queen of the iron universe. She knew it was ultimately all of her own making. Her fears and desires, hopes and anger, formed this deranged landscape's bedrock. Surely that knowledge could help her escape.

Sally set off towards the shops, not particularly caring whether Eva followed her or not. Yet when she reached the ring road, Eva was still beside her, face grim and gaze fixed on the cartoon skyline. They made their way past the row of shops lining Harrogate Road. Only the newsagents by the roundabout had a proper door and window. That figured. It was where she'd bought her Saturday sweets and comics as a kid, so it loomed large in her six-year-old imagination. Several pairs of pale grey eyes watched her from among the moulded newspaper racks and counters inside. All the other shops had roof-high screen-printed drawings stuck to the front of the buildings, with badly drawn doors and displays of groceries peeling away from the greasy

Bakelite. The road itself was empty, though the shadows down the streets on either side were full of twisted shapes, bopping up and down in that endless hallucinatory Betty Boop dance. She remembered visiting a dentist half a dozen houses along when she was little, and wondered what horror he and his drills had become.

It wasn't until the road curved down to the bottom of the hill leading to Chapeltown that creatures began to emerge from the high Victorian blocks of flats on either side. They drifted down the long deformed gardens and onto the pavement. All distances were mightily compressed in this version of Leeds. If memory served, after clearing the brow of the hill ahead they'd be within spitting distance of the city centre. Sally remembered how the roads shifted last time. They'd opened and closed, trapping Angus's squad, until she'd commandeered the plastic car and forced a path through.

Far away to the east, a column of darker mist disappeared into the low cloud above the houses. Could that be the control stick? But where was the vehicle itself? It had been left jammed against the front of her old home when she and the squad first approached Backenforth Heights. That was the last time she'd seen it. Sally didn't remember coming across any cars in this Mystery Planet version of her childhood. They'd have to go on foot. First they needed to deal with these twisted, bug-eyed things shambling back and forth, waving their cartoon hands in the air and mouthing nonsense words.

"What are they?" Eva asked. A crowd filled the top of the rise, all staring down at them with an assortment of distorted faces. Her friend pulled out an exploding bullet, put it into the sling's pouch, and let it dangle by her knees.

"Creeple Peeple. Remember?" Sally said. "You made one the first time I visited Backenforth Heights."

Blank look.

"Are they friendly?" Eva said.

"I don't know."

Sally walked up the slope. The line of creatures looked two-dimensional, fashioned out of pungent chemicals and tapped out of shallow moulds onto Formica kitchen tops. They had squashed plastic heads with sticking out ears and bulbous noses. Their bodies were made of chewed pencils wrapped in brightly coloured wool with giant feet stuck on the end. Purple and green tabards, covered in badly drawn skulls and cross-eyed goblins, hung from their necks and bendy arms.

"Oi. Shift out of the way," Sally shouted.

They jiggled and bounced and gurned.

"See my friend down there? She throws exploding bombs designed to take out storybook monsters like you lot. I've got the Wodaran's raygun. It'll rip your made-in-Hong-Kong bodies into toxic confetti, so let us through."

"She betrayed you," a Creeple Peeple said, pointing at Eva with its translucent sausage-finger hand. It spoke in the hollow, tremulous voice of one of Betty Boop's freakish enemies. The crowd bounced up and down in unison, all chanting, bursts of ink-drop sweat spraying out of their heads in perfect semi-circles.

She betrayed you.

She betrayed you.

"Sally, move out of the way," Eva called.

The bullet whizzed round and round, faster and faster. Sally could see past the crowd, down the slope to Chapeltown. The dreaded church steeple curled like a claw. The streets were full of cartoon toys, as if every grotesque plastic monster ever to pop out of a Thingmaker tray had gathered for one stomach-churning riot. They filled all the lanes leading into the suburb. Their busy, jerky movements reminded her of the room of bugs in the Blocko Tower, and memories of that buzzing, slimy migraine hell made her skin crawl.

"There's too many of them," she yelled over her shoulder. More of the things crowded in from the houses, pushing aside polystyrene doors and popping out of chimneys and cellophane windows like maggots fleeing rotten meat.

"She didn't betray me. Eva's my best friend," she tried, panicking at all those bulbous fingers pointing towards the other woman.

She betrayed you.

She betrayed you.

Give her to the funny men.

Give her to the strange men.

"This is my world. You'll do what I say." She pulled the Wodaran's raygun out of her pocket. "Back off or I'll blow you all to pieces."

No batteries, no batteries and all the shops are shut.

The Creeple Peeple surged forwards, crowding around Sally. She staggered backwards in a cloud of stinking chemicals, tripped and ended up flat on her arse. Thinking they were attacking her, she curled up for protection, but the plastic feet merely pattered by. She heard yelling and shouting, and the dull crump of an explosion. Through the waddling pipe-cleaner legs and giant chewed pencils she saw roiling dust and smoke. Eva must have managed to loose one of the bullets before they got to her. It didn't seem to have had any effect. More attackers poured up from Chapeltown, over the crest of the hill, and towards her friend.

Sally reached out and grabbed a lime green foot, struggling upright as she wrenched the creature's leg out of its moulded socket. A train whistle shriek nearly burst her eardrums. Wielding the limb, she lashed out around her, clearing a space as the Creeple Peeple staggered away, mouths and eyes dead cold circles. She laid into the repulsive fuckers, scything back and forth like a sword-wielding barbarian. The crowd broke in seconds, splitting down the middle as the monsters fled en masse into the houses and alleyways on either side. There was no sign of Eva.

They've carried her off to the funny men.

She tossed the broken leg to the side of the street and examined the Wodaran's raygun. The twittering little buggers were wrong, not all the shops were closed. She ran back along the main road. The destruction brought on by the imprisonment of Professor Backenforth had already reached this part of town. Buildings slumped into red and brown clots, edges melting and mixing like wax crayons left on a classroom radiator. All the trees and houses north of the shops had vanished. The Maharal's synagogue rose out of a lake of green slime.

The newsagents by the junction still stood open. The roof sagged down inside the shop, almost reaching the floor in places. The interior looked like a decaying mouth. Sally didn't have time to hesitate. She ducked under the lintel and found herself between a rack of fake comics and sagging shelves covered in spilled sherbet and rotting sweets. A ragged shape rose up against the far wall. In the growing darkness it was impossible make out any details. Four AA batteries sat on a shelf just next to it.

Sally didn't mess about. She jumped onto the counter and swiped the cells. As she reached out, her hand caught the edge of the roiling protoplasm. It was as if she'd been stung by the queen of all wasps. She snatched her arm away, trying not to drop the batteries, lost her footing and fell. The tumble knocked the breath out of her. For a second she lay stunned, watching the roof droop closer. Something grabbed her foot and started to slide her into the darkness. The ground around her softened, as if an acid ate at the floor. The ceiling touched her chest. Sally turned her face to the side, terrified she'd be smothered by the melting plastic. Her hands fumbled frantically with the batteries, trying to jam them into the handle of the raygun, praying the points hadn't been corroded to destruction. The pressure built up on her torso. The dull pain of her damaged rib began to eclipse the poisoned throbbing in her wrist. It was all she could do not to thrash and scream in panic. Forcing her breathing to slow, she focussed on getting the heavy AAs into the sockets. They slid home. She clicked the hatch shut and pressed the button, aiming somewhere at the rear of the shop and hoping she wasn't going to take her toes with it.

The seconds before the sparkling circles took half the building with them were the longest in Sally's life. The explosion pushed her in the opposite direction, out from under the sagging polystyrene and into the road. The entire row of shops slumped into a steaming ridge of phosphorescent slag. The blast from the raygun carved a semi-circular trench diagonally across the side road and through two more rows of houses. It petered out on the edge of a wide space populated with a dozen plastic trees.

Now to find Eva.

Where do all the funny men hang out?

Roundhay Park was their obvious stamping ground. In 1977, Peter Sutcliffe beat one of his victims to death at the back of the sports pavilion. Long before then, popular imagination filled the bushes and winding tree-lined paths around the lakes with legions of gaberdine-clad perverts, all with pockets full of sweets and homes stuffed with cute puppies and kittens. Sally headed for the Driving Test Game version, hoping the AAs carried more than one charge's worth of destruction.

Her hunch proved right. A red plastic Monopoly house sat bang smack in the middle of the park. It was coated in grey and black paper designed to represent sinister brickwork. Threads of sour smoke trickled out of its crooked chimney. At least she wouldn't have to hunt them down. It had pervert's den written all over it. The only challenge was finding a way in. Her weapon was far too destructive to make a hole in the wall. She'd end up obliterating the building and taking Eva with it.

Sally didn't see the hinges at the bottom of the facade until it was too late. As she approached, the entire front swung down like a lorry's tailgate. It wasn't the impact that knocked her onto her backside in heart-stopping slow-motion. It was the face filling the whole interior, crushed into a greasy cube, eyes bulging and garage mouth spitting tobacco fumes and hate across the plastic park.

"WHERE HAVE YOU BEEN? YOU'VE BEEN GONE EIGHT HOURS YOU STUPID WICKED LITTLE SHIT."

A pit inside Sally swallowed everything - breath, thought, sense. It sucked her identity into a vortex of infant abjection and despair. Every moment spent alone, from the playground to the filthy Portslade bed-sit, crowded in on her, pushing away the rest of the world, turning her into nothing more than a wretched insect pinned to an infinite sheet of cardboard under her mother's relentless stare.

"WHERE HAVE YOU BEEN?"

It took Sally all her strength to push herself over onto her hands and knees, fighting the grinding in her bladder that told her she was about to piss her knickers yet again, humiliate herself in front of the absolute judge of her entire life. She so wanted to run forwards, arms out for a cuddle, desperate for the last shreds of love she'd ever feel before the rest of her days closed in, but she knew it was hopeless. She stared down at her fingers and sobbed.

Calloused knuckles from punching walls, trees and makiwara boards.

"LOOK AT ME WHEN I'M TALKING TO YOU."

Sally summoned up the energy to reach up and touch her nose.

Broken by Bogdan the bit of a cunt.

All grown up now.

She staggered to her feet.

"Fuck you."

"WHAT DID YOU SAY?"

"I said, fuck you. You lied to me, time and time again. Eva's real."

It was oh so hard to stare down that face. Once it had filled the world, roofed the entire universe with implacable adult anger while a storm rained down blows on her. In Toy Town her old Mummy's head was literally as big as a house, squeezed into a life-size plastic model of a Leeds semi. But didn't that make it look trapped? The eyes, suddenly uncertain, swivelled side to side, skin pulling back at the edge of the sockets. The ragged edges of the walls dug into her mother's cheeks, forcing the broken mouth into a half-pout.

"What did you say?"

And she wasn't shouting anymore. Her voice, rasping, irritated beyond endurance, betrayed uncertainty.

"You told me I'd imagined Eva."

"Who?"

"Eva. My Jewish friend from the Blocko Tower."

"You little cretin. Of course it was all made up. You couldn't be a normal daughter could you? You were difficult and awkward from the start, and playing with that lot made it a thousand times worse. Going on and on and on about all their woes and worries. What about my woes and worries, saddled with a disturbed child and a husband who didn't give a toss?"

"She is real."

"No she's not. None of this is. A magician's castle full of stolen children? Flying saucers? A rotting monster in a bonnet instead of your proper mother who actually gave birth to you? An infinite universe of iron ruled by the Queen of the Dead, who feeds you fish and chips while telling you the future of everything rests on your scrawny, spotty shoulders? Ridiculous. You're sick in the head, disturbed, mentally ill. Just look at the state of you. The psychiatrists hadn't a clue. We should have sent you to a mental hospital and had done with it."

Mummy couldn't move, but her gaze roved over the plastic trees and buildings. Sally glanced behind her. More houses slumped as the polystyrene and tin realm of the Driving Test Game continued to fall apart.

"This is madness, Sally. Lunacy. What's that in your hand? Another toy?"

She looked down at the raygun, trying to focus. When she was little, every word her mother had uttered had bound reality with their uncompromising law. Grownups spoke the truth. Was it true what she said? Was all this nothing but sad insanity? Grownups spoke the truth. Right up to the point they lied. Sally lifted the Wodaran's pistol and fired at the house.

The button clicked. That was all. The batteries were only good for one shot and she'd wasted it in the newsagents.

"See? Utterly pathetic," Mummy sneered. "Silly Sally in Toy Town. It's all in your witless little head."

The ground shuddered.

"What's happening?"

Sally ignored her. A wall of fire blossomed behind the houses to the south, towards the city centre. Cartoon silhouettes flew into the air, arms and legs stuck out at ridiculous angles. Creeple Peeple. The collapse must have accelerated.

Sally wanted to run away, head for the edge of the board beyond the station where she and the others had first entered, but what was the point? Mother would still be waiting out there in the real world. The creature might have turned into a disappointed old woman, but her shadow was as all-consuming and grotesque as this thing in front of her. Why bother?

A figure limped into the park, outlined by the last of the detonations behind it, dragging something across the ground as it approached.

"Who's that? I can't see. Sally. Who is it?"

The eyes flickered right and left, up and down, panicking.

"It's Eva. You miserable bitch, it's Eva, and she's alive."

CHAPTER TWENTY-FOUR

Sally and Eva stood shoulder to shoulder in front of Mummy. Her friend looked as if she'd staggered off a battlefield. Most of the armour had been ripped away. Many of the remaining panels appeared dead, the glowing Hebrew confined to shimmering columns along one forearm, the side of the neck and the small of her back. She reeked of plastic smoke. Her right eye had swollen shut. She'd dragged a torn bin bag full of spikes halfway across the park, dropping it a few yards off. It wore a hat and the remaining scraps were held together with Gaberdine patches.

A funny man.

"We have to go," Eva said. "I got rid of those monsters but I think there's worse that way."

"Who's this, Sally?" Mummy asked.

"This is Eva, my best friend. I went with her to play in the Blocko Tower. When I came home you beat me and told everyone I'd made her up, that she was imaginary."

Sally took her friend's hand in her own.

"See? She's real."

"Ridiculous. You're talking nonsense."

The skin puckered and dark gaps opened up on either side of the temples, as if the head had started to deflate.

"What the hell is that thing?" Eva asked. Sally could feel her trying to tug away, to get back from the bloated head glaring down at them. With every bellow, more tobacco smoke puffed out of the chimney in clammy grey donuts. Heavy with toxins, they only managed to rise a few feet before collapsing back down over the roof and filling the park with their nicotine stink.

"That's my mother. She told me you were a figment of my imagination, that I was mentally disturbed enough to think I was best friends with Anne Frank's ghost."

"You always were a difficult child," the head whined.

"Look, Mummy. Here! Eva's right in front of you."

But the eyes juddered in their sockets, hunting this way and that, as if struck blind. Blood and tears leaked down the sagging face. The mouth drooped as if the house had suffered a massive stroke.

"Biffiful biled. Ickle shit."

"Fuck you." Sally strode past the building, pulling Eva along with her.

"Ally. Ally. Ork oo urr vaver. Eee on't ork u me. O ad. O onry."

Sally risked one glance behind. Something dribbled out of the bottom of the house, forming a pool of sludge on the painted grass.

"Seriously. What was that?" Eva asked. It was hard to see the exit from the park. The Marlboro fumes covered everything with a stinking fog.

"Nobody, anymore," Sally managed to say as she wiped her face with the back of her hand.

The monster's death triggered chaos in the rest of the Driving Test Game. Walls of darkness scythed down from the clouds behind them, sealing off Moortown and Chapeltown to the west, and Harehills to the east. Sally picked up the pace as much as she could, Eva limping along beside her. The woman didn't complain even though she was in evident pain, face strained beneath the soot.

They made it through the park gates and back onto the street. A few minutes took them to the north edge of the city centre. Sally really didn't want to head straight on. The lions might be sleeping quietly on their plinths. Somehow she doubted it.

She decided to turn east. A few yards further along an

immense block slammed into the ground. Houses broke open like ripe fruit, spraying molten plastic across the road. Writhing shapes swam on the other side of the translucent wall. The same thing happened when they headed west. They were being steered towards the town hall. It took all of Sally's energy not to panic. Everything happening in this nightmare world, the disintegration and monstering of her childhood, stemmed from her own mind. Did that mean she could control any of this? Slow the chaos down? She scrabbled around inside her memories but came up with nothing more useful than echoes of playing with toys on a brand new wool carpet, in a room scented with bleach and furniture polish.

The area in front of the town hall looked empty. No Creeple Peeple, funny men or other monsters. If memory served, crossing the square would lead them to the ring road. Beyond that lay Angus's woods and the way back to reality. So far so good, but the long platforms where the lions slept were empty. That meant they were on the hunt for naughty children. Sally and Eva had two choices. They could sprint across the middle or edge around the periphery, hoping they wouldn't be spotted in the shadows if the beasts returned.

Eva saved them by glancing over her shoulder. She grabbed Sally, yanked her into the square and to one side. A plastic lion as big as a double-decker bus cannoned past them, so fast and so close the slipstream nearly knocked them over. It must have been stalking them. The creature dug its malformed paws into the ground and twisted to glare at its prey from mismatched eyes set in a face bulging with poorly moulded tumours. Eva made to go back the way they'd come. It jumped again, blocking the exit. As they watched, the lion paced up and down, its prowling made worse by the uneven gait and grotesque limbs. The mouth worked, grunting sounds through the stiff polystyrene. Sally realised it was actually talking to them. She caught her own name once or twice but the rest was gibberish.

"What's it going to do?" Eva asked.

"Eat bad little girls."

"I've nothing to take it down. I used up the last of the explosives on those cartoon monsters and that spiky thing they tried to feed me to."

The lion swiped over their heads. The razor-sharp flash on its paw ripped long streamers of badly-printed plastic from the building behind them, exposing dark lumps beneath. Sally hunted through her memories again, desperate for any clues. Professor Backenforth's magic and the queen's machine virus powered these monsters, not her. They didn't stand a chance.

A smooth ball under her palm. A control stick.

Just a nudge - jerk it too quickly and it'll crash.

Eva guided my hand until I learned to manage the tiny movements by myself.

"Take my hand," Sally said.

"What?"

"Hold my hand, like this."

Another explosion above their heads as the lion savaged the front of Leeds City Art Gallery. Torn sheets of cellophane decorated with screen-printed bricks flew through the air. Sally wrapped her friend's fingers around her own and closed her eyes, hunting for the click of magnets.

There. It's in Kirkstall Road. Just outside the Yorkshire TV building.

No time for finesse. She rammed the control stick in her head over to the right and prayed the wheels wouldn't come off.

The Driving Test Game car hurtled into the town square. It hit the lion in the stomach. The blow threw the cat down a side street. It scrabbled and thrashed against the houses, struggling to get back onto its feet. One of the front legs looked twisted, although that probably didn't count for much given that the entire body was a warped mess. The beast finally righted itself, slavering more unintelligible accusations, and crouched to pounce. Sally tried to reverse the vehicle, misjudged, and sent it sideways into an empty plinth. It teetered on two wheels. If the monster knocked it over they'd be trapped.

A black sheet fell out of the mist and guillotined the creature in half. Filling spurted from its severed abdomen, full of brown worms thrashing in hysterical agony. Sally and Eva raced for the car, put their shoulders to the nearside and heaved it back onto four wheels.

"Get in," Sally yelled. Even with its back end missing, the monster was getting closer. It rolled and flailed, shredding acres of printed vinyl from the surrounding facades. Sally and Eva dived through the passenger window into the slimy cabin. It reeked of cheap hydrocarbons. Eva grabbed the wheel but the wonky circle was just an extruded lump of polythene. Sally took hold of the control rod in her head, fixed her gaze on the far exit of the town square, and nudged. The red car lurched across the plaza, throwing its passengers backwards into the slippery interior.

Sally scrambled upright, grabbing the windscreen pillar for support. The mutilated lion's body heaved up against the rear window. It was trying to turn round, bring its deformed muzzle or claws to bear. She tried once more. The vehicle skidded further away but she lost control and it ended up jammed diagonally across the street. A twitch, and the magnet under the board flicked them around so they faced the right way. At the same instant the lion lashed out and caught the side of the car, sending it tumbling onto the ring road. It hit the portico of the railway station and thumped over onto its side.

Winded, Sally and Eva half climbed, half fell out of the empty rear window. Not only were the houses melting but immense holes began to appear in the ground, full of midnight black like cracks in cartoon ice. The mangled creature lay at the edge of the town square, on the far side of a trench that had opened up between them. That gave some respite, but not much, for more facades were falling away in all directions, while the remainder disappeared behind adamantine walls dropped from the clouds.

The ring road was blocked on both sides. Sally glanced around and spotted a tunnel leading into the station concourse. Like the Merrion Centre, the toy makers had hollowed out the building in a vain attempt to make it more realistic to infant eyes. She saw light in the distance. Praying this gap would be big enough, she grabbed Eva. Together they entered the glutinous colonnade, dodging past malformed lumps extruded from the ground pretending to be passengers. Her friend was limping badly now, practically hopping, and several times Sally had to slow down so Eva could keep up. The ceiling sagged, touching their heads. As the polythene distended it turned translucent and she could see the fabric of the station was full of writhing worms.

They nearly didn't make it. The cheaply moulded floor sloped upwards for the final few yards. They ended up on hands and knees, slipping backwards several times. Once, Sally's leg almost got trapped under a collapsing wall. In the last instant, she hooked her fingers around the edge of the exit and yanked herself out. Eva followed, twisting on her back and holding her calf in pain as she slid down the steps upside down. The pair of them fetched up against a barrier. It gave way under the pressure. Looking up, Sally realised it was made of cardboard. Tree branches projected over the top - real ones, filled with softly rustling leaves. Eva took a knife from her belt and together they worked a hole big enough to step through. On the other side, they found themselves in woodland, staring down long corridors dappled with sunlight. The shadows of the leaves flickered in a breeze that no longer stank of burning plastic.

As they limped away from the edge of the Driving Test Game, the wall behind them turned soggy and slumped to the ground. Sally thought she could still make out the shapes of collapsing buildings on the other side. An odd smoky darkness transformed them into brief glimpses that rapidly faded, pulling back between the trunks, until they were lost from sight. The last thing to disappear was the indistinct column with the red ball on top, merging with the clouds like the ghost of a tornado.

They carried on through the woods, Eva leaning on Sally. A little further on, they found Angus's house among the trees. Sally left her friend propped against an elm while she went to investigate. It was locked and no amount of hammering on the doors or windows got a response. If Chisum and the Scotsman had made it safely down the Backenforth Heights stairwell, there was no sign of them here.

The noise did alert a gamekeeper. He came thundering through the bushes just as Sally spotted the gate at the end of the path. For a second she thought it might be Angus doing his deranged wino impression, but it wasn't. He wasn't moulded out of plastic either, or a Krazy Kreature from Outer Space with boggy eyes. The man was nothing more than a florid pompous arsehole who'd had his day made by two punks lurking on his private land. He yelled and bellowed and shook his fist, threatening to set dogs on them, followed by the police. Sally told him to piss right off, and something in Eva's face made him edge away, grumbling that he'd be back with others to sort them out. He didn't reappear and they got over the fence and to the bottom of Sally's street without anyone else trying their luck.

The Fiat sat outside the old house, a normal pebble-dash semi with no hinges or clouds of Marlboro smoke coming out of the chimney. Sally hadn't a clue where her car keys were. She managed to jump the door lock and Eva showed her how to hot wire the starter. As they headed for the main road out of town, Sally switched on the radio to find out what day it was.

The 6 o'clock news told her that she'd been away for exactly 48 hours and sod all had happened in the real world, apart from the last headline which made them both sit up. Baffled astronomers had located a new cluster in the constellation of Lyra. It consisted of ninety-eight stars that had seemingly popped out of nowhere.

"They did it," Sally said.

"Who did what?"

"The queen's companions. I asked them if they could drop the planets into our universe so nobody died. Pash and Anthony and the others are still alive, out there." She nodded at the sky.

Sally drove back to Otley, taking the long way round. Leeds was the last place on Earth she wanted to drive a car through. It was dark by the time they got to the flat.

"What are you going to do now?" she asked as she handed over a can of Tetley's.

Eva sprawled back on the tatty old sofa, took the beer and

shook her head. If she didn't want to talk now, fine. There'd be plenty of opportunity later. Sally fetched a bowl of warm water and some tissues so her friend could bathe her eye. She helped her out of the wrecked armour. The ankle didn't look so bad. There was a bag of peas in the freezer compartment. Sally scraped it out and slapped it on the injured foot. Eva kept nodding off. Her skin and hair reeked of burnt plastic, as did Sally's. She went into the bathroom and took off her shirt. A giant sticking plaster covered her stomach. Gritting her teeth, she peeled it off and read the word scratched on her stomach.

Lie.

After smearing a palm-full of stinging Dettol over the cuts, she put her shirt back on, ran a bath and rummaged around for a spare set of clothes. She piled a pair of jeans and a Clash t-shirt on the floor beside the settee.

"Get yourself washed before you pass out," she told her friend. "I'll grab some fish and chips for dinner, then we can crash, and in the morning come up with a plan."

Standing in the chippy queue, Sally felt her spirit empty into the night. The bright noise, the reek of oil, and the heat, left her drained of all thought and emotion, like a damp shirt hung over a radiator to dry. A couple of notions flitted through her skull. Find a synagogue and talk to the rabbi. Maybe there were Jewish charities or friendly societies that would help Eva. No chance of her going to Latvia, not while the Berlin wall still stood. In the meantime she'd have to get work and a place to live. They could share, maybe.

When she returned home, Eva had gone, leaving nothing behind. She'd taken Sally's old clothes. There was no armour, no note, no evidence she'd ever been there. The bathwater hadn't been touched. Only the Wodaran's raygun remained, sitting in the middle of the table next to a half-empty can of Tetley's. Sally ran out into the night and spent a frantic couple of hours pacing the streets, checking in pubs, chippies, bus shelters, church porches - anywhere someone might take refuge on a cold evening. Once she thought she spotted a shadow at the end of a ginnel, but it was only a twisted traffic bollard.

Next, she drove along the road to Pool, turned 180 degrees to head over the bridge Harrogate way, then up the hill towards Golden Acre Wood, on to Otley Chevin, and round the streets of Guiseley, before finally heading down to Menston and Ilkley. The later it got, the fewer the people, and none of them looked like Eva. It was four in the morning by the time an empty petrol tank forced her to return to the flat. She dumped both uneaten portions of haddock and chips into the bin and cried herself to sleep.

She never saw Eva again. The West Yorkshire constabulary didn't give two shits about some homeless foreign woman who'd disappeared. When Sally attempted to contact Sergeant Harry Mutherington directly, she got blank looks followed by instructions to sod off. She tried calling him but his phone had been disconnected. When the coppers started suggesting she'd made the whole thing up to waste police time, and threatened to arrest her, Sally stopped bothering.

Six months later the *Wharfedale Clarion* merged with the *Otley Advertiser*. A week after that, George was sent down for gross indecency and assault after defecating in the lobby of the *Yorkshire Post* and punching the arresting officer. Sally found herself out of a job. Eventually, she managed to grab some part-time work at the local record store, sufficient to meet the rent at least.

One day she came across Hannah Able's third album, *Tigerheart*, while rummaging through the untouched contents of a forgotten cupboard. There'd still been enough budget for a passable piece of cover art - a gatefold showing the singer in a sari, riding a clearly stuffed white tiger along a mountain ridge. Disappointment and loneliness had only begun to touch the woman's face. When Sally checked the sleeve notes, she noticed that Spektrum hadn't dumped her yet. They'd also massively over-engineered the music. Hannah's voice was drowned out in a storm of electronic mush, losing all the resonant beauty Sally had heard in those brief moments in the Blocko Tower. She played it through once, took it back to the shop the following morning, and stuck it in the discount section.

That Friday, Sally headed over to the chippy and bought herself fish and chips and a bag of scraps. As Fat Kevin pushed them across the counter, she asked if he'd ever served anyone in a mask.

"What kind of mask?"

"A tall, skinny lass in a full face mask made of silver or gold, like some fancy dress outfit from a Venetian carnival."

"In here? Get out of it you daft bint. This is Otley tha' talking about," he snorted, and moved on to the next customer. Sally stood under the lamppost, eating her chips and staring up at the old *Clarion* office, with its *To Let* sign in the window. It was a clear night for once, and she tried to locate the star cluster with all those perfect planets orbiting new suns. By the time she'd winkled the last of the batter out of the bag, the decision was made.

The next morning, Sally didn't bother going to work. Instead she headed over to the newsagents and picked up half a dozen double A batteries. On the way home she stopped off at the Army and Navy Stores and bought a green webbing haversack. Back in the flat, she packed the batteries, a toothbrush, three spare pairs of knickers, and the Wodaran's raygun. She took one last look around, locked the door behind her and left the key under the mat.

She toyed with visiting her parents and decided not to bother. All the arguments she'd been having in her head with her mother since she was six had evaporated when the slime dribbled out of the toy house in the Driving Test Game. If she told them that Eva had really existed, or that she'd finally found the Blocko Tower, they wouldn't have a clue what she was talking about.

Sally drove over to Moortown and parked the car by her old school. She stood looking up at the playground, until some jobsworth's suspicious expression at one of the windows warned her she was being pegged as a potential troublemaker. Up round the back and past the garages, everything looked so small. This was no longer the epic landscape of her childhood, or the dreams and nightmares that came after. Tarmac, concrete and weeds clustered around the bottom of chain link fences and low sandstone walls. Rusting nubs marked where the council had hacked off the iron railings for the war effort half a century ago. More recently, they'd replaced the Belisha beacons on Nursery Lane with a pelican crossing. A sign further along the road advertised the local synagogue. She could just make out the building through the trees by the water tower. Curving blue brick. No evidence of any medieval fortress filled with alchemical magic.

Somebody had bought her old home and was in the process of gutting it. A skip sat in the drive, full of broken fittings, dirty lino from the kitchen and nondescript lumps of plaster. Sally spotted bits of the wardrobe where she'd kept all her toys.

"What d'you want?" the builder said, clumping out of the front door with a roll of old carpet under his arm.

"I used to live here as a kid."

"So?"

He went back inside. Sally stuck two fingers up at the house and headed down the street.

The *Keep Out* signs were as officious and pompous as before, threatening all sorts of doom on any poor bugger daring to step foot in the woods. She heaved her bag over the fence and climbed after it. The path leading towards Alwoodley Lane formed a pale line, stretching between the oaks, elms and ash trees. The bastards obviously had no intention of keeping it clear, hoping their so-called private forest would eventually wipe the right-of-way from memory. Sally pushed past the tangled bushes around the locked gate and headed north.

The gamekeeper caught up with her after five minutes. He burst out of the undergrowth ahead, red faced, half furious, half smirking at what he thought was easy meat.

"What the hell are you doing here? This is private property. I'll have you arrested."

"This is a public right of way," Sally said, seemingly all nervous and reasonable.

"You need teaching a lesson, you snotty little bitch."

She made to walk past him and he grabbed her by the arm.

"You're coming with me, sunshine. I know how to deal with your type."

Sally broke his nose with the heel of her hand. A kick to the side of the leg shattered his thigh. He didn't even cry out, just collapsed in the mud like a wet sack of meal.

Further on, she noticed the house among the trees to the left. By now it was too dark to make out the shape. It was impossible to tell whether it was a cottage slumped under a mountain of brambles, or a Victorian semi full of World War Two ordnance. No time to get distracted. A weight was growing in the sky and she needed to latch onto it or she'd end up on Alwoodley Lane with nothing to show but assault and battery to her name.

It's all in your bloody imagination.

Face down, eyes on boots, feeling the shadow loom up above the trees.

Don't dilly dally Sally.

Packed earth and grass gave way to tarmac. For a few moments she didn't believe what she was seeing, and kept trudging on, waiting for the vision to clear and show her mere pebbles and mud. A shallow puddle appeared between her Doc Marts. It held the reflection of a wall spattered with faint lights. Sally stopped and looked up at the vast shape piercing a different sky. Laughing, she began to run, aiming for the lobby and the lifts.

THE END

John Guy Collick was born in Yorkshire, England. When he was 10 years old his grandfather gave him a copy of *A Princess of Mars* by Edgar Rice Burroughs, and from then on he was hooked on science fiction and fantasy. He worked for Scotland Yard before moving to Japan for ten years to lecture in literature and philosophy. On his return to England he worked for twenty-five years in the New Media and Education Technology industry. Now he spends his time writing, leading players through various horrific ruins as a RPG gamesmaster, and perfecting his archery scores.

The Blocko Tower is his seventh novel.

He currently lives in Hampshire, England.

Other books by John Guy Collick:

Thumb

Ragged Claws

AntiHelix

Dark Feathered Hearts

The Star Tsar

Slaves of Titan

Shakespeare, Cinema and Society